DEATH & TEXAS

DEATH & TEXAS

WILLIAM W. JOHNSTONE

AND J.A. JOHNSTONE

PINNACLE BOOKS
Kensington Publishing Corp.
www.kensingtonbooks.com

PINNACLE BOOKS are published by

Kensington Publishing Corp.
119 West 40th Street
New York, NY 10018

PUBLISHER'S NOTE
Following the death of William W. Johnstone, the Johnstone family is working with a carefully selected writer to organize and complete Mr. Johnstone's outlines and many unfinished manuscripts to create additional novels in all of his series like The Last Gunfighter, Mountain Man, and Eagles, among others. This novel was inspired by Mr. Johnstone's superb storytelling.

All Kensington titles, imprints, and distributed lines are available at special quantity discounts for bulk purchases for sales promotion, premiums, fund-raising, educational, or institutional use.

Special book excerpts or customized printings can also be created to fit specific needs. For details, write or phone the office of the Kensington Sales Manager: Attn.: Sales Department. Kensington Publishing Corp., 119 West 40th Street, New York, NY 10018. Phone: 1-800-221-2647.

PINNACLE BOOKS, the Pinnacle logo, and the WWJ steer head logo are Reg. U.S. Pat. & TM Off.

First Printing: June 2019
ISBN-13: 978-0-7860-4850-2
ISBN-13: 978-0-7860-4371-2 (eBook)

10 9 8 7 6 5 4 3 2

Printed in the United States of America

CHAPTER 1

Cullen McCabe knelt beside a stout oak tree, watching the door of the tiny cabin perched on the opposite side of a no-name stream halfway between Austin and Corpus Christi. It was early morning and he waited patiently for the man inside to come outside to answer the morning call from nature, thinking he would surely have to soon. But there was no indication that he had even stirred. There was no need to caution himself not to become impatient at this point. By nature, Cullen was a patient man, especially since the man now sleeping inside the cabin was the last of the men he hunted. He had tracked this man for the last three days, a trail that had changed direction four times in an obvious effort to lose anyone who might be on his tail. Now it had ended at this shabby cabin with the last of the five men who had murdered Cullen's wife and children, burned his house to the ground, stolen his extra horses, and slaughtered his milk cow. He could be patient, no matter how long it took at this point, for nothing else mattered.

For the better portion of the last six months, Cullen had tracked the gang of outlaws with no purpose in life beyond destroying the men who had taken away his reason for living. In relentless pursuit of the five, he had tracked them down, one by one, to exact the vengeance that had driven him on to this final place of reckoning. The man inside the cabin was Troy Camp. His was the only name of the five that Cullen knew. As sheriff of the small town of Sundown, Cullen had arrested him for drunken behavior once, but surely this was not motive enough to slaughter Mary Kate and the children. This was an act of purely malicious men, bent on satisfying their evil pleasures.

Cullen felt the muscles in his forearms tightening as he clenched the 73 Winchester in his hands and stared at the door of the cabin. There was still no evidence of anyone stirring inside. The thought occurred to him that maybe he had been tricked, and Camp had sneaked out the back window during the early-morning hours. That possibility was enough to cause him to forsake earlier thoughts of patience. He could wait no longer. Rising from his position by the tree, he pulled a coil of rope up on his shoulder, then walked down the bank of the creek, his rifle ready to fire. When he reached the water, he walked through it, straight toward the cabin door. When he reached it, he raised his foot, and with one powerful thrust, he kicked the door open.

Shocked from a drunken sleep, Troy Camp bolted up from his bedroll, his pistol in hand, firing wildly and as quickly as he could manage. His shots ripped into the log walls around the door until a shot from Cullen's rifle cut him down. Camp grabbed his stomach and dropped to his knees. "You idiot," he cursed as Cullen walked over and kicked Camp's .44 out of his reach. "What are you waiting for?" he demanded painfully. "I'm gut-shot. Go ahead and finish it."

"I'm in no hurry," Cullen said, and took the coil of rope

off his shoulder, stepped behind Camp, pulled his arms behind him, and tied his wrists together. Disregarding Camp's painful protests, he pushed him over on his face, then quickly tied his ankles together.

Not only in pain, but confused as well, Camp realized that the sheriff was not going to shoot him. "Whaddaya gonna do?" Camp whined. "You arrestin' me? You can't take me in. I'm bleedin' bad. I won't make it back to Sundown. I'm hurtin' bad."

"Yeah, Camp, I'm arrestin' you, for murder, theft, and arson, but don't worry, you won't be in pain very much longer. I'm gonna take care of that right now." He cut the rope after Camp's feet were tied and began making a noose in one end of it.

Camp realized at once what Cullen had in mind. "Hey, wait a minute, Sheriff, I didn't take no part in killin' that woman and her kids. That was all them boys I was ridin' with. They just started out to have a little fun, and I reckon it kinda got outta hand. I swear." He tried to wiggle out of reach, but Cullen pulled the noose over his head and tightened it around his neck. Helpless to resist, Camp was pulled up on his feet by his powerful captor, his pleas for mercy falling on ears long deaf to him and his kind.

Oblivious to the moaning from the condemned man, Cullen threw the free end of his rope over the center beam running the length of the small cabin and began to draw Camp up from the floor. The beam was just high enough to lift the struggling victim up about a foot off the floor. Silent and expressionless, Cullen stood and watched until Camp ceased to struggle and quiver. Then he kicked the small stove over on the floor and fed the glowing coals with anything he could find that would burn. When he felt assured that it was enough to catch the whole cabin on fire,

he turned and left. He had not told Troy Camp that the
house he and his friends had burned was his house and
the family he murdered was his family. He didn't want to
give the man that satisfaction to take to hell with him.

Suddenly, he was awake!

Looking all around him in the darkness of the unfinished cabin, it took a moment for him to realize that he
had once again relived in a dream the execution of Troy
Camp. It seemed that his mind would forever hold every
detail of that fatal encounter with the last member of the
murderous pack of animals that had brought an end to all
happiness in his life. He released a weary sigh and lay back
on his bedroll, reluctant to try to go back to sleep, fearing
that he might be drawn back to that encounter yet again.
As he lay there, he wondered if he should have remained
the sheriff in Sundown. Jason Barrett, the mayor, had almost
begged him to stay, but Cullen could not bear the thought
of living there with his family gone. He stayed only until
Tom Hawkins agreed to take the job. Then Cullen left to
find someplace where he wouldn't see the people he knew
in Sundown, to be constantly reminded of what he had lost.
For want of anything better, he settled on this lonely bank
of the Brazos, downstream from the little town of Two
Forks, where no one knew him. He was aware of the fact
that he would have to find some means of surviving, but
at the moment, he didn't care what happened to him. He
also knew that he would eventually decide to do whatever
it took to go on.

"Jimmy!" Leon Armstrong, telegraph operator in Two
Forks, Texas, called to his son. "Yonder he goes!" When
Jimmy hurried into the telegraph office, his father pointed

to a lone rider on a bay horse, leading a sorrel packhorse. He handed a telegram to the boy. "Looks like he's fixin' to pull up at Thornton's. Hurry on over there and give him that wire. He don't come into town that often, and it's been settin' here since Monday." Leon was especially anxious to see the telegram delivered, because he was sure it had to be important. The telegram even said it was important. It read:

GOVERNOR HUBBARD REQUESTS THAT
YOU REPORT TO HIS OFFICE IN AUSTIN
ASAP STOP IMPORTANT THAT YOU MEET
WITH GOVERNOR AND MYSELF STOP

And it was sent by Michael O'Brien, assistant to the governor. Leon couldn't recall anyone else in Two Forks ever receiving a telegram from the governor's office. He remained standing in the doorway, watching Jimmy, as the boy ran across the muddy main street, hopping over the deep wagon ruts left by the recent rainy weather.

When the message had arrived, Leon was not really sure who Cullen McCabe was. He had never received any telegrams addressed to him before. He would not know now, had he not asked Ronald Thornton if he knew who the somber-looking stranger was. Thornton's general store was the only place he had seen McCabe patronize, and Thornton wasn't able to tell him much about the man beyond his name. He said he seemed to be a serious individual, who never smiled and never dallied in the store, called off his needs, paid for them, then promptly left. Thornton said he was a big man, said you didn't realize how tall he was until you walked up and stood next to him. Ronald speculated that he was a loner, because of the basic supplies he bought. Nothing ever indicated he was calling off a list of things necessary to prepare a meal that a woman might create. "He sure as hell don't waste words," Thornton had said. "When I asked him if he had a place near town, he just said, '*Down the river a piece*.' He wasn't impolite, though. When Clara came in from the back room, he didn't say nothin'. But when he left, he tipped his hat to her on his way out the door."

Thinking back on that conversation, Leon grinned as he thought, *Wait till Thornton finds out this fellow got a request to come talk to the governor*. He watched then as the stranger got down from his horse, and Jimmy ran up to hand him the telegram. *Damn, he is pretty tall*, Leon couldn't help thinking when he saw Jimmy standing next to him. It appeared to Leon that this Cullen McCabe hesitated to take the wire at first before finally accepting it. Then, when Jimmy turned to leave, McCabe called him back, reached in his pocket, and came out with a coin for the boy. The somber man paused on Thornton's front step for a couple of minutes to read the short message again before folding it and putting it in a vest pocket.

"He gave me a nickel, Papa," Jimmy exclaimed when he ran back into the office. "Ain't nobody else ever done that."

"What'd he say when you gave him the wire?" Leon asked.

"He didn't say much of anything," Jimmy replied. "At first, he didn't think it was for him, till I showed him his name on it."

I reckon I'll have to wait till I talk to Thornton, Leon thought.

Across the street at Thornton's General Merchandise, the proprietor glanced up when Cullen walked in the door.

"Afternoon," Thornton greeted him. "Glad to see you came back to see us."

"Afternoon," Cullen returned. "I need a few things." He took another look at the telegram Jimmy Armstrong had delivered. "Maybe more than I thought," he added. He was still deciding whether or not to ignore the wire. Even though it was a polite summons and not an order to turn himself in, his first thought was that he had nothing to discuss with anybody in the state capital. Two days after he had killed Troy Camp, he rode down to the Texas Ranger station in San Antonio to report what he had done and where all the bodies could be found. He was told that there were wanted notices out on all five of the men he had tracked down and killed. He spent two more days in San Antonio while his actions were being discussed. After those meetings, a decision was reached, and he had been advised that the Texas Rangers would not seek charges against him. This, in spite of the fact that he, as sheriff of the town of Sundown, had not been authorized to try and execute the five outlaws without benefit of a jury. He had tracked down and hung every one of them, but the commander of the Rangers said they would have hung all five of them, anyway. And McCabe was acting in his capacity as sheriff, so it wasn't as if an ordinary citizen had done it. In the end, they decided that he had done a job that the Rangers would have had to do, and they were stretched too thin as it was. It was not officially noted, but the lenient decision was greatly influenced by the fact that it was Cullen's family that had been so savagely destroyed. When they asked where they might contact him in the event any more information was needed, he told them Two Forks, since he had decided never to return to Sundown.

"You got a list or somethin'?" Thornton asked when Cullen seemed to have his mind somewhere else.

"No," Cullen replied. "No list." Then he called off some things he needed: bacon, salt, coffee, flour, primarily. He considered sugar for a moment when Thornton suggested it, then declined. As in the case of his every visit to the store, the transaction was simple and quick, with no time spent on small talk. Within a few minutes' time, he took his purchases and was gone, leaving Thornton with a growing curiosity about the man.

Still watching from across the street, Leon Armstrong remained in his doorway until McCabe wheeled the big bay away from the hitching rail and rode back the way he had come. As soon as McCabe passed by the River House saloon at the end of the street and continued on out of town, Leon called to his son, "I'll be back in about five minutes—just be across the street, if anybody needs me." Without waiting for a reply from Jimmy, he hurried across the street to Thornton's store.

Thornton looked up when Leon came in the door. "I figured it wouldn't be long before you showed up," he said, "but I don't know any more about him than what I told you before. I don't reckon he said more'n five or six words the whole time he was in the store."

Thornton's wife, Clara, walked in to join them. "You two are working up a lot of steam about that fellow," she said. "If you ask me, I think he's an outlaw, hiding out somewhere down the river."

"Well, I don't know about that," Leon was quick to challenge. "I thought you might be interested to know he got a telegram from the governor's office, tellin' him the governor wanted to have a meetin' with him—telegram said it was important." He looked at Clara and grinned. "So I don't reckon he's an outlaw. If he is, they've got a new polite way of arrestin' folks." Leon was right—Ronald and Clara found that news worth further speculation.

As for the mystery man they puzzled over, Cullen McCabe had nothing on his mind beyond taking care of his horses and completing a small log cabin he had been working on before winter set in over the Texas plains. He had built a three-sided shed for Jake and his packhorse before starting the cabin, so his horses had shelter. Taking care of them was his major concern now that his family was gone. And with the men who had destroyed his family now having been dealt with, there was no longer any purpose to his life. So he had no thoughts on what he would do now that vengeance was done. He had found it impossible to think beyond each day that passed. That was before he received the telegram. As he rode back down the river on this late afternoon, he thought about the summons again. What could the governor possibly want to talk to him about? Maybe there was some problem with the Rangers over their decision not to prosecute him for the five hangings. Although he consciously thought he didn't give a damn what the governor wanted, he could not deny a curiosity to at least know why the governor would think it important enough to send him a wire. These were the thoughts that captured his mind as he guided Jake down through the stand of oaks that shielded his primitive homestead on the riverbank.

He paused for a few moments to look at his cabin and shed. It was a far cry from the solid home he had built for Mary Kate and their three children, that was now no more than a pile of burnt timbers and ashes. It was a place he could not bring himself to return to, so he had carried the bodies of his loved ones over eight miles away from there, until finding a little spot on a hillside that seemed appropriate. It had been since the first of spring that his world had been destroyed, but he came to realize that the burned images of what had been left of his wife and children would forever be in his conscious mind. He thought again of the telegram in his vest pocket. The fact that it made no sense that the governor of Texas sent for him was enough to spur his curiosity to find out why. Still puzzling over the unlikely circumstance that the governor even knew who he was, he decided to ignore the wire, figuring it had to have been a mistake. As soon as he made that decision, he immediately changed his mind, his curiosity having gotten the best of him. *What the hell*—he shrugged—*there ain't nothing keeping me here.*

CHAPTER 2

"What is it, Ben?" Michael O'Brien looked up from his desk when his secretary, Benjamin Thacker, tapped on his open door.

"There's a man out here who says the governor sent for him," Thacker replied.

"What about?" O'Brien asked.

"I asked him that," Thacker answered, "but he said he didn't know, just that the governor wanted to see him."

"Did you get his name?"

"He didn't give it," Thacker said. "I'll ask him." He stepped back to the outer office, and in a few moments, stuck his head back in the door. "His name's Cullen McCabe. He said you sent him a telegram."

"Oh hell, yes!" O'Brien immediately exclaimed. "Send him on in here." He got up from his chair to greet him. It had been quite some time since he had sent the telegram, and he had all but given up on ever hearing from McCabe. Having formed an image of a rugged small-town sheriff who had hunted down and killed five ruthless outlaws, O'Brien was still surprised by the formidable man filling his doorway. Tall and rugged, with shoulders that almost touched each of the doorjambs, he caused O'Brien to think of a cougar on the hunt. At the same time, he was aware of a look of quiet authority. "Cullen McCabe?" O'Brien asked to be sure.

"That's right," Cullen answered. He remained standing in the doorway.

"Well, come on in, man," O'Brien said, walking around his desk to meet him and extending his hand. "I sent you that wire about a week ago, maybe longer. I'm glad to see you decided to come in."

"I didn't get it till yesterday," Cullen stated. "I came in to see what you wanted."

"Well, like I said in the telegram," O'Brien said, "the governor wants to talk to you, but first, let's you and I talk a little bit." He wanted to get to know McCabe a little better before he chanced wasting Governor Hubbard's time on a bad idea. The idea was all O'Brien's, which made it more important to him to get a bigger picture of the fabric the man was made of before he paraded him before the governor. "Have a seat." He nodded toward a chair across the desk from his and thought about commenting on the rifle and sidearm Cullen wore. It struck him that they were inappropriate in the state offices, but he decided not to say so. Instead, he asked Cullen to tell him about the pursuit and ultimate capture of all five of the men responsible for his family's demise.

"There ain't much to tell," Cullen replied. "I tracked 'em till I caught up with 'em, then I hung 'em. I've already squared it with the Rangers. Is this what this meeting is about, the fact that they didn't get to stand in front of a judge?"

"No, no," O'Brien was quick to assure him, "but it does

have a bearing on why you were contacted. I take it you're no longer the sheriff in Sundown. Is that right?"

"That's a fact. I'm done with Sundown."

O'Brien continued, "What are you doing now?"

Cullen hesitated before answering, "Not much of anything—buildin' a cabin down below Two Forks—takin' one day at a time, I reckon."

"Do you have family somewhere?"

"Not anymore," Cullen answered. The only family he knew had been taken from him in one horrible act of fate. He refrained from going into detail about the fact that he had been orphaned when a young boy.

O'Brien began to believe McCabe could not be more qualified for the position he had in mind. "It sounds to me like you don't really have any plans for what you're going to do now." When Cullen shrugged indifferently, thinking that was what he had just said, O'Brien continued, "You ever think about maybe doing something positive with your life, something that might help the people of Texas?"

"Like what?" Cullen asked, already thinking this a pointless meeting he had been summoned to.

"I'll tell you what," O'Brien replied. "Why don't we go in and talk to the governor about that?" When Cullen's silent reaction seemed to indicate he wasn't particularly enthusiastic about it, O'Brien said, "If the governor thinks the same as I do, then he might offer you a job. Just bear with me, all right?"

"A job? What kinda job?" Cullen couldn't think of a thing he could do to help the state of Texas.

"Let's let the governor talk to you about that," O'Brien insisted. "From what you've just told me, you're pretty much adrift on what you're gonna do. So you might as well listen to a possible job that would do some good, all right?"

Cullen shrugged. "I reckon." He decided, since he had gone to the trouble to come this far, he would listen to what the governor had in mind.

"Might be best to leave your weapons here," O'Brien said as he got up from his desk. "They'll be all right. We're just going up to the end of the hall to the governor's office. Sit here a minute while I go see if he's available right now. He's been in a meeting all morning, but he should be out of there by now." He hurried out the door, leaving Cullen to wonder what he had walked into and whether or not it might be best to be gone when O'Brien returned. He hadn't decided before O'Brien came right back and beckoned him to follow.

"Mr. McCabe." Governor Hubbard got to his feet and greeted Cullen when he walked into his office. "Michael tells me you might be the man to fill a job we're considering." He reached out across his desk to shake Cullen's hand. "Right now, I'd have to say you sure as hell look capable."

"Thank you, sir," Cullen replied respectfully. "Tell you the truth, I didn't have any idea I was comin' up here to apply for a job."

"I know we hit you kind of sudden-like," Hubbard said, "but I think you should consider the offer. Before we get into that, tell me why you didn't just shoot those outlaws when you caught up with them, instead of going to the trouble of hanging them."

"What they did was a hangin' offense," Cullen replied. "There wasn't any doubt, they were guilty, and I didn't have a courtroom handy, but I wanted them to experience the same fate they woulda got from a judge."

Hubbard nodded as he considered that, then said, "Michael says, from what he has been able to learn, that there was practically no lawlessness in the town of Sundown while you were the town marshal. Is that right?"

Cullen shrugged. "Sundown's a peaceful town. Lotta good folks there."

Hubbard nodded thoughtfully. He was impressed by the lack of boastful bravado on the part of the quiet man. Needing no further speculation, he made his decision on the spot. "I'm sorry to say I've got another meeting that I'm already late for, but I'm offering you the job. Michael will tell you all about it and I hope you'll give it some serious consideration. He'll be your contact here if you decide to take the job." He grabbed his coat and was out the door in a moment, down the hall to his meeting.

With Hubbard's hasty, although official, approval, O'Brien was ready to make the actual job offer. It was not what Cullen would have imagined, but he listened with no small amount of interest. As O'Brien explained, Cullen was to be appointed as a special agent, answering to the governor alone, or O'Brien on the governor's behalf. He would not be subservient to any law enforcement agency in the state and would be sent on assignments where no other agency was close by. "In the great, wild expanse that is now the state of Texas," O'Brien went on, "there are more and more settlers moving into territory that used to be controlled by Indians. Small settlements are sprouting up all over the state and there are frankly not enough law agencies to handle all the trouble." He shook his head thoughtfully. "Unfortunately, there are plenty of outlaws making their way into Texas, as well."

O'Brien stressed that Cullen was to be, in effect, a troubleshooter, sent to help in any way he could, and authorized to make arrests if he deemed it necessary. O'Brien made it clear that there would be no restrictions on how he handled the assignments as long as he put an end to the trouble he was sent to quell. "Let me make it perfectly clear to you," O'Brien emphasized, "the governor is not interested in hiring an assassin. You are to use your weapons only as a last resort. Is that clear?" Cullen said he understood, so O'Brien continued, "You would receive a salary of seventy-five dollars a month, plus a certain amount for expenses." This caught Cullen's interest right away, for he had no foreseeable source of income since he had left his sheriff's job in Sundown. And the little amount of money he had saved was close to running out. Seventy-five dollars a month was a healthy salary. It was enough to make the decision for him. When he asked what part of the state he would be working in, O'Brien answered, "The whole state of Texas— wherever there's a problem and no law in place."

With a considerable amount of skepticism as to how effective he might be, he accepted the job primarily for the salary and expense money. He and O'Brien shook hands to seal the agreement. "I have to warn you, though," O'Brien said. "We're not signing any contract for any specific length of time, so if either party is dissatisfied with the performance, we'll call the whole thing off. Agreed?"

"Sounds fair to me," Cullen replied, thinking he would most likely be the one to call it off. "What's my first job?"

"The governor and I want to discuss that before we send you out. Come back to my office in the morning. I should know by then."

After shaking hands with O'Brien again, Cullen picked up his weapons and went out the door, aware of Ben Thacker openly eyeing him as he passed through the outer office.

* * *

Since he was not sure what time O'Brien customarily started work each morning, Cullen left his horses overnight at a stable near the capitol with instructions to give them each a portion of grain and see that they were watered. The owner of the stable directed him to a small hotel where he could get a bed and a bath for a reasonable price. After a night competing with a colony of bugs for possession of the straw mattress on the wooden bunk bed, he was more than happy to see morning light make its way through the dingy glass window. He made it a point to inspect his clothes thoroughly before he put them on to make certain he departed the room alone. Satisfied that he had accomplished that, he headed for the capitol, arriving outside O'Brien's office door at six o'clock. It was a little after seven when O'Brien, carrying a briefcase, walked down the hall to his office. "You're here early," he greeted McCabe. "Have you been waiting long?" When Cullen replied that he had been there since six, O'Brien looked surprised. "I should have told you what time to come," he said. "I just came by the office to drop some papers off, and then I was planning to go to breakfast. I usually get to work at eight." Seeing no reaction from his somber new agent, he asked, "Had your breakfast yet?" He didn't wait for Cullen's answer before suggesting, "Why don't you come with me and we'll talk over breakfast—big fellow like you could probably handle some breakfast, right?"

"I reckon," Cullen answered, and gave up his weapons to be put inside the door when O'Brien unlocked it. Then he waited in the outer office while O'Brien went inside and left the briefcase on his desk.

When O'Brien came out, he locked the door again. "Come on," he said. "We'll grab a little breakfast at the restaurant down the street. The eatin's good and the coffee never runs out."

It was a short walk down a side street to a small building with two large windows in front. A sign over the door identified the business as THE CAPITOL DINER. When they went inside, Cullen immediately felt a little out of place because all the customers he saw at the two rows of small tables were dressed in suits and ties, like O'Brien. O'Brien exchanged good-mornings with several of them as he and Cullen walked past to a vacant table in the back of the room. All of the patrons, as well as the women waiting the tables, paused to gape at Michael O'Brien's breakfast companion. When they were seated, a young lady brought them coffee and O'Brien ordered breakfast for both of them, without asking Cullen what he wanted.

While they waited for their breakfast to be prepared, O'Brien proceeded to tell Cullen what his first assignment was to be. He continued on while they ate their eggs, sausage, and grits, with biscuits and gravy, not finishing his briefing until the plates were cleared away. "Well, whaddaya think?" O'Brien concluded. "You think that's something you can handle?" He waited for McCabe's response, not sure if the job might be more than he was willing to tackle.

Cullen didn't answer right away, pausing to decide if he wanted it or not. After he stroked his chin thoughtfully for a couple seconds, he finally asked some questions to make sure he had it straight. "This fellow, the mayor, what was his name?"

"Mitchell," O'Brien answered. "Percy Mitchell."

"Right, Mitchell," Cullen said. "He's wrote three letters

to the governor complainin' about the hands from the Double-D causing trouble in town?"

"Right, and there's been some trouble between the Double-D and the smaller ranchers near the river, too," O'Brien replied.

"Why didn't he write the Texas Rangers about the problem?"

"He said he did," O'Brien replied, "and he got no reply from them at all. And that's the reason he started writing the governor." He shrugged and added, "These folks just don't understand that the Texas Rangers are stretched too thin to cover every complaint that comes up, especially when the town has its own sheriff. That's why we need someone like you to handle those cases that would just be ignored otherwise."

"Does this town have a sheriff?" Cullen asked, wondering how big a problem the town had, if the sheriff couldn't handle it.

"Yes, the town has a sheriff, but evidently the trouble is too much for him," O'Brien replied. "For the most part, your job will be to determine the extent of the problem and whether or not we need to send a party of Rangers in there. On the other hand, most of the time the problem isn't as big as the letters make out, and you might be able to help the sheriff take care of it without calling in the Rangers." He paused, watching Cullen closely and waiting for his response. "McCabe, the governor and I are trusting you to do what is morally right. But if you have to use violence against one or more of the troublemakers, then so be it." He paused to emphasize, "As long as it solves the problem and stops the trouble. So, do I tell Governor Hubbard we've found our man?"

Cullen hesitated a long moment while he thought about

everything O'Brien had told him. He could not honestly say he was the right man for the job. Being frank with himself, he admitted that he wouldn't know for sure until he rode into the little town of Bonnie Creek and saw, firsthand, what had to be done. He wasn't sure what one man alone could do, and his only experience had been as a sheriff in a small town. Finally, he decided. "I'll give it a try, then maybe you can decide if you've found the right man or not. I'll see what I can do."

"Good man," O'Brien responded. "Let's get back to the office and I'll give you your official badge and papers to back it up, plus a cash advance to cover what supplies and ammunition you might need." They got up from the table and, as they went out the door, he told the waitress to put the breakfast on his account.

When they returned to the office, O'Brien walked over to a large Texas map on the wall to show Cullen where the town of Bonnie Creek was. He pointed to an X he had marked on the map, northwest of the city of Austin. "The town's located on the San Saba River where the river's joined by Bonnie Creek," he said. Cullen studied the map for a few minutes before asking how far Bonnie Creek was from Austin. "About one hundred miles," O'Brien said, after measuring the distance with a ruler from his desk.

"Two good days," Cullen said. "I reckon I'd best get started right away." When he had left his cabin on the Brazos, he had closed it up tight, figuring he might not be returning for a while, so there was no need to go back there before starting out for Bonnie Creek. He continued to study the map while O'Brien got some things out of the briefcase he had carried. Since Cullen was not familiar with that part of the state, he made mental notes of any rivers or creeks depicted on the map. He thought he could possibly use them to help guide him in the right direction. When the briefing was finished, O'Brien handed him a badge that simply identified him as a special agent of the state of Texas. Along with that, he gave him a paper officially stamped and signed by the governor, verifying his right to wear the badge and make arrests, if necessary.

Lastly, he was given a check for fifty dollars, written on the First Bank of Austin, for any supplies he might need. "I hope to hell you're the man I think you are," O'Brien couldn't help saying when he handed him the check. "You can cash this at the bank, right on the corner. While you're there, open an account and that's where we'll deposit your paycheck every month."

"Much obliged," Cullen said. "I'll be leavin' for Bonnie Creek this mornin'." He strapped on his Colt .44, picked up his rifle, and with a final nod to Ben, walked out the door.

O'Brien stood in the doorway and watched him walk down the hall to the stairs. *It's gonna be my ass in the grinder if I've made a mistake about that man*, he thought. *That fifty dollars might all be spent in a saloon if I'm wrong.* Somehow, the solemn bearing of the man gave him reassurance and told him that he had not made a mistake. A major factor in his estimate of the man was the fact that McCabe had not simply ambushed the men he had killed with the rifle that appeared to be a permanent part of him. He had made it a point to capture each one of the five and perform a hanging, just as a court of law would have ruled. Without a doubt, he could not have found a man more qualified for the job, he decided.

As for the newly appointed special agent, Cullen was

aware that he had made a serious commitment to the governor and the state. There were no guidelines he could follow for the position he now held, because there had been no such position before. He had decided to undertake the task in most part because he had no future plans of any kind. In fact, he had to admit that he didn't care if he lived or died anymore, so why not try to see if he could help some honest folks who *did* dream of a future. He would approach this job as he had approached the job as sheriff of Sundown, and enforce the rights of those honest people, being well aware that there were no restrictions on his methods.

When he got back to the stable to get his horses, he returned the Winchester to his saddle sling, then took a few moments to look again at the shiny badge O'Brien had given him. With no plans to wear such a badge, he wrapped it with the official document bearing the governor's signature and seal and put it in his saddlebags. After paying the stable owner, he led his horses down to the corner of the street and tied them to the rail in front of the bank while he went inside to convert his check to cash, except for a small amount to open his bank account. With his horses now rested, he set out at once, riding out of Austin on a road heading west for about three miles before he swung off it to follow a creek that ran in a more northwest direction.

Behind him, Michael O'Brien sat in the governor's office to discuss the meeting he had had with the newly appointed special agent. "Do you still feel confident that this McCabe fellow has the integrity to know when not to go too far?" Governor Hubbard asked. "You know the man just tracked down five outlaws and hanged them. I wonder about the chances he might turn rogue and kill without regard to guilt or innocence." After the fact, he was not entirely comfortable with the possibility that people might see this as the equivalent of the governor appointing a hired gun.

O'Brien was not comfortable with the governor's doubts, now that the die had been cast. He had certainly been enthusiastic over the possibilities during their last discussion on the matter, this before he had made McCabe the official offer. O'Brien had no choice but to confirm his confidence in McCabe, knowing that in the event Cullen did go rogue, the governor was sure to dump the whole blame in his lap. "Yes, sir," he answered. "I think we've got the right man. Just in the short time I've met with him, I don't believe he ever gets excited about anything. I think we can count on him to use proper judgment."

Hubbard stroked his chin as he considered what O'Brien had done that morning. Knowing there was nothing to be done about it now, he finally exhaled a sigh of resolve. "I think it's best that we keep this between the two of us for the time being," he said. "And for Pete's sake, don't let Fulcher know about McCabe. He'll start raising hell about it. If the problem warrants an action by the Rangers, then we'll let Fulcher know about it."

"It'll remain just between us," O'Brien assured him, well aware that William Fulcher, commander of the Rangers, would not likely appreciate a gunman running loose anywhere in the state, official government agent or not.

CHAPTER 3

After leaving Austin while the morning was still relatively fresh, Cullen hoped to reach Bonnie Creek in two days. If the distance was what O'Brien had estimated with his ruler, it was going to take two full days of hard riding for Jake and the packhorse. Cullen knew the bay gelding was up to it, but it would be hardest on the sorrel packhorse. Two days gave him a long time to consider the job he had undertaken and how he was going to approach it. Since there was no road from Austin to Bonnie Creek, he had set his course in a general northwest direction, thinking he was bound to strike the San Saba River in two days. By the time he reached the river, he had decided not to inform anyone that he was a special agent, acting on the governor's behalf. He figured it would be best to get a feel for the town and the people running it before he decided what he might do to help them. He was fairly certain that there was a better than average possibility that the sheriff would not appreciate any interference with his job.

As for the river, the question was in which direction the town of Bonnie Creek might lie, upstream or down, and how far was it? There was a wagon track running parallel to the river with evidence of a fair amount of use, so he figured the town must not be too far from where he now was. Going on pure gut instinct, he decided to follow the river road north. If he was wrong, he'd just turn around and go the other way tomorrow. Whatever the direction, he was not willing to push his horses too much farther on this day. They had already worked hard enough, so he turned Jake downstream and started out parallel to the riverbank. After a ride of about half an hour, he was about to call it a day for the horses when he caught sight of the buildings of the town in the distance. "Just a little bit farther, Jake," he said, "and if there's a stable there, I'll see that you get some grain."

He pulled Jake up to a stop before riding down the one short street that was the town of Bonnie Creek. He wanted to take a look at the town before he rode down to the stable he could see on the other end of the street. The first store was on his left and carried a sign that identified it as MITCHELL GENERAL MERCHANDISE. There was a wagon tied out front. He wondered if the owner was the same Mitchell who was the mayor. He decided it was a good bet they were one and the same, as small as Bonnie Creek was. There was an empty space between the general store and a small shop with a barber pole out front and what appeared to be a larger shop behind. Across the street, one of two buildings that were two-story structures proclaimed itself to be a hotel, its back to the river, the other being the Bonnie Rose Saloon, next to the stable. *About the same size as Two Forks*, he thought as he nudged Jake forward. Slow-walking his horses down the middle of the street, he passed a blacksmith's shop, where the blacksmith stopped his work to watch him pass. Next to the blacksmith, he saw the sheriff's office and the jail. He rode on, passing the saloon, where a couple of horses were tied at the rail, and a man sitting on a stool fashioned out of a nail keg and a short board, stared him past.

When he reached the stable and dismounted, he was met with a cautious, "How do? Somethin' I can do for you?" Cullen was aware that the man had been watching him from the time he had passed the blacksmith.

"I need to put my horses up for the night," Cullen answered. "Dependin' on how much you charge, I might wanna keep 'em here for a while."

"How long a while?" the stable owner asked, still cautious, almost as if he suspected mischief of some kind.

"Well, I don't know for sure how long I'll be here," Cullen replied. "I reckon it'll depend on whether everybody else in town is as friendly as you are."

The stable owner suddenly relaxed his guarded posture. "I'm sorry, mister, I reckon everybody in town's been kind of edgy lately. My name's Ross Horner and I'd be happy to board your horses while you're in town."

"Cullen McCabe," Cullen introduced himself. "My horses worked pretty hard yesterday and today. I need to rest 'em up and give 'em a good portion of grain."

"Yes, sir," Horner said. "I'll take good care of 'em. What brings you to Bonnie Creek?"

"Nothin' in particular," Cullen replied. "I never been here before, and I reckon I just wanted to look at the country around here."

Horner suddenly became suspicious again. "You ain't lookin' for the Double-D, are you?"

"Nope. What's the Double-D?" Cullen responded, as if he'd never heard of it.

Horner seemed relieved. "The Double-D's a cattle ranch, owned by a man that's doin' his best to close Bonnie Creek down. I was afraid you was another one of them gunmen ol' man Nathan Dixon hired to work for him."

"Why does he wanna close the town?" Cullen asked.

"It's the land he's wantin'," Horner replied at once. "His range already runs two or three miles along the west side of the river, but he's wantin' this piece where the town sets, where Bonnie Creek empties into the San Saba. There's a heap of folks, small farms and ranches, that depend on the town for their supplies and other needs, and the river for water. And we got here first, at least Percy Mitchell did. He built a tradin' post here before most of the settlers came, and the town grew up from there."

"Sounds to me like there ain't much the Double-D can do about it," Cullen said, "as long as the land claims were filed and approved."

"You'd think so," Horner commented, still warming to the subject, "but Dixon don't think that way. He's got his own set of laws and I think he's tryin' to make it so tough for some of us to stay in business that we'll pull up stakes and go somewhere else." He paused to spit, as if the words left an unpleasant taste in his mouth, then he continued. "We ain't gonna let him and his rowdy crew run us out, though. Most of us have sacrificed too much to get our businesses goin'. I know I ain't in no shape to start over somewhere else." He paused again, realizing how much he was complaining to the stranger. "I'm sorry. I didn't mean to start bellyachin' about our troubles to you. What line of work are you in? You don't look like a farmer. You lookin' for a place to settle?" He was afraid if the stranger was looking for a place to settle, he might have just talked him out of the notion.

"Like I said, I'm just lookin' the town over. I had a place down between Austin and San Antonio, and I reckon I'm just takin' time to see parts of Texas I ain't seen before. I'll most likely stay here a day or two."

Horner nodded as if he understood, but he was thinking that was a fancy way of saying McCabe was a drifter. He didn't seem like the typical drifter, however. Although a stranger to these parts, he didn't act like an aimless drifter. There seemed to be a serious side to him, so Horner suggested that if McCabe was going to stay for a couple of days, he might want to get a room in the hotel. "And the hotel dinin' room serves up some good cookin'," he added.

"I expect I'd like to try the dinin' room out," Cullen said, "but if you don't charge too much, I'll sleep with my horses tonight. Then if I decide to hang around awhile, I'll see about a room tomorrow."

I was right the first time, Horner thought. *He's a drifter*. In reply to Cullen, however, he said, "I won't charge you nothin' to sleep in a stall if you're payin' for two horses."

"I 'preciate it," Cullen said, and promptly paid him for his night's board. Horner led him into his stable and helped him unload his horses, then helped carry his saddle and other possessions into one of the stalls. When they were finished, Cullen pulled his rifle from the saddle and said, "I'll go try that diner out now. What time do you lock this place up?"

"I won't leave here till about seven," Horner said.

"Good. That oughta give me time to get some supper and maybe a drink after that," Cullen said after looking at his pocket watch.

Horner pointed to a cabin behind the corral. "If you ain't too much later'n that, you can knock on my door and I'll let you in the stable." He walked out the front door with

Cullen and stood there a few moments, watching him walking up the street toward the hotel. *He's a strange cuss for a drifter*, he thought. *Mighty damn serious and he paid in advance for his horses.*

Daisy Lynch glanced up when she heard the door open and paused to take a longer look at the formidable individual standing in the doorway. He was a stranger in town. She was sure of that because she was certain she would have remembered if she had ever seen him before. "Come on in, if you're gonna," she called out, "and close the door. You're lettin' a lotta cold air in."

Not sure if she was naturally cross or merely joking with him, he closed the door and said, "Sorry." He paused to look the room over before starting toward a small table against the back wall.

"Whoa, cowboy," she said, stopping him. "If you're gonna eat in my dining room, you'll have to leave those guns on the table beside the door." When he turned to look at her, she pointed to a table just inside the door. He saw no weapons on the table, so he glanced around the room to see if any men were wearing their guns. When he saw no weapons, he went back and placed his Colt on the table and propped his rifle against the back of it. Then, instead of heading for the table against the back wall, he took a seat at the table closest to his weapons. His change of mind brought the hint of a smile to Daisy's face, so she came over to his table and asked, "Double-D?"

He hesitated a moment to study the woman before responding. A strong-looking woman, it was hard to guess her age. She wasn't old, but she was not a girl. There was no sign of gray in her dark brown hair. It was obvious that she was a no-nonsense woman, and he felt sure she was capable of managing her dining room. "No," he answered her. "Why do you think I work for the Double-D?"

She chuckled and replied, "Because you look like the kind of man that rides for the Double-D, instead of what most cowboys look like." She paused to see if he had any response to that. When he made none, she asked, "You want coffee?" He answered with a nod, so she called out to a young woman who was carrying a coffeepot around the room, refilling cups. "Fanny, grab a cup and bring this fellow some coffee." She turned back to Cullen. "You just get in town?" Again, he answered with a nod. "You're a talkative devil, aren't you?" She stepped aside then, to let Fanny pour him a cup of coffee. When once again he made no reply, she continued, "Passing through, or are you here on business of some kind?"

"Fellow down at the stable said I could get some good food in your dining room," he said, ignoring her question. "Any truth in that?"

Aware that he seemed disinclined to volunteer any information, she smiled and said, "We'll serve you up a plate and let you decide for yourself." Then she nodded to Fanny, who was still standing there, eyeing the stranger. When Fanny scurried off to the kitchen, Daisy returned her smile to Cullen. "Since you ain't working for the Double-D, let me welcome you to Bonnie Creek. My name's Daisy Lynch. What do folks call you when they ain't mad?"

"McCabe," he answered, "Cullen McCabe."

"Well, Mr. McCabe, I hope you enjoy your supper." She left him then and went to talk to some of the other customers in the room, most of whom were just as curious about the rugged stranger as she was.

One of the customers she stopped to talk to was especially

curious about the man who was now concentrating on the generous plate of beef stew Fanny had brought him. Any stranger was cause for speculation in Bonnie Creek, but this one inspired some questions from Norman Freeman, who served as the town's barber, doctor, and undertaker. "You were talkin' to him for a good while," Freeman said to Daisy. "Who is he?"

"He said his name's Cullen McCabe," she replied.

"Double-D?"

She smiled, thinking that was her first question upon greeting him. "He says not."

"No, huh?" Freeman replied. "Is he passin' through, or is he here for some reason? What did you learn about him?"

She had to laugh at that. "Not a helluva lot. He ain't exactly a chatterbox, but maybe if you go ask him, he might tell you his whole life story."

Accustomed to Daisy's sharp tongue, Freeman thought about it for a couple of moments before expressing his opinion. "I'm tellin' you, Daisy, that's a hired gun, if I've ever seen one, and I've seen one or two. He didn't like it much when you told him he had to park his guns, did he?"

"Well, don't let him upset your stomach," Daisy said with a chuckle. "He doesn't act like he's fixin' to cause any trouble. I think he ain't got nothing on his mind but Bertha's stew right now." She left him then to go to the kitchen.

When she came from the kitchen again, she noticed that Cullen had evidently finished his supper, so she picked up the coffeepot and went to his table. "Well, how was it?" she asked as she warmed up his coffee. "Looks to me like you cleaned your plate. It must notta been too bad."

"It was as good as that fellow at the stable said it would be," Cullen answered. "It was well worth the price."

"I'll tell Bertha you said so," Daisy said. "She's the one who cooked it." She paused a moment to study his face, thinking about what Norman Freeman had said. She wasn't sure he was right about the serious man seated at her table. He had a quiet way about him that suggested the capability to take care of trouble, but not the smirking demeanor of one who causes it. "Come see us again," she said.

He finished his cup of coffee and went to the table to collect his weapons. There was at least one more call he wanted to make before retiring for the night, so he left the dining room and walked to the Bonnie Rose Saloon. He didn't particularly want a drink of whiskey before he went to bed, but he wanted to see the saloon, because that was the most likely place for trouble.

It seemed quiet enough inside the Bonnie Rose when he stepped inside and paused to look the room over before going to the bar. A couple of men were sitting at one table and having a quiet drink. In the back of the room, there was a five-handed card game under way. A bored-looking woman stood by the table, watching the game. *Peaceful enough*, he thought, and walked up to the bar under the curious eye of the bartender. "Howdy," Chubby Green greeted him. "What's your poison?" Cullen asked for corn whiskey, so Chubby pulled a shot glass from a shelf under the bar and poured. Then he waited until Cullen tossed it back, then hovered the bottle over the empty glass. Cullen nodded and Chubby poured another one. "Ain't seen you in here before," Chubby commented. "You passin' through?"

"Ain't made up my mind yet," Cullen answered. "Reckon it depends on what I find here."

"Whatcha lookin' for?" Chubby asked.

"I don't know. Peace and quiet, I reckon."

Chubby laughed. "I don't know if you'll find that or not. Ain't been much of it lately. The Double-D's done drove their cattle north, so their hands are all back in Texas now. And when they're back on the home range, there ain't much peace and quiet here in town." He picked up the bottle again, but Cullen waved him off, so he put it down and corked it. "If you're lookin' for cattle work, you got here at the wrong time of year. Double-D ain't hirin' this time of year and the smaller ranches ain't likely to, either."

"Sounds like this town depends on the Double-D pretty much to survive," Cullen commented, just to hear how the bartender responded.

"Not hardly," Chubby replied. "When it comes right down to it, that rowdy bunch from the Double-D drives more business away than they bring. They don't buy any supplies here in town. Mostly they just come in to raise hell. There's a lot of small farmers and ranchers on this side of the river, and half of 'em has got to where they're scared to come into town on a Saturday or Sunday." He paused then when someone walked in the door. "Speak of the devil," he muttered softly. Cullen turned to see what had distracted Chubby. Two men, obviously cowhands, ambled in and looked the room over, then stood leering like two conquering warriors. The two patrons who had been quietly drinking when Cullen walked in, immediately got up from the table and hurried out the door.

"You'd *better* get the hell outta here," one of the cowhands blurted. "That's my table and you saved me the trouble of throwin' your ass out." He was a big, heavyset man with a full beard. When he reached up and flipped his hat off to rest on his back, the hat held in place by a rawhide cord, he exposed a shiny bald head. His companion, a dark-haired, rail-thin man wearing two pistols, butts forward in the holsters, grinned in appreciation of his partner's antics. "Chubby!" the bald man yelled out. "Get us some whiskey over here!" They sat down, yanking the chairs out to scrape noisily on the rough floor as if to make sure everyone was aware of their entrance. The five cardplayers in the back of the room had stopped playing when the two men made their noisy arrival but resumed the game after the two sat down.

"I'm comin'!" Chubby yelled back. He lowered his voice then and said to Cullen, "That's two of the Double-D crowd. The big one with the bald head's name is Curly. The other one is Tom Yates. That'll take care of my business for this evenin', soon as everybody else knows they're here."

To this point, the two boisterous cowhands had paid no mind to the lone patron standing at the bar, although Cullen McCabe was hardly a man to go unnoticed, even had the saloon been crowded. The two Double-D riders had other interests in mind, and they had barely finished their first drinks when they pursued them. "Hey, Lilly!" Curly yelled. "Come on over here and have a drink with us." Lilly Bloodworth winced visibly when she heard him call, an obvious sign to Cullen that she must have had contact with the obnoxious brute before. She ignored his invitation and moved around a little farther behind the table to stand behind one of the cardplayers. Her response did not go over well with Curly, so he yelled at her again. "Lilly! Damn it, get your ass over here."

Afraid not to respond again but determined not to subject herself to his brutal behavior, having evidently been subject to it before, she walked toward his table, but stopped several feet short. "I can't right now, Curly. I've got a customer." It was not true, but she hoped the fact that there were five men seated at the card table would discourage Curly from making trouble.

"Is that so?" Curly replied. "Which one is it?"

Lilly hesitated to answer, afraid she might cause trouble for one of the regular customers seated at the table, but she was more reluctant to risk any more of Curly's treatment. With Curly's malicious sneer locked on her, she hurriedly pointed toward the biggest man in the card game. He happened to be Shep Blackwell, the blacksmith. Blackwell was a husky man, and with one eye on the two unwelcome customers, he was startled to see Lilly point him out.

"Well, you just tell him you got yourself another customer and get on over here like I told you," Curly said, loud enough to make sure the men at the table heard him. Tom Yates, seated at the table with Curly, wore a wide smirk on his unshaven face to show his amusement with his partner's antics. When Lilly failed to respond quickly enough to suit him, Curly warned, "If I have to come over there and tell him myself, it ain't gonna go too well for you."

Lilly stood terrified, her last encounter with the cruel cowhand still too fresh in her mind. She took a quick look back at Shep Blackwell, who was staring at her as if waiting for her to tell Curly the truth. She glanced quickly away, unable to confess that she had made the story up. Caught between her fear of Curly and Yates and the terrible twist of fate she had brought upon Shep, she froze.

Curly got to his feet, a smug smile of anticipation parting his full beard. He headed straight for the card game, pausing only to deliver a backhand to Lilly's cheek as he passed her. "Get over there and sit down with Tom," he ordered. When he reached the card game, now brought to an abrupt halt, he pointed a finger at Shep Blackwell. "I reckon it's up to me and you to settle this little problem. What's it gonna be—knives, fists, or six-guns? It don't matter to me, but if you don't get up outta that chair, I'm gonna shoot you where you set."

The threat was enough to force Shep to his feet to stand behind his chair. "I'm not wearin' a gun," he said.

"Then it's fists or knives," Curly said, not giving Shep time to say more. "I'm partial to knives, myself, but I get just as much fun with fists."

"Why don't you just go on about your business?" Shep said. "I've got no reason to fight you."

"Is that so? Well, I reckon I'll give you one," Curly taunted. "You ain't gettin' outta this whippin'." He started to move toward him.

An interested spectator, standing at the bar, Cullen had made no motion to interfere, waiting to see what would be done to prohibit flagrant bullying like that he was witnessing. The bartender had made no sign of stopping the senseless confrontation. Surely he must have a shotgun handy under the bar, but he had stood as if turned to stone. Cullen suspected the cause to be the sneering Tom Yates and his two pearl-handled six-guns. As for the other men in the card game, none showed the slightest inclination to rise to Blackwell's aid. Cullen decided it had gone far enough. He stepped away from the bar. "I expect that'll be about enough," he stated evenly.

"What?" Curly demanded as both he and Yates jerked their heads around to see who dared to stick his nose in their fun. "Who the hell are you?"

"I'm the man who's gonna put a stop to the trouble you're tryin' to start in here," Cullen said calmly. "The man said he ain't got any reason to fight you, so I think it's best if you and your friend just pay your bill and get on outta here."

Scarcely able to believe his ears, Curly looked the stranger over. He was taken aback by the challenge from the tall somber man. Expressionless and confident, he was a big man, but Curly thought he was bigger, and he was damn sure he was meaner. With a confident grin, he started walking toward the bar. Cullen looked at Chubby, who was as frozen as Lilly now. "Take that shotgun out from under the bar and hold it on the fellow at the table. If he makes a move for those guns he's wearin', give him both barrels. Can you do that?"

"Yes, sir!" Chubby exclaimed, shaken out of his trance. "I sure can!" He came up with the shotgun in a second and laid it on the bar, aimed at Yates.

"All right, big man," Curly threatened, "I'm fixin' to carve you up real good." He drew a long skinning knife from a sheath on his gun belt and assumed a crouched position. Then he came toward Cullen, shifting his knife back and forth from hand to hand, a smile of anticipation on his ugly face, meant to intimidate. He hesitated for a moment when Cullen stood waiting for him, holding his rifle in both hands. "Put the damn rifle down and draw your knife," Curly demanded.

"Druther not," Cullen replied patiently.

The big stranger's indifferent attitude tended to infuriate Curly. "Suit yourself," he spat, confident he could move in fast enough to keep Cullen from raising the rifle to fire. With no further warning, he lunged forward, his knife in his right hand, with the intent to thrust it up under Cullen's ribs. Still holding his rifle in both hands, Cullen blocked the upward thrust with his rifle, then caught Curly under the chin with the butt of the weapon. The impact on Curly's chin produced a sound like that of a whip across a horse's rump. Curly slumped to the floor, knocked senseless.

Anticipating the possibility that Chubby might hesitate, Cullen turned at once to level his rifle at Yates, who was slow to reach for his pistols, hampered by the fact that he was sitting at the table. "That'd be a mistake," Cullen warned as he and Yates locked eyes. There was a standoff for a long moment, then Cullen spoke again. "You're wonderin' if I cranked a live round in the chamber, right?" He pulled the hammer back with his thumb. "You didn't see me crank a cartridge in the chamber. Maybe I didn't, but then, maybe I did. Maybe you're a gambler. Are you willin' to pay the price to find out?"

He could tell Yates was thinking it over. While sitting in a chair it would be a little easier to draw from a holster like his, which held the gun butt forward, than it would be with a typical holster. After another moment, a smile appeared on Yates's face. "You're right, I didn't see you crank a cartridge in that Winchester." The smile became wider. "But you was just standin' at the bar, havin' a drink when we came in. You wouldn't hardly be walkin' around with that rifle ready to shoot. I think you're bluffin'. I think if you pull that trigger, that hammer's gonna fall on an empty chamber." He glanced at Curly on the floor, trying to get to his hands and knees. "Besides, you've still got two of us to worry about."

Cullen shook his head slowly. "I'm warnin' you, don't do it." He barely got the last word out before Yates made his fatal move. He was fast, but he got only one gun halfway out of the holster before the .44 slug from Cullen's rifle slammed into his chest, knocking him hard against the back of his chair. With eyes opened wide, he stared down at his chest in shocked disbelief. Knowing he was fatally wounded, he tried to get up, but sat back when he found he was unable to. "I warned you," Cullen reminded him.

"Look out," Chubby exclaimed, and pointed at Curly struggling to get up off all fours. "He's fixin' to get up!"

Cullen reached down and grabbed the hat on Curly's back. Using the rawhide cord like a noose, he pulled back hard, threatening to strangle him, until Curly went over backward to land on the floor again. Choking, he clawed frantically at the rawhide around his neck, but Cullen held him there until he was close to passing out. He released him then and stood over him with his rifle aimed directly at his face. "The only reason I don't kill you is because I want one of you bastards alive, so you can ride back to the Double-D and tell 'em they're gonna have to act like civilized men if they come to Bonnie Creek. Do you understand, or do I have to explain it to you again?"

Still not recovered from the blow he took on his chin, Curly struggled up on his hands and knees again, staring glassy-eyed at Cullen standing over him. He tried to speak but found it too painful to try with a broken jaw. Feeling in no shape to try to resist, he managed to get to his feet after a couple of tries. While he was doing that, Cullen said to Chubby, "Check on that other one, the one you were gonna shoot if he made a move." Unaware he was being chastised, Chubby came from around the bar and went to Yates, slumped in his chair.

"He's dead," Chubby announced.

"Figured he might be," Cullen said, still covering Curly with his rifle. "You might as well look in his pockets to see if he's got the money to pay what they owe you." Back to Curly then, he said, "The drinks are on your partner this time. Now you can get on your horse and take that message I gave you back to your boss." When Curly just stood there, still trying to figure out what had happened, Cullen stuck his rifle in his back and, with a shove, started him toward the door. They almost bumped into a man standing just outside the door, who stepped back quickly to let them pass. He took a long look at Cullen, then looked quizzically at Chubby, who answered his look with nothing more than a shrug and a shake of his head. Like the card-players and Lilly Bloodworth, he was finding what had just happened hard to believe.

When Curly missed the stirrup on his first try, Cullen helped him up into the saddle, then untied Yates's horse and handed the reins to him. "Here," Cullen said. "You might as well take his horse with you. It most likely belongs to your boss." He stepped back then, his rifle trained on him in case he wasn't as dazed as he appeared to be. When Curly rode off toward the other end of town, Cullen went back inside the saloon, where he found Chubby and the man he had almost bumped into at the door standing beside the body slumped in the chair. They stopped talking when he came back in.

"This here's Bob Bartlett," Chubby announced. "He's the sheriff. I never caught your name."

"McCabe," Cullen said. "Cullen McCabe." He looked at the young man wearing a badge, and his first impression was not a favorable one. He hoped he was wrong.

"I heard the shot from that Winchester," Bartlett said, "so I came over here to see what the trouble was. Chubby told me about the shooting." He took another look at the corpse. "That's Tom Yates. I don't know what the major's gonna do when he hears about it."

"Who's the major?" Cullen asked.

"Major Nathan Dixon," Chubby answered for him. "He's the owner of the Double-D. All his crew call him major 'cause he's supposed to have been a major in the Confederate army."

Cullen eyed the sheriff closely and wondered why it took him so long to investigate the cause of a rifle shot in the middle of his town, especially since the jail was right across the street from the saloon. When Bartlett continued talking, Cullen was convinced that his first impression of the sheriff was an accurate one. "Mr. McCabe, it mighta been better if you hadn't shot Tom Yates. It might stir up a lot of trouble we don't need."

"You figure it woulda been better if I had just let him shoot me," Cullen said. It was not a question, for he was convinced the sheriff would have been a lot more comfortable had that been the case.

Chubby was quick to point out, "Tom Yates was goin' for his gun. This feller warned him not to go for it."

Bartlett shook his head, glanced at Chubby, then back at Cullen. "I reckon I'm just sayin' it's too bad he got shot. Chubby said you sent the major a warnin' back with Curly." He paused to think about the possible results of that. "We could do without gettin' the major riled up over this. Chubby said it was self-defense and I believe him, you didn't have no choice. So you ain't gonna have no trouble from me. Anyway, I expect you'll be movin' on in the mornin'."

"Why do you think that?" Cullen asked.

Bartlett started to fidget. "Well, I just thought you would, so you wouldn't be here if some of the Double-D men show up here tomorrow."

Growing more disgusted by the moment with the sheriff's obvious lack of a backbone, Cullen asked, "Are you thinkin' about runnin' me outta town?"

Bartlett hesitated for a long moment while he considered the risk of ordering the big man to leave town. He was fearful of finding himself caught between this intimidating individual and the whole Double-D gang. "Why, no, I didn't say anything about running you outta town. Like Chubby said, Yates was fixin' to draw on you. I figured you were just passin' through town, and after this little mix-up with Curly and Yates, it'd be healthier for you to keep on goin'."

Cullen nodded as if considering the sheriff's advice before he spoke. "No, I think I'll stay over for a while. My horses could use a good rest and I kinda like the feel of the town. Besides, if I'm the cause of some trouble comin' to town tomorrow, I feel like I oughta at least be here to face it. Maybe give you a hand, if you need it." His statement was met with a look of undisguised disappointment all over Bartlett's face. "So I reckon I'd better get myself back to the stable. Ross Horner told me I'd best not be too late, or he might be locked up." He nodded toward the late Tom Yates. "Fellows wearin' their guns with the handles out like that are usually pretty fast."

"Yates was fast, all right," Chubby spoke up. "I hear tell ain't nobody stood up to him and walked away." He paused, then added, "Till now, anyway. There's gonna be talk about this at the Double-D tonight."

Cullen nodded. "He was a gambler, too, just not a very good one." He looked at Bartlett, who was still thinking about the trouble he could anticipate. "I expect you'll take care of the body."

"What?" Bartlett replied, still engrossed in his thoughts

of Nathan Dixon's possible reprisal for the killing of one of his men. "Oh yeah, I'll get Norman Freeman to come get him."

"Well, then, good night, gentlemen. I reckon I'll see you tomorrow." When Cullen turned to leave, he found the blacksmith waiting for him.

"Mister, I reckon I owe you an apology for gettin' you into trouble with those two," Shep Blackwell said. "And I reckon you mighta saved my life. I don't know how I woulda come out if I'da had to fight Curly Cox."

"You don't owe me an apology," Cullen said. "That lady over there owes us both one." When he walked outside the saloon again, he spotted Ross Horner standing among a small crowd of people who had heard the shot fired. Horner stepped forward to meet him. "Damn, McCabe," he remarked, "that was bad luck to run into them two, but I'm mighty glad to see you still on your feet."

"Thanks for your concern," Cullen responded drily. It was obvious that Horner wanted him to tell him all the details of what had taken place inside the saloon, but Cullen didn't offer to do so. Horner decided he was going to have to wait and talk to Chubby to find out. Cullen left him standing there and went back to the stable alone. Horner need not have worried. He would get every detail of the incident inside the saloon from Chubby and the cardplayers. In a matter of minutes, it would be all over town about the mysterious stranger and the two Double-D riders. Of special note was the way he handled the notorious bully, Curly, but the thing that spawned the most speculation was his duel with Tom Yates. Yates enjoyed quite a reputation as a fast gun. The general feeling was already leaning toward the speculation that a notorious gunman had hit town.

CHAPTER 4

"What is it, Consuelo?" Nathan Dixon looked up from the Bible he was reading when his cook and housekeeper tapped timidly on the door of his study. She was reluctant to bother him when he was reading after supper.

"Excuse me, sir," the petite Mexican woman replied. "Reese say he need to talk to you. He say it important."

Dixon closed the Bible and laid it on the table beside his chair. "Well, tell him to come on in." It was well past the supper hour. He wondered what could be so important that his foreman couldn't wait until morning. "And, Consuelo," he called after her as she went out the door, "tell Mateo he's let my wood box get low."

"Yes, sir," Consuelo responded. "I tell him at once." She paused only briefly when she passed Reese Cochran standing in the hallway. "He say for you to come in," she said, then hurried to tell her son the major wanted more wood for his fireplace.

"Sorry to bother you, Major," Cochran began, "but I thought you'd wanna know about somethin' that happened in town tonight." He paused, but Dixon didn't say anything, so he continued. "Tom Yates got shot . . ."

Dixon interrupted then. "Dead?"

"Yes, sir, dead," Cochran replied.

"Who?" Dixon demanded, his interest fully aroused now. Tom Yates was lightning quick with a .44. "Who shot him?"

"Some feller in the Bonnie Rose Saloon, a stranger. Curly said he ain't never seen him before."

"Curly was with him?" Dixon responded, then paused to consider that. "So I suppose Curly took care of the stranger?" When Cochran didn't answer right away, seeming to think before composing his answer, Dixon asked, "Where is Curly?"

"He's down at the bunkhouse. Smokey's tryin' to give him a little doctorin'. Smokey says he thinks Curly's got a broke jaw. He can't hardly talk, so Smokey's tryin' to fix him up as best he can."

Visibly upset now, Dixon got up from his chair. "How in hell did that happen? Was Curly drunk?"

"No, sir," Cochran answered. "Curly said he weren't—said it was a big feller—hit him on the chin with his rifle butt. Then he turned and shot Tom when he went for his guns." He paused then when Consuelo's son, Mateo, carrying an armload of firewood, came into the room.

"Where was that sheriff of theirs?" Dixon asked, ignoring the young boy. "Was he there?"

"Curly said he showed up after Tom got shot, but he didn't do nothin'," Cochran answered. "He didn't even *say* nothin'. That's what I thought Curly said. It's hard to understand everythin' he's tryin' to say with his jaw all busted up like it is."

This was all disturbing news to the major. It represented the first real challenge to his dominance over the town and the settlers around it. His first thought was the possibility that a gunman had ridden into town and decided he would set up camp there. If that was the case, it was important to shut him down right away. He didn't want any stray gunslinger moving in on his territory. It also occurred to him that the town might have hired themselves a hired gun. If he was raising hell in town, however, that was probably not the case. "I want to talk to Curly," he decided. He needed to know more about this stranger.

"Yes, sir," Cochran replied. "I'll go see if Smokey's got him patched up, and I'll bring him here."

"No, I'll go down to the bunkhouse," the major said, and started pulling on his boots.

When they walked into the bunkhouse, they found Curly with a wide piece of a sheet wrapped under his chin and tied on top of his head. Already marks of bruising were developing and there was considerable swelling around his mouth. "Can you talk?" Dixon asked.

Smokey answered for the obviously miserable Curly. "He can talk a little bit. I told him he's got to keep his teeth clamped shut to try to keep them jawbones in place till they can get to healin'. It ain't real plain, but you can make out what he's tryin' to say."

Dixon nodded, but he really wasn't that concerned about Curly's discomfort. He was more interested in the stranger that put him in this condition. "How the hell did he get the jump on both you and Tom?"

Curly tried to offer an excuse, but could not make the major understand him, so after a few minutes of painful grunts and groans, Smokey took over for him again. "I got to where I can understand him a little bit," he offered. "I think he said the feller surprised 'em when they was havin' a drink in the saloon."

Dixon figured that may or may not have been the case.

"You say he was a big man?" Both Curly and Smokey nodded. "Was he wearin' a badge?" They both shook their heads. *A damn, hotshot gunslinger*, Dixon thought, *had to be fast to beat Tom Yates*. He turned to Cochran. "We'll take a little ride into town in the mornin' and see if this gunman is still hangin' around. Maybe I might wanna hire him, since it sounds like he was fast enough to beat Tom Yates, or maybe we might just run him outta town. We'll take a couple of the men with us—start right after breakfast."

Jeff Hammond crossed over the San Sabo River some thirty yards short of its confluence with Bonnie Creek, guiding his horse up the bank and into the trees almost directly behind the Winter House Hotel. It was pitch-black among the trees along the banks, but Jeff had no trouble following a path through them. He had been here on more than one occasion, and always at night. His passage caused no effect on the chirping and singing of what sounded like thousands of night critters. He paid no attention to the cricket chorus as he dismounted at a familiar spot, where a large oak had been tilted over in a long-ago storm. The angle of the tilt caused one large limb to grow parallel to the ground, making it a natural bench. He looped the reins over a small branch of the oak and proceeded to the edge of the trees on foot, where he stopped to make sure all was quiet behind the hotel. Satisfied that it was, he walked out into the clearing just short of the alleyway and stopped beside a smokehouse sitting behind the hotel kitchen. Taking another look around to make sure he was alone, he placed two fingers on his tongue and softly blew what sounded like the call of a bird.

Inside her room behind the kitchen, Fanny Wright

turned from her right side onto her left, not realizing why. After a few minutes, she turned back over, half-awake, and tried to go back to sleep. Another few moments brought her completely out of her sleep and she realized that something had disturbed her, but she was not sure what. Then she heard the clear sounds of a night bird's song, and a smile immediately graced her face. She hurriedly rolled out from under the quilt and slid her feet into her slippers. Grabbing her robe, she pulled it on while trying to smooth her hair down at the same time. At the door, she slid the bolt back as quietly as she possibly could and slowly pushed the door open just far enough to make sure there was no one in the tiny hallway. Marvin Winter had built this addition onto the back of the kitchen to house the women who ran his dining room. While they were not much larger than jail cells, the rooms at least provided a sense of privacy for them.

When she saw no one in the hallway, Fanny crept out and quietly closed her door behind her, then tiptoed past Daisy's room to the outside door at the end of the hall. Again sliding the bolt as quietly as possible, she went out the back door and ran to the smokehouse, where her lover was waiting.

When he saw her coming, he stepped away from the corner of the smokehouse and waited with open arms and a wide grin she could not see in the darkness. As if on cue, the moon broke through the heavy cloud coverage as she flew into his arms, giggling like a young schoolgirl. After a short embrace, he took her hand, and they ran back to the oak tree and their natural bench by the river. "You musta been sound asleep," he told her, laughing as he helped her onto the limb. "I thought I was gonna have to shoot my gun a couple of times just to wake you up."

"You do, and you'll most likely have Daisy out here with her shotgun," Fanny replied with a giggle. "You must be riding nighthawk again."

"Yep, me and Seth are ridin' nighthawk, and he'll cover for me if anything comes up, but I can't stay away too long. If somethin' was to happen that I shoulda caught, the major would most likely string me up to a tree."

His remark made her frown. "I don't see why you don't quit that job," she said.

"And do what?" Jeff replied. "Where am I gonna get a job this time of the year? I'd be out ridin' the grub line, just tryin' to get a meal once in a while. The major hires you year-round, feeds you, and gives you a horse to ride. I can't get that nowhere else."

"Yes, but Jeff, the man you work for is an outlaw and he's made all his men outlaws, too." She frowned and took his hand. "You're not an outlaw. I know you're not."

He shook his head slowly as he considered her words. "All the men were outlaws long before he hired 'em. That's the reason he hired 'em. I ain't no better. I got hired 'cause I was a friend of Seth's and I helped drive a herd up from Mexico. And I reckon that makes me an outlaw, at least in Mexico, but I needed a job."

"I know you're not an outlaw," she said to him again. "I wouldn't be out here holding your hand if you were." She had to laugh then. "Daisy would skin me alive if she knew I was sneaking off at night to meet a Double-D cowhand. That man is trying his best to destroy this town and everybody in it."

"I reckon I can't say you're wrong about that. He wants his cattle grazin' right where we're sittin'." He shook his head slowly when he thought about it. "And he'd nail my hide to the barn door if he knew I was tryin' to court a gal in Bonnie Creek."

"Oh," she said, pretending to be surprised. "Is that what you're doing—courtin' me?"

"You know blame well that's what I'm doin', and I'd ask you to be my wife right now if I had some way to support us without ridin' with a gang of outlaws."

She knew there was a longing in his heart to share his life with her and her heart ached for him, for what he said was true. He had nothing to start a family with. He didn't own much beyond his saddle and his weapons. They wouldn't make it six months. She snuggled up under his arm and thought about the circumstance that caused them to know each other. He came into the dining room with three other hands from the Double-D to eat supper one night. The men he was with were typical of the rough cowhands the town of Bonnie Creek had come to despise. Their behavior was crude and loud, causing Daisy's other customers to eat quickly and leave. She remembered that he had not taken part in their coarse behavior and sat quietly throughout their stay in the dining room. She had caught him stealing peeks at her, only to quickly look away if she looked in his direction. It struck her at the time that he was not like his companions. When they finally left, he returned alone to apologize for his friends' behavior. They talked for a short while and it was obvious that at some point in his life he was taught to respect women. After that night, he would sometimes find a way to lose his friends long enough to come to the dining room for a meal whenever he was in town. It wasn't long before he asked if he could call on her sometime. Although it seemed their relationship was heading in that direction, still she was surprised when he actually asked her. She was very aware that she was not a beautiful woman, plain as a tabletop, in fact, but he seemed not to notice. So she said yes to his proposal, but she didn't want the town folk to know she was friendly with anyone that rode for Nathan Dixon. And that's what led them to this point of frustration in both their lives.

"What?" she asked, suddenly aware that he had said something that broke into her reverie.

"I said, as much as I don't want to, I reckon I'd best get myself back on the job," he said. "Seth might not be able to cover for me if I stay too long."

"Just as I was getting comfortable sitting on this rough oak bench," she joked.

He hesitated, thinking about what he was about to tell her. "Fanny, I need to tell you why I made it over here tonight. I need to warn you." When he said that, she immediately gave him her attention. "What I wanna tell you is to be real careful tomorrow and don't go out of the hotel if you can help it. The major is plannin' to come into town in the mornin' and he's takin' Reese and Sam and Harvey with him. He's plannin' to kill that fellow that shot Tom Yates, and anybody else that gets in the way, even if the sheriff's got him in jail. He don't want folks in Bonnie Creek thinkin' they can kill a Double-D rider. I just don't want you or any of the folks at the hotel to get hurt. If you're lucky, maybe that fellow will be gone before the major hits town." He could see that his warning had a sobering effect upon her, and he was prompted to ask, "Who is that fellow, anyway? He ain't nobody we've ever heard of—Cullen McCabe. That bunch I ride with has been doin' business in dang near every part of Texas, Oklahoma, and some parts of Mexico. But ain't none of 'em ever heard of Cullen McCabe and it looks like they would have—from somewhere. Reese says he mighta changed his name. It wouldn't be the first time a gun-slinger got a little too well-known for his own good and got his name on a wanted poster."

"Nobody in town knows him," Fanny said. "He just showed up yesterday in the Rose and managed to stir up trouble right away." She paused as she thought about it. "The odd thing about him is he doesn't seem like he's look-ing for trouble. He was in the dining room and was quiet as a mouse, even with Daisy giving him some sass about leaving his guns on the table." She got up off the oak limb and walked with Hammond to untie his horse. "Chubby Green told Daisy that McCabe didn't get into it with Tom Yates until that monster, Curly, called Shep Blackwell out. And after McCabe stopped Curly from cutting Shep up with his knife, Tom Yates tried to shoot McCabe, but he wasn't fast enough to do it."

Jeff thought about that for a moment. "That ain't ex-actly the way Curly told the story. He said him and Yates was just havin' a drink and this fellow jumped 'em." He shook his head when he recalled Curly's version of the in-cident. "Well, it don't make no difference. If he ain't gone in the mornin', I expect he's a dead man," he said. He turned to face her and she stepped into his arms for a brief embrace "You just be sure you stay outta the way." Then he climbed on his horse and headed back to the Double-D. She watched him until he rode down the bank into the river, sighing as she wondered what could become of their relationship.

"Good mornin'," Ross Horner called out cheerfully when he opened the front door of the stable. "You were already turned in with your horse by the time I got back here to close up." Cullen returned the greeting and Horner continued talking. "That was quite a little party you were in last night at the Rose."

"Where?" Cullen asked.

"The saloon, the Bonnie Rose," Horner replied. "Most folks call it the Rose. When Malcolm Howard built it, he called it the Rose for his wife, Rose. She passed away last year. She was a fine and gracious lady. Most folks thought she was too good for ol' Malcolm, so the good Lord called her back home." He paused to shake his head out of respect for her before resuming his original remarks. "I heard the shot from that rifle of yours, so like everybody else in town, I ran up to the saloon to see what happened. And like I told you last night, you sure as hell picked a pair to tangle with. I got here a little bit early this mornin' 'cause I figured you might wanna get an early start outta town."

"Well, I appreciate it, but I ain't leavin' town just yet," Cullen said. "I'd like to keep my horses here for a while."

His comment left Horner to wonder if the somber man had good sense and caused him to hesitate before continuing. "I ain't one to tell another man his business," he finally came out with, "but I ain't sure you know how big a wasp's nest you stuck your nose in last night. You might be thinkin' you settled that business with Yates and Curly, but more'n likely you set the hounds on you, sure enough. I don't usually like to run customers off, but the healthiest thing for you right now is to get on your horse and put some distance between you and Bonnie Creek. Nathan Dixon ain't likely to let that piece of work you done last night go by without somebody payin' for it."

"'Preciate the advice, Horner," Cullen said as he strapped

on his gun belt and picked up his rifle, "but I think the best thing for me to do right now is to get up to the hotel dining room. I'm kinda curious to see if those ladies up there cook as good a breakfast as they do supper."

Astonished by the man's ignorance of his situation, Horner could only gape for a moment before he thought to say, "You suppose you could pay me for boardin' your horses before you go to breakfast?"

Cullen couldn't help smiling. "I suppose I could, but if something happens to me, you'd have my horses, wouldn't you?" Horner nodded and smiled, as if he hadn't thought of that. Cullen reached in his pocket and pulled out some money. "I'll be leavin' my horses here, but I might take a room in the hotel. I'll let you know later." Horner walked outside with him and stood there to watch him walk up the street toward the hotel. Then he turned to stare down the road out of town, halfway expecting to see a band of riders approaching.

There were only a couple of customers in the dining room when Cullen walked in the door. Both of them stopped eating to watch him as he placed his weapons on the table, then quickly returned their attention to their plates when he went to the same table he had picked the night before. He had just settled himself in the chair when Daisy Lynch, carrying a stack of plates, came in from the kitchen. "Well, good mornin'," she greeted him. Like Ross Horner, she was somewhat surprised to find him still in town. She placed the stack of plates on a long sideboard, then walked over to his table. "That supper you had last night must not have been too bad, if you've stuck around for breakfast."

He gave her a slight smile and replied, "I figured there was a fifty-fifty chance the breakfast might be good, too."

She studied his face for a long moment before admitting, "To tell you the truth, I didn't expect to see you still in town this mornin'." She turned her head far enough to tell Fanny to bring him a cup of coffee before continuing her conversation.

"I don't know why not," he said. "It seems like a nice little town."

She pulled a chair back and sat down. "Listen, mister . . . What was your name?"

"McCabe, Cullen McCabe," he said.

"Yeah, well, listen, Mr. McCabe, you seem like a decent man, so I feel like I oughta tell you a few things about Bonnie Creek. It could be a nice little town, all right, if it wasn't for that Double-D gang of hoodlums that think it's their playpen. Everybody in town knows what you did last night in the Rose. And there's sure as hell gonna be some riders from the Double-D in town today lookin' to settle up for what happened to Tom Yates. Nathan Dixon ain't used to havin' his men come out on the losin' end of a fight."

"Don't get me wrong, I appreciate what you're tryin' to tell me. It's mighty nice of you to care, but Tom Yates caused his own death last night, so I reckon I was within my rights to defend myself. The most important thing I've got on my mind right now is to try some of that hash those fellows are eatin'."

"Fanny," she instructed her waitress, who had paused to hear some of the conversation. Fanny turned and went immediately to the kitchen to fetch his breakfast. Turning her attention back to Cullen, Daisy resumed her plea. "Sure, you were in the right with Yates, and everybody in town was tickled to see Curly shut up for once. But damn it, McCabe, I'm tryin' to save your ass. You might think you've got the law on your side, but I'm tellin' you, you best not depend on Bob Bartlett to take care of things." As if on cue, the door opened and the sheriff walked in.

Bartlett stopped abruptly when he saw Cullen and Daisy sitting at the table. Cullen thought he could see the disappointment in the sheriff's face at finding him there. "Well, good mornin' there, Sheriff," Daisy sang out. "You're early this mornin'."

Bartlett nodded and said, "Good mornin'." He nodded again in Cullen's direction. "McCabe," he acknowledged. "I see you're still here."

"I said I would be," Cullen replied.

Bartlett turned his attention back to Daisy. "I'm afraid I ain't got time to set around for breakfast. I got a message about some rustlin' on one of the ranches down the river and I expect I'd better go see about it. So I just stopped by to get a couple of biscuits and ham, and I'll just take 'em with me." Fanny, still standing within earshot, didn't wait for Daisy's instructions, but went to the kitchen to get the ham and biscuits.

When the sheriff walked over to stand by the kitchen door to wait for his breakfast, Daisy looked directly at Cullen, her raised-brow expression needing no words to convey her message. "Like I said," she whispered.

Cullen was not really surprised that the sheriff was going to conveniently be called out of town. When first meeting Bartlett, he didn't have much confidence in the sheriff's ability to perform the job of protecting the town. Now he found that Bartlett was a little short on courage, also. Just as well, he figured, he'd be better off without him. *Well, there's no need to hurry my breakfast now*, he thought, for he had planned to visit the sheriff's office next, in case Bartlett was inclined to enforce the peace.

In a few minutes' time, Bertha came to the kitchen door and handed the sheriff his ham and biscuits, wrapped in a light towel. Bartlett paid Fanny and hurried to the door. "Thank you, Sheriff," Daisy called out. "You be careful with those cattle rustlers, they might be some dangerous outlaws." He didn't bother to look around behind him. Daisy turned her full attention back to Cullen then. "Now whaddaya say, McCabe? There goes every bit of the town's law and order out the door." She figured the message should surely be loud and clear.

"I reckon I'd best get ready for a visit from the Double-D," he replied. "How much do I owe you for breakfast?"

"Not a damn thing," she declared impatiently. "I don't charge dead men." She got up from the table, seeming to be disgusted with what she perceived as mule stubbornness, or at worst, plain suicidal tendencies.

He remained at the table long enough to empty his coffee cup, thinking all the while of what he should do to prepare for the visit that everyone, including himself, was expecting. This was going to be a hell of a test to see if he could survive. For a brief moment, his thoughts were shifted to think about his late wife and children. *Maybe this will be the day we'll see each other again*, he thought. *But I'll damn sure make it expensive for the Double-D.* In spite of Daisy's offer of a free meal, he left some money on the table, deciding that he wasn't going to qualify for her charity. As he strapped on his Colt .44, he was aware of Fanny near the kitchen door, staring openly at him. He put on his hat and picked up his rifle, turned, and started toward the door. "Mr. McCabe," she called after him. He stopped and waited while the young girl hurried to him, looking from side to side, hoping no one would notice. When she reached him, she started talking as fast as she could, anxious to give him her message before Daisy came back from the kitchen. "They're comin' to town this morning. I don't know what time, but Dixon and three men are coming in to find you and kill you."

"How do you know that?" Cullen asked. She seemed so sincere that he didn't doubt her word; he just wondered her source.

"I can't tell you that," she whispered, "and don't tell anybody I told you." She turned her head quickly when she heard Daisy yell something to Bertha in the kitchen. "You'd best run while you still have time," she urged, then turned and retreated to the other side of the room. She obviously was in contact with someone on the Double-D. It was little wonder that she wanted to keep the relationship secret, but she was evidently loyal to the town. He appreciated the fact that she felt conscience-bound to alert him.

Fanny Wright hadn't told him anything he hadn't already assumed, but he was confident now that there would be four of them. She was a surprising source for a tip-off. His guess was that she might have a romantic relationship with one of the Double-D hands. He hoped that it wasn't someone he might be called upon to face. After leaving the hotel dining room, his first stop was the sheriff's office. He figured that it was the best place to make his defensive stand, if there was to be one—and according to Fanny, there was. At this early hour, there were few people on the street. Some of the merchants were getting ready to open their doors. All of them paused to stare at him as he walked down the middle of the street, enforcing the feeling that he was a stranger, and as such, he was very much on his own.

As he expected, he found a padlock on the office door when he reached the sheriff's office. With no concern for who might be watching, he kicked the door open, ripping the latch off the door to leave it dangling from the door-jamb. Inside, he found a desk and a couple of chairs, a cabinet, a stove, and a gun cabinet on the wall behind the desk. In one corner of the room, there was a pump and a dry sink. The gun cabinet held a twelve-gauge, double-barreled shotgun and a Henry rifle, plus cartridges and shotgun shells. *They might come in handy*, he thought, so he opened the desk drawers and searched through them until he found a key for the cabinet. The stove was still warm, so he put a few pieces of wood on the glowing coals, then opened the door at the back of the room. It led to a cell room with two cells, each one with one barred window that looked too small for a man to crawl out. He went back into the office, leaving the cell room door open, in case something might come flying through the back windows later on, like a flaming torch.

He had a strong hunch that any riders from the Double-D would most likely look for him at the hotel or the saloon first. When they didn't find him, they would probably look for the sheriff to complain about the killing of one of their hands. Just in case they didn't, he picked up a bucket in the corner and walked down to the end of the street to the horse trough. He took his time filling the bucket before walking back to the sheriff's office. There was no doubt now that there were plenty of eyes on him, watching him go inside, so they could readily direct anyone looking for

him. Nothing to do now, but wait for the arrival of the
Double-D. He loaded the shotgun and the Henry, then,
noticing a coffeepot and a sack of coffee on the little sink
beside the pump, he decided to try it out. He was sampling
his first cup when he glanced out the front window and
saw four men on horses pull up before the saloon and tie
their mounts at the rail. One man, obviously the boss,
started toward the saloon door. An older man than the other
three, he strode straight and tall. Wearing a Boss of the
Plains hat, a buckskin jacket, and cavalry boots, he
marched into the Rose. Cullen felt sure he had just had his
first glimpse of Major Nathan Dixon. "It shouldn't be long
now," he muttered, "just like Fanny said." He took another
sip of coffee, somewhat relieved to confirm that there were
only four of them.

Also drinking coffee, Chubby Green almost choked on
his when the door to the saloon was flung open and Nathan
Dixon led three range-hardened cowhands inside. It was
still early in the morning, so there was no one in the saloon
but Chubby and Lilly Bloodworth. Both became instantly
nervous. They often saw men from the Double-D come in
the saloon, too often in fact, for it usually meant trouble
for some poor soul, and destruction of a table or chair. But
Chubby could recall seeing the major only once before.
That was enough, however, for him to know who he was.

Looking much like a commander at the head of a military column, Dixon strode straight to the table where
Chubby and Lilly were seated. "Are you the owner of this
flytrap?" Dixon demanded, his eyes blazing under heavy
gray eyebrows.

"No, sir," Chubby gulped. "Mr. Malcolm Howard's the

owner, only he ain't here. He's outta town this week and won't likely come back before tomorrow or the next day." He glanced nervously at Lilly, who was staring, wide-eyed, at the imposing rancher. She was oblivious to the mischievous grins directed at her from Sam King and Harvey Bush, who had taken advantage of her services on friendlier occasions.

Not satisfied with Chubby's answer, Dixon said, "Then that makes you in charge here, right?"

"I reckon so," Chubby replied, not sure if his admission would get him into trouble or not.

"Was the owner here yesterday or last night?" Dixon pressed.

Chubby looked at Lilly for help, but she offered none. "No, sir," Chubby said, "he weren't here last night a-tall."

"So you were in charge last night, too," Dixon stated, "and that makes you answerable to me. One of my men was murdered in here last night, and I want to know what you've done about it."

Chubby was struck dumb, but Lilly spoke up. "It weren't murder. Tom Yates tried to draw on that man and he weren't fast enough." She was immediately struck across her face with a backhand from Dixon.

"Keep your mouth shut, whore, unless I tell you to speak," Dixon roared at her. Turning back to Chubby, he stormed, "I want that man! Where is he? Did that pitiful sheriff of yours arrest him for murder? Is he in jail?"

The questions were coming too fast and furious for Chubby, intimidated as he was by the major, so he blurted the answer to the last one. "Yes, sir, he's in jail." That much he was sure of. It had been the topic of discussion between him and Lilly ever since they saw McCabe kick open the door of the sheriff's office. "Yes, sir," he repeated,

"McCabe's in the jail." Dixon seemed surprised by that, knowing the sheriff's reputation. The fact that the sheriff might have arrested McCabe had no effect on the plans that the major had for him, however. With no further use for Chubby, he turned around and marched out the door.

"I hope you ain't just put McCabe in the grave," Lilly said, after they were gone, her cheek still stinging from the major's backhand. She was thinking about the night before and the fix she had almost gotten Shep Blackwell in. "I damn near got Shep killed last night."

"I didn't mean to do it," Chubby replied. "It just fell outta my mouth before I thought about what I was sayin'." They both rushed to the front window to see what was going to happen.

CHAPTER 5

Well, that didn't take long, Cullen thought when he saw the four men storm out of the saloon and head straight for him. He didn't know what to expect, but in case they charged in with guns blazing, he prepared to receive them the same way. He went back to the desk and laid his Winchester and the sheriff's Henry on it, aimed at the door. In the event that wasn't enough firepower, he placed his Colt .44 in front of him on the desk. With all three weapons, cocked, he sat down in the desk chair and waited.

In a few short seconds, he heard the four men's boots when they struck the short boardwalk in front of the office. The men paused there for another few seconds, no doubt contemplating the door latch dangling from one end, the padlock still locked. He figured it must have puzzled them, but it wasn't enough to inspire them to be cautious. In the next instant, the door was flung open wide to reveal the imposing figure of Major Nathan Dixon. Stopped by the sight of the powerful man seated at the desk, with each hand resting on the trigger guard of a rifle, and the muzzles of those rifles pointed straight at him, Dixon stopped cold. It was not the reception he had expected, for after Chubby had told him that McCabe was in the jail, he expected to find him in a cell. Having heard many descriptions of Sheriff Bartlett, he was reasonably sure the man he was facing was not him. He now found himself standing in the doorway alone, because when they saw what was waiting inside the room, the three men with him ducked to the sides of the door for cover.

For a long few moments, there was a standoff, as each man sized up the other. "Somethin' I can help you with?" Cullen broke the silence.

"Where's the sheriff?" Dixon asked.

"Outta town, is what I heard," Cullen said. "Some kinda trouble with some cattle rustlers is what he told some of the folks here in town. I thought I'd give him a hand keepin' the peace till he gets back."

Dixon remained standing there, one full step inside the door, his three men outside hugging the wall. "You'd be McCabe," he finally said, a thin smile parting his lips now, as he regained some of his confidence. "You're the fellow who shot Tom Yates."

"I am," Cullen answered. "If you've come to get the body for burial, your business is with a fellow named Freeman. He's the undertaker."

"No," Dixon replied. "My business is with you." He was still studying the man behind the desk. He was not at all what he had expected him to be. Calm, with no sign of fear or panic, this was no ordinary gunslinger. But in Dixon's mind, he was nothing more than a gunslinger and he had commanded many of his kind before. "Tom was fairly handy with that pair of matched pistols he wore—take a pretty fast man to outshoot him—that is, if he was facin' him at the time."

"There's fast and there's foolish," Cullen replied, his

somber tone never wavering. "Your man Yates was foolish. I gave him fair warnin' that he'd be better off if he kept his hands away from his pistols. If you're wonderin' about the shot that killed him, it's in the middle of his chest. Freeman can let you take a look if you want to."

Dixon already knew that Yates was shot facing McCabe, so he was surprised when Cullen felt no inclination to boast about it. This was not the typical saddle tramp who worked for him. He made his decision. "I came into town this mornin' with the clear intention to kill you for what you did to my two men. But I believe that would be a waste of a man good enough to take Tom Yates down. I could use a man like that at the Double-D. I don't know what you had in mind when you rode into Bonnie Creek, don't know if you're just driftin', or you're plannin' to stay. But you need to know that the town of Bonnie Creek is dyin' on the vine. I can guarantee that. I aim to close this town down. It's right in the middle of my range and sitting on the water I need for my cattle. I can use a man like you to help me." He paused to judge how Cullen was taking his little speech. When there was no sign of interest in the somber face looking back at him, he issued a warning. "Don't make the mistake of picking the wrong side to fight on. I'm holdin' my men off right now, but when I leave here, I'm through talkin'. My advice to you is to come work for me or ride on out of town while you can."

There was no doubt in Cullen's mind that the letters Percy Mitchell had sent to the governor, asking for his help, were legitimate complaints. "That was an interestin' job offer, Dixon," he responded. "I reckon I might be interested, if I was the same kind of troublemakin' saddle trash you've got ridin' for you. But from what I've heard, the folks in Bonnie Creek are determined to make it a successful town. And I'd kinda like to hang around to see if they can do it. Now, since you were considerate enough to warn me, I'll return the favor. The merchants are tired of havin' to repair all the damage your men make when they come into town, so that's gonna stop today. I ain't sayin' your men can't come to town. They just have to learn to act like respectable human beings."

"Respectable human beings, huh?" Dixon mocked. "That's awful strong talk for a damn drifter who's got no business in Bonnie Creek at all. What in hell makes you think you have anything to say about what goes on here? If I decide to bring my whole crew in here one day and wipe out this entire little nuisance of a town, there ain't very much anybody can do to stop me."

"I ain't sure you could afford the losses you would take, if you tried that," Cullen said. "Maybe the best thing I could do would be to shoot you down right now, since you've gone to the trouble to walk in here." He grasped the Winchester, raised it from the desk, and pointed it straight at Dixon's chest.

"Whoa!" Dixon couldn't help exclaiming, caught totally by surprise. He had never even considered the possibility that the troublesome stranger could have the audacity to threaten him. Feeling completely powerless with his men still outside, he was caught helplessly fumbling for words. "That would be your death warrant," he finally managed. "My men would string you up to a tree." He took one step backward, but was still not clear of the door, as he quickly glanced from side to side, looking for his men to come to his rescue. He still could not see them, however, because they were pressing close against the outside wall to avoid being shot. Dixon stared at the expressionless face so calmly watching him, his rifle ready to fire, and he realized that his life was dependent upon the stranger's whims. "I'm going to back away now, and you can think about what we've said here today. I'll tell my men to holster their weapons." He took another tentative step backward. "You just hold your fire, all right?" Cullen made no reply. Dixon took another step backward, clearing the doorway, and as soon as he did, he dived for cover. "Kill him!" he ordered frantically.

Reacting immediately, Sam King charged in the door, only to catch a .44 slug in the throat from Cullen's rifle. Stopped cold, he nevertheless tried to shoot his pistol, succeeding in putting a slug into the heavy oak desk before another round from the sheriff's Henry stopped him for good. Cullen cranked another cartridge into the chamber of his Winchester, swung the rifle around to fire at Reese Cochran, who had moved to the front window, preparing to shoot. Cochran was spun around by a bullet in his shoulder and showered by broken glass from the window pane before he could take a shot. There was no need for Dixon to order a retreat. He ran for cover in the saloon with Cochran, holding his wounded shoulder, and Harvey Bush running after him.

Cullen came from behind the desk and moved quickly to the door, in time to see them disappear into the Rose. He could not be sure what to expect now, but he decided he'd better be ready for their retaliation. Somehow, he didn't expect Dixon to retreat to his ranch. So to have a chance against the three of them—and he still counted Cochran, even with a shoulder wound—he needed to be out of the jail. And there was no way out of the jail but the front door. They could hole him up in there until they shot the place to pieces or burned him out. He decided right away that he would rather be outside, free to move about. Wasting no more time, he grabbed a couple of boxes of the sheriff's .44 cartridges and came back to the door. There was no sign of Dixon or his men as yet, so he stepped over the body lying in front of the door and slipped around toward the back of the building. Half expecting a series of gunshots to immediately follow him as he ran along the side of the jail, he stopped when he reached the safety of the back corner. So far, there was no sign of Dixon and his men scurrying for firing positions to attack the sheriff's office. He hoped that meant he had not been seen leaving the building, so he ran behind the black-smith's forge next door.

"What the . . ." was as far as Shep Blackwell got before Cullen told him to find cover or run. Shep was already wary, having been startled by the gunshots at the sheriff's office next door, but he had not known whether to run or hide. Still undecided, he stood there, trying to make up his mind.

"I've got three men across the street at the Rose that are gonna be shootin' in this direction pretty soon," Cullen quickly alerted him. "So it's best for you to get outta here and find some cover somewhere. I'm gonna wait here and see if I can get a decent shot at 'em." Without further dis-cussion, he dropped down on one knee behind the forge, his rifle ready to fire, his eye upon the door of the saloon.

Blackwell knew the three men Cullen referred to, so he decided to flee, but hesitated before actually making a move. This solemn stranger had landed in their town yesterday and was already at war with the Double-D. He had bla-tantly stepped into the trouble with the town's adversary, not knowing if the town would back his move. He had asked for no help in what could be a battle with the entire Double-D crew and showed no signs of withdrawing and dropping his trouble in the town's lap. Blackwell thought about the night before, when the stranger interfered with Curly's plans to carve him up. Seemingly without reason, McCabe saw it as his responsibility to stand up to the major's gang of horse thieves, robbers, and murderers, even if the men of the town wouldn't. Blackwell decided then that he would take a stand beside McCabe. It was high time somebody did, so he spoke up. "I'll lend you a hand." Cullen's attention was immediately captured. He had not anticipated help from anyone since no one had defied Dixon before this time. "I've got my rifle," Blackwell went on, as he knelt down behind the anvil. "Where are they comin' from?"

"They're in the saloon," Cullen said, "but I don't know if they'll come out the front or not. I don't think they saw me slip out of the sheriff's office, so they'll most likely concentrate their fire there. Best keep an eye on the back corners of the buildin'. I don't think they'll take a chance out front." He turned his full attention back to the saloon, then paused to say, "I appreciate the help."

"I figure I owe you some help for what you done last night," Blackwell replied, then hesitated before continuing. "I'll tell you the truth, mister, I don't know why you landed here and managed to stir up that mess with the Double-D, but it's been long overdue. It was bound to come to a head pretty soon. I reckon I was like everybody else in town, just hopin' it would go away by itself." That was as far as he got before they saw Reese Cochran, his sleeve red with blood, run out of the saloon and take cover behind their horses. Not sure what he was up to, Cullen cautioned Blackwell to hold his fire until he had a clear shot. "He's gettin' the horses out of the way!" Blackwell reported when Cochran led the four horses around behind the saloon, using them

as cover in the process. "Maybe they're fixin' to hightail
it," he exclaimed. But a couple of minutes later, they saw
Reese come from behind the saloon and run to the barbershop next door. "Get ready!" Blackwell exclaimed.

"Hold on a minute," Cullen said. "Let's see where the
other two are before we show 'em where we are." He had
no sooner said it when they saw Harvey Bush run from the
rear of the saloon to the back of the stable, which sat on
the other side of the saloon. It was obvious they were planning to attack the sheriff's office from three sides, maybe
with hopes of one of them getting around to the rear of the
jail. If that was the case, then either Bush or Cochran
would be making an attempt to sprint across the street.
Cullen figured it would be Bush, since Cochran was hand-
icapped by his wounded shoulder, so he shifted his position
to give himself a better angle to shoot toward the stable.
"One of 'em's gonna be tryin' to make it across the street,"
he said to Blackwell. "You keep your eye on the street in
front of the barbershop. I'll take the stable."

The wait was not long, for all at once, Dixon started
firing from the corner of the front window of the saloon
into the open door of the sheriff's office. The object of his
assault was no doubt to keep Cullen pinned down long
enough to allow Bush to sprint across the street to gain
cover behind the post office. Dixon was obviously under
the impression that Cullen was still in the sheriff's office.
It might likely have worked had Cullen still been there. As
it happened, however, Cullen, having an excellent line of
fire from the blacksmith shop, cut Bush down before he
reached the middle of the street. Cullen's shot prompted
Cochran to open up from the back corner of the barbershop. This, in turn, caused Blackwell to concentrate his

fire on that spot, while Cullen poured shot after shot toward the saloon window to silence Dixon.

With no safe position to shoot from, Dixon was effectively stopped. Furious to have been so totally defeated, he was left with no alternative other than to retreat. In frustration, he backed away from his position beside the window and emptied the last two rounds in his pistol toward the bar, behind which Chubby and Lilly had taken cover. As fast as he could manage, he reloaded his gun as he backed away toward the rear of the saloon, taking one last shot at the bar before escaping out the back door. As soon as he was outside, he yelled for Cochran and jumped up into the saddle. In a second, Reese ran across the small alley to join him, with bullets kicking up the alley dirt behind him. When Reese saw the major in the saddle, he exclaimed, "Harvey!"

"Harvey's dead," the major blurted. "Get the horses!" He then kicked his horse hard and galloped off behind the stable, leaving his foreman to take the two extra horses. There was no time to fashion a lead rope for the two horses, so Cochran grabbed the reins of both, then climbed into the saddle and started out after his boss. With .44 slugs snapping through the air around him as he galloped across the open space between the saloon and the stable, he found he couldn't handle the two extra horses. His wounded shoulder made it too difficult to hang on to both sets of reins with that hand, and the horses trying to gallop while so close together, added to his difficulty. Almost immediately, he had to let go of one set of reins and leave one horse behind.

"They're runnin'!" Cullen shouted to Blackwell, and left the cover of the forge to give chase. With Blackwell close behind him, he ran past Bush's body toward the stable in time to get a glimpse of the horse Cochran was leading before it disappeared from sight into the trees. He looked at Blackwell, his eyes wide with the excitement of the unexpected skirmish. "Thanks for your help. I don't know how it woulda turned out without it," Cullen told him.

Blackwell puffed up a little but thought to question his contribution. "Hell, I don't know how much help I was. I didn't hit nobody." His eyes shifted back to the body lying in the middle of the street. "I don't know what Dixon's gonna do now. We might be in real trouble." He paused, then added, "Or maybe he'll think again when he talks about runnin' us outta town."

"I wouldn't bet on it," Cullen said. He figured Dixon would be more determined than before to take vengeance upon the town. He had delivered a message that day, but it was most likely a declaration of war. He had hoped for a totally different outcome after today's fight. If he had managed to kill Dixon, instead of two of his men, that might have been the end of Bonnie Creek's problem with the Double-D. He shouldn't have hesitated to shoot Dixon when he had him standing helplessly in the doorway. Instead of threatening to shoot him, he should have pulled the trigger. With this day's fight, the problems would more than likely multiply. A shout from Chubby interrupted his thoughts then and acted as an all-clear signal. The town, which had appeared to be deserted, was now busy with curious spectators. Cullen was reminded of a giant anthill that suddenly had its top knocked off.

Leaving Blackwell to tell the onlookers what had just happened, Cullen went inside the stable to check on his horses. Like most everyone else in town, Ross Horner had gone to join the small crowd of spectators in the street in front of the saloon. Cullen found both his horses in good shape and apparently well cared for. How long he would be staying in town would be hard to predict, so he figured he might as well get himself a room in the hotel. He picked up his saddlebags and went back up to the hotel, walking behind the buildings to avoid the people out front.

While Cullen was on his way to the hotel, the owner of that establishment, Marvin Winter, was one of those gathered around Shep Blackwell and Chubby Green, as they recounted what had taken place. "It was ol' Nathan Dixon, hisself," Chubby brayed loudly. "After he got blasted away from the front window, he ran like a scalded dog—emptied his gun at Lilly and me behind the bar—didn't hit nothin' but the bar."

After hearing Shep's accounting of the shootout, during which Shep helped Cullen, Winter walked over to discuss it with Percy Mitchell, the mayor, and Norman Freeman, who was in the process of examining the body lying in the middle of the street. "Got him with one shot," Freeman commented when he looked up and saw Winter approaching. "Looks like he mighta got him right through the lungs."

Winter bent over to take a close look at the corpse. When he straightened up again, he said, "One of the Double-D hands, I've seen him in town before, but I don't know his name." Knowing no one else did, either, he said, "Shep says that fellow that killed Tom Yates is the same one who shot that fellow lying in the front door of the sheriff's office and this one here in the street." He looked at Percy Mitchell. "Anybody know his name?"

"Cullen McCabe," Freeman announced, and got to his feet.

"Cullen McCabe," Winter repeated. "Who the hell is he? Does anybody know?" His questions seemed to be aimed at the mayor.

Mitchell shrugged. "Don't look at me. Damned if I know who he is. Just another gunslinging drifter coming through town, causing trouble, I reckon."

"Whaddaya think we oughta do about him, Percy?" Winter asked. "These three killings could bring that Double-D gang down on us worse than ever. Where the hell is Bob Bartlett?" His question was met with shrugs and blank expressions.

"I don't know," Freeman answered, "but ain't he gonna be surprised when he gets back and finds out that McCabe fellow took over his office and damn near got it shot to pieces?"

The mayor shook his head when he considered what Freeman had said. "I swear, Marvin, I don't know what we're gonna do about him. The sheriff's the one we pay to arrest people."

"How many of those Double-D hoodlums has Bob Bartlett ever arrested?" Freeman couldn't help asking. No one answered his question, since it was pretty well known that Bartlett tended to be scarce whenever there was any altercation involving Dixon's men. The jail seemed to be no more than a place for nonviolent drunks to sleep it off. Freeman looked up at the town's two leading citizens. "Make no mistake about it," he said, "McCabe's done stirred up a nest of yellow jackets—been in town for one night and killed three of Dixon's men." He shook his head thoughtfully. "And wounded two, countin' the job he did on that big 'un they call Curly."

He didn't have to remind Mitchell or Winter about that. It was very much on the minds of both men, since both were heavily invested in the success and growth of Bonnie Creek. Turning to Mitchell, Winter asked, "Have you still not heard from the governor, Percy?"

"Nothing that offers any hope of help coming our way," Mitchell replied. "He acknowledged our complaint and that's all it amounted to. I reckon he's telling us to handle it ourselves."

"Ain't that a fine how-do-you-do?" Winter commented. "My business at the hotel is already down because so many of the folks don't want to get hassled by that Double-D gang of outlaws. They'd rather drive a wagon half the night to get home than stay overnight in town. Just between you and me, I'm keeping John Taylor on out of the kindness of my heart. I don't have the heart to tell him I don't need him. If it wasn't for the dining room, I'd be thinking about closing up and moving on. Thank the good Lord for Daisy and her girls."

"It looks like we're gonna have to form a protection committee if we're gonna keep our town from turning into a hellhole," Mitchell said. "I think we all know that Bob Bartlett ain't got the grit to protect our town, but maybe if we can give him a little help . . ."

That was as far as he got before Winter interrupted. "I don't know about you, but I'm getting a little too old to join any vigilante posse. And you ain't no spring chicken, yourself, Percy."

"I know, I know," Mitchell was quick to agree, "but there are some younger men who should be able to help." He nodded toward Freeman, who was still crouched beside the body. "Hell, Shep Blackwell has already stepped up today to help this McCabe fellow, so we could count on him. Ross Horner oughta be able to help. Wilbur Tate. There's a few others," he said, although no additional names came readily to mind.

Winter was not enthusiastic about the vigilante idea. For one thing, there were too many men working at the Double-D. For another, McCabe, who had stirred this hornet's nest, looked to be no more than another wild gunman. If anything, he'd only served to bring their trouble with the Double-D to a head sooner than it might have otherwise. "I reckon we could stand here and speculate about our problem all day, but I don't know what good it would do us. I expect we'd best have a discussion with Bob Bartlett when he comes back. We're paying him to protect the people of this town and not to ride off whenever some rancher is missing a cow. Right now, I'd better get back to the hotel." Winter paused to point to the shattered window in the front of the saloon. "Malcolm's gonna have a nice little surprise waiting for him when he gets back." He nodded to each of them and hurried off up the street.

John Taylor was standing at the front desk when Marvin Winter returned to his hotel. Taylor, eager to hear about the shooting, looked up when Winter walked in. "Any of our folks hurt?" he asked.

"No," Winter answered, "but there's another dead Double-D hand lying in the street, down in front of the sheriff's office, and another one lying in the sheriff's door. Dixon, himself, rode in with three of his men, looking for that drifter that shot one of his boys last night."

"I declare," Taylor replied, well aware that it was rare, indeed, when the owner of the Double-D came into town.

Then knowing his boss could use some cheerful news, he said, "Well, I rented a room while you were gone, number three, up front. Fellow said he might be in town for a few days—paid up front for the first two nights."

"Well, I hope we don't have any more shooting parties to change his mind, if he heard that shootout at the sheriff's office. And I don't know how he couldn't have," Winter said. "Did he say what he was in town for?" When Taylor replied that he had failed to ask him, Winter asked, "What's his name?"

Taylor glanced at his guest registry to be sure. "Cullen McCabe," he answered, then paused, puzzled by Winter's startled reaction.

Winter grabbed the registry and spun it around to see for himself, as if hoping Taylor had read it wrong. When he saw the strong plain handwriting that spelled out the name, he almost choked on his words. "Lord help us!" he exclaimed. "That's the man who shot all three of the Double-D hands!" At first, he glared at Taylor, angry that he had rented a room to the gunman. Then he realized that he could not fault Taylor. There was no way he could have known who he was. Like Taylor, Winter, himself, had never seen Cullen McCabe.

Seeing his boss's distress, Taylor tried to defend his actions. "He seemed all right to me, kinda quiet-like, but he was a big fellow." His next thought was that he hoped his boss wasn't going to tell him to inform McCabe that he was going to have to get out. He didn't care for the image of himself confronting the ominous man.

"Is he in his room?" Winter asked, not really wanting to, but feeling that he should meet the man to try to get a clue if the hotel was in for any trouble.

"I don't know," Taylor said. "I know he took his saddle-bags upstairs, and he asked when the dining room would open for dinner."

"I'll look in the dining room first," Winter said, talking to himself. "Maybe get an idea why he's in Bonnie Creek and how long he intends to stay." It was still a little too early for Daisy to open for the noontime meal, but he decided to check there, anyway, before going upstairs to find McCabe.

He found Cullen seated at the same table close to the door and the table where firearms were deposited, drinking a cup of coffee. Cullen looked up when Winter stopped before the table and introduced himself. "Pardon me, Mr. McCabe, I'm Marvin Winter. I'm the owner of Winter House."

Cullen greeted him with a cool, steady eye, as if entering him in his mind's depository. Then he nodded. "What can I do for you, Mr. Winter?"

Like most folks, upon meeting McCabe for the first time, Winter found himself unprepared for the aura of quiet confidence that surrounded the somber man. "Ah . . . well . . ." he stammered, not certain what to say. "I just like to meet strangers who check in to the hotel," he finally managed. All thoughts of ordering him out of the hotel were immediately abandoned. "I was wondering if I could ask you what line of business you're in. You planning to settle in Bonnie Creek?"

"I wasn't plannin' on it," Cullen said.

"Just passing through, then," Winter continued. "I just wanted to thank you for your business and hope your room is satisfactory." As soon as he said it, he wished he hadn't, because he felt he was placating the solemn gunman.

"It'll beat sleepin' in the stable with my horse," Cullen replied unemotionally.

Since there seemed to be no hint of the snide demeanor of the typical gunslinger, Winter was encouraged to continue. "It's just downright bad luck you've had with those ranch hands from the Double-D, and it'd be remiss of me if I didn't warn you about the possibility of more trouble with them. The old man, Major Dixon, himself came into town looking for you. That's something that doesn't happen very often, I mean him coming to town at all, and he wasn't very happy when he left." He was interrupted momentarily when Daisy came in to refill Cullen's cup. She asked if Winter would like a cup also and he refused and resumed his appeal to Cullen. "What I'm trying to say to you, Mr. McCabe, is the major keeps a large number of men year-round. He is likely to return with a number too large for one man to fight."

"What you're sayin' is you think it'd be best if I got the hell outta town, or at least outta your hotel," Cullen said. "Then maybe he wouldn't come down hard on you. Ain't that about the size of it?" When Winter answered with a timid sputtering and nothing more, Cullen went on. "Maybe if you don't tell him, Dixon won't know I'm stayin' in your hotel. Even if he finds out, I don't expect to stay in my room. He'll catch me at the saloon or the stable, most likely. I don't plan to hide from him and his men, and I'm findin' it hard to understand why a whole town is tryin' to hide from him."

Slightly flushed with embarrassment now, Winter offered a weak excuse. "Like I said, Dixon has a lot of men, and they're mostly outlaws."

"Well, Mr. Winter, looks to me like it's about time for

the town to get together and stand up to the Double-D. Don't you think?" With that, he got to his feet and dug into his pocket for a couple of coins to leave for his coffee. "Now, I reckon I'd best get outta here. Miss Daisy let me buy a cup of coffee, if I didn't get in her way, and I told her I'd be back when she was ready to feed again. Pleasure talkin' to ya." He walked around Winter and headed toward the table to pick up his weapons. Then he was out the door, leaving Winter to stand there perplexed. He had learned nothing about the man, or what he was doing in town, other than the fact that he didn't scare very easily.

When Daisy came to pick up the empty cup from the table, she paused long enough to comment to Winter, "He's a strange one, ain't he? Tough to figure out. One thing you can say about him is he sure doesn't slip into a town unnoticed."

"He's crazy, if you ask me," Winter said. "He's already lived longer than he should have, and he's still hanging around town. What I'm afraid of is how many innocent town folk are gonna get killed, if they get caught between him and the Double-D?"

"If you ask me, what he said about the town gettin' together to form a vigilance committee sounds like good advice," Daisy said. "Maybe Bob Bartlett would grow a little backbone if he had somebody backin' him." She handed McCabe's cup to Fanny, who had busied herself in the kitchen the entire time Cullen sat at the table drinking coffee.

CHAPTER 6

Cullen stood outside the hotel dining room, watching Norman Freeman down the street as he collected the bodies of the two men killed that morning. Cullen's stop in the dining room was merely to give Freeman time to pick up both of the dead men. When Freeman had loaded them in his wagon and hauled them behind his barbershop, Cullen walked back toward Blackwell's blacksmith shop. The crowd that had gathered was now dispersed, having gone back to their businesses or to the saloon. "McCabe," Shep acknowledged him when he walked in.

"I'd be obliged if I could ask you for another favor," Cullen said. "I need to do a little repair work on Sheriff Bartlett's front door, and I'm wonderin' if I can borrow a hammer from you. Shouldn't take long, and maybe a few nails, if you got some to spare."

"Why, sure," Blackwell responded, then when he thought about the broken latch, he was quick to suggest, "Here, let me take a look at that. I can fix it for you."

"It shouldn't be much of a job," Cullen replied. "I should be able to do it. I figure I sorta took some free liberties by usin' the sheriff's office for that little discussion with Dixon and his boys. The least I can do is fix the latch and make sure everything's back just like I found it."

Blackwell picked up a hammer, a crowbar, and a handful of nails. "Come on, let's go take a look at that latch." As Cullen had said, the damage wasn't much. The main problem was the nails that had been jerked out of the door had left holes that would now be too big. So Blackwell wedged the hasp off the doorjamb with his crowbar and moved the latch up a few inches to drive the nails in solid wood. Before he drove in the final nails, Cullen returned the Henry rifle to the gun case on the wall, along with what cartridges he hadn't used. When he felt sure everything was right, at least to his satisfaction, he gave Shep the go-ahead to nail the latch in place. Cullen looked at the finished repair, the padlock still locked, and he nodded his approval. "Much obliged," he said to Shep. "Now, if you've worked up an appetite, it'd be my pleasure to buy your dinner at the hotel dinin' room." He felt that he owed Shep for his willingness to take up his rifle and commit to protecting the town. He was also curious as to how much he could count on him, if he needed help in the coming days.

"Why, I'll gladly take you up on that," Blackwell replied at once, "but you don't owe me nothin' a-tall. I brought me a cold biscuit and a slice of ham for dinner, but I can eat 'em for supper tonight. Come to think of it, a plate at Daisy's, and I might not need any supper."

"I take it you ain't married," Cullen commented, since Shep had not hesitated to accept his invitation.

"That's a fact," Shep replied. "I ain't ever come close. How 'bout you?" Cullen replied that he had been at one time, but he wasn't now. He offered no details. "That's my abode right there," Shep went on. He pointed to a neat little cabin on the back of his property close to the jail. "It ain't exactly a mansion to bring a woman home to, but it does just fine for me."

"I reckon that's all that counts," Cullen said. He was thinking Shep might be counted on when more trouble started, especially since there was no little woman to worry about him.

It was not fear of pursuit that had caused Major Nathan Dixon to push his horse mercilessly over the four and a half miles between his ranch headquarters and the town of Bonnie Creek. He seriously doubted there were enough men in Bonnie Creek with sufficient nerve to form a posse. He drove his laboring horse out of sheer fury over the damage he had suffered at the hand of one troublesome drifter. *Cullen McCabe*—the very sound of the name caused Dixon to clench his teeth in anger. Three of his men were dead and he, himself, had been threatened by this man who had ridden into town evidently with the intention of taking it over. He even had the audacity to commandeer the office of the town's sheriff when that cowardly individual fled rather than confront the wrath of the Double-D.

"Smokey!" Dixon roared when he charged into the barnyard and pulled the lathered Morgan gelding to a sliding stop in the door of the barn. He stepped down in time to hand Juan Hernandez his reins. "Where's Smokey?" Dixon demanded of the startled Mexican. "Reese has been shot."

Juan blinked in confusion as he gaped at Reese Cochran when he pulled his horse up beside Dixon's exhausted Morgan, leading one horse with an empty saddle. "Smokey's in the cookhouse," Juan said. "I go get him."

"Help me offa this damn horse first," Reese ordered, wincing with pain when he tried to dismount.

"Okay, I help you," Juan replied, and came to him at once, although afraid the major might berate him for not obeying his command immediately.

Cochran's wounded shoulder was of no importance to Dixon as he stormed from the barn on his way to the house. "Reese!" he ordered over his shoulder. "As soon as you get that shoulder fixed up, come on up to the house. We've got some things to talk about. It's time for those bastards in Bonnie Creek to find out who rules this range."

"Yes, sir," Cochran dragged out, "soon as I get the bleedin' stopped." He turned to Juan as soon as Dixon was out of earshot. "Take care of these horses. He damn near killed 'em on the way back from town. I'll go find Smokey."

"Where's Sam and Harvey?" Juan asked as he took the reins of the three horses.

"They're dead," Reese replied. "Shot by the same devil that shot Tom Yates and winged me, and the major's hotter'n I've ever seen him before." He knew Dixon had ridden into town with him and the other two men, to show the people of Bonnie Creek what price they would pay for defying his will. The embarrassment of his exit from the confrontation was more painful to the major than the death of any of his men. Shaking his head in frustration, Reese walked off toward the cookhouse to find Smokey, leaving a confused Mexican to take care of the horses. Like Reese, Juan Hernandez had never seen the major when he didn't seem totally in control. He had a longer history with Dixon, having served as his valet when the major was in the army. Seeing him now, flustered and angry, was a sight unnerving to the faithful valet.

* * *

Four and a half miles away, the cause of the major's frustration had left Shep Blackwell after suggesting they meet at the hotel dining room at noon. Cullen figured it was time to meet the mayor of Bonnie Creek to see what kind of man had been judged the best to hold that office. He was still of a mind not to inform the mayor that he was in Bonnie Creek in response to the letters sent to the governor. Whether or not that was a wise decision, he couldn't say, but he preferred it that way, at least for a while yet. He had to admit to himself that he was still not sure he was comfortable as the governor's special agent. But, as Horner had said after he had killed Tom Yates, he had stirred up a real nest of yellow jackets, so he was bound to stand firm against whatever Dixon threw at him.

Percy Mitchell was in the process of removing the top from a twenty-pound container of dried apples when the formidable stranger entered Mitchell General Merchandise. He did not greet him right away, held speechless for the moment because he and his wife had just been discussing the arrival of one Cullen McCabe in Bonnie Creek. Percy could not deny an eerie sensation that their discussion had somehow summoned the mysterious man to their door. It seemed to him that, of all the town's leading citizens, he and Malcolm Howard were the only ones never to have met the man. The man now standing in the door of his store was strikingly different from the man he had only glimpsed at a distance before. Bigger up close than he had seemed at a distance, he moved with the deadly grace of a mountain lion. Percy cast a nervous glance toward his wife, standing at the end of the counter. She was seemingly as dumbstruck as he. It was Cullen who finally broke the silent impasse. "You open for business?"

The question was enough to jolt Mitchell out of his sudden stupor. For some reason, he had not expected the grim gunman to come into his store. "Yes, sir," he finally blurted. "What can we help you with?"

"I understand you're the mayor of Bonnie Creek," Cullen said.

"Yes, sir, that's right," Mitchell answered, wondering if he was endangering himself by admitting it. "The business owners decided I should be the mayor. I guess nobody else wanted the job." Then remembering his manners, he said, "This is my wife, Jane."

His wife, not nearly so intimidated by the somber stranger, greeted Cullen. "Pleased to meet you, Mr. McCabe—I think."

There was no mistaking the sarcasm in her remark and Cullen was quick to realize it. "Ma'am," he acknowledged with a nod. "I reckon I owe you folks an apology for the shootin' I caused in town. At the time, though, I couldn't see any way to avoid it, seein' as how all three men took a notion to kill me. I guarantee you, I didn't come to town lookin' for trouble. I just didn't know that this town is where trouble lives."

"The trouble ain't in the town," Jane Mitchell was quick to respond. "It's coming from the Double-D and everybody knows it. We'd have a real thriving little town if it wasn't for Nathan Dixon terrorizing the merchants and the small farms and ranches."

Cullen waited patiently for her to vent her anger before asking a question. "If everybody knows that, why don't the town people get together to put a stop to it?"

"That's easy enough to say," Percy answered, "but we're merchants and family men. We're not vigilantes. And those men of Dixon's are hardened outlaws. I've written the governor for help, but he keeps telling me he doesn't have the help to send." Warming to his subject, he had the courage to say, "It's easy for you to tell us to fight, while you're just a drifter who's stirred up a storm for us to weather, while you just ride on to the next town."

"I'm not goin' anywhere," Cullen calmly stated. "This latest trouble started when I rode into town, so I reckon I'll stick around to see if this town has the guts to survive. I've broken no laws in defending myself except, I reckon, maybe breakin' and enterin', when I kicked the sheriff's door open. But I did repair the damage, with the help of Shep Blackwell, so I reckon that'll be between the sheriff and me."

"It's my understanding that Shep helped you fight Dixon and his men," Mitchell said.

"That's a fact," Cullen replied, "and he didn't have to, he coulda run, but I reckon he figured it was time to fight the Double-D. He's a good man, and if you and the other folks decide to stop Dixon, he'll most likely join you." He could tell from Mitchell's troubled expression that the mayor was thinking about that possibility.

"We've talked about that some," Mitchell confessed. "At least Marvin Winter and I have, but we haven't gotten very far with it. Like I said before, Dixon has a small army of outlaws working for him. I'm not sure we could round up enough men in town to have a chance against that gang of murderers." He paused then when his wife interrupted.

"Are you saying you'll stay and fight with the men of this town?" she asked. "You were just passing through Bonnie Creek on your way to I don't know where. Why would you stay here and take a chance on getting shot?

You just suddenly appeared one day, you might just as suddenly disappear if it gets too hot in town."

"You've got a point there," Cullen replied, "and I don't blame you for thinkin' that. But I ain't ready to leave yet. The weather's already startin' to get a little chilly and I ain't anxious to get back to sleepin' on the ground right now. If Mr. Winter don't go up on his rates, I think I'll hang around for a while—at least till my money runs out." Judging by her expression, he figured she didn't put much faith in what he said. There seemed to be no more to say, so he tipped his hat to her and said, "Well, I reckon I'd best be movin' along, I'm gonna meet Shep Blackwell at the hotel dinin' room. It was nice meetin' you folks."

"Glad you dropped in," Mitchell said, and walked to the door with him. He remained there, watching Cullen as he crossed the street toward the hotel.

Stepping up behind her husband, Jane said, "That man scares me. What in the world does he expect to get outta helping us fight Nathan Dixon?" She slowly shook her head when another thought occurred. "For all we know, he might really be one of Dixon's men."

"If he is, he's got a funny way of showing it," her husband responded, "killing three of them."

"Yeah, well you notice he didn't shoot Dixon," she insisted, aware that her argument was a weak one.

"Well, you are right about one thing," Mitchell said. "It's hard to trust a man like that. But I'm afraid he's right, it's time we called everybody together to decide what we're gonna do to save our town. Maybe him hitting town has brought this war with Dixon to a head, but it was coming sooner or later. We were just acting foolish, thinking the governor was gonna send the Texas Rangers here to help us. And if McCabe is really willing to lend his gun to our cause, we oughta be damn glad to get it. I'll go over and talk to Marvin about calling a meeting."

Cullen found Shep Blackwell waiting in the dining room. He was talking to Daisy and Fanny when Cullen walked in. "Well, here he is now," Daisy announced, so Cullen figured he must have been the topic of conversation. Had he given it any thought, he should have surmised that he was almost everyone's topic. "I even sat Shep down at your favorite table," Daisy went on. "I told him you don't like to set too far from your guns."

"I 'preciate it," Cullen replied, and nodded to both women. Fanny, whose eyes seemed to have gotten wider when he walked in, gave him a quick nod in return, then promptly excused herself, claiming to have duties in the kitchen. It didn't take a lot of thought on Cullen's part to realize she was fearful that Daisy and Bertha might guess her secret. If he got a chance to speak to her alone, he would thank her for the tip-off and assure her that her secret was safe with him.

When Daisy went off to the kitchen to tell Bertha to put a couple of steaks on for them, Cullen made it a point to thank Shep again for his help earlier that morning. The discussion naturally led to speculations about what to expect in retaliation, and Shep assured him that there was bound to be some. "He'll do somethin'," Shep assured him. "Dixon ain't accustomed to gettin' his ass whupped. Last fall, he sent a bunch of his men in to set fire to the new bank buildin' that was almost finished. They was gonna open a bank here, but after Dixon's men burned it down, the folks from Fort Worth said to hell with Bonnie Creek, they'd open their bank somewhere else." He cocked his head to one side and winced at the memory. "The town was all excited about havin' a bank here. It was bound to help the town." He looked at Cullen and shrugged. "Can't blame 'em, though, they most likely figured they'd get robbed about once a week."

"You took a stand this mornin'," Cullen said. "Will anybody else stand up to Dixon, if he decides to make war on the town?"

"I don't know," Shep replied. "There ain't many, I'd think—maybe Ross Horner, Norman Freeman, me, Wilbur Tate—course, there's the sheriff. Tell you the truth, though, I didn't really take a stand. I reckon I helped you 'cause it just seemed wrong not to."

Cullen found it interesting that Bob Bartlett was named last, almost as an afterthought. Normally he would have thought the sheriff would be the first name to come to mind. It only served to strengthen the initial opinion he had formed of the sheriff. *Maybe he'll fool me*, he thought hopefully. *I'm gonna need all the help I can get.* "I just came from the mayor's store. Talked to Mitchell and his wife about the need for the town to organize to protect it. Don't know if anything'll come of it. I wanted to let him know that I planned to be here to help what I evidently started." The conversation was interrupted when Daisy arrived with two steaks. Fanny was right behind her with the coffeepot.

"Well, lookee yonder," Daisy said when she glanced up from the table and caught a glimpse of a rider in the window. "Our sheriff's back in town—wonder if he's plannin' to come eat with us." Cullen turned to look, but the sheriff had already passed by the hotel. Fanny filled Shep's and Cullen's cups, then quickly moved to the other tables to fill theirs.

"I expect I'd best go see him," Cullen said. "He might wanna know why the hasp on his door ain't in the same place he left it." He made no move toward hurrying his dinner, however, thinking there might be the possibility that Bartlett would come there to eat dinner, too.

When their meal was finished, and after a slice of apple pie and a final cup of coffee, Bartlett had not made an appearance. So Cullen and Shep walked back down to the blacksmith shop to find the sheriff standing out in front of his office, talking to Ross Horner. Their conversation was centered on the many bullet holes in the siding of the building, and Ross was relating the circumstances that caused them. "Here's Cullen and Shep now," Ross said when he saw them approaching. "I was just tellin' the sheriff how them bullet holes got in the wall behind his desk." He chuckled and added, "I told him he was lucky he warn't settin' there at the time."

"I reckon I owe you some explanation for breakin' into your office," Cullen said to Bartlett. "I needed a place to hole up, and I figured Dixon and his men wouldn't come to the sheriff's office lookin' for me, but I figured wrong. Anyway, I think I put everything back like I found it." He was not prepared for Bartlett's reaction. He expected one hell of a forceful response and probably an attempt to arrest him for kicking in his door. He anticipated being forced to expose his hand before it was over and show his badge and official papers.

However, that was not necessary, for Bartlett hardly flinched. "It don't make no difference to me," he said. "I just came back to get my belongings. I'm quittin' as sheriff—headin' back down to El Paso. If you want the job as sheriff, I'm sure Mitchell and the town council will be glad to give it to you. Ain't nobody else wants it, that's for sure, 'cause there's gonna be some hell to pay for what you've done since you hit town."

His statement caused Shep and Ross to blink in surprise, speechless at first until Ross pleaded, "You don't mean that, Bob." He looked at Shep for support. "Why, hell, me and Shep will give you a hand. You don't wanna run out on us and let that damn Double-D crowd run over the town. Hell, even Cullen, here, says he'll stay till we get somethin' settled."

Cullen was not as surprised as the other two, but he had not expected Bartlett to surrender so shamefully. "I don't want your job," he said to Bartlett. "I'm just passin' through Bonnie Creek, but I was willin' to stick around long enough to give you and the other folks in town a hand."

Showing a flicker of spark, Bartlett said, "I reckon that's only fair for you to offer, since it was you that started this trouble."

"Now hold on, Bob," Shep objected. "It weren't Cullen that started this trouble. It was that Double-D bunch. When Lilly Bloodworth pointed me out in the saloon and that damn Curly was fixin' to carve me up for fish bait, Cullen stepped in. He didn't have to."

"It was just McCabe this time," Ross said. "Next time, it'll be somebody else. They just look for any excuse to bust somebody up or shoot 'em down, if they get a chance. We need to stop 'em for good and then we'll start to build the kinda town we all want. You can be a part of that." When Bartlett simply shrugged in response, Ross asked, "When you thinkin' about leavin'? I reckon you'll be wantin' to tell Percy Mitchell you're gettin' ready to quit."

"I ain't gettin' ready, I've quit. I'm leavin' today, just as soon as I pack up my possibles," Bartlett said. "I reckon Percy will know I quit when he don't see me around no more. I'll leave my badge in my desk drawer with the keys to the cells and the gun cabinet. The padlock on the door belongs to me, so I'll be takin' that with me." He turned to go inside the office, pausing long enough to say, "Good luck to you boys."

He left two astonished town citizens standing in the middle of the street. Bartlett had a reputation as a somewhat timid lawman, but no one thought he would simply cut and run when the first real showdown occurred. After a long moment's silence, Shep turned to Ross and said, "I reckon I'll be settin' up in my cabin with my rifle ready tonight."

Ross nodded. "I reckon I will, too. Ain't no tellin' what they're gonna try to do." He looked at McCabe. "I wish you hadn't moved out of the stable and took a room in the hotel. I wouldn't mind havin' you in the barn tonight. I won't even charge you nothin'."

"I might end up there," Cullen said. "You just take good care of my horses." He planned to keep an eye on the town that night from the window of his room. It was upstairs at the front of the hotel and he could get a good view of anybody riding up the street.

"I think it'd be a good idea for all of us to stay awake tonight," Shep said. Ross agreed. They looked at each other, both with the same idea. It was Shep who voiced it. "I think I could use a drink right now."

"Me, too," Ross quickly seconded it. "How 'bout you, McCabe?"

"Maybe just a short one," Cullen replied. They walked across the street to the Rose. Behind them, Bartlett came out of the office with the last sack to tie on his packhorse. When it was tied on to his satisfaction, he stepped up into the saddle on the sorrel he rode and turned the horse's head toward the south end of the street.

"Howdy, boys," Chubby Green called out cheerfully when the three men walked into the saloon. "What'll it be?" When Ross and Shep replied "whiskey" at the same time, Chubby reached for the glasses, pausing only a second to ask, "How 'bout you, McCabe?"

"I'll have the same," Cullen answered, but refused the second one when it was offered. He wasn't sure what kind of night he might have, but whatever happened, he intended to meet it with a clear head.

While the three men stood at the bar, a middle-aged man with gray hair and mustache came from the back room and walked over to join them. "I thought it was about time I met the stranger who rode into town and killed three men before suppertime the next day," he said, and offered his hand. "Don't get me wrong, that's perfectly all right as long as they're Double-D hands." He flashed a wide smile. "My name's Malcolm Howard. I own this establishment, no matter what Chubby mighta told you."

Cullen shook his hand. "Cullen McCabe," he said.

"You cost me a ten-dollar gold piece," Howard went on. "I bet Buford Tate you'd be out of town before dinnertime today. And here you are, still in town and everybody thinking Nathan Dixon is gonna rain hell down on us." He grinned good-naturedly. "Let me tell you, I'm proud to meet a gunslinger who doesn't run when the odds aren't in his favor. That's what you are, ain't it? A gunslinger?"

Cullen was taken aback slightly by Howard's blunt approach, but decided he had no intention to be sarcastic. Without answering the question, Cullen asked one of his own. "Who's Buford Tate?" That was a name he hadn't heard since he came to town.

"He's the postmaster," Howard replied. "He's like me, too old to do anything but get into trouble. Drinks too much, but I encourage that, of course, and both of us are ready to pick up a weapon to defend our town. Ain't nobody had the guts to do that until you rode in and made us all think about it, which reminds me." He looked at Shep and Ross. "I was talking with Percy Mitchell a little while before you came in. He's calling a meeting tonight, right after supper, wants every responsible citizen there, so we can decide what to do to defend our town. I think it'd be a good idea if you were there, Mr. McCabe. It'll be at the hotel, in the dining room."

That was good news to Cullen, because he was of the opinion the town was doomed to be destroyed if they did not organize. "Will everybody be at that meetin'?" He asked the question thinking that if everyone was at the meeting, there would be no one watching the town.

"I see why you ask that," Howard responded. "Good question. Buford's son, Wilbur, is gonna keep an eye on the street and give a signal if he sees anything suspicious."

"How old is Wilbur?" Cullen asked, and was told he was twenty. That was more good news to Cullen, for that meant one more man who might be willing to fight. If everyone was willing to stand in defense of their town, they might end up with numbers more closely matching Dixon's gang of outlaws.

CHAPTER 7

Once the tables were cleared, the three women, following Marvin Winter's instructions, moved several of the tables together to create one long one for the meeting. Since the meeting was of grave concern to all the residents of the town, it was already under way while Bertha and Fanny were still cleaning the supper dishes in the kitchen. Mayor Percy Mitchell sat at the head of the table with Marvin Winter and Malcolm Howard on either side of him. The mayor opened the meeting with an introduction of Cullen for those few who had not met him close up. He wrapped it up by saying, "We're mighty glad you're willing to stand with the folks of Bonnie Creek." He had no sooner finished when an elderly man with long gray hair and a mustache and beard to match, sounded off.

"It appears to me that Mr. Cullen McCabe dang sure oughta be willin' to stand with us, 'cause from what I've heard, he started the trouble in the first place. We wouldn't be havin' no meetin' if he hadn't gunned down three of Dixon's men. Ain't that right?"

"Now, Poss," Mitchell replied, "that ain't exactly right.

McCabe didn't have any choice in the matter. He had to defend himself."

"The way I heard it, he was arguin' with one of 'em over that whore at the saloon, then him and Tom Yates got into it," Poss insisted. "Two gunslingers fightin' over a whore, and now the whole dang town has got to worry about what Dixon is gonna do." As brash as only an old-timer can be, he aimed an accusing stare at Cullen, who remained solemn and expressionless. "I'm wonderin' what McCabe is gonna gain from this. It's bound to be more'n just lendin' a helpin' hand."

"Now, hold on, Poss." Shep Blackwell got to his feet. "Whoever told you about that shootin' in the Rose must notta been there to see it. Cullen was standin' at the bar, mindin' his own business when Lilly Bloodworth pointed me out to that crazyman, Curly, and told him she was with me. She weren't, but that's what started it, and if it hadn't been for Cullen, I'd most likely be dead right now. He stepped in when Curly was fixin' to cut me up with a knife."

"Oh," Poss responded. "That bein' the case, glad to have you with us, Mr. McCabe." Without a pause, he asked, "Where's the sheriff? He oughta be here."

"He cut and run," Shep answered. "Got out while the gettin' was good."

"Damn," Poss swore, and paused for a moment before declaring, "I reckon that's about what everybody expected of him." He shifted his gaze back toward Cullen. "What about you, stranger, you want a job as sheriff?"

When Cullen made no reply, Mitchell said, "Meet Poss Rooks, McCabe. He owns the harness shop on the other side of the stable. He's been here longer than anybody but me, and he never did learn to keep his mouth shut when he didn't know what he was talkin' about. And I don't know why he thinks it's his place to offer the job of sheriff to anybody."

"As long as he can pull a trigger, he can talk all he wants," Cullen said, "but I ain't lookin' for the job of sheriff."

The meeting got under way at that point, with Mitchell predicting an uncertain future if things remained as they now were. "He has been sitting on our shoulders like a buzzard waiting for the town to slowly die. We'd have a bank now, if his men hadn't burned the damn thing down before it was finished. And that was when we had a sheriff. Now, when the town quit showing signs of dying and for the last six months has started to show a little growth, that ol' buzzard has started sinking his claws in a little deeper. As brazen as he was when we had a sheriff, you can imagine how he'll be now that we don't have one. This business yesterday and today would have happened sooner or later and now I'm afraid we're gonna see more trouble from Dixon sooner rather than later. And it ain't likely to be subtle. I expect his men will be provoking fights, just like Curly did when he tried to call Shep out. The question is, and the reason I called this meeting tonight is, what are we gonna do about it?"

"Hell, we've got no choice," Malcolm Howard said as he took the floor. "We've got to fight, and we've got to win, else we're all ruined. If he turns his crew loose to come in here and raise hell, pretty soon the word will get around that Bonnie Creek is a wild, lawless town. I don't know about the rest of you, but I've sunk everything I own into my business. I'm too damn old to start over somewhere else."

"What if he just sends all his men in here and raids the town, burns everybody out?" Ross Horner asked. "He might decide to shut us all down once and for all."

Cullen had remained quiet, preferring to listen to the discussion between the business owners, but he felt he should answer Horner's question. "I don't see that happenin'," he said. "He might like to do that, but I think he's got sense enough to know if he did, it would bring the military into this fight. The governor would likely get some response from the army if a whole town was wiped out. I figure Dixon knows he would be destroyed if he does enough to attract the army's attention. So he'll most likely keep sending his boys into town to raise hell and do as much damage as he can and hope you all get fed up with it and leave."

"I think McCabe's right," Shep Blackwell said. "We're gettin' all riled up thinkin' we've got to fight the whole damn bunch of 'em at the same time. They ain't likely to hit us with more'n four or five at a time, just out to cause mischief. We can fight that many if we're ready for 'em."

"Well, I ain't as young as some of you fellows," Marvin Winter spoke up. "I don't know how good I'd be in a gunfight with those outlaws that work for Nathan Dixon."

"I'm as old as you are," Poss Rooks blurted, "maybe older, and I ain't too old to fight."

"I think we oughta have a show of hands on who we can count on to fight," Malcolm Howard suggested, but before the hands could be counted, Wilbur, the postmaster's son, burst into the room.

"Shep!" Wilbur exclaimed, his eyes wide with excitement. "They're here! They set fire to your cabin!"

"How many?" Cullen asked.

"I counted three," Wilbur said. "They set it to blazin' before I ever saw 'em, and I think they're tryin' to set the jail on fire now!"

His alarm started a stampede toward the door, with

Shep leading. Cullen heard him moaning to himself, "Oh Lordy, Lordy, Lordy . . ." as Shep fumbled with his rifle, thinking about his losses as he headed toward the door. Cullen went into the kitchen instead, passing three frightened women as he ran down the narrow hallway past their rooms and out the back door. *Three men*, he thought as he ran across the clearing toward the river, *and not the sizable raiding party the town men had feared*. His first thought had been that this was not the real attack Dixon planned to launch on Bonnie Creek. That was yet to come, but speculating on the major's arrogance, he figured this was a mission of punishment for Shep Blackwell for his part in helping him at the fight in the sheriff's office. Why else would they pick Shep's plain little cabin to burn? If punishment was the case, those three arsonists were not likely to stand and fight the mob storming down the street toward them. Very likely, they crossed over the river behind the blacksmith and left their horses in the trees. *They'll be leaving the same way*, he thought, and waded across to the other side in an attempt to get between them and their horses.

Running through the shadows of the oaks that lined the riverbank, he heard shots ring out, and they sounded like they may have come from the outlaws. There were no return shots from the street right away, but soon he heard answering gunshots. In his mind, he pictured the mob of citizens scattering for cover when the outlaws fired at them. The flames from Shep's cabin soon grew large, lighting the yard behind it. They also provided light enough for him to make out the dark forms of three horses, tied to the branches of a couple of small oaks in the center of a line of larger trees. With little time to look for the best place to ambush the three Double-D hands, he ran to the horses with the intention of using them for cover.

The black horse he picked was skittish at first when Cullen suddenly appeared and took hold of its bridle. After a quick calming of the horse, Cullen laid his rifle across the saddle, aimed it at the burning cabin, and watched for the three men to show up. There were only a few random shots from the street in front of the cabin now as the would-be vigilantes shot at targets they could not see behind the burning cabin. In a short while, all firing ceased and Cullen got set to receive visitors. He heard their feet thrashing the shallow water as they splashed across the river, then the three were silhouetted against the flaming cabin behind them as they scrambled up the bank. "That's far enough!" Cullen commanded. "Put your hands—"

Their reaction was immediate, with all three firing at the sound of his voice in the darkness of the trees. Given no choice, Cullen squeezed off the first round, his .44 slug knocking the man on his left back down the bank. His muzzle blast drew fire from the other two and he could hear their bullets snapping the air around him. One of the horses screamed and reared when it was struck by a bullet. And as it tore its reins loose from the branch, Cullen dropped one of the remaining arsonists to his knees. Seeing his two partners shot down, the third outlaw turned tail and ran.

"What the hell?" Poss Rooks blurted. "Them shots come from across the river." He was lying behind the watering trough across from the blacksmith shop, where he and two others had taken cover. They lay there a long moment, listening. "The shootin's done stopped," he declared.

"McCabe," Shep said. "I'll bet that's why it stopped. He got over there behind 'em."

"You reckon?" Poss replied. "I was wonderin' what happened to him. I thought he mighta stayed back there with the women."

"You think they're gone?" This from Percy Mitchell, who had dived behind the trough with them when the outlaws started shooting at them.

"You could stick your head up over this trough and find out," Poss said.

Shep looked to his side to see what the other men were doing. He could just see Ross Horner's elbow from that angle where he and Wilbur Tate had taken cover at the corner of the saloon. Looking in the opposite direction, he couldn't see anyone, but he knew that Buford Tate and Malcolm Howard were somewhere behind the barbershop. "Well, we're gonna have to do somethin'," Shep said. He had no sooner made the statement when they heard McCabe's voice ring out from across the river.

"Hold your fire. It's over!" Cullen yelled. "You'd best see about the fire before it catches onto the jail!" Shep jumped up immediately and ran toward his cabin, which was engulfed totally in flames now. When no one fired a shot at him, the rest of the Bonnie Creek posse came from their hiding places and ran after him to gather around the bonfire that was his home. He picked up a bucket from his forge, filled it with water from his pump, then ran back to frantically toss the water at the flames. It had little effect upon the fire and it was obvious to those standing near him that he was wasting his time and effort. There was no chance of saving the cabin, but at least the jail next door wasn't in danger as Wilbur had feared. After repeating his first efforts even Shep realized the futility of it. "I could use some help with these horses," Cullen called out again from across the river. "One of 'em got shot."

Poss Rooks stepped up close enough to the fire to pull a piece of burning timber from it to use for a torch. Following his example, several others tried to snatch some more pieces out of the flames. Then they splashed across the river, where they encountered the two bodies on the opposite bank, one of which was still on his knees. This effectively halted the advance of the posse until Cullen assured them the man was dead. He walked down the bank, leading the wounded horse, a dun gelding. "There were three of 'em, all right," he said. "I gave 'em a chance to come peacefully, but they went for their guns. The other one took off on foot, headed up the river. I chased him till I couldn't see him anymore, then I stopped, in case he decided to stop runnin' and ambush me." He calmed the dun gelding when it started to shuffle its hooves nervously. "This one took a bullet in the neck, just above his withers. Thought maybe you might do some doctorin' on him," he said to Norman Freeman.

"I can dig a bullet outta him, if it ain't in too deep," Freeman said, and took the reins.

"Anybody recognize 'em?" Ross Horner asked while standing by the body that had rolled down the bank. "Bring one of those torches over here. Hold it up close to his face." No one could name the corpse, but several remembered having seen him in town before. "How 'bout the other one?" He pointed to the body still on its knees.

As if hearing him, the body picked that moment to keel over, face-first, causing Percy Mitchell to jump, startled. This prompted a comment from Poss. "Look out, there, Percy, he's liable to grab you." Mitchell responded with a nervous giggle.

"If it was up to me," Cullen said, "I reckon I'd say these horses they left behind oughta belong to Shep to help pay for the cabin he lost—and whatever was in it." That seemed to be all right with the rest of the men. No one was thinking of claiming them. "Maybe he could use the sheriff's office till he gets fixed up with a new cabin," Cullen suggested. He didn't express it, but he was thinking that, of all the men he had met in town, Shep might be the closest one suited to take on the job of sheriff. So he might get comfortable living in the jail and decide to stay there permanently.

They stood around the remains of Shep's cabin until certain the fire was no longer a threat to any of the other buildings. While watching the fire, the talk continued regarding the organization of a citizen's watch committee. The general consensus was that everyone should keep their shotguns and rifles ready to use to defend their own property against any drunken hell-raisers. "Of course, every man's gonna defend his own property. We don't need a committee to decide that. We need a damn sheriff," Malcolm Howard charged. "Who the hell is gonna lock up the drunks who ain't tryin' to kill us? At least Bob Bartlett could do that, even if he wasn't worth a damn when it came to anything else."

"You're right, Malcolm," Mitchell answered him, "and we'll have to find us one. But that ain't gonna do us any good right now. Right now, we've got a fight against the Double-D. He means to destroy the whole town, so we're at war. If this fire tonight ain't enough to warn us about what we have to expect, then I don't know what will. We've got to fight him until he gives up on his plans to run us out." He paused to emphasize his next statement. "And make no mistake, gentlemen, there isn't anyone to help us. As for the governor's office, there's no response."

As sobering as it was, there was no question with anyone there that what the mayor said was the sad truth of their situation. "What do you think we ought to do, Percy?" Marvin Winter asked.

"I think for the time being, until this thing with Dixon is settled, we need to make up a roster with one of us taking the responsibility of watching the town at night to give the alarm when something else like tonight happens," Mitchell replied. "There's enough of us so we wouldn't have to be the night watchman more than once a week."

"What about you, McCabe?" Poss wanted to know. "Are you gonna take a turn watchin' the town?"

"You can put me on the list," Cullen said. "I'll stick around till you folks get control of your town." His answer appeared to bring some relief to everyone, especially the older men. The solemn man's emotionless confidence in facing a dangerous situation had been witnessed by the citizens of the town on more than one occasion in the short time since he had suddenly appeared. While there was some speculation about his motives for involving himself in Bonnie Creek's fight to survive, most of the men didn't care at this point. Protecting their families and property was the concern now, and they would welcome the devil, himself, if he would stand with them against the Double-D.

Most of the men remained there at the blacksmith shop until the fire died out to leave only small flickering flames, before moving to the Rose to draw up their watchman duty roster. Cullen walked the captured horses down to the stable with Ross Horner, while Freeman went to his shop to get his surgical tools. All three would return to the saloon to see which night they were responsible for watching the town. As far as sleep for most of the men, this night was already destroyed, so there was still plenty of talk and speculation concerning the chance of another attack before morning. As for Cullen, he was of the strong opinion that the burning of Shep Blackwell's cabin was the extent of the violence for this night. He saw it as an immediate retaliation against the actions of one man, so he went to his room to get some sleep. As he prepared to leave, Percy Mitchell caught his arm. "How about meeting me for breakfast at the hotel in the morning? I'd like to talk over some things." Cullen agreed to be there early.

While the men of Bonnie Creek were still filling out their duty roster, some four and a half miles away, a weary man stumbled into the barnyard of the Double-D ranch. Reese Cochran, his arm in a sling, walked out of the barn in time to see Seth Wiley staggering from the pace he had tried to maintain to get home safely. "Seth! What the hell . . ." Reese exclaimed, and ran to meet him. "What happened? Where's Benny and Bill?"

"Dead," Seth answered, and kept walking, heading for the watering trough by the pump.

Reese followed him and waited impatiently by the trough until Seth finally lifted his head from the water. "Both of 'em dead?" he asked again. "How?" He gave that only a second's thought before asking, "McCabe?"

Almost choking on the water he had gulped, Seth looked at him and replied, "Damn right, McCabe! Who the hell else? He was waitin' for us on this side of the river. We never had a chance. He caught us comin' up the bank, cut Bill and Benny down, and woulda got me, too, if I hadn't took off through the trees." He gaped wide-eyed at Reese and demanded, "How the hell did he know to wait for us across the river? I'm tellin' you, Reese, that man's got me spooked."

"The major ain't gonna like this news," Reese said.

"You were supposed to burn that blacksmith's cabin down, just to let him know we knew it was him helpin' McCabe. He didn't say nothin' about gettin' in a gunfight with anybody."

"We burnt the damn cabin down!" Seth exclaimed. "They started shootin' first. A bunch of 'em come runnin' down the street, blazin' away, so we shot back and sent 'em scurryin' for someplace to hide. Then we hightailed it outta there, back across the river, but he was waitin' there between us and the horses. How'd he know to be there?" he demanded again.

"He just got the jump on you," Reese said. "Don't go makin' somethin' special out of him, he ain't nothin' but another hired gun, same as you and the rest of the boys here at the Double-D. He got lucky, that's all." He bit his lip and shook his head, not looking forward to what had to be done. "We're gonna have to go tell the major about this, and you tell him everything that happened. He ain't gonna like it. He's still burnin' about what happened in town at the jail." He looked Seth in the eye. "He ain't gonna like losin' three horses, either."

"I don't like it much, myself," Seth responded, with a hint of irritation now. "I lost my saddle and saddlebags, too. I reckon I wouldn't have my rifle if I hadn't been totin' it in my hand."

"Let's go up to the house," Reese said with no attempt to hide the reluctance he felt for the job. With twice that amount of reluctance, Seth accompanied him across the barnyard to the kitchen door, where Reese knocked politely. In a few minutes, the housekeeper opened the door. "Consuelo, has the major gone to bed?" Reese asked, his voice low, as if fearful he might disturb him if he was in bed.

When she informed him that the major was in his study, smoking a cigar while reading, Reese told her that there was something important that the major would want to know. "I go tell him," Consuelo said, and stepped back, holding the door for them to enter. "You wait here." Standing there, hats in hand, they could hear the major growling in response to her message, although they could not make out the words. In a few seconds, she appeared in the kitchen door and motioned for them to come.

Dixon was standing by the fireplace when they entered the room, a half-smoked cigar in his hand, and an open Bible lay on the table beside his chair. Knowing that Seth was one of the men sent to perform his act of immediate retaliation against anyone helping Cullen McCabe, he demanded, "Did you burn that place to the ground?" He at once saw the fear in his men's faces.

Reese didn't wait for Seth to answer. "Yes, sir," he said. "They burnt it to the ground, but they ran into some trouble while they was doin' it." He could see Dixon's heavy brow wrinkling and his dark eyes narrowing in anticipation of bad news. "Bill Pardee and Benny Doyle are dead," Reese pushed on. "Seth, here, was lucky to get away without gettin' shot." He paused then before adding, "And we lost the horses they was ridin'."

"All three of them?" Dixon asked, his eyes almost closed in anger. Reese nodded in reply. "So you came back here on foot?" he asked Seth directly.

"Yes, sir," Seth stuttered. "I had to walk back . . . you see, he was between us and the horses . . . there wasn't no way I could get to my horse."

"So you just turned and ran," Dixon finished the sentence for him in disgust. When Seth couldn't find words to answer, Dixon asked, "McCabe?"

"Yes, sir," Seth replied, his head bowed, afraid to look the major in the eye. "It was that feller named McCabe."

Dixon turned his anger on Reese. "What kind of gutless men am I paying good wages for? You send three men to start one fire, and they're stopped by one man, two of them killed and the other one chased off like a cowardly dog." He returned his fury to Seth again. "When I was commanding a regiment of fighting men in the war, I would have a man shot for running away from a battle!" Back to Reese again, he roared, "Get him out of my sight! Out of this house!"

"Yes, sir," Reese responded, and turned immediately to follow Seth, who was already on his way out the door. As they hurried through the kitchen, they went past Consuelo, who was shaking her head slowly.

Having heard the uproar from the study, she knew that she could anticipate a night of constant profanity and no hope of pleasing him with any chore he asked of her. She was afraid not to ask him if he needed anything, however, so she stuck her head inside the door. "Do you want anything from the kitchen?"

"No, damn it! I don't need anything from the kitchen," he roared at her. "Get the hell outta here and leave me alone!" She backed quickly away and hurried back to the kitchen.

Outside and on their way to the bunkhouse, Reese and Seth could only speculate on what this latest defeat would cause the major to do. "Dang it, Reese," Seth complained. "What did he jump on me for? He had us out in the open and we couldn't even see where he was. I threw some shots at where I thought he was, but I ain't dumb enough to stand there on that open riverbank, waitin' for my turn to get shot. We shoulda throwed our hands up when he told us to, but we didn't. Hell, you and the major done the same thing after McCabe shot Sam and Harvey. You came back without them, and from what Juan Hernandez said, he damn near rode that Morgan of his to death."

"I'm glad you didn't remind him about that while we were in there," Reese said. "He ain't too happy about what's happenin' in Bonnie Creek ever since that McCabe feller came to town, and anything's liable to set him off. I don't know what he's gonna do now, but you'd best pick out a new horse. We might be gettin' rousted out for another visit to Bonnie Creek. I don't know when we're gonna get back to workin' cattle." When Seth reminded him that he had lost his saddle and saddlebags as well, Reese said, "You can use Harvey's rig. It's in the barn."

"I wish you'd been able to bring Sam's horse back with you," Seth said. "I always admired that chestnut of his and he had a fairly new saddle, too."

"Yeah, too bad we lost that one," Reese said. He and the major had galloped away from Bonnie Creek. But he soon decided that he couldn't handle both of them, what with his wounded shoulder, so he just let go of one set of reins. When Seth asked why Dixon couldn't have led the other horse, Reese quickly told him he wasn't fool enough to tell the major he needed help. When he thought back on the morning, he remembered the major galloping away without looking back.

"Doggone it, Reese," Seth blurted, "how much is it gonna take before the major realizes he can't run everybody outta that town? How many more of us are gonna have to get killed by that damned hired gun before he gives up?"

"Don't be talkin' that kinda talk," Reese replied at once, concerned that Juan or Consuelo might overhear it and tell the major. "We've had some bad luck, but the major knows what he's doin'." He was afraid to confess to Seth that he had worrisome concerns, himself, and he was finding it harder and harder every day to retain his confidence in his judgment.

"Dang!" Jeff Hammond exclaimed when Seth walked into the bunkhouse and sank down hard on his bunk. "What happened to you? You look like you're wore out. Where you been? Smokey said he saw you ride out with Benny and Bill, said the major sent you into town."

Seth gave his friend a limp smile and a shake of his head before he answered. "We went to town for a house-warmin'." When his remark was met with a questioning expression from Jeff, he spelled it out. "The major sent us to burn the blacksmith's house to the ground, but we got ambushed by Cullen McCabe, and I walked back alone."

"You don't say!" Jeff blurted. "Benny and Bill dead? This keeps up and there ain't gonna be none of us left to run this ranch, much less ride down to Mexico to rustle more cattle." Then the second part of Seth's statement registered in his brain. "You walked back?" Seth replied that he certainly did and proceeded to tell him all that had happened.

"The major told us to burn the cabin down and we did but a mob of town folks came runnin' down the street, shooting at us and ran us right into that McCabe feller. I'm tellin' you, they were all set up to chase us right where he was waitin' for us." When he was done, Seth shook his head, as if to indicate he didn't know what was going to happen next.

"And you walked back?" Jeff asked again.

"Had to," Seth replied. "He was usin' our horses for cover." He locked eyes with his friend and spoke frankly. "I'll tell you what's the truth, Jeff, when that man said to stop, and we drew on him, he cut Bill and Benny down so quick it was like he shot both of 'em at the same time. I was damn lucky to get away."

"I didn't have no idea the major was gonna send you to town to burn that cabin. I was thinkin' about slippin' off tonight for a little visit to town, myself," Jeff confessed.

"Well, it wouldn'ta been a very good night for it," Seth said. "Those folks were pretty riled up when they saw that fire. We mighta set the house on fire and got outta there before anybody caught us, but Benny wouldn't leave till he was sure it was gonna catch up good. I lost my horse, saddle, and saddlebags, damn near everything I own, and had to run all the way back." He thought about what he just said and couldn't help an additional remark. "That gives me and Reese somethin' in common, don't it? I wonder which one of us ran that four and a half miles the fastest, me or his horse?" He gave Jeff a wink. "That little gal you're so sweet on mighta even took a shot at you if you had showed up there tonight."

"Nah," Jeff replied. "She wouldn't never do that. Me and her's got an understandin' about each other."

"Is that so?" Seth came back. "What kinda understandin' have you got? Has she got an understandin' that you're an outlaw and might find yourself on the end of a hangman's rope one day?"

His question caused Jeff to turn serious for a moment. "It might not always be like that," he said. "Somethin's bound to come along and change it. The major might forget about Bonnie Creek, especially if the people over there have got themselves organized like you said."

Seeing his friend's seriousness, Seth couldn't help feeling sorry for him. "Maybe so," he said. "Maybe it will change." As for his own philosophy, he was content to ride on the wrong side of the law. He had since he was a boy and it was the only way he had ever gained anything of value. After his dressing-down by the major that night, he might have wished he had hooked up with another outfit, but he knew there was nothing he could do to change it now. Consequently, he would just try to roll with it and stay out of Dixon's sight as much as possible. He sometimes wished Jeff was more like him, but Jeff was burdened with a conscience and that was liable to get him in trouble one day in this business. Of the Double-D crew, he and Jeff were the youngest, not counting Consuelo's thirteen-year-old son, Mateo, but Mateo wasn't one of the riders. He just did chores around the house for his mother. "Hey, I didn't get any supper," he blurted suddenly to bring his thoughts back. "Reese grabbed me to ride into town with Benny and Bill before I got a chance to eat. Let's go see if Smokey saved any cold biscuits."

"I figured I'd see you boys before I finished cleanin' up tonight," Smokey said when they appeared in the cookhouse door. "I didn't hear you ride in," he directed at Seth. "Where's Benny and Bill? You boys didn't get no supper." Seth repeated the story he had just told Jeff, and Smokey was as amazed as Jeff had been. "There's gonna be some hell to pay around here," Smokey commented. Like everyone else on the Double-D, he was accustomed to the major running over everybody who blocked his path. Two days ago, there were fourteen men riding for the Double-D. Now that number had been reduced to nine, and all of them done in by one man. Seth, Jeff, and Smokey speculated on what the major's next move might be for a short while before Smokey removed a cloth covering a plate of cold biscuits and pork belly. "Here," he said, "this'll keep your belly from rubbin' itself raw against your backbone. There's still some coffee left in that pot. It's been settin' on the stove for a good while, oughta be gettin' pretty rank by now, just right for drinkin'."

Jeff was glad to help Seth put away some of the biscuits. Since Benny and Bill didn't make it back from town, there were plenty. The talk about the deaths of two more of their partners continued with Smokey summing it up. "I reckon we'll find out somethin' in the mornin'. Now, get outta here so I can finish up tonight."

The clanging of Smokey's iron triangle dinner bell was heard earlier than usual the next morning, and when the men ambled into the cookhouse, they found Reese Cochran waiting for them. By then, everybody had heard about the deaths of Benny Doyle and Bill Pardee, so no one was really surprised to see Reese waiting for them. "Before Smokey puts breakfast on the table," he told them, "the major wants to tell you somethin'. He'll be here in a minute."

In less than a minute Major Nathan Dixon strode into the cookhouse. He was wearing his Boss of the Plains hat, cavalry boots, and a buckskin jacket that was given to him when his regiment defeated a concerted Comanche attack against an army outpost near the end of the War Between the States. The men guessed that he was about to raise hell with them or tell them to get ready for an expedition into Mexico to steal cattle. On this morning, it was neither. Before speaking, he looked around the room to make sure every man was there. All of his men were present, except

Ike Roper, who had already moved his gear out to the line shack before winter set in.

"It seems we have an obstacle in our path to make this the biggest cattle empire in the state of Texas," he began. "The reason I hired men of your particular skills was because I wanted to be prepared to destroy obstacles in our path. Now I'm beginning to wonder if I picked the right crew to handle this, because we've lost five men in our attempts to remove this obstacle, this one man, this Cullen McCabe. Nobody's ever heard of him, he just showed up one day, a damn drifter, far as anybody knows. Who the hell is he? If he's got a reputation as a fast gun, it sure ain't in Texas. I'm thinking he's just a killer and not a gunfighter at all. But if he is a gunfighter, I'm thinking about sending for Deacon Pratt, somebody I *have* heard of." The mention of Pratt's name caused a few grunts and murmurs from the eight men gathered around the table. Dixon let them consider that for a moment before continuing. "Pratt's gonna cost me a lotta money, money I'd rather give to one of you men, so I'm offering two hundred dollars to any of you to gun down Cullen McCabe. I don't care how you kill him— gunfight, ambush, any way you can put the man in the ground. But the total bounty is two hundred dollars to kill him. Whether it's one of you or more than one, two hundred is all I'm paying." He stood there and let that sink in for a few moments before issuing some additional orders. "I want everybody ready to move the main herd off the north range. I want 'em moved over to the east range, next to the river."

This was news to Reese. The major hadn't talked about that when he met with him the night before, so he questioned him. "All of 'em?" He knew he was talking about moving the cattle to the section right across the river from the town.

"All of 'em," Dixon emphasized. "I want to keep 'em there for a while, till there ain't any grass left to graze." It was a puzzling move to Reese and the men, but Dixon had reasons other than moving the herd to new grazing. He had decided it was time to make the people in the little town aware of the fact that they were sitting on his range. In truth, his range ended at the river, but he had always fully intended to claim the land beyond the river as part of his range. He knew that, if the town kept growing, there would be a bigger and bigger draw on the water from the river, and in his vision for expansion, he needed that water.

"I expect it won't take longer than a week before the grass will be gone from that one spot," Reese felt the need to point out.

"Maybe so," Dixon replied, "but we're gonna work it just like any cattle drive. We'll be on the range with the cattle and we're gonna stay right there until it is all grazed out. Smokey, you get your chuckwagon packed up with everything you need for at least a week. It'll do you boys good to sleep on the ground for a little while. So get your gear together, I want those cows moving this morning." He promptly left the cookhouse then and returned to the house for his breakfast.

"What the hell's the sense of that?" Curly was the first to question the move, his words still garbled due to his injured jaw. "This time of year? It's gonna be pretty cold sleepin' on the ground." Every man knew that when they were on the home range, there was no need for the whole crew to watch the cattle.

"I know it's gonna be a helluva short cattle drive to the river," Reese said, dutifully backing his boss. "But the major's got his reasons. He don't do nothin' unless he's got good reasons."

Dave Crouch, one of two brothers who rode for the Double-D, was still thinking about the major's offer of a two-hundred-dollar bounty on Cullen McCabe's head. The brothers, nicknamed Big Crouch and Little Crouch, were normally tight-lipped when it came to any conversation, even when drinking with other members of the crew. They seldom spoke, except to each other, and that was usually too low to be overheard by anyone else. Jimmy, the younger brother, and about half the size of Dave, was usually the one to make important decisions for the two of them. When breakfast was finished and the crew went to the barn to get their saddles, Big Crouch confided to his little brother that he had been thinking about collecting that bounty. "I know you have," Jimmy said. "I have, too, and I'll tell you somethin' else. I know the major says he's havin' us move the cattle over beside the river so the town will know they're in the way. Now, here's the part that tickles me, and I know dang well that's what he's thinkin'—we'll be campin' right across the river from the town. And that's right across the river from the saloon and bound to give us a chance to catch up with this McCabe feller. That's what I'm thinkin'."

Big Crouch's eyes opened wide with enlightenment. "I hadn't thought about that," he confessed in his simple-minded way. "We can go to town every night." He grinned, thinking about it, and was dumb enough to believe no one else had.

CHAPTER 8

"Well, ain't you up mighty early this mornin'?" Daisy Lynch remarked when she walked in the kitchen door to find Fanny helping Bertha prepare for breakfast. Bertha was always the first up in the mornings, but it was unusual for Fanny to appear until after the stove was hot and coffee was starting to boil.

Fanny laughed as she replied, "I guess I am a little bit early this morning. It turned out cool last night and that floor was cold on my bare feet when I got up. Won't be many more days before I'll be wearing socks to bed. I slept good, though, under a pile of quilts."

When Bertha went out the door to get more wood for her stove, Daisy winked at Fanny and said, "Maybe you slept so good 'cause you didn't sneak out the back door to try to catch that bird that keeps comin' around here makin' those birdcalls."

Startled, Fanny gaped wide-eyed at Daisy. "Why, whatever are you talking about?"

Daisy chuckled, delighted with the embarrassed girl's reaction. "Honey, those ol' floorboards creak when a mouse walks down that hall, especially after dark." Fanny started to respond, but Bertha came back in at that moment, so she quickly pressed her forefinger to her lips to shush Daisy. Her panic only caused Daisy to chuckle harder. "Hell, Bertha knows about your little sleepwalkin' problem, don't you, Bertha?"

Bertha stuck a stick of firewood in the stove, then paused to answer. "You talkin' about Fanny's trips to feed the birds at night? Yeah, I know about 'em. I've been thinkin' about goin' out there one night, myself, and see what that bird has to say about that. If I was as young as you, I might give you a little competition."

Fanny covered her face with her hands, too embarrassed to have them see her blush. After a moment, she came up for air, still thinking to deny it. "You two old witches are just hearing things in the middle of the night, maybe ghosts, I don't know what. Even if you did hear somebody going down the hall, how do you know it's me? And even if it was, how do you know I ain't going to the outhouse?"

"'Cause you keep a pot under the bed, same as me and Bertha," Daisy responded, then got suddenly serious. "Honey, I don't blame you for slippin' out to see some young feller. It's the natural thing to do, and I reckon you're doin' it on the sly 'cause you don't want nobody to know about it. But I'd be wrong not to warn you to be careful. There ain't no young men in town worth foolin' with, except maybe Wilbur Tate, so I hope it's one of the boys from one of the farms on this side of the river."

Having held her tongue longer than usual, Bertha had her say. "Fanny, honey, me and Daisy don't want you to get hurt. That's what she's tryin' to tell you. And if you're seein' one of that gang from the Double-D, you're liable to get your little heart broke."

Fanny knew they meant well, but it was hard not to be

mad at them for knowing about her meetings with Jeff Hammond. Her face, flushed before with embarrassment, was now red with defiance. "You two old busybodies need to stuff the covers in your ears when you go to bed, so you don't hear things that aren't there." There was no more conversation for a long moment until Fanny could no longer keep from defending her lover. "Everybody that works for Nathan Dixon isn't an outlaw," she suddenly blurted. Bertha and Daisy both stared at her in surprise. She stared back in defiance. "Well, they're not," she insisted.

"Jeff Hammond," Daisy pronounced calmly, one eyebrow raised in a smug expression. Judging by Fanny's shocked reaction, she knew she wasn't wrong.

"Why do you think I'm talkin' about him?" Fanny sputtered.

"'Cause he's the one that always shows up in here every time he's in town, even when none of the other men come in," Bertha contributed. Daisy smiled and nodded in agreement.

At first determined not to admit anything, Fanny was finally forced to yield to their accurate perception of her affair. "Jeff's not like those ruffians he's riding with," she insisted.

"Maybe so," Daisy replied, "but he's ridin' with 'em. It's hard not to paint the whole gang with one brush."

"You don't know him, Daisy," Fanny pleaded. She looked at Bertha for support. "You've seen how he acts when he comes in here. He's not rowdy and crude like the rest of them."

"No," Bertha replied. "I gotta give you that. He does behave better'n the rest of his pals."

Daisy glanced at the clock on the wall and decided they'd better stop gabbing and get busy. "Listen, honey, me and Bertha are on your side. You know Jeff better'n we do. We just want you to think about how bad things are liable to get around here now that real trouble has got stirred up between the town and the Double-D. A lotta folks are gonna get hurt. We just don't want you to be one of 'em." She turned her attention to Bertha. "Now, you'd best get to cookin' on that stove. I'll help you roll out your dough for biscuits." Satisfied that something had been said that needed to be said, she went back to her morning routine, glancing only once at Fanny to make sure the young girl was all right.

The sign on the door proclaimed that the dining room was open for breakfast at six a.m., but Cullen walked in at about five forty-five. He had arrived a little early the day before and had not been turned away, so he figured Daisy would serve him again. She was standing near the door when he entered. "Well, good mornin', McCabe," she sang out upon seeing him. "I declare, you fooled me again. I thought for sure you'd be gone this mornin' after shootin' those two men last night."

He was never quite sure how to take Daisy. She had a naturally sharp tongue and she was prone toward sarcasm, and it was hard to tell if she was being sarcastic or simply japing him. So he answered her greeting with a simple "Reckon not."

"What you want for breakfast, same as yesterday?" When he answered with a nod, she called it out to Bertha, then returned her attention to him. "I'll get you some coffee." A few minutes later when she came back with his coffee, she said, "We'll get you fed as quick as we can. I know you've got places you need to be."

"No hurry," he said.

She gave him an impish grin. "To tell you the truth, I'd just as soon you didn't sit around in my dinin' room too long. I've noticed folks got a habit of gettin' shot when you're around."

"Hate to disappoint you," Cullen said, "but I told Percy Mitchell I'd meet him here this mornin'."

"Is that right?" Daisy replied. "His Honor, the mayor, is fixin' to grace my humble establishment? He don't as a rule. You wanna wait for him?"

"No, I reckon I won't." Then deciding to return some of her sarcasm, he said, "I don't know if he'll take a chance on eatin' here. He might be a little more particular than me."

That made her throw her head back to laugh and he realized that she was still japing him. "We'll give him a cup of coffee when he gets here. That's all he ever has, anyway. I reckon that's the reason he's skinny as a hoe handle."

At half past six, when the mayor walked in, he found Cullen seated closest to the weapons table, drinking coffee. He signaled Fanny to bring him a cup of coffee, then sat down at the table. "How about some breakfast?" Mitchell asked, thinking he would pay for it.

"I've already had some," Cullen replied. "I'm just workin' on coffee now."

"Oh . . . well, I'm sorry I've kept you waiting. I had intended to buy your breakfast, since I asked for this meeting."

"Thanks, anyway," Cullen said. "What did you wanna talk about?"

"Well, you might tell me right off that it's none of my business and that would be the end of it," Mitchell began, then paused as if not sure he should continue. "Let me put it this way—as mayor of the town, I feel it my responsibility to put the town's interest ahead of everything else." After he got that out, he paused again to take a breath.

"Why don't you just ask me what you wanna know?" Cullen suggested.

Mitchell paused again to wait while Fanny placed a cup of coffee on the table before him, her eyes averted to avoid Cullen's gaze. When she left, Mitchell blurted out, "We don't know anything about you, except you've killed five men since you rode into town."

"Their choice, not mine," Cullen replied.

"I know, I know," Mitchell quickly agreed. "I'm not saying it was your fault." He hesitated, thinking it might not be wise to continue the line of questioning he had in mind. He was not sure what might trigger the somber man's rage. He was already beginning to regret the conversation he had with Marvin Winter the night before, but Marvin had expressed something that troubled him about McCabe. It troubled Mitchell as well. What could they expect if the town, with McCabe's help, was successful in repelling Nathan Dixon's attempt to destroy them? Judging by McCabe's cold sober reaction to threats from Dixon's men and his obvious ability to eliminate them, who could say what his plans for Bonnie Creek might be after Dixon was driven back to his range? As Marvin had suggested, even though McCabe had said no to the job earlier, he might actually be thinking about setting himself up as sheriff, and in effect, taking over the town. It had happened before in Kansas and Colorado. This whole thing might simply be a battle between McCabe and Dixon for control of the town. Bonnie Creek could be on the verge of jumping out of the frying pan into the fire.

Afraid that his hesitation was showing his reluctance to proceed with his questions, Mitchell steeled himself to continue. "What do you expect to gain from this conflict?"

It was the same question Poss Rooks had asked. "Nothin' more than a good supper and a peaceful night's sleep before I leave town," Cullen said.

It was something along the lines the mayor would have hoped to hear, but he was still not sure he could believe him. "You don't think you'll stay, if things come out the way we hope?"

"Hadn't planned to," Cullen answered. "Is that what you wanted to find out?"

"Yes . . . I mean no," Mitchell stammered. "You're certainly welcome here. I don't want to give you the impression that you're not welcome. Right now, you're the only police force we've got." He hesitated again, thinking that might have encouraged his plan to become sheriff, but he decided to press on. "It's just that nobody can figure out why you'd want to involve yourself in Bonnie Creek's troubles."

Realizing the mayor's, and the rest of the town's, consternation over his sudden appearance to join in their fight, when there was nothing of obvious gain for him, he was tempted to confess. Still, he was reluctant to inform them that he was there as a representative of the Texas government. Acting on his own, he would not be subject to questions and complaints about the state's failure to actively protect them with Rangers or soldiers. Besides, wearing his official badge would have little or no effect on the outlaws riding for the Double-D. "It ain't the first crazy thing I've ever done," he finally said, answering the mayor's question. "I reckon, if we're done here, I'll go see to my horses."

"Yes, I guess we are," Mitchell said, although he was

not sure he had learned much about the man. At least, he had said he didn't plan to stay around long. "I insist, let me pay for your breakfast. I surely owe you that for delaying you."

Already digging in his pocket for money, Cullen hesitated. "Obliged," he said, and got to his feet.

After he strapped his .44 on, picked up his rifle, and walked out the door, Daisy came over to stand by Mitchell. "Well, Mr. Mayor, what did you learn about the mysterious Cullen McCabe?"

"Not any more than I knew before I walked in," Mitchell answered, shook his head, and started toward the door. "The money for his breakfast is on the table," he said in parting. He didn't express it, but the notion occurred to him that McCabe might simply enjoy the act of shooting people. The thought was more than a little disturbing to him.

When he walked in the stable Cullen found Ross Horner cleaning out a stall. "Damn!" Horner blurted, startled when he turned to discover Cullen standing in the door. "I didn't hear you come in."

"Sorry, I should have sang out," Cullen said. "I just thought I'd visit my horse and see if I'm gonna need to see Shep Blackwell anytime soon. It might be time for Jake to get new shoes. I don't like to let him stand around too long, anyway. He might get to thinkin' he likes it."

"I turned him out in the corral with your other horse this mornin'," Horner said. "You fixin' to take him out?"

"Maybe this afternoon," Cullen answered on his way toward the back door. "Right now, I'm just gonna take a look at his hooves." The bay gelding plodded over to meet him when he opened the corral gate, as if expecting to be led out to be saddled. "How ya doin', boy?" Cullen muttered softly, and stroked the bay's neck. "We ain't goin' anywhere, I just wanna take a look at your feet." After a couple of minutes petting the horse, Cullen started to check his hooves. "I believe you ain't quite ready for new shoes," he said after checking all four. About to drop the last hoof to the ground, he paused to listen. He dropped the hoof and looked toward the river, thinking the sound came from that direction. It was the sound of cattle in the distance, and in the few minutes he stood there listening, it became quite clear and seemed to be getting closer.

"I thought I heard cattle bawlin'," Horner said as he walked out of the stable to join him.

"I thought I did, too," Cullen said, "from over yonder." He pointed toward the river. They both walked out to the front of the stable. Across the street, Buford Tate came out of the post office, having heard the same sounds, which were steadily becoming more distinct.

"That sounds like a herd of cattle, instead of a few strays," Horner declared. "Once in a while, some of the Double-D cattle will stray this far north of their usual waterin' hole. But they don't move the main herd this close to town—mostly 'cause they don't want it to be too easy for us to help ourselves to some fresh beef," he joked.

They were soon joined by others coming out of the stores and the saloon to stand in the street as the first of the cattle came into plain view across the river. Shep Blackwell ran over from his forge to join Cullen and Horner. At first, the growing crowd of spectators gawked in simple curiosity, thinking the Double-D cowhands were going to have to round up a lot of strays. There were even jokes exchanged about the opportunity to cross the river to get some cheap beef. Still, the size of the herd running toward the river continued to grow until the drovers came into view. "Hell, those cows ain't runnin' loose," Shep declared. "They're drivin 'em this way."

"Now, what the hell?" Malcolm Howard blurted as he ran up to join the three of them. Already some of the foremost cows were being pushed down the bank into the shallow river by those behind them. "They're bunchin' up right behind my saloon! We gotta keep 'em from comin' across and runnin' right through the middle of town!" It was obvious to most of the merchants who were now out in the street that this was Nathan Dixon's intention.

In Cullen's mind, Howard had called it right and that was exactly what was going to happen if they weren't somehow stopped. "How are you at herdin' cattle?" he asked Horner and Shep, and when they were puzzling over the question, Cullen said, "Get a horse saddled!" Without waiting for Horner to question him, he ran back to the corral. Horner dutifully followed, still uncertain about what he was supposed to do. Shep ran back to his shop to get his horse. When he returned, he found Cullen and Horner leading horses back into the stable in order to empty the corral of all but Cullen's and Horner's horses, which were now saddled.

"If Dixon wants to run his cattle through town," Cullen declared, "he's gonna have to pay a tax. Now, let's see how many cows we can pack in this corral."

Realizing then what Cullen had in mind, Shep laughed and yelled, "Ride 'em, cowboy!" Cullen stepped up on Jake and his two cowhand partners followed him out of the empty corral.

Pulling up short when he came to Malcolm Howard still frantically walking in circles in the middle of the street, Cullen said, "Go get your gun and get down to the river.

Tell everybody you see to get their guns and go with you. Maybe, if we make enough noise, we can turn those cattle down the riverbank. Understand?" Howard nodded rapidly and ran to get his gun.

When the lead cows went into the water, they tried to stop to drink, but the drovers pushed the rest of the herd onward. Firing their pistols in the air, they created a near stampede and the cattle were driven into the river. By the time Cullen reached the riverbank behind the town, some of the cattle were pushing across and clambering up the near banks. Firing their guns into the air as well, Cullen and his two cowboys tried to turn the herd downstream, away from the town. Following his example, many of the merchants joined Malcolm Howard and ran along the banks, firing into the air. Their efforts seemed to have some success as the main herd turned downstream, but they could not prevent small groups of cattle from breaking off from the others and running toward the street. These were the cattle Cullen and his two partners went after, and when a bunch of about thirty cows charged between the post office and the saloon, Cullen was there to turn them back toward the stable. With Horner and Shep on either side as swing riders, they, after a fashion, were able to drive the cattle into the corral. Wilbur Tate ran over from the post office and closed the gate for them. "There's room for a few more," Cullen said. He wanted to make it an expensive tax for Dixon to pay for his stampede. "Wait here," he instructed Wilbur, "and we'll try to bring you a few more." Then he galloped off to intercept about a dozen cows that had split off and were now running in the street by the hotel.

When Horner tried to cut them off, hoping to drive them back toward the herd, they scattered, causing Cullen and Shep to ride hard to get in front of them and head them back in a bunch. Once they got them moving together, they were able to drive them down the street to the corral, where Wilbur was waiting to open the gate. "Looks like we mighta turned 'em downriver," Shep exclaimed. With the exception of a few stray cows now milling about the street, it appeared that he was right, for the rear of the herd was now clear of the town, although on the side of the river opposite the Double-D range.

Now that the excitement was over and the town was spared the damage a runaway herd was capable of, Cullen, Shep, and Horner went to join the people gathered on the riverbank. They arrived as the men from the Double-D crossed over in pursuit of their cattle. Mayor Percy Mitchell was foremost in waiting to confront the riders, who simply rode around him and continued off after the herd. Among the last, Reese Cochran pulled his horse to a stop in front of the gathering of town folk, his arm still in a sling. "You're off your range!" Mayor Mitchell charged. "You've got no business driving cattle on this side of the river."

Reese shrugged and replied, "You have to tell that to the cows. Me and my boys were tryin' to stop 'em. Tried to turn 'em back before they got to the river, but they stampeded."

"They stampeded because you did it on purpose, firing your guns in the air," Malcolm Howard charged. "You were tryin' to drive 'em right into town where women and children were liable to get run over by your damn cows."

Reese tried to smile as he answered. "Nah, we wouldn't never do that. The major wouldn't want that. It's just a bad place to try to build a town. Shouldn'ta started here in the first place. This is cow country." He was simply repeating what he had heard Nathan Dixon rant about for the past year, not convinced that it was right or wrong. While he talked, he kept an eye on Cullen, who had pulled up to listen.

"You've got plenty of range to graze those cattle and plenty of river downstream from here," Mitchell said.

"Well, it's like this," Reese replied. "We need every bit of our range and we ain't grazed this part of it where the creek empties into the river. The major says to graze 'em here for a while—give the rest of our range a chance to catch up. So we'll be movin' the herd back up closer to the creek for a while, but don't you worry, I'll keep the men right here with 'em." He glanced at Cullen again when he said, "I'll send some of the boys to pick up those strays you penned up at the stable."

Silent to that point, Cullen spoke up. "Those cows will remain where they are. You tell your boss that's the price he'll pay every time he decides to stampede a herd through town."

Reese didn't reply right away, but continued to study Cullen closely. "Mister," he finally said, "you've got a lotta hard bark on you and you're mighty quick to pull a trigger. I don't know who you are or what business this is of yours."

"He speaks for the town," Malcolm Howard spoke up. "It's gonna cost you every time you try to drive a herd through town." Several of the men voiced their agreement. Encouraged by their support, Howard said, "You tell Dixon it's gonna be a costly tax every time he tries a stunt like this."

This show of resistance was not expected by Reese and it occurred to him that the major was not going to be pleased when he reported the results of his planned attack on the town. Instead of discouraging the citizens of the town, they appeared to be more determined since they successfully turned the cattle away. And the troublesome gunman who had popped up out of nowhere seemed to be among the leaders of the resistance. "All right," he finally conceded. "I'll tell him what you said, but you might be bitin' off more than you can chew." He wheeled his horse and loped off after his men.

After Cochran had gone, Howard came up to stand beside Cullen. "That was damn good thinkin', McCabe. Let ol' Dixon think about that every time he gets a notion to run his cattle through Bonnie Creek."

Percy Mitchell was not so sure. "I hope you're right, but I'm afraid he's just as likely to send his men in here and take his cows back."

"We've gotta move 'em somewhere else," Horner said. "I need my corral."

"Where's the closest cattle ranch?" Cullen asked, knowing there were several small outfits fairly close by.

"I reckon Frank Carver is the closest, about six miles," Mitchell answered. "He's got a small herd. He might be glad to get them."

"Six miles," Cullen said. "We've got enough daylight left to drive that bunch that far."

"I wouldn't want to bring any trouble from Nathan Dixon down on Carver," Mitchell worried.

"Hell," Horner said, "if we drive 'em on up to Frank's place right now, Dixon won't know where to look for 'em. Besides, I took a look at some of those cows when we drove 'em in my corral. They're wearin' all different brands on 'em. It'd be hard for Dixon to know which ones were his." He paused to chuckle. "Some of 'em mighta belonged to Frank in the first place." His comments met with agreement from most of the men there, so Cullen, Shep, Horner, and Wilbur started out right away to move the cattle. Most of the other men retired to the Rose.

* * *

"What the hell . . . ?" Frank Carver started when he looked up the river road to see what looked to be a small herd of cattle approaching. He and his brother, Jesse, had ridden down near the river earlier that morning after hearing a multitude of pistol and rifle shots coming from the direction of Bonnie Creek. There was immediate concern upon seeing the cattle. The automatic first thought was that this was some possible aggressive action from the Double-D. If that was the case, Frank wasn't sure what the two of them could do to stop them.

"Hold on," Jesse said, just then recognizing a couple of the drovers. "That ain't Double-D cattle. That's Shep Blackwell and Ross Horner ridin' with 'em."

"Damned if you ain't right," Frank said. Both men were relieved, but now curious to find out what was going on, since neither of the men they recognized were in the cattle business.

They waited there beside the road until Shep caught sight of them and signaled with his arm, then cut away from the small herd and rode up to talk. "You boys interested in takin' on a few more head of cattle?" Shep sang out as he reined his horse to a stop.

"What the hell are you talkin' about, Shep?" Jesse replied, laughing. "We ain't buyin' no cattle right now. Where'd you steal 'em, anyway?"

"That's right," Frank said. "We thought they was Double-D cattle at first when we saw you comin' down the road."

"Is that a fact?" Shep asked, then turned to look at Ross when he rode up. "Frank thought we were drivin' Double-D cows." When Ross laughed, Shep turned back to the Carver brothers. "As a matter of fact, they used to belong to Nathan Dixon, but the town of Bonnie Creek has took 'em for taxes. And we're willin' to let you have 'em at a mighty reasonable price."

It was obvious that Shep and Ross were enjoying themselves with their sales pitch, but Jesse repeated, "We ain't in no fix to buy cattle right now." He cut his eyes over to look at the rugged stranger on the bay horse, now riding over to join them, thinking right away that he must be the mysterious gunman he had heard about. Cullen merely nodded a greeting to each of the brothers, leaving the talking to Ross and Shep. They ended the japing then and explained the circumstances that caused them to be in possession of forty head of Double-D cattle, and their intention to give the cows to them.

"Well, I'll be . . ." Frank reacted. "Tried to drive the whole herd right through town, did they? We was wonderin' what all the shootin' was about." He looked at his brother and grinned, then said, "Hell, yeah, we'll be glad to take 'em off your hands. We'll drive 'em over to the eastern part of our range and thank you kindly."

"And take any more you come up with," Jesse added. Cullen and his "cowboys" stayed long enough to get the cattle started deeper into the Carver brothers' range before breaking off and heading back to Bonnie Creek.

CHAPTER 9

"Hey, Señor Reese," Juan Hernandez sang out when Reese Cochran rode into the barnyard, "how the folks in Bonnie Creek like it when the cows come to town?"

"The cows never got to town," Reese answered. "The whole damn town turned out and got 'em turned downriver before we could catch up to the lead steers."

"They don't get to town?" Reese answered him with a shake of his head. "The major not gonna like that," Juan said, shaking his head slowly as well.

"I don't like it, myself," Reese said, "but that's what happened. Now I gotta go in and tell him." It seemed that all he had to tell the major in the last three days was bad news. *Ever since that dirty dog came to town*, he thought. "Has he et yet?" Dixon got especially cross if disturbed while eating his supper, so Reese preferred to wait until he was sure that he had.

"I think so," Juan replied. "I see Consuelo come out the back door to throw dishwater out. She don't usually do that till she wash up all the dishes."

"Good, then maybe he won't get his belly upset when I tell him what that prissy mayor said to tell him." He handed his reins to Juan. "Leave the saddle on him, I expect I'll be goin' back to bed down with the cattle." He wished he had eaten before he rode back to the ranch house, but he didn't want to delay his report to Dixon. And Smokey was just getting ready to cook when he left the crew at the river.

Going to the kitchen door, as he usually did, Reese was met by Consuelo, who led him to the den, where Dixon was enjoying his after-supper cigar. Reese was greeted with a single-word greeting. "Well?"

"Well, sir," Reese started, "things didn't go exactly like we wanted." That was as far as he got before Dixon's brow lowered, anticipating another report of failure. Reese hurried to continue. "We drove the cattle right on down into the river behind the town, but there was half the town waitin' on the other bank and they raised so much hell, shootin' and hollerin', till they turned the whole herd down the river. We tried to get up to the front of the herd, but couldn't get there before they was turned away from town."

As he stared at his foreman, Dixon's eyes glowered from under heavy dark eyebrows, the veins in his temples swelling with his fury. "McCabe?" Again, a single word.

"Yes, sir, he was right there with 'em." Reese hesitated again, reluctant to convey more bad news. "That's another thing. We lost thirty or forty head that made it across the river and ran into town."

"What do you mean, you lost them?" Dixon questioned.

"Well, you see, when they made it across, that feller McCabe and a couple of other men rounded those cows up and drove 'em into the corral at the stables." Dixon's silence at this point was frightening as he continued to glower at Reese. "I told 'em I was comin' to get those cows, but McCabe said they was gonna keep 'em and to tell you that was the price you're gonna pay every time we run cattle into town."

Dixon smoldered visibly while he thought that over for a long moment, trying to keep the anger building up inside from overcoming him. "Was anyone else talkin'? Or was McCabe runnin' the whole show?"

"No, sir, it weren't just McCabe. Looked like everybody in town was there. That feller Howard that owns the Rose Saloon done some talkin', too. He said Double-D territory stops at the river and we got no business on their side of it."

Dixon threw his half-smoked cigar into the fireplace in disgust and stood there staring into the flames for what seemed several minutes before muttering to himself, "They're standing in my way." He appeared to be so deep in his anger that Reese was afraid to ask him to repeat what he'd said, even though he had been unable to hear it. He would not think it possible for the major to admit that he might be defeated, that maybe he could not fight the entire town and win. Dixon fretted over that same distasteful conclusion, however, before deciding what his next move would be. Since he could not storm into the town and shoot them all down, he decided to go back to his previous attacks on one merchant at a time. The more he thought about it, the more he was convinced that it was the only solution without attracting the attention of the Texas Rangers, or worse, the army. As soon as he harassed one merchant to pack up and leave, it would be easier to press the others until they decided to leave, too. It had worked well with the people from Fort Worth when they started to build a bank in Bonnie Creek. He told himself that he should have continued with that plan until he had burned enough of them to discourage the others. At the time, he had expected the other merchants to follow the bank out of town. Instead, they went out and hired a gunfighter, but they were going to sing a different tune when their hired gun was dead. Satisfied that he had arrived at an effective plan of attack, he turned to face Reese again. "I'll tell you what I want you to do, then you can go on back to the herd tonight."

Reese pulled up by the chuckwagon as soon as he returned to the herd on the chance that Smokey had a biscuit or two left over from supper. Traveling back and forth between the river and headquarters, he had missed supper at both places. He had hoped that Consuelo would have some food left over, but the little bit left after the major had finished was eagerly consumed by her son, Mateo.

"You missed a good 'un," Smokey told him. "I fried up a mess of beans and fresh beef from one of the cows that got crippled in the stampede. I made pan biscuits. There weren't but two left. You can have 'em, and you're lucky that Curly's jaw is still ailin' him, or you wouldn'ta had them."

"Right now, I ain't choosy," Reese assured him. "I see the boys rounded up the rest of the cattle and got 'em back on this side of the river. Any trouble?"

Smokey said there was none. "I think them people in town has had enough excitement for one day. One thing that ain't gonna make you happy, though, is them cows they penned up in the corral at the stable are gone. They drove 'em off somewhere while we weren't lookin'."

Smokey was right, that didn't make Reese very happy, but he didn't know what he could do about it. "Who's ridin' night herd?" When told that Seth and Jeff were,

Reese asked where Curly and the Crouch brothers were, since he didn't see them sitting around the fire.

"Gone huntin'," Smokey said with a big grin.

"Huntin'? Huntin' for what?"

"A two-hundred-dollar bounty on Cullen McCabe," Smokey answered, and chuckled.

"They better go loaded for bear," Reese advised, "and they better shoot him in the back." He shook his head slowly when he thought about that day at the sheriff's office and how quickly McCabe whipped that rifle around and shot him through the window. "I just hope we don't lose any more men because of that damn reward. We've got about five hundred head of cattle now, and we've got barely enough hands left to drive them. The major's gonna have to hire more men, if we're gonna build up a herd to drive north next summer. I wish to hell he'd quit thinkin' about closin' that town up and get back to raisin' cattle." He stopped talking suddenly when he realized he was criticizing the major's leadership. It did not escape Smokey's awareness of a rare moment when Reese expressed his innermost thoughts. That was not typical of the foreman's usual backing of the major's every decision. Reese took the two rock-hard biscuits Smokey handed him and asked, "Any coffee left in that pot?"

"No, there ain't," Smokey replied, "but I'll make another pot and drink a cup with you. Besides, Jeff and Seth will most likely show up sometime later on, lookin' for a cup."

When the coffee was ready, they sat down by the fire to drink it. The two oldest men in Nathan Dixon's crew of outlaws, they were both concerned over the future of the Double-D. Both felt they were too old to move on to somewhere else if the major's plans were unsuccessful, so they had no choice except to back Dixon's every decision, whether it made sense or not. When a much younger man, about the age of Seth Wiley and Jeff Hammond, Reese had ridden with a gang of stagecoach bandits. And he had rustled some cattle, but as the years mounted up, he sought to find a better way to spend his life. He soon found out there was little opportunity for honest endeavor for a man with his background. When, because of that background, he was approached by the major in a saloon in Galveston, he eagerly accepted an invitation to help him build a cattle empire. "*We'll walk over this valley like kings*," Dixon had promised.

After the Civil War, there were millions of cattle roaming wild in South Texas. They were there for the taking by anyone who wanted them. The Double-D was not one of the first to take advantage of these free cattle, but they were able to round up five hundred or so. That was only the start. The rest of the herd was to be built by rustling stock from other ranches, mostly in Mexico, which Reese felt was not really unlawful. Dixon told him that the rustling was only in order to build a core herd to start with, and after that, there would be no need to steal cattle. They would raise their own. During the three years since then, however, that had never come to be. They were still stealing cattle, and the major's desire to become the biggest cattle baron in Texas had increased to approach insane proportions. Of great concern was the major's tendency to react violently when something or someone crossed him, on some occasions settling the incident with an unprovoked shot from his Army model Colt handgun. Consequently, the men feared him and relied on Reese to maintain a buffer between them and the major. Reese had managed to perform that position, but it was getting harder and harder to do. This latest blunder, when the major drew him into that fight at the sheriff's office and nearly cost him his life, was enough to make him question the sanity of staying on at the Double-D.

Smokey, simple soul that he was, could appreciate the strain put upon Reese and could fairly well guess what was on Reese's mind during the long pauses in their conversation. "Reckon the major is gonna start givin' the boys orders to pick as many fights as they can with those folks across the river?"

Reese looked up from the coffee cup he had been concentrating on. "I'm damned if I know," he flatly stated.

"We're liable to start up one helluva range war," Smokey speculated. "No tellin' where we'll end up."

"Looks like we're headin' straight to hell, anyway," Reese stated. "I reckon we might as well go at a gallop." He emptied his coffee cup with one long gulp and got to his feet. "I think I'll get some sleep—as soon as I get rid of all this coffee I drank." He paused to look back at Smokey, still seated by the fire. "At least, that's one thing I know to do that makes sense." Smokey watched him as he walked away from the camp to answer nature's call. He wasn't happy to witness the lack of confidence he was seeing in Reese. It made him wonder if he should be thinking about moving on, but every time he did, he was prone to remind himself that he wasn't young anymore and the money was good where he was.

Chubby Green looked up from the bar when he heard someone come in the front door. There was no one in the saloon at the moment and he was beginning to wonder where the usual customers were, unaware that the arrival of one of the Double-D riders had discouraged them. "Uh-oh," he muttered softly to himself when he saw who had come in. Curly Cox barged into the saloon with the swagger of a pirate. After the recent trouble with the Double-D and their cattle, Chubby didn't expect to see any of them in the saloon, if not forever, at least until that affair had a chance to cool down. Now, here he was, a rag still tied around his jaw, with the knot under his hat, his face still swollen from his last visit to the Rose, yet still wearing the same insolent expression that characterized him. When he walked up to the bar, Chubby greeted him. "Curly," he said cautiously, "I hope you ain't come in here lookin' for trouble."

"Why, hell, no," Curly brayed. He had thought to find McCabe in the saloon, but since he didn't, he decided he would settle another score. "I'm a peaceable man, always was. I just came in to visit with Lilly, since we kinda got interrupted last time I was here. Where the hell is she?"

"She ain't feelin' so good tonight," Chubby lied as he glanced beyond the rough brute facing him and spotted Lilly at the top of the stairs. About to come down, she had stopped when she spotted Curly and was now slowly backing away from the stairs as quietly as she could manage and hoping Curly didn't glance in her direction. "I think it's her time of the month and sometimes that treats her pretty poorly. She'll be sorry she missed you. I'll tell her you came in to see her."

The foolish grin remained on Curly's face, the expression somewhat crooked now because of the injury to his jaw, but the deep frown and the intense look in his eye told Chubby he didn't believe him. "Hell, she's too old to get the female sickness," Curly scoffed. "I just wanna tell her I'm sorry 'bout the misunderstandin' we had in here the other day. Where is she, in her room? I'll just go up and tell her how sorry I am she's feelin' so poorly." Without waiting for Chubby's response, Curly turned and started for the stairs.

"Hold on a minute!" Chubby exclaimed. "She ain't in her room. She's gone to stay with a friend till she gets to feelin' better. She told me she ain't got no hard feelin's about that trouble, anyway."

Curly turned back to face him again, the crooked smile still in place. "Stay with a friend?" he blurted. "Lilly ain't got no friends. Chubby, you ain't worth horse turds as a bartender, and you're worse than that as a liar." He turned his head back toward the steps and yelled, "Lilly! Get your ass down here. If you ain't down here in two minutes, I'm comin' up there to get you, and it ain't gonna be to your likin'." His attention back to Chubby then, he said, "When I'm through with her, I'll be wantin' a little talk with you, you lyin' piece of dirt." With that threat, he waited for no more than a minute before turning toward the stairs again. "You make a move for that shotgun under the bar and I'll shoot you down," he called back over his shoulder when Chubby was about to make just that move. The threat was enough to freeze Chubby right where he was.

Halfway up the steps, Curly was surprised by the appearance of Lilly standing at the top, a two-shot derringer in her hand, pointed at the bull-like brute. "You can just stop right there," she stated. "I ain't got nothin' to say to you, so turn right around and get outta here."

He stopped and smirked. "Well, well, ain't that a nice way to greet a gentleman who's come to see you? I don't know how much you can do with that little popgun before I get my hands on that scrawny neck of yours. But I guarantee you it ain't enough to keep me from chokin' the life outta you, so you'd best put it down." He waited for her to drop it, and when she didn't, he took another step toward her. Seeing her hand shaking and the derringer wavering from her fright, he sneered and said, "Where's your hero, McCabe, now?" His grin returned when he saw the tears form in the corner of her eyes and he knew she was helpless to defend herself. He took another step up, stopping abruptly when she pulled the trigger.

The bullet caught him in the shoulder, causing him to recoil with the impact, but failed to stop him. "Damn you!" He roared like a wounded mountain lion and started toward her again. She screamed, too terrified to run away as he reached for her. But he stumbled when the blast of the shotgun sent a tight pattern of buckshot into his back. Knocked facedown, Curly landed hard on the steps, only a few steps below the terrified prostitute. He struggled briefly, managing to get to his hands and knees before tumbling backward, over and over, all the way to the floor below, like a tremendous boulder rolling down a mountainside. Chubby, at the foot of the stair, stepped aside to keep from being bowled over by the oversize bully. Shaking almost as much as Lilly, he stood with his shotgun aimed at the body until he was absolutely certain Curly was dead. With her knees threatening to fail her, Lilly sank down to sit at the top of the stair and tried to pull herself together.

The two of them remained unmoving for what seemed a long time, both of them in a state of shock, neither of them having ever shot anyone before. The small crowd that had remained at a safe distance when they saw Curly go in the saloon, now waited after hearing the gunshots until finally Wilbur Tate went up to the door and opened it wide enough to peek inside. "They got Curly!" he exclaimed to the spectators, and led them all inside. Norman Freeman was right on his heels. When they saw *what* had happened, everybody wanted to know *how* it happened.

"There's another one I won't get no pay for" was Freeman's first remark upon seeing Curly's body at the foot of the stairs. Since McCabe had arrived in town, Freeman had buried five bodies and now he was looking at number six. They were all Nathan Dixon's men, but Freeman didn't have the courage to seek payment from him. At least he was spared the cost of coffins, because he just dug holes in the ground and dumped the bodies in the holes, settling for anything of value he found on them.

Malcolm Howard pushed through the gathering just inside the saloon door to discover his bartender still standing over the body at the foot of the stairs and the prostitute sitting weeping at the top. "Chubby! What the hell happened?" Howard blurted. His outburst served to bring Chubby out of his state of shock, but before he could respond, Lilly answered for him.

"He saved my life," she sobbed. Still holding the derringer, she pointed it at Curly's body. "He was comin' to kill me and Chubby shot him. Chubby saved my life."

"Well, you can put the gun down now," Howard said when she continued to use it to point. She looked down at the derringer, just then remembering she still held it, and dropped it on the floor, as if she were holding a snake. He looked around the room then, as if searching for someone. "Where's McCabe?" Howard had been in the hotel dining room when he heard the shots. McCabe had been eating supper at a table close to the door at the same time.

"I'm here," Cullen answered him, aware of the fact that Howard had wanted to know where he was, first thing. It was not the first hint that many of the town's citizens had started to look toward him as their protector. He had entered the saloon through the back door. Since there was a gang of people going in the front, he thought it best to cover the back to intercept a possible killer trying to escape. He walked over to take a look at the body. After a moment, he looked up at Lilly, who hadn't moved from the top of the stair. "There's a bullet hole in his shoulder. You put a shot in him with that pocket pistol?"

"Yes, I did," she whimpered. "He was comin' for me, so I shot him. But it didn't even slow him down."

"Well, that twelve-gauge of Chubby's stopped him, all right," Cullen said, and glanced at the bartender, who was rapidly getting over his first killing, enjoying the pats on his back and the cheers for his heroic actions. Cullen was satisfied to see another of the townspeople stepping up to take action against the outlaws. Maybe it would inspire more of the timid citizens to resist Dixon's aggression.

Malcolm Howard, seeing an opportunity with the people crowding in to look at the body of the notorious bully, walked over behind the bar. "Looks like Chubby and Lilly know how to deal with anybody who thinks they can run over the folks of Bonnie Creek," he announced loudly. "The bar's open!" His announcement brought a cheer from the men and a surge of drinkers to toast Chubby and Lilly. After a while, Lilly recovered enough to descend the stairs and join in the celebration.

Behind the post office, which was long since closed for the day, two men knelt in the darkness, watching the front door of the saloon and the spectators going in. They had not gotten there in time to see Curly walk in, but they recognized his horse tied out front. A short time later they heard the shots, but Curly didn't come out, so their focus now was to try to spot Cullen McCabe and hope he was still alive. "I don't see him anywhere," Big Crouch whispered. "Why the hell ain't he runnin' over there like ever'-body else? Maybe he went in the door and we didn't know it was him." He and his brother had had only glimpses of Cullen McCabe. That was from across the river and most of the time he was on a horse.

"We ain't missed him," Little Crouch declared. "I'd know him, if he was there."

"Maybe he's layin' low, since the major put a two-hundred-dollar reward on him," Big Crouch speculated.

"No, hell, he ain't," Little Crouch insisted. "How would he know there's a reward out for him?"

"Maybe he was already in the saloon and Curly shot him and we won't get that two hundred dollars," Big Crouch worried.

"He coulda been in the saloon when Curly walked in," Little Crouch said. "If he had, though, most likely it woulda been McCabe who done the shootin', but I didn't hear nothin' that sounded like that Winchester Reese said McCabe favors."

Always a mental step behind, Big Crouch had to ask, "Why do you think it was Curly that got shot?"

"'Cause there weren't but two shots, one from a shotgun and one from a gun like one of them little pocket pistols," he said impatiently. "I didn't hear nothin' that sounded like that .44 Curly carries. Besides, all them people wouldn't be crowdin' in the saloon if Curly was still alive."

Big Crouch nodded thoughtfully as he considered that.

"I hadn't thought about that." He grinned. "I knew you'd figure it out."

"That's right," Little Crouch said, "and if we set here awhile, McCabe's bound to show up sooner or later." He reached over and gave his brother a playful punch on the shoulder. "When he does, one clean shot and we'll split that two hundred dollars, 'cause ain't none of the boys come across the river tonight but Curly and us."

Big Crouch beamed a wide grin at his younger brother, enjoying the fact that they had put one over on Curly Cox. Their plan had been the same as Curly's—to simply ride into town, find McCabe wherever he was, and shoot him down without warning. Also, like Curly, they had planned to look in the saloon first, since that was where they would be if they were McCabe. But Curly got there ahead of them. He'd finished up his supper while Big Crouch was still eating, so he beat them across the river to town. Unlike the two brothers, Curly had ridden right up to the saloon and tied his horse at the rail. The Crouch brothers had taken a more cautious approach, at Little Crouch's suggestion, and taken cover behind the post office to wait and see if Curly was successful. Now, after the shooting, it looked as if Curly had done them a favor, because McCabe was bound to show up at the saloon, if he hadn't been there already. There would be no need to search the town to look for him. As it turned out, Little Crouch was right, he finally showed up, but not exactly from the direction they expected.

"There he is!" Big Crouch suddenly blurted. "That's him—ain't it?" He was not positive, but the man walking out the door of the saloon looked like McCabe. Both brothers immediately readied their rifles to take aim, but their target was surrounded by some other spectators standing around the door.

"It's him, all right," Little Crouch said, "but don't shoot till you get a clear shot. We gotta make sure we hit him, then get the hell outta here before they come after us."

"Right," Big Crouch replied, and promptly fired.

Buford Tate, the postmaster, stepped up to talk to McCabe mere seconds before he was struck in the arm by the .44 slug meant for Cullen. The shot scattered the spectators gathered at the front door of the saloon as everyone ran for cover behind anything they could find. Tate was spun around by the shot and dropped to the steps. With no time to find better cover, Cullen grabbed the back of Tate's collar and dragged him roughly off the steps onto the ground behind the hitching rail where Curly's horse was tied. "Lie flat as you can," he said to Tate, who was partially in shock and confused, but hugged the ground for all he was worth.

"He's over behind the post office!" someone crouched behind the corner of the two steps up to the boardwalk yelled out, having seen the muzzle flash from Big Crouch's rifle.

Flat on the ground beside Tate, Cullen brought his rifle up before him and aimed it at the little board shack that served as a post office. With nothing for protection but darkness and four legs of a horse, he was not in a very good position for a gun battle. He peered under Curly's horse toward the back corner of the post office, straining to pick out the shooter. There had been no second shot, so he figured the shooter could not see well enough to find his target. And he had a pretty good idea who that target was.

Having quickly backed away from the rear corner of the post office, the two Crouch brothers squatted against the rear wall. "You big dummy!" Little Crouch scolded. "I just said wait till you get a clear shot!"

"I thought I had one, I thought I could hit him," Big Crouch replied sheepishly.

"Yeah, well, the last time I looked, he was movin' pretty fast for a dead man. Now they know we're here and they're liable to come chargin' over here to get us."

"I thought I could hit him," Big Crouch repeated, remorseful for having displeased his brother. "At least they ain't nobody shootin' back at us."

Little Crouch shinnied back to the corner and stuck his head around the edge. "I can't see a blame thing," he complained. "They've all scattered. We better get the hell outta here before they decide to do somethin'. Come on, let's get back to the horses."

"Ain't we gonna try to get that two hundred dollars?" Big Crouch complained, hanging back. When his brother replied that they had missed their chance, Big Crouch persisted. "They ain't even shot back at us." He crawled back to peek around the corner of the jailhouse. "There still ain't nobody comin' this way," he persisted, reluctant to leave a chance at that reward money.

"They ain't shot back at us 'cause they don't know where we are," Little Crouch insisted. "Now, come on before they figure it out and we have the whole damn town on us."

"They ain't gonna come runnin' across that open street if they can't see us," Big Crouch persisted. "We might get another shot at him. This time, I'll make sure it's a clean shot."

While the two brothers wasted time arguing, Cullen was not content to lie there behind the hitching rail. Since someone had seen the muzzle blast from behind the post office, he decided to take the risk of trying to get around behind him, even though he was not sure the shooter was still there. *I reckon I'll find out when I get up from here*, he thought. "You stay right there and hug that ground till we find out that shooter's gone," he said to Buford Tate.

Buford winced with pain as he whispered, "You ain't got to worry about that. If I could get any flatter, I dang sure would."

Cullen got to his feet then, expecting rifle fire as soon as he did, and ran toward the barbershop next door. To his surprise, there were no shots, so he kept running until he reached the safety of the barbershop. Once he got there, he ran across the street to circle around the jail, hoping to cut the shooter off before he got to his horse, just as he had done when he caught the two that set fire to Shep's cabin. It was unlikely the shooter was still behind the post office. Failing that, Cullen hoped to maybe get a shot at him as he crossed the river. Running at a steady lope, he plunged into the dark shadows of the trees on the riverbank, only to stop abruptly when he almost ran into two horses tied in the bushes. The first thought that struck him was there were two shooters, not just one. The second thought, and the more important one, was that they were behind him. He spun around at once, dropping to one knee as he did, with his rifle aimed toward the back of the post office. There was no one there, but in a few moments, he heard the sound of the two men grumbling as if arguing, and they were coming toward him. It was obvious that they could not see him in the shadow of the trees, so he waited for them to approach.

It was not long, but it gave him time to think about his next move. It was an opportunity to eliminate two more of Nathan Dixon's men by simply shooting them down. He could justify that action by the fact that they had obviously just tried to kill him. Of that, there could be little doubt. He felt sure they were not aiming to assassinate the postmaster. He could make out their forms now as they crept toward the river. It was not the same as when he had methodically hunted down and killed every man of the gang who had participated in the murder of his wife and children. These men were outlaws, true, but he had spent too many years as a lawman to simply execute them, so he reluctantly decided to give them a chance to surrender. He had an empty jail waiting to accommodate them.

He waited until he could see them clearly, while they could still not make him out, kneeling in the shadows. Then he spoke. "Halt right there and drop your weapons! You're under arrest!" Their reaction was as he expected. One of them, the larger man, immediately raised his rifle and fired blindly into the trees, wounding one of the horses. Startled even more by the scream of the wounded horse, he swept his rifle wide in the opposite direction and fired another round into the trees. Cullen had no choice. He took careful aim and shot him in the upper thigh, just below the hip. Big Crouch collapsed to his knees, yelling out in pain as he dropped his rifle. "Best not!" Cullen warned, having already cranked in another round, ready to fire when Little Crouch raised his rifle to shoot at Cullen's muzzle flash. Hearing the warning voice coming from a different spot in the darkness, Little Crouch realized then that Cullen had moved as soon as he fired the first shot. His brother had been shot when he had fired. Little Crouch feared the same would happen to him if he threw a wild shot into the darkness, so he dropped his weapon when Cullen told him to.

"Help your partner up on his feet," Cullen ordered.

"I can't walk!" Big Crouch wailed. "You crippled me!"

"You either walk or I'll put the next shot where I won't have to worry about you anymore," Cullen threatened. "It's up to you." Big Crouch tried to get to his feet at once. When he was obviously feeling too much pain to stand on the wounded leg, Cullen again ordered Little Crouch to help his partner walk.

"He ain't my partner," Little Crouch said. "He's my brother."

"Help him anyway," Cullen said.

The next five or ten minutes saw Little Crouch struggling to get his brother up to limp on one foot while he acted as his crutch and Cullen herded them back toward the jail. By the time they reached the back wall of the jail, the folks taking cover across the street realized that whatever had happened seemed to be over. Shep Blackwell was the first to call out. "Cullen! Is that you back there?" When Cullen answered and assured them that the shooters were under control, there was soon a crowd there to help herd the prisoners. "What are you gonna do with 'em?" Shep asked.

"Well, that's what the jail is for, ain't it?" Cullen replied. "I figure we'll put 'em in jail."

Shep hesitated for a moment before answering, "But we ain't got a sheriff."

"That's right," Little Crouch spoke up. "There ain't no sheriff, so you can't put us in jail. Besides, my brother's been shot. I gotta take him to the doctor."

"We ain't got a doctor, either," Shep pointed out.

By this time, most of the town's citizens had gathered to witness the goings-on and Percy Mitchell questioned, "We don't have a judge, either, so how are we gonna try them, and on what charges?"

Losing his patience with the incompetence of the whole town, Cullen asked the mayor a question. "So, whaddaya think we oughta do, let 'em go?" He waited for a few moments while the mayor sputtered over an answer. "I didn't think so," Cullen said. "These two shot into a crowd of people and wounded the postmaster, and they shot at me when I tried to arrest them. So we'll put 'em in the jail that was built for that purpose. After he takes care of Buford Tate, Norman Freeman can dig a bullet outta the big one's leg. When he's done with that, he can dig one outta one of those horses back yonder in the trees." He turned his full attention to Percy Mitchell again. "Mr. Mayor, I reckon it would be your responsibility to get up a jury to decide how the prisoners should be punished. Maybe the town council can help you with that, if you've got one."

There followed a short silence while Mitchell and the others considered what Cullen had said. "We still don't have a sheriff," the mayor said. "There should be one to watch the prisoners and feed them and such."

"Then I reckon it's time to appoint one," Cullen said. "I'd recommend Shep Blackwell. He's shown me that he'll step up to the job."

Everyone, including the two prisoners, turned to look at Shep, who was as startled by McCabe's recommendation as they were. He thought for only a moment before commenting, "I'da thought you mighta been a better choice," he said to Cullen.

"I'm not in the runnin'," Cullen replied. "I'm just driftin' through town—ain't plannin' on bein' here much longer."

"We need a sheriff," Marvin Winter spoke up. "That's for sure. What about it, Shep, you wanna take the job? We'd pay you the same as we paid Bob Bartlett. Wouldn't we, Percy?" The mayor nodded his agreement and looked to Shep for his answer.

Shep looked at Cullen, who nodded his approval, then looked back at Marvin Winter. He shrugged and said, "I reckon." With that settled, they hustled the prisoners inside the jail and into the cell room. Cullen found the sheriff's badge and the keys in the desk drawer and Shep took possession of both. Ross Horner went to fetch the two horses, and Norman Freeman went to get his medical instruments, and the sheriff's office was officially back in business.

With the position of sheriff finally filled, Marvin Winter and Percy Mitchell were able to breathe a little easier. The worry that had concerned them, namely, that Cullen McCabe might be planning to take on the job as sheriff and consequently use it as a strong base to take over the whole town, evidently was not what McCabe had in mind. Instead of lifting the aura of mystery about the man, however, his recommending Shep for the job served only to make Cullen's motives more mysterious. With nothing obvious to gain, why would he subject himself to a high risk of getting shot? Most of the rest of the town was not burdened with Winter's and Mitchell's concerns. They were just happy that McCabe had lingered.

CHAPTER 10

"Where the hell is Curly?" Smokey asked Reese. "And the Crouch brothers, they ain't here, either," he added. "They didn't come back from town last night." He had heard the shots fired across the river in town and was afraid the three had gotten into some trouble.

"Don't look like it, does it?" Reese replied, not surprised since their camp was just across the river from the saloon. There was bound to be trouble, and he had thought it was a mistake when the major ordered him to bed the herd down so close to town. He was still not one to tell the major he was making the wrong call, however.

"I'm gonna throw most of this chuck out if they don't show up here in the next five minutes," Smokey threatened. "Any you other fellers want some more?" He looked at Seth Wiley and Jeff Hammond, who were finishing up their breakfast after riding nighthawk all night. "I'm gonna throw it out," he threatened again. "They oughta miss breakfast," he grumbled. "Most likely still drunk."

Jeff Hammond had held his tongue up to that point, while he tried to decide whether to say anything or just play dumb. When Reese stood up, peered out toward the river, and wondered aloud where the three missing men were, Jeff could keep his silence no longer. "Curly's dead and the Crouch brothers are in jail," he announced. He had been reluctant to tell them because he would have to confess that he had slipped off to town while he was supposed to be watching the herd.

"How the hell do you know that?" Reese asked.

"Fanny Wright told me," Jeff answered.

"That little gal in the hotel dinin' room?" Reese demanded. "How the hell . . . ?" He started but was too confused to finish. "You were supposed to be watchin' the herd. What the hell were you doin' in town?"

"Jeff weren't gone more'n half an hour," Seth spoke up quickly when it looked like Reese was beginning to get the picture. "Not much longer than it would be if he had to go take a dump."

"Curly, dead?" Reese exclaimed, more concerned by that news than he was with the way he found out. "What happened? Who done it, that damn McCabe? Whaddaya mean the Crouch boys are in jail?" His questions came with the speed of a Gatling gun, with no space for answers.

"Tell him what Fanny told you," Seth said, and Jeff repeated the story of Curly's demise at the hands of Chubby Green and Lilly Bloodworth.

"It wasn't McCabe that shot Curly," he said, "but he did put a bullet in Big Crouch's leg." He went on to tell Reese about Big Crouch and Little Crouch getting arrested when they tried to shoot McCabe.

To Reese, it was the very thing he had feared might happen when the major placed a reward on Cullen McCabe's head. Reese didn't say anything for a long moment while he ran it over in his mind. Then he looked around him at what was left of his crew—himself, Seth,

Jeff, and Smokey—they were all that was left to work the cattle. He would have to call Ike Roper in from the line shack and put Juan Hernandez to work with them. *And the major's gonna expect me to build another herd with half a crew*, he thought. "Damn it to hell," he cursed loudly, causing the others to come to attention. "I reckon I'll have to go tell the major his intimidation plan ain't workin' worth spit." He caught himself before complaining further, lest someone might think the major didn't know what he was doing. "I know you boys have been up all night," he said to Seth and Jeff, "but I'm gonna have to go tell the major about this. So, I need you to keep an eye on the cattle. I'll bring Juan back with me. Smokey, you might have to get your ass in a saddle and help out, and I'll be back just as soon as I can. And stay the hell away from that town!"

"Good mornin', Mr. McCabe," Daisy Lynch sang out when Cullen walked into the dining room. "You're early, as usual, but I'm always happy to see you walkin' around every mornin'." She picked up the coffeepot and went to his usual table near the door. "Another exciting night in Bonnie Creek last night," she said as she filled his cup. "Every night's pretty much exciting ever since you hit town."

"Good mornin'," Cullen replied, ignoring her attempts at playful sarcasm.

"You gonna have your usual breakfast?" Daisy asked. "Bertha's makin' sausage biscuits this mornin'. You oughta try some. Ain't nobody makes 'em like she does."

"All right," he said, surprising her, as well as Fanny Wright, who was standing near the kitchen door, timidly watching him, as was her habit.

"I'll tell Bertha to make 'em special for you," Daisy said, and went at once to the kitchen. "What you standin' there like a scared doe for?" she asked Fanny as she passed by. "He ain't gonna bite you. He always looks that way."

In a couple of minutes, Daisy came back to visit. "Those sausage biscuits will be ready in a jiffy," she said, then lingered, since he was the only one in the dining room at this early hour. "Understand we got us a new sheriff," she began. "I'll bet ol' Shep didn't have any notion about bein' the sheriff. He oughta make a good one, though. I hear he's already got a couple of guests in the jail, and we'll be feedin' 'em." She looked around at the empty tables. "It's kinda sad when the jail's got more guests than the hotel has." She laughed at her attempt at humor, then said, "You know, a conversation usually takes place between at least two people. You don't do a helluva lot to hold up your end of it, do ya?"

"You didn't sound like you needed any help," he commented drily.

She placed her hands on her hips and gave him an appraising stare. "When was the last time you ever cracked a smile?"

"The last time somebody brought me my breakfast on time," he replied with no hint of a smile.

She shook her head and returned to the kitchen in time to see Bertha flip a couple of huge biscuits onto the plate Fanny was holding. "I'll take 'em to him," Fanny said, and went at once to deliver them.

"'Mornin', Fanny," Cullen said when she set the plate before him.

His polite greeting was enough to fluster the timid girl, but instead of quickly returning to the kitchen, she forced out the warning she was determined to give him. "Nathan

Dixon has put a two-hundred-dollar reward up for anybody who kills you."

He was surprised by her warning, but not really surprised that Dixon had placed the bounty on him. He didn't doubt that to be the reason for the three Double-D hands in town last night. It verified his initial belief that Big Crouch's shot had been meant for him. "I 'preciate you tellin' me," he said to her, but didn't ask her where she got her information. He thought he could see the appreciation in her eyes before she turned and fled to the kitchen.

In a few minutes, Daisy came with the coffeepot. He pushed his cup over toward her, so she wouldn't have to reach over with the large pot. She filled it, then asked, "What did you say to Fanny? She looked like she'd seen a ghost when she came back in the kitchen."

"I said, 'good mornin','" he answered solemnly. Then, without a change of expression, he said, "Tell Bertha these are the best sausage biscuits I've ever had." *Except for maybe some that Mary Kate used to make*, he thought. He tried not to dwell on thoughts of his late wife. He found it too hard to accept her loss, and sometimes it was impossible not to recall. His wife often made biscuits like those he had just finished. Flapjacks were the breakfast treat every Saturday morning for him and the kids. The memory of that brought a mental picture of his little family gathered around the breakfast table. He was glad when Daisy had a comment in response.

"Well, I know that'll just make Bertha's day for her," Daisy said. "I'm tickled we were able to please you this mornin'."

As she walked away, it occurred to him that everything Daisy said sounded like sarcasm, and he wondered if she was the same with everyone or was it just him? It made little difference, however, so he finished his coffee, put some money on the table, and left. Outside, he paused for only a second or two to consider what kind of day it was going to be weatherwise, then he started walking toward the jail.

The first thing he noticed was a shiny new padlock on the front door. Inside, he found Shep rolling up his bedroll. The door to the cell room was closed, but Cullen could hear the grumbling of the two prisoners beyond and they sounded unhappy. "Shep," Cullen responded when Shep said, "Good morning." "Havin' trouble with your guests?"

"Not much," Shep replied. "They've been whinin' about wantin' to eat for about an hour. I told 'em they were gonna get some breakfast just as soon as Daisy finds time to send it down here. But they got to bellyachin' so bad that I had to close the door."

"Is that right?" Cullen asked. "Makin' a lot of noise, huh? How 'bout the one I shot, is he up and around?"

"That big fleabag?" Shep was quick to respond. "He's hoppin' around fit as can be. Norman cut the slug outta his leg last night and he's limpin', but he ain't as bad as you'd expect. I know the two of 'em was makin' so much noise till I had to close the door to keep from wantin' to shoot both of 'em."

"That a fact?" Cullen asked. "Let me take a look at your prisoners." Shep got the keys out of the desk drawer and followed him into the cell room. As soon as the heavy door between the two rooms opened, the prisoners shuffled quickly over to their bunks to sit down.

When they saw who had entered the room, they both sat up. "Well, well, Dave," Little Crouch said to his brother, "if it ain't the stud horse, himself, come to call on us."

"How you know it's him?" Big Crouch asked, not sure,

since this was the first chance he had to take a close look at the man in the shadows on the night just passed—and that was only seconds before he went down with a shot in the leg.

"It's him, all right," Little Crouch said, having had plenty of opportunity to identify Cullen. "Ain't that right, McCabe?" When Cullen didn't answer, Little Crouch sneered. "Maybe he's the boy they sent down here with our breakfast. How 'bout it, McCabe, is that why you're here?"

Ignoring the taunting intended to rile him, Cullen didn't answer him. Instead, he asked Shep for the key to the cell door. Not sure what Cullen had in mind, Shep nevertheless handed him the key. "Now draw your weapon and cock it," Cullen said. "Hold it on those two and if one of 'em so much as twitches a finger, shoot him."

"Right!" Shep responded. He did as Cullen said and held his .44 aimed at the bunks while trying to watch Cullen at the same time.

Cullen went to the small window in the back wall and found what he had expected. He looked around on the floor then and found a piece of heavy wire from under the mattress of one of the bunks. He picked it up and came back out of the cell, locking it again behind him. "I'll give you boys a little education," he said to the brothers. "You can dig and scrape all around that little window with something like this." He held the wire up. "But if you took a look at the outside of the window, you'd see those heavy pieces of flat iron holdin' the window frame in. It wouldn't have made any difference if you cleaned out the whole frame around the inside of the window, you'da had to have some dynamite to get past those iron plates." He glanced at Shep and said, "I expect the sheriff, here, mighta been the one to put 'em on that window, since he used to be a blacksmith." The look on Shep's face told him the sheriff was totally confused, but the pained expressions on the faces of the two prisoners told him he had hit the nail on the head. "I doubt you'da been able to squeeze the big 'un through that little window, even if you had managed to push the frame out." He glanced toward the front door when he heard it open. "Might as well sit down and eat your breakfast now and behave yourselves. Maybe the sheriff will let you use his broom to sweep that little pile of plaster out from under your bunks."

Shep holstered his pistol and took the two plates of food from Bertha's son, Jordan. "Mama said Sheriff Bartlett usually made coffee for his prisoners, and I didn't have to wait for 'em to eat. She said I can pick up the plates when I bring 'em some dinner." He lingered for a few moments to get a look at the two prisoners before he went out the door.

Leaving the Crouch brothers to eat their breakfast, Cullen and Shep went back into the office, closing the cell room door behind them. As soon as it was shut, Shep said, "I didn't put those iron plates around that window frame."

"There ain't no iron plates around the window," Cullen said, "but now they think there are. Maybe it'll discourage them from tryin' to remove the window frame."

"Oh . . ." Shep drew out a long breath and nodded thoughtfully. "But how did you know that's what they were up to, scratchin' out around that frame?"

Talking softly to make sure he wasn't overheard by the prisoners, Cullen answered, "When you told me they were makin' a constant racket in there, so you had to close the door, I figured they mighta been makin' noise, so you *would* close the door."

Again, Shep nodded slowly. "Looks like I've got a lot to

learn about bein' sheriff. Maybe me bein' sheriff ain't such a good idea." He picked two cups off the shelf behind the desk chair and filled them with coffee for his prisoners.

"You'll make a good sheriff," Cullen said. "You just have to use common sense." He opened the cell room door for him. "Little piece of advice," he said. "Don't hand that coffee to 'em—set the cups on the floor between the bars, but not until they both back away from the bars."

"Right," Shep replied. He cocked an eye at Cullen as he passed through the doorway, thinking about the possibility of someone like Big Crouch slapping a cup of hot coffee all over him—then grabbing him while his brother snatched his gun out of his holster. "You know a lot about sheriffin'. You sure you didn't used to be a lawman?"

"Just common sense," Cullen answered. "That's all it is. You'll see." When they came out of the cell room, Cullen asked, "You got anybody to help you? Somebody you could make a deputy maybe, somebody to watch the jail when you're out doin' something else?"

"Matter of fact, I've been thinkin' about that very thing," Shep replied. "I was talkin' to Wilbur Tate, you know, the postmaster's son. There ain't really anybody else, but he said right off he weren't interested in it. He did say he'd help out until we could find somebody else. Whadda you think?"

"I think he might be all right," Cullen said. "You know him a lot better than I do, but from what I've seen of him since I came to town, he seems like he might be a dependable young man. He was right there to help with the cattle we rounded up. You think he could shoot somebody if he had to?"

"I don't know," Shep replied, "but I know he's honest and a hard worker." He gave a little shake of his head and confessed, "Hell, I ain't sure I can shoot anybody if I have to."

"You'll be fine," Cullen said. "Just like you were when we sent Nathan Dixon runnin' outta town. You were shootin' to kill then, weren't you?" When Shep merely shrugged in answer, Cullen asked, "Why don't you offer Wilbur the job? Marvin Winter told me the mayor wants to have a meetin' at the hotel tonight after supper to talk about what the town needs to do about your prisoners. I'm sure he'll want the sheriff there. Wilbur can watch the jail while you're gone. Make sure you talk to the council, or whatever they call themselves, about a salary for your deputy."

"You gonna be there?" Shep wanted to know.

"I don't know," Cullen answered. "The mayor ain't said a word to me about it. He might want a meetin' of just the town citizens. I expect I might drop in to see what's what, though." He took his leave then, telling Shep he wanted to go across the street to the stable to check on his horses.

He had a good feeling about Shep. He felt sure he would grow into the job in a short time, just as he had when Jason Barrett persuaded him to take the job as sheriff in the town of Sundown. That thought created another one, one he regretted to call up—Mary Kate had not wanted him to take the job. She feared that it would put him in constant danger, but he was big and strong, he was sure he could take care of himself. He was to find that he could be hurt, not his physical being, but by having something taken from him that was more precious to him than his life. What they took from him could never be replaced. He had extracted his vengeance from every member of the gang of savages who killed his family—hunted them down, one by one—but it brought no peace. *The sooner you get that off your mind, the better off you'll be*, he reminded himself and returned his thoughts to Shep. Maybe a dedicated sheriff and deputy would prove to be a big step in solving some of the town's problems. He had to think it was in line with what the governor hoped for when he sent him to Bonnie Creek. *There's still one hell of a problem to fix*, he thought. *Nathan Dixon was not likely to pull back on his determination to own Bonnie Creek, or destroy it.*

At the same moment Cullen was walking to the stable in Bonnie Creek, Nathan Dixon was standing in his barn four and a half miles away. Facing him and trying to weather the storm of anger emanating from his boss, Reese Cochran was hard-pushed to come up with an explanation that satisfied him. It seemed that the major blamed him for every stroke of misfortune that had befallen the Double-D. "I need Juan here to take care of the place," Dixon charged when Reese said he wanted him to help with the cattle. "You've got to take care of the herd without his help. Damn it, man, I gave you men to work the cattle, and one by one, you're losing my whole damn crew!" Pressed for an answer to that, but reluctant to place the blame on his boss, Reese shifted nervously from one foot to the other. "Curly Cox dead!" Dixon continued to rage. "The Crouch brothers in jail? What the hell were you thinking—letting them go into town?"

"I wasn't there till after supper," Reese replied. "When I got back to the herd, they'd already gone."

"If you were doing your job, they would have known not to go into town," Dixon insisted.

"Well, sir, that two-hundred-dollar reward money was too temptin', I reckon," Reese offered lamely. Even as he said it, he marveled at the fact that he had to say it. It seemed to him that anyone would expect that to be the case.

"I pay you to control your men," Dixon fumed, ignoring the reason the men were drawn to the town. "When are the Crouch boys gonna get out of jail?"

"Well, now, that's hard to say. They locked 'em up for shootin' at that feller McCabe. They ain't likely to let 'em go anytime soon. More'n likely they'll hang 'em. One of 'em, I don't know which one, shot into a crowd of folks and hit the postmaster."

That served only to further infuriate Dixon. Every move he had made against the town had been met with disaster and the loss of his men. And it had all begun with the arrival of Cullen McCabe. The town had been cowered by the very presence of his ruthless men until McCabe showed up to stir the town people's confidence to defend themselves. And now it appeared that his bounty on McCabe's head had resulted only in more losses for the Double-D. It was apparent to him, after losing most of his hired gunmen, that he was going to have to pay an expert to eliminate McCabe. That meant sending someone to contact Deacon Pratt, and Pratt might not be at Poole's Place, the saloon that was his usual haunting spot this time of year. It would be an expensive contract—Pratt didn't work cheap. But Dixon knew Pratt was one he could count on for results, for there was no one faster with a six-gun than Deacon Pratt, a man with over a dozen duels that had been verified. Rumor had it that there were possibly as many, if not more, that were unreported. Dixon's mind made up, he gave Reese his orders. "You go on back to the men, what's left of them, and see if you can take care of the cattle I still have. Go to the line shack and get Ike

Roper to help you. I need Juan for something else." He paused for a moment. "And see if you can find out what they intend to do to Big Crouch and Little Crouch."

Juan Hernandez had been a silent witness to Dixon's angry tirade over Reese's report of the latest setback. He had listened from the safety of the corral several yards away and he snapped to attention immediately when Reese departed and his boss beckoned. "Juan," Dixon said, "I've got an important job for you. I want you to ride to Waco with a message for Deacon Pratt. Pick a good horse and you can make it up there in two and a half days or less. I'll write the message and you can take it to him. I'll give you enough money to pay for any food you need, and I want you to get started right away before it gets any later. You remember the way to Waco?" Juan replied that he did. He remembered, for that was the way he had come with the major on their way out to this land. "Good," Dixon said. "I trust you to do the job for me."

"Yes, sir," Juan said. "I not let you down, but I be gone for four days, maybe more. I worry who take care of the ranch."

"No need to worry," Dixon assured him. "We can make out for that long, and in the meantime, I'll have Mateo to do some of the jobs you normally do." When he said it, he was hoping that Deacon Pratt was still using Poole's Place as his usual haunt. It had been a while since he had last talked to the man. He had once offered Pratt the job that Reese Cochran now held, but Pratt had no desire to work on a cattle ranch. *If he had taken the job*, Dixon thought, *I wouldn't have been bothered with Cullen McCabe for more than one brief encounter.*

"How I find Deacon Pratt?" Juan asked. He knew the

major had met with Deacon Pratt, but he had never seen the man, himself.

"You remember the big bridge they built across the Brazos River?" Dixon asked, and Juan nodded. "You ride across that bridge to the east side. About half a mile beyond it there's a two-story building with a big sign on the front that says 'Poole's Place.' It's a saloon. Can you remember Poole's Place? The man that owns it is Roy Poole." He had to ask Juan if he could remember the name because Juan couldn't read. Juan repeated the name several times, then assured Dixon that he would remember.

"What I do if Pratt not there?"

"Leave my message with Roy Poole and come on back," Dixon said. "This time of year, Deacon will likely be there. If he is, then you bring him back with you. If he's not, I'll write directions for him in thc message."

Later that afternoon, Juan, with an envelope in his coat pocket, climbed on his horse and, leading a packhorse, left the Double-D. It was not a trip he wanted to make, certain as he was that Deacon Pratt would only cause matters to get worse. However, it was not in him to defy the major's orders. He planned to make the trip to Waco in two days, if possible, wishing to get it over with as soon as possible and hoping that Pratt was not in Waco.

CHAPTER 11

"We've got two prisoners in the jail for attempted murder," Malcolm Howard said. "What are we gonna do about it? We don't have a judge, so what do we do with 'em—try 'em ourselves and sentence 'em to hang—or let 'em go, so they can try it again?"

"We can't just let them go," Marvin Winter responded, taking Howard's remark seriously. "Because they'll surely try something like that again, especially if they see they're not gonna be punished for it."

"Well, we sure aren't set up to keep 'em in our jail for any length of time," Percy Mitchell said. "The jail wasn't built with that in mind, and we can't afford to feed prisoners long term. We'll just have to get word to the Texas Rangers to send somebody to pick 'em up."

"Good luck with that," Poss Rooks interjected. "I say hang 'em and we won't have to worry about 'em causin' any more trouble. We get a chance like this to get rid of two more of that bunch of rattlesnakes, that's two more that won't be takin' potshots at us." There were a few voices in agreement with Poss among the small gathering of merchants. However, there were some in disagreement.

"If we hang those two, then we aren't any better than vigilantes," Winter commented.

"Ain't nothin' wrong with that," Poss came back. "Hell, ain't no doubt they're guilty. Might as well get on with the hangin'."

"There wasn't but one shot fired when Buford got hit," Mitchell reminded them. "So maybe the one doing the shooting is the only guilty one, and we should let the other one go." His comment caused some concern among them, since no one had considered that. "We're trying to build a respectable town here, so we oughta be fair in cases like this," he added.

"I see what you're sayin'," Horner said, "but the other one ain't innocent of tryin' to commit murder. So you can't let one of 'em go free."

"In most towns in this territory, those two would already be swingin' from the limb of a tree," Poss insisted.

"We ain't gettin' a helluva lot done here," Ross Horner spoke up again. "Poss may be right, but Percy's right about bein' a civilized town. So, why don't we appoint three of us to decide what to do with the prisoners, and whatever they decide, that's what we'll do." His suggestion was met with general approval from the rest of them, and the review board was quickly voted on. Percy Mitchell, Marvin Winter, and Malcolm Howard were easily elected to try the prisoners.

With that issue tabled for the time being, there was another point of some concern for several at the meeting. It was Norman Freeman who brought it up. He got to his feet and, before speaking, looked around the room to make sure Cullen was not present. "Do we need to talk about this fellow McCabe? Does anybody know who the hell he is? Don't get me wrong," he quickly injected. "He's cleaned up a lot of trouble since he blew into town, but why is he doin' it? He says he's just passin' through, but he don't ever say to where. He ain't got no family and no particular business, so what's in it for him to risk his neck, if he ain't gettin' anything out of it?" He turned then to look at the sheriff. "How 'bout it, Shep? He's spent more time with you. Have you got any idea what he's thinkin'?"

Shep scratched his chin whiskers to help himself think. "No, not no more than you do," he replied. "All I know is he's helped me settle into this sheriff's job. Without his help, I don't know what I woulda done with those two prisoners. He might be another gunslinger, but I don't think he has any ideas about stayin' in Bonnie Creek." He paused, then added, "I don't know about the rest of you, but I'm damn glad Nathan Dixon has lost half of his gang of outlaws." His statement brought lots of nods and grunts of agreement.

Malcolm Howard took the floor. "It's good to have all this talk about doing the right thing with these two no-account dogs. But I say to hell with what Cullen McCabe's reasons are for standing with us against Dixon. I'm just damn glad he is. It's hard to deny that he has damn near single-handedly brought Nathan Dixon to his knees. And we wouldn't be in the position of strength we are right now if he hadn't showed up when he did." He looked at Mitchell and said, "Hell, Percy, your store mighta been the next one Dixon burned down—or my saloon—so I say thank the Lord, or the devil, whoever sent him." He sat down to a chorus of *amen*s from half of those in attendance.

With nothing more to add on that subject, the meeting moved on to the usual issue of Nathan Dixon's designs on the future of Bonnie Creek. The last item to be discussed was introduced by Shep Blackwell and that was the matter of hiring a deputy sheriff. Shep said that he had discussed the job with Wilbur Tate and Wilbur's reaction was not entirely positive, but he had agreed to help Shep for a while until they found someone else to fill the post permanently. The council agreed on a salary for Wilbur and hoped he would decide to keep the job.

Thinking about the same thing, Cullen McCabe sat in the hotel dining room. Shep needed a deputy. Cullen remembered acting as a sheriff without the help of a deputy. It was a lonely job. Having finished a plate of steak and potatoes, he was taking his time drinking a second cup of coffee. The women were cleaning up the dishes after supper, happy to have him help empty the pot before they cleaned it. Like the men meeting in the hotel parlor, Cullen was wondering if Dixon was going to draw back a little, since he had lost so many of his men. He wondered if his job here was done, or was this merely a lull before Dixon added more men and resumed his harassment of Bonnie Creek? There was no way to predict what a man like Dixon would do. Cullen was already prone to call him insane for thinking he could destroy a whole town just to add more territory to his home range. *I guess I'll hang around a while longer*, he thought when Daisy, holding the coffeepot and an extra cup, strolled over to the table.

"Want some company?" Daisy asked, then sat down without waiting for his answer. "You looked like you were doin' some serious thinkin' over here, but then, you always look serious—or maybe it was your supper that ain't settin' right in your stomach." She filled his half-empty cup, then poured a cup for herself. "That oughta about do it for that pot, so if you're plannin' on sittin' around here drinkin' more, you're gonna have to pay me to build another one." When he managed a slight smile for her attempt to engage him, she jerked her head back in a mock show of amazement.

"Thanks for the coffee," he said. "I'll get outta here and let you close up."

"There's no hurry," she said. "I'm ready to sit down for a while and rest my bones." She chuckled then and added, "At least until Bertha and Fanny start yellin' for me to get my behind in the kitchen to help them." Unlike the men in the parlor, she was not too shy to ask, "How long are you gonna hang around Bonnie Creek?"

He gave her a long, patient look. "Until it's done," he said. Then he downed the last few swallows of his coffee, got to his feet, and walked out the door.

Fanny walked out of the kitchen just as the door was closing behind Cullen. "Did you find out anything about him?" she asked because Daisy had said she was going to make him open up and at least tell her if he had changed his mind about leaving.

"No," Daisy replied, "not a damn thing." She got up from the table. "I'm more convinced than ever, though. That man's runnin' from something that's keepin' him from settlin' in one spot for very long. I bet there's a price on his head and I ain't talkin' about the two hundred dollars Dixon put on him. I bet that ain't even his real name. He musta changed it to hide from the law."

Fanny listened with interest, yet she was not sure she agreed. "He don't really seem like a bad man to me," she said. "He's always been nice and polite to me."

"That's the way those men are, the ones who like to kill women," Daisy said. "Nice and polite, till they get their hands around your throat." She made an imaginary twisting motion with her hands, stuck her tongue out, and made a face like she was being choked.

"I don't think so," Bertha said, coming into the dining room in time to hear Daisy's comments. "He'd kill you in an instant, but he'd do it quick so you wouldn't feel much pain, kinda like squashin' a bug."

"How do you know it don't hurt to get squashed?" Daisy asked, always ready for a harmless debate. "I bet if you asked a bug, he'd say it hurt like hell."

"I think you're both wrong about him," Fanny interrupted before they got started. "I think he's a good man."

Daisy laughed and remarked, "This is comin' from the gal who thinks Jeff Hammond ain't an outlaw like the rest of that Double-D crowd."

"Well, he's not," Fanny replied, heating up a little. "You shouldn't judge people when you don't really know them."

Realizing she had hit a nerve with her teasing, Daisy eased off a little. "You're right, honey, I don't know Jeff well enough to judge him." She glanced over and locked eyes with Bertha. They had been concerned about Fanny's infatuation with the young Double-D rider, fearing that she was in for some heartache. "I reckon he'll show his true colors before this mess with Dixon is settled."

Jeff Hammond was very much on Fanny's mind because he had told her, when they last met, that he was going to try to slip over to see her on that night. As it turned out, however, his plans had been changed and their planned rendezvous was not to be. The major had instructed Reese to try to find out what was going to happen to the Crouch brothers. And since Reese was too well-known in Bonnie Creek, he decided to first send someone in after dark to try to make contact with the brothers. The men he picked were Ike Roper and Jeff Hammond—Ike, a half-breed Comanche, he picked because he was a loner who never went into town, so the town folk would not be sure who he was. To go along with him, Reese picked Jeff, because he had never caused trouble in town, so if they happened to be seen, there was a good chance nothing would come of it. In addition to that, Reese figured Jeff could talk to the prisoners better than Ike, who was not good at communicating with anyone.

Jeff was not especially friendly with Ike, but then nobody else was, either. Since Ike was a loner, he was the obvious choice to camp in the line shack all winter. The rest of the crew wholeheartedly supported that decision, happy to have him out of the bunkhouse. As Benny Doyle had once commented, Ike Roper gave off a scent like a wolf with rabies, and not just because he never took more than two baths a year. Jeff shared that opinion, so he was not happy with the assignment, although it was a simple mission that Reese had charged them with. After dark, they were to sneak up to the small windows in the back of the jail to see if they could talk to Big Crouch and Little Crouch without anyone else knowing. Reese figured they might have been told what was to be done with them, and then he would know if there was a chance to plan an escape for them. To Jeff, the mission seemed to be a waste of time as far as the possibility of springing them. He had learned from Fanny that the town had a new sheriff and deputy, and there was still the problem of dealing with Cullen McCabe. On the positive side of this *mission* was the fact that it shouldn't take too long just to talk to the Crouch brothers, then he and Ike would head back. He would tell Ike to go on back alone and he would still have time to see Fanny. These were the thoughts that occupied his mind as he and Ike crossed over the river.

"Yonder's the jailhouse," Jeff whispered as he pulled his horse up beside the half-breed's. They dismounted and tied their horses in the branches of the trees, then jogged across the open space behind the buildings.

Before approaching the back windows, Ike wanted to slip around the side to see if there was anyone in the sheriff's office. Jeff waited, and in a few seconds, Ike returned. "There's a man in the office," he said. "Maybe we kill him and get them outta there."

"Best not try that," Jeff said, thinking the man in the office might be Cullen McCabe. "Reese was pretty plain about it," Jeff told the half-breed. "Just find out how they're doin' and if anybody's told 'em what they're gonna do with 'em." The half-breed shrugged, but made no objection, so Jeff started to move up under the window, only to be stopped by a warning from Ike.

"Be still," Ike whispered. "Somebody comin'."

They both lay flat on the ground to keep from being seen by the man walking down the street. He looked to have come from the hotel, possibly heading to the saloon across the street from the jail. When he was almost in front of the jail, Jeff recognized him. "It's McCabe," he whispered, not expecting what followed immediately. Without hesitating, Ike got up on one knee, raised his rifle to his shoulder, ready to fire. Jeff saw at once that the half-breed was not just being cautious, he was preparing to shoot McCabe in the back. "Hold on!" Jeff blurted. "Don't shoot!"

Ike turned his head toward Jeff and said, "I shoot. If

that's McCabe, I get two hundred dollars." He had heard about the reward. He looked back toward the unsuspecting target and cocked the rifle. From that moment and during those that followed immediately after, time seemed to stand still for Jeff. Afterward, he could not remember what had happened during the few seconds that followed the cocking of the rifle. He only remembered thinking it was wrong for the half-breed to shoot McCabe. Snippets of memory flooded his brain—Ike recoiling, trying to get to his feet and stumbling a few steps before falling to the ground—the recoil of the six-gun in his own hand—then the chain lightning reaction by Cullen McCabe, his rifle aimed at him.

"Drop it," Cullen demanded, "or I'll cut you down!" Jeff immediately dropped his weapon and Cullen walked toward the body on the ground, his rifle ready in case he was still alive. One look was enough to verify the death, even in the poor light, so he turned his attention to Jeff. He could see that the young man was shaken by what he had just done. "Why'd you shoot him?"

"I don't know," Jeff at first replied, still confused. "Because he was fixin' to shoot you, I reckon."

"Well, I appreciate that," Cullen said. "What's your name?"

Before he could answer, Wilbur Tate came from the front of the sheriff's office and answered for him. "He's one of the Double-D hands!" His pistol already in hand, he immediately aimed it at Jeff.

"Put it away," Cullen told him. "He just saved my life." He turned to Jeff and asked again, "What's your name?" Jeff told him, then Cullen asked, "Who is he?" He motioned toward the body. When Jeff said it was Ike Roper, Cullen asked, "He work for the Double-D, too?"

"Yes, sir," Jeff replied, "only I don't reckon neither one of us work for the Double-D no more." He swallowed hard and added, "When they find out I shot Ike."

"You got that right, you low-down coward!" The shout came from the little window in the rear of the cell room. "You can kiss your ass good-bye 'cause you're a dead man."

"Shut up in there!" Wilbur yelled back at the window.

"He's a dead man!" Little Crouch yelled again. "Just wait till Reese finds out what you did, you yeller dog!"

"If you don't shut up, you'll get no breakfast in the mornin'," Cullen threatened. A hushed conversation could be heard in the cell as Big Crouch pleaded with his brother to be silent. Cullen waited a few moments to see if the threat worked, and when it obviously did, he turned his attention back to the completely confused young man standing rigidly by the back corner of the jail. "Now, tell me, exactly why did you shoot one of your partners from the Double-D?"

"I told you, he was fixin' to shoot you." Jeff hesitated, trying to figure it out, himself. "He didn't even know who you were a couple of days ago. It didn't seem right for him to shoot you. And he didn't really know it was you, till I told him who you were. We were only supposed to try to talk to Big Crouch and Little Crouch to find out what you were gonna do with 'em. But to shoot a man down for two hundred dollars—it just ain't right."

Cullen hesitated, not sure if he should believe him, but it was hard to argue otherwise when Jeff had obviously shot Cullen's would-be assassin. He had been totally unaware of the two men hiding in the shadows beside the jail. There was no reason he had not been shot other than Jeff's twinge of conscience. Cullen bent down and picked up

Ike's rifle. It was cocked and ready to fire, further evidence to support Jeff's story. A small crowd of people began to gather in the street between the jail and the saloon, curious to find out what the shooting was about. Cullen motioned to the still-shaken young man and said, "I think you could use a drink. Pick up your pistol and I'll buy you one." Side by side, they walked through the little gathering of spectators, who flocked to look at the body they'd left behind them.

Chubby Green was standing in the door when Cullen and Jeff stepped up on the board stoop of the Rose. Chubby took a step back and held the door for them, eyeing Jeff openly. "Well, I shoulda figured that shot had somethin' to do with you, McCabe. Anybody hurt?" He continued to eye Jeff, his curiosity about to get the best of him.

"Yeah," Cullen answered. "One dead, one of the Double-D gang, fellow by the name of Ike Roper."

"What was he up to?" Chubby asked. "Why'd you have to shoot him?"

"I didn't. Jeff did," Cullen replied, and started to explain.

"He shot him?" Chubby blurted before Cullen could continue. "He rides for the Double-D! I don't know nobody named Roper, but I've seen this feller in here a time or two with some of that Double-D crowd."

Cullen went on to explain that Jeff had saved his life when he stopped Roper from shooting him in the back. "Now, I'd like to buy him a drink." He turned to Jeff, standing beside him, his eyes wide as if still in a state of shock and wondering what was about to happen to him. "Whiskey?" Cullen asked. Jeff nodded, thinking he could use something strong at this particular moment, especially when he thought of the image Nathan Dixon had painted of McCabe. A hired gunman, Dixon had labeled him, a ruthless killer, maybe no better than the late Tom Yates. When Chubby poured two whiskeys, Cullen picked one up and said, "Come on, we'll take it over to a table and sit down. Better give me the bottle," he said to Chubby, which disappointed the chunky bartender, since he was burning with curiosity.

Judging by the tears brought forth in Jeff's eyes by the first shot of the strong whiskey, Cullen figured him not to be a steady drinker, even though he nodded again when Cullen offered a second one. There were no words spoken until after Jeff knocked back a third shot of whiskey. Studying the young man with interest, Cullen thought to ask a question. "You've never shot a man before, have you?"

"No, sir, I haven't. That was my first and I don't feel very good about it." This in spite of the fact that no one on the Double-D would grieve the death of Ike Roper.

"Well, if you're lucky, maybe it'll be your last," Cullen said. On a hunch, he asked, "You're the one who told Fanny Wright about the four riders comin' after me, and the bounty on my head, right?" Jeff didn't answer the question, but lowered his head and, after a moment, reached for the bottle. Cullen moved the bottle out of his reach. "You've had enough. Any more and you'll be sick. You ain't used to drinkin'." That much was obvious to Cullen. "What the hell are you doin', ridin' with that gang of outlaws on the Double-D?"

Jeff looked up at him. "It was either that or ride the grub line," he said.

"Now, after you just saved my life and shot one of Dixon's men, what are you gonna do? It's gonna be kinda hard to explain to him why you shot Roper instead of me, ain't it?"

"Yes, sir," Jeff replied. "I can't hardly go back there." He thought about what his reception might be after they found out he'd killed Ike. Even his friend Seth would be hard-pressed to forgive him for that. Ike was little more than a crude animal, but he was a member of the Double-D crew.

It was a short time to judge a person, but Cullen trusted his intuition about the young man sitting at the table with him. He was convinced that Jeff was a good man who had landed in the wrong place with the wrong crowd. He had seen it his duty to give Fanny warnings of harm coming Cullen's way on two separate occasions. Now Jeff had shot Ike Roper because it was the right thing to do. And especially at this particular time, Bonnie Creek could use all the right-thinking men they could find. So Cullen made a suggestion. "Well, seems to me you've got to make a decision. You can get on your horse and ride as far from here as fast as you can, or you can stay right here and help the good people of Bonnie Creek save their town from Nathan Dixon." Jeff looked up at him in surprise. It was obvious that he had never considered the possibility of staying in Bonnie Creek. To add further enticement, Cullen said, "And Fanny Wright is lookin' to build her life right here."

Jeff's eyes opened wide, amazed by what he was hearing from the man who had driven Nathan Dixon to such desperate measures. A man who was supposedly a conscienceless killer who had coldly cut Tom Yates down and was responsible for the loss of half of the major's men. "I can't find a way to make a livin' in Bonnie Creek," he finally said. "Besides, the folks here ain't gonna want me here, knowin' I worked for the major. They're more likely gonna wanna hang me."

"There's that possibility," Cullen admitted, "but after they get to know you wanna do the right thing, they might change their minds." He knew it was a hell of a gamble, but he felt he could trust his thoughts about the young man. He didn't tell Jeff, because he wanted to make sure before he proposed it, but he knew that Wilbur Tate was definitely not interested in filling the job of deputy permanently. He might have to do one hell of a job selling the town council on the idea of hiring Jeff as deputy sheriff. If he could do that, it might be a big step in establishing law and order in Bonnie Creek. There sure as hell shouldn't be any question about any loyalty he might feel toward the Double-D. Jeff had pulled the trigger when the time came. That told Cullen he would do it again if called upon. His mind made up, he finally said, "Go on back and get your horse, and Roper's horse, and meet me down at the stable. We'll put 'em up there, then we'll get you a room in the hotel where I'm stayin' till you get something permanent."

"Whoa!" Jeff blurted. "I ain't got money to spend on stables and hotels! I ain't got but forty dollars to my name and it took me a year to save up that much." It occurred to him then that he would be spending some of that money right away. "I'm gonna have to buy some more stuff, too, to replace some stuff I left in the bunkhouse."

"I'll stand good for you for a little while till you get yourself squared away with what you wanna do for the rest of your life. Maybe we'll even have breakfast in the hotel dinin' room in the mornin'." He almost cracked a rare smile when he saw the look on Jeff's face after his last remark.

CHAPTER 12

There had been little trouble in boarding Jeff's horses with Ross Horner. He took Cullen's word as bond for the two horses. Cullen's first challenge in Jeff's swapping of sides in the battle for Bonnie Creek came when they went to the hotel. Marvin Winter's clerk, John Taylor, was not sure what to do when he recognized Jeff as the Double-D man who liked to eat in the hotel dining room. Having already been called on the carpet when he rented a room to Cullen, he went to get the owner. Winter's reaction was predictable as he was reluctant to turn any of the hotel's rooms over to the lawless vandals who rode for the Double-D. It took Cullen's guarantee that he would stand good for any damage caused by Jeff in addition to paying the room rent. Even that might not have been enough, save for the fact that the hotel was nearly empty of guests. This even after Cullen explained that Jeff had taken a stance against the evil of the Double-D when he saved Cullen's life by shooting down a would-be assassin. It promised to be a hard sell to convince the rest of the merchants that Jeff had come to fight for their cause.

It was a different story, however, the next morning when

Jeff walked into the dining room, causing two of the three women who worked there to pause frozen in midstep. They were even more amazed when he nodded politely to Fanny, then walked over to take a seat at the table where Cullen was sitting, drinking a cup of coffee. Daisy was the first to find her voice. "Well, I'll be double damned and hog-tied," she muttered. "I reckon you can wait on him," she said to Fanny. "I'm goin' to tell Bertha. She's gotta see this." As she had expected, Bertha had to come to the door to see for herself, and she was still not sure she wasn't seeing things.

"Good mornin'," Fanny said rather faintly when she came to the table, then stood speechless.

"Good mornin'," Jeff returned, his voice almost quaking. He wanted to explain why he had not come to see her the night before since he was not sure if word had gotten around town about the shooting of Ike Roper. It was impossible to convey his thoughts with his eyes when she was too shy to meet his gaze, so he was forced to sit there with no chance to explain.

There followed an awkward moment of silence and Cullen looked from one of them to the other, then finally spoke. "Good mornin', Fanny. I reckon you know Jeff Hammond. He's likely wantin' breakfast, same as me." That seemed to shake her out of her trance.

"Of course," she quickly replied. "I'll get you some coffee." She spun on her heel and hurried to fetch the coffeepot. Then, holding the heavy pot, she returned to stare dumbfounded at the table.

"He could most likely use a cup," Cullen advised her. "I ain't through with mine, else he could use it." She flushed visibly and ran to get one, leaving the big coffeepot on the table. Cullen casually picked it up and filled his almost-empty cup.

After Fanny returned with a cup for Jeff, she retreated to the kitchen, where Daisy and Bertha were already in a huddle speculating on the surprising occurrence. "They want breakfast!" Fanny exclaimed as if it was a phenomenal thing. "Do you think he has Jeff under arrest?" she asked then.

"Well, I doubt he'd bring a prisoner to breakfast," Daisy said. "Besides, he ain't the sheriff. Jeff came in by hisself. McCabe was already here." Far too curious to remain silent and wait for Fanny to tell her the story, she grabbed the plates when Bertha filled them and delivered them to the table, herself. Placing them down before the two men, she couldn't help commenting, "I swear, I didn't know you two knew each other." Her remark was met with a shy nod from Jeff and nothing from Cullen, which seemed to agitate her into further comments. "You do know that Jeff, here, rides for the Double-D, don't you, McCabe?"

Cullen thrust a fork loaded with potatoes into his mouth before answering. "He used to, but he quit after he shot Ike Roper when he was fixin' to shoot me. Anybody who saves my life is a friend of mine."

"Well, I'll be . . ." Daisy started, then paused to think about it. "That was the shot we heard last night?" Cullen nodded without looking up from his plate, more intent upon consuming the slice of salty ham occupying half of it. Daisy, still finding it hard to believe, turned to Fanny, who was standing a few feet away. "That shot we heard was Jeff," she said. "It was him that shot that feller."

"I heard," Fanny replied. They had been told that a Double-D man had been killed last night and speculated that it was probably Cullen who did the shooting.

Daisy turned back to look at Jeff. "Good for you," she blurted. "That's one less we have to worry about. Fanny, bring some more coffee over here." Then she looked at Cullen again. "I'll let you boys eat your breakfast."

"'Preciate it," Cullen said as she walked away. He waited while Fanny topped off their coffee, almost spilling it when she and Jeff locked eyes. When she took the pot back to place it on the stove, he commented, "Now, there's some more friends you've already got in town." He studied Jeff carefully as the outlaw-turned-respectable was obviously thinking hard about his unexpected situation. Cullen was sure Jeff was trying to make up his mind about what to do. "It's your decision to make," Cullen said, "but my advice is to take a couple of days to see if you can make it here."

"I ain't sure I can," Jeff said. "I know I'd like to, but with the Double-D right across the river, I'd have to be lookin' over my shoulder every minute. The major will likely put a bounty on my head, too. He ain't gonna let me get away with killin' one of his men."

"That's a possibility, all right, but how many men has Dixon got left?" Cullen asked. This was something he was very interested in knowing.

Jeff paused to think. "With the Crouch brothers in jail, that only leaves Reese Cochran, Seth Wiley, Smokey Jones, and Juan Hernandez," he said. "That's not enough men to work that ranch, but the major will most likely hire more men. He'll have to, with winter comin' on."

"It'll take him a while to find enough men." Cullen was thinking out loud. "There are always out-of-work cowhands ridin' the grub line this time of year, lookin' for work. But finding the kind of men he's lookin' for, outlaws and cutthroats, will make it a little harder. In the meantime, we've got just four men to contend with, and they've still got to take care of his cattle."

"That's right," Jeff said, "but right now, he ain't got but about five hundred head of cattle, so they could handle that many. He usually builds his herd up to a couple of thousand, most of 'em rustled in Mexico."

"Maybe they can handle that many," Cullen suggested, "but they likely can't handle the cattle and make war on the town, too."

The discussion continued on through breakfast, and by the time they were finished, Cullen had gathered a great deal of information about the running of the ranch and the likely nature of each man still there. From Jeff's rundown on each man, he concluded that the teeth of Dixon's ruthless gang of outlaws had been pulled, leaving a foreman who was the conveyer of Dixon's orders. Then there was Smokey, who was really a cook, and Seth, who was the closest to a friend that Jeff knew and more a thief than a killer. That left Hernandez, who was little more than a valet for Dixon and hardly a gunman. The evil behind the Double-D ranch was Dixon, himself, a man who would sacrifice all those who worked for him, as he had already demonstrated.

Based on the information he had just gathered, Cullen decided it was time to make a scouting visit to the Double-D camp across the river. With Dixon's men down to a skeleton crew, now was the best opportunity he was likely to get. The first step was to fully recruit Jeff Hammond, and he was already halfway there. With the expense money the governor's aide had advanced him, he could afford to pay for Jeff's room and board for a few days until he persuaded the town council to give him the job as deputy. First addressing Jeff's concern about Dixon placing a bounty on him, he said, "I'm thinkin' right now neither one of us has to worry too much about a shot in the back. Who would Dixon send to shoot you now? The cook doesn't sound like he'd come after you, nor the Mexican, either. That leaves Reese Cochran, who's already come out on the short end when he came in with Dixon before—and Seth—what did you say his name was?" When Jeff told him, Cullen continued, "From what you've told me, he was the only friend you had. Do you think he would come after you?" He waited while Jeff pondered that thought.

"I don't know," Jeff finally answered. "I'd hate to think so."

"I think there's a good chance he won't, but that's just a guess. If you're willin' to take a gamble on Seth and hang around for a few more days, I'm willin' to pay for your room and a couple of meals a day. In the meantime, we'll take you to talk to some of the folks who run this town, so they'll know you're on their side." He paused to judge Jeff's reaction to the proposal before continuing. "How do you feel about takin' the job of deputy sheriff?"

"What?" Jeff responded, stunned by the question.

Cullen continued before Jeff could say more. "The job is open, you've got the makin's of a good lawman, and that would give you a payin' job. It ain't a very high-payin' job, but it might be enough to ask Fanny Wright to marry you—if that's what you've got on your mind. Whaddaya say?"

Jeff couldn't speak for a few moments, still astonished by Cullen's proposal. "You've already got a deputy sheriff," he replied. "That fellow in the jail last night."

"That was Wilbur Tate," Cullen said. "He's just fillin' in till Shep finds a deputy. He ain't interested in the job at all."

Deputy sheriff was a job Jeff had never considered before, nor would he ever have, if it had not been suggested. He answered honestly, "I don't know." Cullen let him think about it. After a long second, Jeff allowed, "I reckon I could try it."

"Good," Cullen said. "Come on, we'll go talk to the sheriff." He wanted to make sure he could sell Shep on the idea before he approached the others on the prospect.

The rest of the morning was spent introducing some of the merchants to the idea of seeing Jeff in town in the company of McCabe. There was no objection from Shep Blackwell, since Jeff had gunned Ike Roper down. He knew Wilbur wouldn't take the job and Jeff looked to be a better candidate for the job, in spite of his prior association with Nathan Dixon. Cullen pointed out that it was not unusual for a lawman to have been on the other side of the law at some time in his life. He was reminded of several successful town marshals who had stepped over the line prior to beginning a career protecting the people.

Percy Mitchell was a little more difficult to persuade, but the more he thought about it, the more he was willing to accept the notion that Jeff could not in good conscience work for Dixon. Malcolm Howard thought it was a hell of a good idea and welcomed another gun to fight Dixon. It was early afternoon when Cullen suggested that Jeff should go back to his room to think about everything they had covered that morning. "Go to the dinin' room, if you're hungry. Tell Daisy I'll pay her next time I'm in."

"You don't eat no dinner?" Jeff asked.

"Not today. I'll be there for supper," Cullen said. "I've got something I need to take care of." They parted company then with Cullen heading for the stable. He didn't tell Jeff, but he thought it was time that he took a look at the

Double-D camp, if only to let them know that they were vulnerable to attack. Jake needed to get a little exercise, anyway. The big bay gelding hadn't been ridden in a couple of days. Cullen thought it a good idea to give Jeff some time to think about the decision he was about to make. It was a hell of a jump the young man was considering, swapping sides in a range war. The wild card in this game was Fanny Wright. The path many men took was for no other reason than to follow a woman.

Smokey mumbled to himself as he set a pot of beans to soak in the back of the chuckwagon. He was thinking of the difference between the number of men hc had to feed now compared to the meals he had to fix before McCabe came riding into the middle of the major's plans to build an empire. "Helluva note," he mumbled when he thought about the steady reduction in the number of Double-D hands. *Dixon ran into a tornado when Cullen McCabe came to town,* he couldn't help thinking. It was the middle of the afternoon and still no sign of Ike Roper and Jeff Hammond. Reese sent them into town the night before to see if they could talk to Big Crouch and Little Crouch. Smokey didn't give a damn about Ike, but Jeff was a decent young man and he hated to think he might have been gunned down by that devil McCabe. *They left us in a hell of a fix*, he thought. *Nobody but Reese and Seth to try to keep the herd together*. "Why the hell didn't Hernandez show up to help? I reckon the major has to have somebody to do for him," he mumbled to himself, a trait that had become a habit whenever he was alone. He was unaware that Dixon had sent Juan to Waco to deliver a message. "We're every one of us gonna wind up in hell before this is over." Shooing a large horsefly away from his pot of beans, he prepared to fetch some more wood for his fire. "Jumpin' Jehoshaphat!" he suddenly blurted when he turned to encounter a grim figure mounted on a bay horse, no more than ten yards away. A big man, he sat silently watching the startled cook and his idle babbling.

Terrified, Smokey reached for his gun, only to discover he wasn't wearing it. In a panic, for he was certain he was facing the man called McCabe, he backed away to collide with the corner of the tailgate of his chuckwagon, sending him stumbling to the ground. On his hands and knees then, he started crawling as fast as he could toward the front of the wagon and his gun and holster on the seat. Cullen nudged Jake with his heels and the big bay walked slowly after the crawling man. When Smokey reached the front of the wagon, Cullen warned him, "Reach for it and you're a dead man."

Thinking all was lost, Smokey rolled over and sat on the ground, his back against the wagon wheel, waiting for the bullet he knew was coming. When Cullen just continued to watch him, his Winchester rifle resting across his thighs, the frightened man blurted, "What are you waitin' for? Get it over with!"

"What makes you think I'm gonna shoot you?"

"'Cause that's what you do, ain't it? Sooner or later, one by one, you're gonna kill every one of us!"

"Is that what you think?" Cullen replied. "Well, you're a damn fool. Every man who was killed came to town lookin' to kill somebody."

Smokey realized that he might not be going to meet the devil in the next few seconds after all, so it emboldened him to argue. "Is that so? What about Jeff Hammond? He ain't never gone lookin' to kill nobody. Where is he?" Then he remembered. "And Ike Roper, what about him?"

"Roper's dead." That was all he said about him for the moment. "Jeff's in town. I expect he's most likely still in the hotel dinin' room. At least that's where he said he was goin'. He's decided he ain't comin' back to the Double-D. He's got sense enough to know that Nathan Dixon is the man responsible for the deaths of every man he's lost. Too bad you ain't got that much sense."

Smokey didn't answer right away. What Cullen said was enough to make him realize he was speaking the truth. Smokey had known it for some time, he had just been too stupid, or maybe too afraid, to admit it, even to himself. It struck him that Reese was close to admitting it as well. "What are you aimin' to do with me?"

"That's up to you. I'm not aimin' to do anything to you. I just wanted to see what kind of men would keep volunteering to die for Nathan Dixon's greed. I didn't come over here to do you any harm, but I will shoot you down if you go for that gun on the wagon seat. Do you understand?"

"Yessir, I sure do," Smokey replied immediately, feeling as if he had been given his life back. "And I ain't goin' nowhere near that gun."

"Not even for a shot at two hundred dollars?" Cullen couldn't resist asking.

"No, sir, not even for that. There ain't no place in hell to spend two hundred dollars." He was truly convinced that he would be killed if he tried anything with the grim horseman. At this point, he just wanted him to leave before Reese returned. He was afraid Reese might try something foolish and get them both killed. Convinced by now that McCabe meant it when he said he didn't come to do harm, he was emboldened to ask a question. "Is that the truth, what you said about Jeff joinin' up with the town people?"

"Yep," Cullen answered. "It didn't take Jeff long to see who was gonna come out on top of this big mistake your boss, Dixon, is makin'. He ain't got the message that the people of Bonnie Creek are tired of his harassment. They ain't scared no more and they're ready to fight back. The only difference is, they're aimin' to fight by the rule of law and order. Those two boys of yours, the Crouch brothers, are gonna get a fair trial, and then I reckon they'll hang 'em. If Dixon sends anybody else over to town, lookin' for trouble, I expect they'll end up just like the Crouch brothers—if they ain't shot down first. The thing of it is," he concluded, "Bonnie Creek's got more fightin' men now than the Double-D has. That's something you oughta think about." Judging by the apprehensive look on Smokey's face, he figured he had triggered some questions in the simple cook's mind. Hopefully they would be enough to spark thoughts of desertion. With that thought, he decided he had done what he came to do. Whether it was worthwhile or not would remain to be seen.

"Well, I reckon I'll be seein' you again pretty soon," Cullen said. "Where's your rifle?" When told it was behind the wagon seat, Cullen guided Jake over beside the wagon and reached in and picked up the rifle. He picked up the gun and holster from the seat and threw them over into the wagon. Then he replaced his Winchester in the saddle sling and held Smokey's rifle up for him to see. "I think we have an understandin', but just in case we don't, I'll leave your rifle by that tree yonder." He pointed to an oak tree about forty yards away. He wheeled Jake and loped off toward the tree, leaving a relieved cook to stand staring after him, his shirt wet with sweat in the chilly air.

After a minute or two, Smokey slowly recovered his senses, although still confused by the fact that he was still breathing. From all he had heard about the sinister gunman, he had come to expect that any man opposing him faced instant death. "Lord-a-mercy," he uttered, thankful to still be alive, and started walking toward the oak tree to retrieve his rifle. As he walked, he thought about Jeff Hammond and wondered if what McCabe had said about him was true. If it was, then he would have to conclude that Jeff had gone over to the other side. Normally, that would have placed a bounty on Jeff's head and a definite attempt by Dixon's men to claim it. But, in Smokey's mind, there was no one left to go after it. Not himself, probably not Seth, and he couldn't see Reese inclined to risk going into Bonnie Creek to challenge him. Reese would not likely get out of town alive, with McCabe on the scene. That left Juan Hernandez, and the nonaggressive Mexican had never been a violent man. "I reckon if the major wants Jeff dead," he decided, "he's gonna have to do the job himself, and that ain't likely to happen."

A couple hundred yards away, Cullen rode along the edge of the trees that lined the river. He had nothing in mind beyond his curiosity to see how far down the river Dixon's cattle had been driven. Within a mile or so, he came upon the first pockets of strays that had lagged behind the main herd. The farther he rode, the more strays he discovered until he decided he had seen enough to substantiate what Jeff had told him. Dixon was short of help to tend his cattle, almost to the point of desperation. It was Cullen's opinion that Dixon would now be forced to draw back and try to concentrate on saving his cattle business. The next few days should tell for sure.

CHAPTER 13

The cards weren't falling right for Whit Dawkins. It seemed to him that every time he looked to have a winning hand, one he was confident to bet heavy on, the smug horse's ass across the table managed to draw out to fill a straight or pair up an ace. *One more time*, he thought, *and I'm going to call him on it*. Nobody could be that lucky. "I'll take two," he told the man dealing the cards, hoping to catch a lucky pair to go with his three jacks and fill in a full house. Whit's partner, Muley Price, threw his cards in, his luck running as poorly as Whit's. The man to his right, a whiskey salesman from Fort Worth, folded as well. The dealer, whose dark features seemed to suggest a mournful disposition, even when he occasionally smiled, took two as well. He gazed up at Whit from under heavy black brows and smiled, waiting for the bidding to begin. When it was finished, Whit moved everything he had left to the center of the table for the final call. "Three jacks," he announced, and spread them in front of him.

"I reckon this just ain't your lucky night," the dealer said as he spread three aces.

Whit didn't say anything for a full minute, his eyes

almost glazed as he stared at the cards faceup on the table, not even blinking when the baleful-looking dealer raked his sizable winnings off the table into his hat. Muley, knowing his partner well enough to know he was burning inside, made an attempt to reach him. "Come on, Whit, let's get outta here. Like he said, this just ain't our lucky night." Whit, still staring at the table, gave no indication that he had heard him.

The stranger, his somber gaze fixed on Whit, spoke after a moment. "That's hard luck, friend. Tell you what, let me buy you a drink."

"That last ace came off the bottom of the deck," Whit stated solemnly. Suddenly the room went totally silent.

"What was that you said?" the stranger asked, his voice low, his words distinct.

Muley grabbed Whit's arm in an attempt to pull him out of his chair, but Whit refused to be moved. "I said that last ace came off the bottom," he repeated. The whiskey salesman pushed his chair back, stood up, and quickly moved away from the table. Roy Poole, standing behind the bar, smiled, knowing what was to come. It would not be the first cowboy that got dusted in his saloon. Poole's Place was notorious for gunfights.

Totally unperturbed, the sinister stranger said, "It sounds like you're callin' me a cheat."

Fully irate now, Whit replied, "Damn right I am. You've been cheatin' every time you dealt the cards. Ain't nobody that lucky, every time it was their deal."

Poole came out from behind the bar and walked over to the two men now standing and facing each other. The sinister man was no stranger to him, and he cared not at all how the dispute was settled, but he thought he would at least let Whit know who he was facing. "Maybe you oughta listen to your partner and get the hell outta here, cowboy. The man you're callin' a cheat is Deacon Pratt."

"Maybe you oughta stay outta this, Roy," Pratt said as he pushed his chair back and stood up. "The man oughta stand up to what his mouth gets him into. I don't like bein' called a cheat and I want an apology. And I mean down on your knees and beg me to forgive you." He directed that last requirement toward Whit.

Whit was beginning to realize what he had stepped into, but he was reluctant to grovel for forgiveness. He had never heard of Deacon Pratt, but from the way Poole had said the name, maybe he should have. Still, he was cursed with stubborn pride. "I meant what I said," he stated.

"No man calls me that and walks away," Pratt said. "You're wearin' a gun, so you'd best get ready to use it, else I'm gonna gun you down where you stand." He backed away from the table toward the center of the room. With his baleful gaze zeroed on Whit, he pulled his coat back and took hold of it with his left hand and held it behind his back, clearing the .44 on his right hip. "Whenever you're ready," he said, "draw your weapon, or get down on your knees and crawl outta here like the yellow dog you are."

The remaining few patrons in the saloon quickly got up from their chairs then and cleared the center of the room, leaving Whit and Muley standing alone to face Pratt. "Come on, Whit," Muley begged. "It ain't worth it. Tell the man you're sorry and let's just get outta here."

Whit hesitated, reluctant to being branded a coward, but more convinced by the second that he had challenged a notorious gunfighter. He turned slowly away and started to follow Muley when Pratt commanded, "I said on your hands and knees!" Whit halted, but did not turn around, his brain whirling with a tornado of thoughts and his hands tingling with nerves. It occurred to him that there was still a chance to save face, if he could take Pratt by surprise. It being the only chance he had, he started to crouch as if about to get down on his knees, at the same time dropping his hand on the handle of his pistol. Then he suddenly spun around, pulling the weapon as he turned, just in time to catch a .44 slug in his chest before he could pull the trigger. Without pause, Pratt fanned the hammer back and sent the next shot to strike Muley in the chest as well. Whit dropped to his knees before falling over on his side, shot through the heart. Muley staggered a couple of steps before falling facedown.

An eerie silence fell upon the saloon, a silence that was more deafening than the sound of the two shots just fired and was not broken until Pratt spoke. "You all saw it," he said. "The other one was goin' for his gun. I've seen that trick before. They thought I couldn't watch both of 'em, but they weren't fast enough to pull it off."

"I reckon that's the way it happened, all right," Roy Poole spoke up. He looked around at the few customers who had witnessed the murder and nodded in agreement. "They were definitely tryin' to double up on you." Not one of the other witnesses offered any different version of the face-off, in spite of the fact that no one had seen Muley Price make any attempt to draw his weapon.

The smirk on Deacon Pratt's face slowly became a satisfied smile. He replaced the two spent cartridges and holstered his .44. "Too bad about those sore losers, but seein' as how I came out pretty good in the poker game, set up a round of drinks on me, Roy." The usual noise of the saloon resumed immediately with most of the conversation about the lightninglike speed of Deacon Pratt's draw. Having seen all he needed to see, the whiskey salesman gathered up what little cash he had left and scurried out the door, causing Roy to chuckle. "Hey," he yelled after him, "don't run off, we might get us another game goin'." He laughed heartily when the salesman picked up his pace. A couple of Roy's regular customers gave him a hand in dragging the two unfortunate cowboys out of the saloon to be left for Roy's son to dig a hole for them.

Deacon Pratt was in no hurry to leave the scene, confident that the spectators of the face-off would say that Whit Dawkins went for his six-gun first. Pratt was smug also in the knowledge that there was no law in this little pocket across the river from town. The closest law was in Waco, across the river, and the marshal there had no interest in what happened on the east side of the river. It was the reason Pratt kept a room upstairs over the saloon when he was in Texas for the winter. Feeling in a good mood now, he joked with Roy as he enjoyed a drink of whiskey at the end of the bar. "That damn cowboy was lyin', he didn't see that ace come off the bottom."

Roy laughed. "Hell, I saw it from over here at the bar," he japed, and they both laughed. They were still laughing when Juan Hernandez walked in the front door and paused to look the room over. Still wary, after seeing the two bodies parked by the front porch, he eyed the two men talking at the end of the bar. The one behind the bar was most likely Roy Poole, so he pulled the envelope from his coat pocket and went straight to the bar.

"I got a message for Deacon Pratt," Juan announced, speaking directly to Poole. "It's from Major Nathan Dixon."

Both Poole and Pratt eyed Juan up and down with some

skepticism before Poole responded, "Well, whaddaya tellin' me for? Why don't you give it to him?"

"You are Deacon Pratt?" Juan asked, turning to the smirking Pratt.

"Yeah, I'm Pratt," he said, and took the envelope. He knew who Nathan Dixon was, he had talked to him before in Waco. "Pour him a drink, Roy," he said after he looked at the message inside. It was a lengthy one, with instructions on how to find the Double-D and a rich reward for doing a job. *Bonnie Creek*, he thought. *Never heard of it, but I know where the San Saba River is*. Looking up at Roy, he said, "Looks like I'm gonna take a little trip. I expect I'll be gone for a spell."

"That a fact?" Roy replied. "Well, you know you've always got a room here when you get back."

"I'll be leavin' in the mornin'," Pratt said, then he reached in his hat, which was sitting upside down on the bar beside him. Taking out some of the money from his poker winnings, he handed it to Roy to pay for the drinks he had bought the house. Looking back at Juan, he said, "Accordin' to what's written here, you know the way to the Double-D, so I don't need all these written directions, right?"

"I take you back," Juan confirmed.

"Good, you take me back," Pratt said, mocking the Mexican's broken English. "How far is this place?" When Juan told him it was two hard days, or two and a half easy days, Pratt said, "I reckon we'll make it in two days, then, but I ain't leavin' till the mornin'. I'm gonna have to go into Waco to buy some supplies. He didn't give you any money to pay for them, did he?" Juan shook his head. "Well, I reckon I'll have to trust him to cover my expenses.

If he ain't lyin' about what he'll pay me for the job, I reckon I can pay my own expenses. You be back here in the mornin' about seven o'clock. I like to eat breakfast before I get started. Maybe Roy will let you sleep in the barn." He glanced at Poole. "Won'tcha, Roy?"

"I reckon," Roy replied, "but it'll cost you a dollar to keep your horse in the barn."

"I have two horses," Juan said.

"Then it'll cost you two dollars," Roy said.

"I camp by the river," Juan decided. Dixon had given him enough money to pay Roy's price, but it was too high a price to suit the Mexican. Nodding to Deacon, he said, "I see you at seven in the morning, Mr. Pratt."

After Juan left the saloon, Pratt hung around for one more drink before he announced, "I expect I'd better ride over the bridge to town to pick up a few things. I don't wanna keep my special guide waitin' in the mornin'."

"Whaddaya gonna do about the two horses those cowboys rode in on?" Roy asked.

"The same thing we did last time somebody drew down on me," Pratt replied. "You get the horses and saddles. I'll take a look to see if there's anything in their saddlebags I want."

"Right," Roy crowed. "You already cleaned them outta their money in the poker game, so I reckon we both made a profit. A pleasure doin' business with you," he said with a wide smile.

About twenty minutes after Pratt had saddled up and set out on the road to town, he spotted the solemn Mexican by the river, about forty yards upstream from the bridge, a fire already burning and his horses grazing.

* * *

Back in the little town of Bonnie Creek, things were beginning to get back to a more civilized pace of life. Since Cullen's visit with Smokey Jones at the Double-D's campsite, the town people were aware that the Double-D was down to less than a skeleton crew. After only a day's time, the council had voted in favor of Cullen's recommendation to hire Jeff Hammond as a deputy to help Shep keep the peace. The night watch by citizens was stopped since it was now the sheriff's and his deputy's responsibility. The main thing on everybody's mind at this time was a trial for the two inhabitants of the jail. It was no secret that, for most of the men of the town, the trial should be no more than a formality before hanging both prisoners. The main dissident to this decision was Percy Mitchell, who strongly believed that punishment for the actual shooter should carry the most severe penalty and his brother should be sentenced to the Texas State Prison. Mitchell's main argument was that a vigilante-like lynching would damage the town's chances of gaining new respectable businesses. His attempts to swing others to his way of thinking were in vain, however, and he was outvoted by Marvin Winter and Malcolm Howard. So a trial was set to be held in the saloon the next day.

Chubby shoved three tables together to form the "bench" for the three judges in the center of the back wall, which left plenty of room for spectators to watch the proceedings while enjoying their favorite libations. The trial was set to begin at two o'clock in the afternoon, and most of the merchants closed their businesses while it was in session. It was a big day for the town of Bonnie Creek—

there had never been an occasion for a trial before. Promptly at a few minutes to two, Shep and his deputy led two disgruntled prisoners across the street to the Rose, their hands bound behind their backs. Their appearance prompted a noisy reception by the spectators, some of them already heavily invested in Malcolm Howard's stock of whiskey. One who was not inside the saloon, Cullen McCabe, was taking a walk around town. He was inclined to believe it a good idea to keep an eye on the deserted street. This just in case one or more of the Double-D men felt bold enough to make an attempt to either free the Crouch brothers or, failing that, cause some damage to some of the stores.

With no notion of how to begin the trial, Percy rapped on the table with a mallet he brought from his store and announced, "The trial of Dave Crouch and Jimmy Crouch is officially open. The charges against them are attempted murder, resulting in the wounding of Buford Tate." Tate got on his feet and took a bow, grinning from ear to car. He received a loud reception of whistles and cheers, which he acknowledged with a wave of his good arm. Percy rapped for order again and when it had quieted down, he addressed the two defendants. "Have you two got anything to say in your defense?"

"Yeah," Little Crouch spoke up immediately. "I got somethin' to say. We didn't murder nobody, so you ain't got no right to try us for murder. This ain't no courtroom, you ain't no judge, and there ain't no jury, so you gotta let us go."

"Is that all you've got to say?" Malcolm Howard asked. When there was no immediate reply, he said, "I vote we hang 'em."

Marvin Winter spoke up then. "I vote with Malcolm, hang 'em. How do you vote, Percy?"

Only slightly dismayed by the failure to even approach a real trial, Percy said, "Looks like it doesn't make any difference how I vote. It's two to one against me." He shrugged as if helpless.

Seeing the way his "trial" was going, Little Crouch's sullen smirk vanished from his face, replaced by an expression of panic. "Hold on a minute!" He sprang to his feet, only to be pulled back down by Shep, but that didn't stop his protest. "This ain't no trial!" When that didn't seem to make any difference to the panel of three, he yelled out again, "I never tried to shoot nobody, never fired my gun a-tall. You can't hang me for somethin' I didn't do. My brother's the one that shot that feller, not me."

"You was with him!" Poss Rooks accused loudly from a table closest to the "bench." "You came to do some killin', same as him. We're just wastin' time, Percy." He was backed by a low chorus of remarks in agreement from the spectators, some getting to their feet, anxious to get on with the hanging.

Through it all, Jimmy's brother, Big Crouch, sat stunned by Little Crouch's plea to save himself. With the trial rapidly getting out of hand, he suddenly exploded. "Damn your soul!" he roared at his brother. "You was gonna shoot, too. You said we would split the money." With one mighty lunge, he dived for his brother, pulling Jeff Hammond off his feet in the process. Unable to hold the powerful brute back, Jeff went down on the floor as Big Crouch drove his huge body into his brother's, straining with the rope that tied his wrists until he snapped it in two. In the chaos that followed, Big Crouch managed to get his brother by the neck and began to squeeze the life out of him. Not quite sure what to do at that moment, Shep pulled his six-gun and shot Big Crouch in his side. When that seemed only to increase his anger and he released his brother's throat to turn on Shep, Jeff fired from the floor, putting a bullet in the big man's chest. Feeling as if he had just been saved from the charge of an angry grizzly, Shep stood staring at the huge body until someone remarked that there wouldn't be a hanging for the big one. He shook himself out of his mental lapse and quickly helped Jeff subdue Little Crouch.

At the end of the street, Cullen was checking by the hotel when he heard the two shots. His first thought was that someone from the Double-D had managed to slip by him, so he hustled down the street to the saloon, his rifle ready to fire. As he approached the Rose, he was somewhat relieved to find no one running out the door to escape a shooter. Still, he was a bit cautious when he pushed the door open and went inside to find the chaotic results of Bonnie Creek's first attempted-murder trial. With his brother lying dead on the floor, Little Crouch was trying to convince the panel of three that they had already executed the guilty one, so they should let him go. His pleas fell on deaf ears, however, for the town was past due to show an act of retaliation against the Double-D. They were finally at a point where they no longer feared Nathan Dixon and his band of outlaws. From Cullen McCabe and Jeff Hammond, they had learned that Dixon had only four men left.

Noticing Cullen come in just in time to see Little Crouch being led outside, Chubby sidled over to the end of the bar to tell him the news. "I was wonderin' where you were," he said, then quickly summed up the action for him. "You missed the big show. The little 'un sold out on the big 'un, the big 'un damn near killed the little 'un, and Shep and Jeff had to shoot the big 'un."

"So what are they gonna do with him?" Cullen asked. When Chubby said they were on their way to string him up, Cullen could hardly say he was surprised. He had to wonder what Nathan Dixon might do with this latest defeat. With just four men left to carry out his orders of retaliation, would it be enough to cause him to act, himself, as he tried to do that day at the sheriff's office? It was doubtful. According to what Jeff had told him, of the men Dixon had left, none were likely real gunmen, and Cullen had seen Smokey Jones. He was inclined to believe his job here in Bonnie Creek was finished. The threat from the Double-D seemed to be dampened, and the town had at last acquired some backbone. To be sure, he decided to saddle Jake up and check on the herd of cattle. He thought that would tell him if Dixon had given up.

"Well, there you are," Shep Blackwell called out when Cullen walked into the dining room. He was sitting at a table with Jeff Hammond. "Come set down with us." Cullen parked his weapons on the table by the door, aware that Shep and Jeff were still wearing their handguns. *I guess Daisy's rule doesn't apply to lawmen*, he thought. *Maybe I should start wearing my badge.* "Where you been?" Shep went on. "I didn't see you at the hangin'. I thought for a minute you'd decided to move on, but John Taylor said you still had some things in your room."

"I took a little ride across the river to see what the Double-D boys were up to," Cullen said. "I don't know for sure if they've decided to back off, or not, but they've moved that herd of cattle on down the river. They left their camp in the same place, with the chuckwagon still there. I think they're fixin' to turn 'em back on their range."

That was definitely a positive sign as far as Shep was concerned. "You reckon Dixon has given up?"

Before Cullen could answer, he was interrupted by the arrival of Daisy at the table. "You gonna eat?" she asked him. He nodded. "Still can't talk," she said sarcastically. "I'll get you some coffee. If you'd gotten here any later, you'd be out of luck."

"'Preciate it," he said, just then realizing the other tables were already being cleared by Fanny and Bertha.

"I'll get it," Daisy said when Bertha started to go back to the kitchen to fix a plate of food. "You and Fanny finish up those tables." She winked at Jeff and said, "Fanny will usually have a cup of coffee after the dinin' room is cleaned up. You might wanna have a cup with her." She gave him a big smile, satisfied with the obvious embarrassment her remark caused him. Then she went to the kitchen, chuckling to herself all the way. Cullen glanced at Jeff, whose face was flushed almost scarlet. *Funny how things work out sometimes*, he thought.

CHAPTER 14

Mateo Sanchez spotted the two riders leading pack-horses when they came through the gate, some two hundred yards from the ranch house. Standing in the door of the barn, he watched them closely until he was certain it was Juan Hernandez returning. Then he ran up to the house to tell his mother. "It's Juan," he exclaimed when he ran in the kitchen door. "He's come home, and he's got someone with him."

"I'll go tell the major," Consuelo said. "You go back to take their horses." She knew that Juan had gone to find the gunman called Deacon Pratt. The major had not told anyone when he sent Juan, but Consuelo knew because she always listened in the hallway outside the study door whenever he called anyone in to talk privately. Mateo said there was another rider with Juan, so she assumed he was successful in finding the man he was sent to find. She went down the hall to the study and tapped lightly on the door.

"What is it, Consuelo?" Dixon replied to her knock.

"Mateo says that Juan has returned," she answered. "He is not alone."

"Good!" Dixon exclaimed. "I'll be right out. Tell Mateo

that I'll be waiting for our guest at the front door. You go make sure the guest room is ready for him." He got up from his desk, slipped into his coat, and went out the front door to wait on the porch for his special guest.

The two riders were pulling up in front of the barn when he came out to wait on the porch. He stood watching Pratt as he dismounted from the flea-bitten gray gelding he rode and handed the reins to Mateo. While Juan took care of the other horses, Pratt talked to the boy for a few minutes, obviously giving him instructions on how he wanted his horse treated. Mateo then pointed toward the front porch, and Pratt turned and started walking toward Dixon, who watched him as he approached. Dressed in black trousers, black coat, and a flat-crowned, wide-brimmed hat, Pratt made Dixon wonder if his attire was because of the name Deacon. The only relief from his dark visage was a white shirt and a silver band around the crown of his hat. He walked with the swagger of a man confident in himself.

"Major Dixon," Pratt said when he reached the steps and started up. "It's been a while."

"Yes, it has," Dixon returned the greeting. "You look like you haven't lost a step since I saw you last in Waco."

"I ain't lost a step," Pratt was quick to inform him, and extended his hand. "Looks like you've got a sizable spread here."

"It's not as big as I intend to make it," Dixon said.

"Somebody standin' in your way?" Pratt smiled. "Is that why you sent for me?"

Dixon smiled. "Let's go in the house and we'll talk about it. I expect you could use a drink after riding all day."

"As a matter of fact," Deacon replied, "I could use a little somethin' to burn the dust outta my throat." The trip had taken two and a half days instead of the two days he had wanted, and he felt the need for a drink after riding with the nearly mute Mexican. He followed Dixon inside, and he led him to his study, where he poured a couple of glasses of brandy, the major's personal choice.

Pratt tested the strong drink cautiously, since he had never tried brandy before. After a couple of sips, he smacked his lips and declared, "That's right tasty, and it's got a good burn. You must have a big job for me."

"One man," Dixon replied, "and anybody else that gets in your way, of course."

"One man?" Deacon repeated. "For four hundred dollars? Who the hell is he?"

Dixon offered a cigar, took one for himself, then walked over to the fireplace and picked a small splinter of burning wood from it. After both cigars were lit, he asked, "You ever heard of a man named Cullen McCabe?"

Pratt paused to think about it before replying, "No, can't say as I have. Who is he?"

"I wish to hell I knew," Dixon answered, already heating up at the mere mention of the name. "Some damn gunslinger is all I can tell you. Nobody knows where he came from or who he is. He just showed up one day and caused me one headache after another."

"Just one man," Pratt repeated. "Where can I find him?" He automatically assumed this man McCabe was a fast gun, out to make a reputation for himself.

"In a little town about four and a half miles from here called Bonnie Creek." When Dixon saw Deacon's lack of concern for the killing of one man, he was quick to point out that McCabe was responsible for the loss of almost all of his men, men who lived by the gun. "That's the reason I'm willing to pay you four hundred dollars to get rid of this man who is standing in my way."

"He must be fast," Pratt speculated, giving the job more serious thought now. "What's his style, holster low on the leg, or waist high? Reversed pistols, or regular?" Deacon had faced all kinds and he had never been beaten, so he feared no one—he was just curious.

"Every man he's killed has been with a Winchester rifle."

"So he's knockin' your men off at long range," Pratt assumed, "waitin' for 'em in ambush. He ain't facin' up to nobody?"

"One of the men he killed, Tom Yates, was the fastest man I've ever seen next to you. Killed him in a saloon. That was face-to-face at close quarters."

"With a rifle?" Pratt asked. Dixon said that it was. "That tells me he ain't fast with a handgun. This town, Bonnie Creek, have they got a sheriff there?" Dixon nodded and Pratt continued. "How the hell's this feller gettin' away with killin' all your men if there's a sheriff in town?"

"Because the sheriff's in it with him!" Dixon blurted. "The whole damn town is in it with him. It's just my men they're killing. They're trying to ruin me." He neglected to tell him that his men were sent to kill McCabe at the time.

"Sounds to me like I'm gonna have to pick me a spot to dry-gulch this devil." He paused a moment while he thought about it. "Any of your men could lay up in ambush somewhere and shoot him, unless there's somethin' you ain't told me about this jasper. Dry-gulchin' ain't my style." He shrugged and admitted, "I ain't sayin' I ain't never done it, but I druther call him out to face me, man-to-man. That way, you don't have to worry about the law tryin' to call it murder. I don't care if he wants to face me close up with a rifle, as long as we lay the rules down that nobody starts with a cocked weapon. I know damn well I can pull and fire before a man can raise a rifle and crank a cartridge into the chamber." In Pratt's mind, there were other factors to consider. To lie in wait to ambush McCabe at a distance would be a lot easier, but it wouldn't do as much for his reputation as a fast gun as a duel would. In addition to that, McCabe was in town, and Deacon would have no opportunity to lie in wait for him without a great risk of being seen. In that case, he could be cited for murder, which would be a hell of a lot different from a face-off. "I expect I need to take a little trip into town and find Mr. Cullen McCabe."

"He won't be hard to find," Dixon assured him. "He hasn't left town ever since he first rode in."

"I'll ride in tonight for a drink at the saloon, maybe find a card game," Pratt decided, eager to get a look at the man he had come to kill. "I'll borrow a horse from you. Mine's been rode pretty hard today."

"Fine," Dixon responded, "whatever you need! Consuelo should have supper ready in a few minutes. You might want to eat before you go." Pratt thought that was a good idea, so Dixon showed him to the guest room, and by the time Deacon had brought his saddlebags in with his personal belongings and insisted upon a pan of water to clean up a little, supper was on the table.

Consuelo, a woman of deep spiritual feelings, could sense a spirit of evil surrounding her employer's guest, despite his obvious attempt to be polite and engaging. She was not unaware of Nathan Dixon's almost insane desire to build his ranching empire, no matter the cost. If she had a choice, she would not serve as his cook and house-keeper, but unfortunately, there was no other position available for her. Since her husband's death, there was nothing in Mexico to go back to. The major had provided work for her son as well, so it would be hard for her to leave. She had resigned herself to the fact that Dixon was ruthless, but it was only since the arrival of McCabe that he had ordered outright murder. She continued to stand by attentively while the two men ate supper until Pratt asked a question. "How do I find this town of Bonnie Creek?"

"I'll have someone show you the trail to town," Dixon replied, and looked at Consuelo. "Send Mateo in here."

She went at once into the kitchen, where her son was seated at the kitchen table, eating his supper with Juan. Since Smokey was with the cattle, Juan and Mateo ate in the kitchen instead of the cookhouse with the rest of the men. When she told Mateo why he was summoned to the dining room, Juan was quick to whisper a warning. "Tell him how to get to town. Don't go to town with him. The man is dangerous, he has the smell of death about him." Two and a half days of travel with Pratt had taught him that. Mateo nodded his understanding as he got to his feet and hurried into the dining room. In the time since he and his mother had lived at the Double-D, he had never been to Bonnie Creek.

"Did you feed and water my horses like I told you?" Pratt asked before Dixon had a chance to speak.

"*Sí, señor*," Mateo replied. "I feed."

"Mateo will show you how to get to town," Dixon said. "Do you want him to ride into town with you?"

"No, I don't want any company," Pratt answered, much to Consuelo's relief, "unless it's hard to find." He was assured that if he followed the trail Mateo would show him, it would lead him straight to town. Then he told Mateo to tell Juan to pick out a good horse and put Pratt's saddle on it. "I'll take a little time to look the town over," Pratt said.

"Most likely I'll be stayin' overnight, instead of ridin' back here so late. If I do, I'll see you tomorrow sometime and I'll expect to be paid for the job then."

"Fair enough," Dixon said. "As soon as I see proof of McCabe's death, I'll pay you."

"Proof?" Deacon responded. "You'll have to take my word for it. I ain't gonna take his scalp for you. Maybe you might wanna send one of your boys into town to witness it."

"I might at that," Dixon said, although he was not inclined to do so. He felt pretty confident that the word of McCabe's death would spread fast.

"I swear, Reese, we've got cattle scattered along the river for miles," Seth Wiley complained as he pulled his horse up to the fire by the chuckwagon. "I've been tryin' to round up some of 'em and get 'em started back this way, but I ain't had much luck by myself. I figured I might as well come on back and get somethin' to eat." He slid down off his horse and went to the fire to get a plate from Smokey. "You have any better luck upriver?"

"'Bout the same as you," Reese said.

"Well, whadda we gonna do?" Seth implored. "We can't keep that herd together with just the two of us, much less move 'em anywhere."

Reese shoved a spoonful of beans in his mouth and slowly chewed them up, then took a big swallow of coffee to wash them down while he thought how best to answer him. "I don't know, Seth," he finally declared. He glanced at Smokey, who paused over the coffeepot to hear his answer. Like them, Reese knew they had more than they could handle, and he couldn't see how they were going to keep the cattle from scattering all over hell and back. Unlike them, he was going to have to answer to the major for it, even though it was not his fault. He could feel Smokey watching him closely, waiting for an answer. It was plain to see that the once-formidable Double-D ranch had been reduced to a pitiful skeleton crew and Seth and Smokey looked to him for answers. It looked to be no more than a few days before the major was going to be forced to see it as they did, and then it would be anybody's guess as to what his reaction would be. It had all happened in the span of a few days, with the coming of Cullen McCabe.

Reese was brought out of his disturbing thoughts by a statement from Seth. "I found a couple of places downstream where some of the cows were crossin' the river onto the range of one of those small ranches," Seth said. "I'll need some help roundin' them up before they get mixed up with somebody else's cattle."

"There ain't much we can do to go after those cows without losing control of the bigger part of the herd we *have got* rounded up," Reese said. "And we've got the remuda to worry about, too. We'll just have to save what we can until we get some more help."

"There's somebody comin'," Smokey interrupted, pointing toward a rider approaching them. All three strained to see who it might be, coming from that direction. The first thought for all of them was that Dixon had finally let Juan come to help them. It was hard to be sure, however, in the rapidly descending darkness. When he was close enough to identify, Smokey asked, "Who the hell is that? It ain't Juan."

"Nobody I've ever seen before," Reese replied, and

all three got up from the fire to stand and wait to see who it was.

Deacon approached the camp at a slow walk and proceeded right up to the fire before pulling his horse to a stop. "Any coffee left in that pot?" he asked as he dismounted.

"Maybe there is and maybe there ain't," Reese answered. "Who the hell are you?"

Deacon flashed a patient smile at him and replied, "I work for the Double-D, same as you, and a cup of that coffee would go good right now, so how 'bout pourin' me a cup."

Smokey picked up an empty cup and filled it while Reese and Seth continued to study the stranger. "When did you hire on?" Reese asked.

Before Deacon could answer, Seth remarked, "I hope to hell you know how to work cattle."

"That right?" Pratt smirked. "Hate to disappoint you, but nursemaidin' a bunch of dumb cows ain't exactly my trade." He stepped down and took the cup Smokey offered. "How far is that town from here?"

Reese turned and pointed. "Right across the river yonder," he said.

Smokey studied the stranger closely as he talked to Reese. His first impression was that he looked nothing at all like a cowhand, even had he not said that he wasn't. "You're Deacon Pratt, ain'tcha?"

"You've heard of me, right?" Pratt answered, his cocky smile telegraphing his satisfaction in being recognized.

"Yeah, I've heard of you," Smokey replied, then exchanged troubled glances with Reese, who remembered the name of the man Dixon had talked about. "The major send you to town lookin' for Cullen McCabe?" Smokey asked. He honestly thought the major wouldn't send for the notorious gunman, but was using the threat of it to inspire his men to go after McCabe.

"As a matter of fact, he did," Pratt said. "Seems you boys can't get the job done, so he sent for my help," he added. "You can help me out a little if you just tell me what he looks like."

"Oh, I don't reckon you'll have much trouble findin' him," Smokey said, his mind immediately calling back the image of McCabe that caused him such a start when he turned to discover him that day in their camp. "He's a big feller, usually holdin' a Winchester rifle in his hand."

Reese couldn't resist asking, "Are you as fast as folks say you are?"

The question caused the return of the cocky smirk to Pratt's face. "Well, now, you ain't the first to ask me that. Most men who wondered about it had to find out the hard way. How bad do you wanna know?"

"Not enough to get myself killed," Reese replied.

"Well, then, I reckon I'll ride on into town and see if I can make Mr. McCabe's acquaintance," Deacon crowed, obviously proud of his reputation. "Yonder way?" He pointed in the direction Reese had pointed out before.

"Follow that same trail you came here on," Reese said. "It'll take you right down to a shallow crossin', and you'll come out right behind the saloon."

"Ain't that somethin'?" Smokey uttered as the three of them watched Pratt ride off into the darkness. "The major went ahead and sent for that stinker."

"I wonder if McCabe is fast with a six-shooter," Seth said.

"Well, we've heard of Deacon Pratt," Smokey pointed

out, "but we ain't heard of Cullen McCabe before he landed in Bonnie Creek."

"If McCabe's got a lick of sense, he won't try his luck against that jasper," Reese offered.

"I'd like to see it, when they do face off," Seth remarked.

"Yep, I reckon it'll be quite a show, but there's a few head of cattle here that need watchin'," Reese reminded them. He was already thinking over the possible results of a showdown between McCabe and Pratt, and he had to wonder if it was too late to restore the fear factor the Double-D had once held over the people in Bonnie Creek. Things had changed drastically in the town since the arrival of Cullen McCabe. It seemed the whole town had taken on more backbone, and all the real intimidators, like Tom Yates and Curly Cox, were dead. The major was going to have to find a new crew, and Reese wondered if he would now settle for working cowhands instead of outlaws—now that his plan to close the town down had been defeated. *Something to hope for, anyway*, he thought. Regardless of what happened between McCabe and Pratt, the town of Bonnie Creek was there to stay.

Pratt slow-walked his horse up past the hotel, then back again, to get a look at the fledgling town on the San Saba River. *Not much of a town*, he thought, surprised that they supported a sheriff and a deputy. Already, at this early evening hour, the little town seemed to have gone to bed. The only visible sign of life came from the saloon, where a couple of horses were tied at the hitching rail. Figuring this to be the most likely place to find Cullen McCabe, he pulled up at the rail. Stepping down, he tied his horse, then before walking up to the door, he adjusted his gun belt to ride comfortably on his hips. As a matter of habit, he rubbed his hands together to wring some of the cold out of them and make sure they were flexible. He eased the Colt .44, riding below his hip, gently up and down a couple of times to make sure it was riding freely. Then he pushed the door open and stepped inside, pausing there to look the room over. Two men, obviously cowhands and no doubt the owners of the two horses tied out front, sat at a table, working on a bottle. A woman sat with them, helping empty the bottle. The rest of the tables were empty, so he shifted his gaze to the bar, where one man stood, engaged in a conversation with the bartender, who shifted his gaze to meet Pratt's.

"Welcome, neighbor," Chubby greeted the stranger. "Whaddle it be?" He looked Pratt up and down as he strolled over to the bar. "Don't think you've ever been in before."

Deacon didn't bother to answer right away, as he took a good look at Norman Freeman, who had been talking to Chubby. Deacon decided at once that he was not Cullen McCabe, so he turned his attention back to Chubby. "You got any decent whiskey?"

"I've got rye and I've got corn," Chubby told him. "Will one of them do?" Pratt chose the corn, and while Chubby poured, he asked the usual questions. "Ain't seen you in town before. What brings you to Bonnie Creek?" When Pratt said he was just passing through, Chubby asked, "Are you headin' for the Double-D?" The question came naturally, since Deacon's appearance was more akin to a gambler's or a gunman's.

"What makes you ask that?" Pratt replied. "Do I look like a cowhand?"

There was no effort to hide the sarcasm in the stranger's

tone, so Chubby was quick to respond. "No, I reckon not. I just naturally asked 'cause the Double-D's the biggest spread around here. No offense."

Pratt's usual smirk relaxed to form a smile. "None taken. I just stopped to warm up a little with a drink of whiskey—kinda chilly night out there."

"It is, indeed," Chubby said, thinking the stranger was showing a friendlier side. "This here's Norman Freeman," he said, nodding toward the barber. "My name's Chubby Green. Welcome to Bonnie Creek."

Pratt didn't offer his hand, nodding instead. "Pleased to meet you, boys. My name's Deacon Pratt." He paused then to see if there was any spark of recognition. When there was none, he thought, *They'll damn sure remember it when I leave here*. He tossed his whiskey back, paused again to test the aftereffects, then slid his glass over for a second shot. "You ain't got many customers in here," he commented. "Is this place always as dead as this?"

"It's early yet," Chubby replied. "There'll be some more folks in when everybody has had their supper. Course, it ain't like a Saturday night, but it'll get a whole lot better when the word gets around that the Double-D ain't got some of them troublemakers they used to have." After he said it, he wondered why the remark caused Pratt to grin. Something told him that maybe this wasn't a subject to talk about with the puzzling stranger.

"Troublemakers?" Deacon asked. "Whaddaya mean, troublemakers?"

Norman Freeman, silent up to that point, didn't experience the same sense of caution about the stranger. "There was a sorry bunch of outlaws that worked for the Double-D. They used to raise a lotta hell here in town, until a fellow named Cullen McCabe showed up and cleaned 'em all out."

This captured Pratt's attention right away. He rubbed his chin thoughtfully and responded, "Is that a fact? Cullen McCabe, huh? He must be as mean as a cross-eyed grizzly bear. Is he still in town?"

"Yes, sir, he sure is," Freeman replied. "And as long as he is, I don't think we'll have any more trouble from the Double-D. Right, Chubby?" Chubby looked at him but made no reply.

Pratt returned his attention to Chubby. "I'd like to meet this McCabe fellow. You think he'll be in tonight?"

"Well, it's hard to say," Chubby was quick to respond. "I don't expect McCabe like I do any of the regulars. Sometimes he stops in and sometimes he don't."

"This town ain't that big," Deacon insisted. "If he ain't here, where would he most likely be?"

Ever more cautious now, Chubby was hesitant to give up more information to the sinister-looking stranger. Even Freeman was now aware of the stranger's unusual desire to find McCabe. "I ain't sure McCabe's in town this evenin'. Matter of fact, I ain't seen him all day," Chubby concluded.

Rapidly becoming aware that Chubby was reluctant to give him any more information on the whereabouts of Cullen McCabe, Deacon's customary smirk was transformed to a smile. "I'll be sorry I missed him," he said. "He sounds like the kinda feller I'd like to meet. I reckon I'll take a little walk around town, to see what's here." He paid for his whiskey and walked out the door.

He left his horse at the saloon and took a walk back up the street toward the hotel. Passing the sheriff's office, he could see Jeff Hammond sitting at the desk. *Young*, he thought, and continued past the barbershop, heading for the hotel. Inside the small lobby, he found John Taylor at the desk. John gave him a quick scrutiny before asking, "Can I help you, sir?"

"Yeah," Deacon replied. "I was supposed to meet Cullen McCabe here tonight. Is he in his room?"

Taylor hesitated a moment, thinking that here was another sinister-looking character, and he was still a little shy after Marvin Winter's response to his renting a room to McCabe when he first arrived in town. "Well, sir, I don't believe Mr. McCabe is in the hotel at the present time."

"Well, where do you suppose he is *at the present time*?" Pratt asked sarcastically, thinking the town wasn't big enough for a man like McCabe to hide.

"I wouldn't know," Taylor replied, then seeing that Pratt was becoming angry, he hastened to suggest, "In the dining room, possibly." He breathed a sigh of relief when the ominous stranger jerked his head with a single nod and pointed toward an open door to the hallway. "Yes, sir," Taylor said, "right through that door—dining room door's at the end of the hall."

Pratt was greeted at the door of the dining room by Daisy Lynch, who scrutinized him more thoroughly than John Taylor had. "If you're lookin' for supper, you're a little late," she informed him. "If you're starvin', we might find something for you to eat, though."

"I don't wanna eat," he grunted as he scanned the empty room. "I'm lookin' for Cullen McCabe. Was he in here?"

It was not necessary to paint a picture for Daisy. Judging by his appearance and his cocky swagger, she figured the gruff stranger was hunting Cullen for only one reason. "Yeah, he was in earlier," she answered, thinking it no harm to tell him that, even though *earlier* meant breakfast. "He was eatin' supper with the sheriff. Why don't you go down to the jail and talk to the sheriff?" she suggested. "Maybe McCabe's still with him." She was hoping that might discourage the man from looking for Cullen.

"I might do just that," he said, and paused to fix his smirk upon her, then he turned and walked out.

Bertha came from the kitchen as soon as he went out the door. "That man's bad news for Cullen," she announced. "He's a killer, if there ever was one. Ol' Dixon hasn't given up yet." Daisy and Fanny were quick to admit they felt the same as she.

"I wonder where the hell Cullen is," Daisy said. "He sure didn't show up here for supper. Come to think of it, we ain't seen him since breakfast. I wonder if he knows this fellow's lookin' for him. I sure wish we could warn him, if he doesn't already know."

"You know, it wouldn't surprise me none if he's just pulled up stakes and moved on to wherever he was goin' when he landed here in the first place," Bertha said. "Right from the first day, he said he was just gonna hang around till the town got done with the Double-D trouble. And it sure looks like we've got the upper hand now, and Nathan Dixon has run outta outlaws."

"I remember you bein' so sure McCabe was runnin' from something," Fanny said to Daisy. "You think that might be the man he's been runnin' from? 'Cause if it is, it looks like he left just in time."

"Why, hell, don'tcha think he woulda said something about it, if he was fixin' to leave?" Daisy asked.

"Not to my way of thinkin'," Bertha replied. "If anything, I'd say when he thought it was time, he'd just pack up and go. That's just his way, if you ask me."

"Maybe one of us better go tell Shep and Jeff about that fellow," Fanny said. "At least warn them that he's runnin' all over town lookin' for Cullen." She didn't express it, but she was mainly worried that Jeff might find himself in the middle of a gunfight.

"That's a good idea, Fanny," Daisy said. "Why don't you do that?" Fanny didn't have to be asked twice. She was out the door in a few seconds' time.

As she approached the sheriff's office, Fanny saw Pratt go in the stable. She hurried her step as she opened the door to the office, surprising Jeff Hammond, who was seated at the desk. "Fanny," he exclaimed joyfully upon seeing her, and immediately got to his feet. "What's wrong?" he asked a moment later upon seeing the concern in her face.

"I think McCabe's in danger," she replied. "We haven't seen him ever since breakfast and there's a man lookin' for him and I don't think it's for anything good." When he asked her why she thought that, she went on to relate Pratt's visit to the dining room, looking for Cullen, and she was pretty sure he was a gunfighter, by his attitude and his appearance.

"Where is he now?" Jeff asked. "Is he still in the dinin' room?"

"No, I just saw him goin' into the stable and I know he's fixin' to turn the town upside down lookin' for Cullen." She glanced toward the cell room door. "Where's Shep?" She didn't like the idea of Jeff checking on the stranger by himself.

"He's at his forge, shoein' a horse," Jeff answered. "He still has blacksmithin' to do, even though he's the sheriff."

"In the dark?" Fanny asked. "Well, go tell him what I just told you," she ordered. "Don't you go down there to talk to that man by yourself."

Taking slight offense to what her remark implied, he at once replied, "That's what the town is payin' me to do, to take care of things like this. If I was afraid to face every gunhand that drifted through town, I wouldn't have taken the job in the first place."

"You go tell Shep," she repeated sternly. "I don't aim to be a widow before I even get married." As soon as the words fell out of her mouth, she realized she shouldn't have exposed her deepest wishes. It was too late, however.

He didn't reply for a few seconds, not sure he was hearing right. "Does that mean you'd marry me?" For the moment, thoughts of a sinister stranger in town were forgotten.

"I don't know," she quickly replied. "Maybe I would, maybe I wouldn't. You ain't even asked me, anyway."

"I'm askin' you now," he immediately responded.

"Not now," she insisted, thoroughly disgusted with herself for losing any leverage she might have held in their relationship. "Right now, there's a dangerous-lookin' man prowlin' around town and you need to make sure you don't get yourself shot. You go get Shep, and the two of you can go look for him. Then we can talk about whether or not I'll marry you."

He took her by the shoulders and planted a kiss on her before she had time to see it was coming. "You go on back to the dinin' room. I'll come see you later." He walked her out the door, a foolish grin still implanted upon his face, and headed her back up the street toward the hotel.

"You be careful," she cautioned again.

CHAPTER 15

He sat by a small stream that emptied into the river, watching the big bay gelding graze upon the grass near the water's edge. Taking his ease, he picked up a couple of the dead limbs he had gathered and placed them on his fire, then pulled another piece of jerky from the spit he had fashioned from a green cottonwood branch. He took a bite of the beef jerky and washed it down with a swallow of coffee from the small pot he carried. It was not the supper he might have enjoyed at the dining room back in Bonnie Creek, but it was satisfying. He felt like he was taking a holiday, just him and Jake, away from the troubles of the small town on the bank of the San Saba River. It felt peaceful, and it had been the first day he had felt it safe to leave Bonnie Creek since arriving there. The Double-D's crew had been reduced to a few men unlikely to cause any trouble for the town, and there were a conscientious sheriff and deputy in place. It had been a bloody battle with Nathan Dixon's men, but the town had been fortunate in that the casualties were all from the Double-D. And while there was no way of knowing for sure if Dixon had accepted his defeat, Cullen thought that surely he had suffered enough to know the town was there to stay and would continue to grow.

The question on his mind now was whether or not his job was finished, according to what the governor expected of him. By his estimation, he had ridden close to fifteen miles and back along the banks of the river this day with no sign of Double-D cattle. It was enough to make him believe Dixon's skeleton crew had managed to drive most of their herd back closer to the ranch headquarters, no longer threatening the town. He decided there was nothing more he was needed for, and although he was not but a few miles from town, he decided to camp where he was and go back in the morning. *Too bad I didn't check out of the hotel and bring my packhorse*, he thought. *I could just head for Austin in the morning.* He had already paid for his room for the night, but he decided the solitude here by the river would be good for him after his time in Bonnie Creek. His last thoughts, before drifting off to sleep, were questions about how Michael O'Brien and the governor would grade his handling of his first assignment. There was a hell of a big body count before the town could see evidence of positive results—maybe a little bloodier than the governor expected. *Well*, he decided, *they told me to handle it my way*.

When the morning light began to make its way through the leaves of the trees he had spread his bedroll under, he roused himself to saddle Jake and prepare to ride the few miles back to town. He would forgo the cup of coffee he might normally make and wait to have it in the dining room at the hotel. He hoped Bertha was making pancakes this morning—he had a hankering for flapjacks. Maybe it was Saturday and that was the reason. Maybe his mind had called back memories of Mary Kate and the kids and the Saturday-morning ritual. He was not really sure what day of the week it was. "It won't do us any good to start thinkin' of things like that," he reminded Jake as he stepped up into the saddle, knowing well that those thoughts would never completely leave his mind.

It was a short ride into Bonnie Creek, so he showed up at the dining room too early. There was no sign of any activity in the small wing of the hotel that housed the dining room, so he rode on down to the stable to put his horse away. He arrived just as Ross Horner was opening the front door of the barn. "Cullen!" Horner exclaimed upon seeing him, as if greatly surprised.

"Mornin', Ross," Cullen responded.

Horner couldn't wait to inform him. "There was a feller in here lookin' for you last night," he said excitedly.

"What fellow?" Cullen asked. "Who was he?"

"Damned if I know," Horner replied. "But he looked like the kinda feller you'd just as soon not run into." He shook his head slowly. "I'm tellin' you, Cullen, there ain't no doubt in my mind, that feller was a professional gun-slinger, and he was gettin' right put out with me when I didn't know where you were."

There was no doubt in Cullen's mind that Ross was probably right—there was no likelihood that anyone other than an assassin could be looking for him. He immediately realized that all his earlier speculation the night just past, that his job was done in Bonnie Creek, had been nothing more than wishful thinking. His mind was immediately alert. "Is this fellow still in town?"

"I don't think so," Horner said. "I talked to Chubby last

night and he said that feller came back to the saloon and sat at one of his tables for a while, then he walked out."

"All right," Cullen said. "'Preciate the information. I'll keep my eyes open in case he comes back." He unsaddled Jake and turned him out in the corral. "He could use a portion of oats," he said before he left. The next thing to determine was if the stranger was still in town. Maybe he just didn't come back to the saloon, so Cullen headed to the hotel to see if the man had taken a room there. He didn't get that far before he was hailed by Shep Blackwell from the door of the sheriff's office.

Shep, obviously as concerned as Horner had been, came out in the street to see if Cullen knew anything about the man looking for him. "Fanny Wright came down here last night to tell Jeff about that fellow. Me and him went down to the stable, that's where she said he went, but he was already gone by the time we got there." Cullen said that he didn't, but he could well guess what he wanted. "I did see him," Shep went on. "He was in the Rose for a little while, just settin' at a table, didn't have but a couple of drinks, then he left. He was a slick-lookin' jasper, dressed like a preacher or somethin'." He stopped to recollect, then said, "More like a preacher from hell."

"Did you get his name?" Cullen asked.

"No, I reckon I shoulda done that," he said, "but Chubby did. He said the feller said his name was Deacon Pratt. I figured that as long as he weren't makin' no trouble, I'd leave him be. Deacon Pratt," he repeated. "Is that anybody you know?"

"Nope, never heard of him. Maybe he'll show up today sometime," Cullen said. "I'm on my way to get some breakfast. I'll check in the hotel, just in case he took a room there last night." He started toward the hotel again, scanning every doorway and alleyway he passed. When he reached the hotel, he found John Taylor just reporting for work.

"Mr. McCabe," Taylor was quick to greet him. "Did anyone tell you there was a man in here last night looking for you?"

"Yeah, I heard. He didn't by any chance take a room in here last night, did he?"

"No, sir, he did not," Taylor replied. "And I'm mighty glad he didn't. That man looked like a disciple of the devil."

"Well, it's almost time for Daisy to open up for breakfast," Cullen said, "so I think I'll go get some coffee." As he walked down the hallway that led to the dining room, he realized that he had underestimated the insane determination of Nathan Dixon. This gunman who was in town looking for him had to have been hired by Dixon, and when the gunman didn't find Cullen, he must have gone back to the Double-D. He would no doubt be in town again today. The question Cullen would like an answer to was, is he an assassin who will shoot him in the back, or a gunfighter building a reputation as a fast gun? *I guess we'll find out today*, he thought. *Oughta be able to recognize him. Either looks like a preacher from hell or the devil's disciple, but right now I need a cup of coffee.* At the end of the hall, he found the dining room door locked, so he rapped politely once, then rapped again when no one came to open the door. After another few seconds, the door opened to present Daisy Lynch's frowning face.

"I shoulda known it was you," she scolded. "We don't open for fifteen minutes yet. Whaddaya comin' in the back door for, anyway?" Answering her own question, she said,

"'Cause I woulda seen it was you through the glass and wouldn't have opened the door."

"Good mornin' to you, too," he said. "I figured you'd let me have a cup of coffee one more time before you flipped your sign over."

She stood back, holding the door open wide for him. "I thought maybe you'd said good-bye to Bonnie Creek, since I didn't see hide nor hair of you after breakfast yesterday. Might be it woulda been better if you had. I reckon somebody's told you there was some gunman lookin' for you."

"Yeah, I heard," Cullen replied. "What makes you think he's a gunman?"

She stood with her hands on her hips, looking at him like a mother might look at a problem child, wondering just what it would take to cause some concern in the man. "'Cause I know one when I see one," she replied, then stood a few moments more, giving him her problem-child look. "Well, set yourself down and we'll get you fed quick as we can. If that fellow comes back to town, I druther he didn't catch up with you in here."

"I 'preciate your concern," he said, accustomed by now to her sarcasm, but convinced she was not as ornery as she liked to convey.

"Bertha's makin' flapjacks," she said. "You want 'em, or you want eggs as usual?"

He almost smiled. "Is today Saturday?"

"Don't you even know what day it is? Yeah, it's Saturday, yesterday was Friday, and tomorrow's Sunday, so that usually makes today Saturday."

"I'll take the flapjacks, then," he said. She went to the kitchen to give Bertha the order, passing Fanny on her way to his table with the coffeepot.

"Did that man catch up with you yesterday?" Fanny wanted to know right away. He said that he did not, that he was out of town all day. "You be careful today," she cautioned. "That man's dangerous, and he might come back to look for you again."

"I will. I'll keep my eyes open," he said, surprised by her seemingly genuine concern. He was surprised again when Bertha brought his pancakes out to him, instead of Fanny or Daisy, and proceeded to encourage him to be alert as well. When he had finished his breakfast and left the dining room, he was beginning to think that maybe the town had finally accepted him and stopped wondering when his evil side was going to emerge.

It was late afternoon when he came up from the river and guided his horse up the middle of the street. His dark features exaggerated by his black trousers and coat, his eyes shadowed by the broad brim of his flat-crowned hat, he seemed the personification of death. A bright gleam of sunlight reflected from the silver band around the crown of his hat as he turned the flea-bitten gray horse toward the hitching rail at the Rose. He dismounted and stood there for a long moment, looking up and down the street, before he looped the reins around the rail and stepped up to the saloon door. *I hope to hell you ain't out of town again today*, he thought. It would be nice to find this so-called hired gun right away, so he could get his money quickly and head back to Waco.

Across the street, Shep Blackwell got up from his desk when he caught a glimpse of the dark stranger and went to the door to peer out. *He's back!* The thought was not a confident one. It was not unexpected, for he had felt that

Deacon Pratt would return, even though he hoped he
wouldn't. As the new sheriff, he supposed he was obligated
to prevent the sinister gunman from causing trouble, but
he wasn't sure how to do that. He considered waiting for
his deputy to return from the stable, but when he left the
office Jeff said he might be a while. "I'll go over there to
let Pratt know we have law in this town," Shep muttered
aloud, then picked up his hat and headed for the Rose,
hoping Cullen would show up.

"You'd best leave that old man alone," Chubby said to
Lilly Bloodworth when she came to the bar to fetch another
drink for Poss Rooks. "Even if you did get him upstairs he's
liable to have a heart attack." They both chuckled at the
mental picture that created.

"Ah, I just tease him a little bit," Lilly said. "That's
about as much as he can handle, but he seems to enjoy it."
They laughed at the thought of the old man even thinking
about a tussle with her. "I ain't sure I've got the stomach
for it, myself." Then, suddenly, Lilly stopped laughing and
her eyes seemed to get bigger. Chubby turned to see what
she was staring at.

"Uh-oh," was all Chubby could gasp when he saw
Deacon Pratt standing in the doorway. "Here comes trouble again," he muttered when he regained his speech. "I
kinda hoped he wouldn't be back when he didn't find
Cullen yesterday."

Pratt remained in the doorway while he scanned the
room, looking for someone who might look like the man
he sought. There were no likely candidates in the sparse
crowd of drinkers. He was disappointed, but he figured
this was still the most likely place to run into Cullen

McCabe, so he decided to wait him out a while. He shifted his gaze to a table near the back of the room where Poss Rooks and two cowhands were playing a game of three-handed poker. *Might as well make a little money while I wait*, he thought, and ambled on back to the table.

"You fellows look like you need another player, so you can have a real game," Pratt said when he walked up to the table. Engrossed in their game, none of the three had noticed him when he walked in.

Poss looked up and, never having seen him before, said, "Hell, my luck can't get no worse whether it's three-hand or four." He nodded toward the other two players. "I don't care, if they don't." His playing companions, two cowhands from one of the smaller ranches on the east side of the river, although somewhat concerned when they got a look at Deacon, reluctantly nodded. "Set yourself down, then," Poss said, then looked toward the bar and yelled. "Hey, Lilly, where's my drink? Better bring another glass, too. We got us another player."

"That damned old fool," Chubby said. "He don't know who that is." He poured a drink and gave it to Lilly. "Why didn't he buy a bottle in the first place?" He glanced toward the door again when he heard it open and was glad to see the sheriff walk in.

"Any trouble?" Shep asked when he walked up to the bar, his gaze fixed on Deacon.

"Well, not so far," Chubby answered. "He just walked in and went back there with Poss, and it looks like he's fixin' to play cards with 'em."

"There ain't nothin' I can do, unless he starts some trouble," Shep was quick to remind him, "but I reckon I'll just wait here for a spell."

Back at the table, Deacon did not fail to notice the man

wearing the badge when he walked in. It caused him no concern as he pulled the extra chair back and sat down. Dixon had told him the town had just hired an inexperienced sheriff, so he didn't expect to have any trouble from him. He pulled a roll of money out of his vest pocket and put it on the table. "What's the money limits?" He glanced around the table to see only modest piles of cash.

His question had a dampening effect upon the two cowhands. One of them, a young blond-haired man, was the first to speak up. "Our little game might not be big enough to suit you, mister. We're just playin' a dollar limit on a raise, just a little game to pass some time."

Pratt responded with a sarcastic smirk. "Is that so? Well, let's play a few hands and pass a little time. Whose deal is it?" Even at low stakes, he couldn't resist the opportunity to separate the three of them from the little bit of money they might have.

"It's my deal," Poss answered him. He picked up the cards and started shuffling them. "Ante up fifty cents." Poss dealt and the game was on. The first hand was won by Poss with two pair, kings over nines. Over the next hour or so, Poss was a steady winner, with one of the cowhands winning once in a while, and Pratt winning every time he dealt. Although the cowhands seemed unaware of the coincidence, it didn't take long before Poss caught on. Finally, when he was certain, he paused when the deal came around to him again. Shuffling the cards casually, he looked Pratt in the eye. "You know what's a curious thing? You've won a few hands once in a while when it's somebody else's deal, but you've won every time when you're dealin'. Now, ain't that a curious thing?"

"What are you sayin', old man?" Deacon replied. "Are you callin' me a cheat?"

"I'm just sayin' it's a curious thing," Poss repeated. He looked at the sandy-haired cowhand seated left of him. "Don't you think it's mighty curious?" The young man didn't respond vocally, but his face seemed to suddenly go pale.

"I don't think I like the way you're talkin', old man," Deacon threatened, irritated now to the point where his voice could be heard by Shep and Chubby at the end of the bar. "I think maybe you'd best shut up before you bite off more than you can chew."

Over at the bar, Shep muttered, "Shut up, you old fool, you never did know when to keep your mouth shut." He was not sure what he should do, or when he should interfere, but he knew he should do something to keep Poss from getting himself shot. It seemed that Poss was determined to do just that, however, because he made another comment. Shep couldn't hear what he said, but it was enough to cause Pratt to push his chair back and challenge Poss to defend his accusation. "Oh shit," Shep muttered, braced himself mentally, and walked over to the table. "What's the trouble back here?" he asked, speaking in what he hoped was a voice of authority.

Pratt gave him a sideways glance while keeping his focus on Poss, not sure at this point how crazy the old man was. "This old sidewinder accused me of cheatin' him, and I'm callin' him out to back it up."

"We can't have no shootin' in here," Shep said. "Poss is just a big-talkin' old man. Best you just forget about it. Why don't you tell him you didn't mean it, Poss, and we'll all settle down."

"Hell, no," Poss came back. "He is a cheat and not a very good one at that."

In a fit of temper, Pratt grabbed the edge of the table

and flipped it upside down on the floor. "All right, old man, you asked for it? You got it! You're wearin' a gun, so get on your feet!"

"All the same to you, I'll just set right here," Poss calmly said, not being quite as insane as he had appeared. "I ain't playin' cards no more with a damn cheat, and I sure as hell ain't plannin' on gettin' shot by one." He defiantly folded his arms in front of his chest and remained seated, further infuriating the irate gunman. "If you're so hell-bent on shootin' me, you're gonna have to do it while I set here. It'd be murder, then, and the sheriff's standin' right here, ready to arrest you."

"Damn you!" Pratt cursed. "I'll shoot you down right there in that chair, if that's what you want."

"Now, hold on," Shep interrupted. "That'll be the end of it! Like he said, that would be downright murder, and I'd have to arrest you for that."

"The hell you will!" Deacon responded. "In this part of the territory, a man's got a right to defend his honor, so it's about time somebody taught this old fool not to make charges he ain't prepared to back up."

Still with no intention of backing down, Poss said, "You ain't got no honor to defend, you two-bit gunslinger."

That was too much for Pratt's temper. "Get on your feet or take it settin' down!" He pulled his coattail aside to clear his gun and holster.

Shep knew he had to act. "That's enough!" he commanded, and pulled his .44. "I think you'd best pick up your money and get on outta here, or I'm gonna have to lock you up for disturbin' the peace."

Fully inflamed now, Pratt cocked his head in Shep's direction and stared at him for a long moment before issuing his challenge. "I've got a right to defend my honor, even if it's against a damn lawman, and if I have to take care of you first, then that's just your tough luck." The slight trembling he saw in Shep's hand encouraged him to push it further. "If you'd ever heard of Deacon Pratt, you'd know that I'm fast enough with a six-gun to draw and drop you before you can cock that gun and pull the trigger." Giving Shep his full attention, he backed away from the chairs toward the center of the room, his back to the front door. With a glance sideways, he told Chubby to stay right where he was standing. "You go for a gun under that bar and you're a dead man," he promised. Chubby believed him and stood frozen beside Lilly, who was afraid to move as well. Back to Shep then, he taunted, "Anytime you're ready, Sheriff."

Shep could not seem to hold the weapon steady in his hand, knowing now he should have cocked it as soon as he drew it from his holster. Pratt was obviously confident in his speed with the .44 he wore, enough so that Shep was not sure he could cock his and shoot before Pratt could. The longer he hesitated, the heavier the gun seemed in his hand, and the harder it became to make a decision. He couldn't back down and still hold the position as sheriff. He was moments before making his move when he heard the voice behind Pratt.

"Put your hands up and turn around."

Pratt acted without thinking. Somehow, he knew the voice belonged to the man he searched for. He spun around, his hand whipping his .44 out of the holster as he turned, in time to feel the slug from the Winchester rifle when it tore into his chest. He stood motionless for a few seconds, staring dull-eyed at the grim figure holding the rifle, ready to shoot again, before he dropped to his knees, then keeled over to land on his side. Cullen walked over and took the pistol from Deacon's hand. He looked up at Shep, still standing there, his pistol in his hand. "You all right?"

As if awaking from a violent dream, Shep gradually came to. He holstered his weapon, fully realizing he had just faced certain death and yet he was still standing. "I don't know," he finally answered, unsure of himself. "I mean, I ain't sure." He stared at the body lying on the floor, still sinister, even as Chubby and the others crowded around to look at it. "Damn, Cullen, I don't know what I'da done if you hadn't come in when you did."

Cullen fully understood. "You woulda done the right thing, Shep. It's hard, the first time you face a man with that kind of reputation. It ain't ever a good idea to stand and shoot it out with a man who makes a livin' drawin' faster than most men can. You didn't back down when a lotta men would have. Next time, you'll be more prepared for it."

"I ain't so sure I'll ever be ready to face somebody like that again," Shep confessed. "I might be tempted to shoot him first, then arrest him."

"That'll work, too," Cullen said. Shep wasn't sure if he was serious or japing, since it seemed he was always serious.

The room, which had gone dead silent a short time before, was now buzzing with conversation as Chubby, Lilly, and the few other patrons stood gaping at the corpse. They were joined in a short time by other curious spectators from outside, who decided it safe to enter the saloon now. Cullen noticed that Shep still looked a little shaken, so he hauled Chubby away from the body and led Shep back to the bar with him. "I think Shep could use a good stiff drink," he said to Chubby.

"I sure as hell could," Shep said, so Chubby poured three shots and they all tossed them down.

After a few minutes, Chubby said, "Well, I reckon I'd best send somebody to get Norman. He's got another grave to dig."

"Not this time," Cullen said. "I'm claimin' this one and the horse he rode in on."

Not sure if he was joking or not, Shep and Chubby exchanged puzzled glances. "I reckon there ain't no doubt, he's your kill, all right, same as a deer or a buffalo," Chubby said.

After another drink of Chubby's whiskey, Cullen looked at Shep and said, "You look like you're gettin' the color back in your face. Come on and give me a hand with that body." Shep set his glass back on the bar and followed Cullen over to the corpse, still the center of attraction for the spectators. "Show's over, folks," Cullen announced, and rolled Deacon over onto his back. Then he took hold of him under his shoulders and motioned for Shep to grab his feet. When Shep asked where he was taking the body, Cullen simply said, "Out the door." So they picked the body up and carried it out the front door, held open wide by Lilly. Outside, they carried the late Deacon Pratt to the flea-bitten gray gelding waiting at the rail and hefted him up to lie across the saddle. Using a length of rope he found attached to the saddle, Cullen tied Deacon's hands and feet under the horse's belly. "'Preciate the help," he said.

"McCabe," Shep said, stopping him when he started to untie the gray's reins from the rail. "Back there, I don't know if I was too scared to pull the trigger or not." He felt he had to confess.

"It was your first time," Cullen said. "If you're in that situation again, you've learned not to pull your weapon unless you're ready to fire it. That means it's cocked as soon as you pull it. You'll remember, but it's never a good idea to face up to a gunslinger if there's any way around it. You'll make a good sheriff." He untied the reins and Shep, along with a small knot of spectators who walked outside then, stood back when Cullen turned the horse away from the rail and led it down the street to the stable.

Halfway there, he met Ross Horner on his way to the saloon. Seeing the obvious cause for the body draped across the saddle, he exclaimed. "I heard the shot a little while ago. Who is it?"

"Mr. Deacon Pratt," Cullen replied. "I believe you've met him before."

"I swear," Horner uttered. "So he finally found you, did he?"

"Reckon so."

"Where you goin' with him?"

"To your place to get my horse," Cullen replied. "Then I expect I'll take him back to where he came from today."

"The Double-D?" Ross exclaimed, surprised. "You're gonna ride right into the Double-D with that corpse?" He was not sure that's what Cullen meant.

"I expect that's where he came from, so I'm interested to see if Nathan Dixon wants him back. I think it's time to have a little meetin' with the major to see if we can't come to a peaceful settlement between him and Bonnie Creek."

More than a little skeptical, Horner turned around and walked back to the stable with McCabe. He didn't think there was much hope for a productive meeting with Dixon. In addition to that, he wondered why McCabe took it upon himself to seek such a meeting. By his own claim, he was just passing through Bonnie Creek.

After tying the gray at a corner of the corral, Cullen

threw his saddle on Jake and led him out beside Pratt's horse. Seeing no logic in returning weapons to the enemy, he removed Pratt's gun belt from his body and took his rifle out of the saddle scabbard. Then with a notion that Pratt should help pay for the cost of some of the trouble he'd caused, Cullen went through his pockets and saddlebags and removed all the money he found. It was a considerable sum and would pay for a great deal of Cullen's expenses. When all was ready, he climbed aboard the big bay and started out across the river and began the four-and-a-half-mile ride to the Double-D ranch headquarters. Horner stood watching him until he rode out of sight, then turned and headed for the saloon, eager to spread the word that McCabe was taking the gunfighter's body back to the Double-D.

CHAPTER 16

Consuelo Sanchez answered the knock at her kitchen door to find Reese Cochran waiting on the back step. "I just rode in from the south range," he said. "I figured the major would wanna know what's what with the cattle. Is this a good time?"

"*Sí*, Señor Reese," she replied. "I just start supper. The major in his study. I go tell him." Reese stepped inside and waited while she went to tell Dixon. In a few minutes, she returned to tell him the major said to come on in.

"Well, Cochran," Dixon greeted him, "have you got anything more than bad news to report?" Although his greeting was negative, the major was in a more optimistic mood than he had been since the beginning of the trouble at the hand of Cullen McCabe. He was almost cheerful, in fact, content with the thought that McCabe was no longer a problem.

"Well, sir," Reese began, "we've moved as much of the herd as we could round up back by the creek on the south range. They'll be a sight easier to keep together with the few men we've got to work 'em." He paused and shook his head slowly. "But we've still got cattle scattered between there and the river, so that's what I left Seth Wiley and Juan Hernandez doin' while I came to report to you. What I'm afraid of is we might still have quite a few head strayed across the river to one of them small ranches. Smokey was helpin' in the roundup yesterday, but he'll be on his way back here tomorrow." Reese would have preferred to keep using Smokey to help with the cattle, but the major was adamant about having a separate cook for his cowhands, instead of using Consuelo to cook for the few men he had left.

Dixon frowned heavily upon hearing of a possible loss of more cattle but took heart in the belief that things were soon to take a positive upswing. "All right," he said. "Just do the best you can. The battle isn't over yet, and I expect we'll be back in control after today. That sorry little settlement will pay the consequences for trying to block the Double-D's expansion. Once Deacon Pratt finishes his work, so we don't have Cullen McCabe to deal with, I'll hire on more men to build this empire we started."

"Yes, sir," Reese said. "I'll get on back now to help Seth and Juan." He took his leave, still worried about the fate of the Double-D. The major, for some reason, still could not realize he was beaten. Instead of weakening the spirit of the town, the people had rallied around McCabe and were now stronger than in the beginning. The major put too much faith in the notorious gunslinger he had hired. At this point, the damage was already done. Pratt might kill McCabe, but the town would still resist Dixon's attempts to close it down. These were troubling thoughts for Reese Cochran and he was past wondering if he wanted to continue with Dixon and his lawless ways. Unable to see any other options for himself at the moment, he had no choice but to return to the cattle.

"Smokey come back?" Consuelo asked when Reese walked back through the kitchen. He told her that Smokey would be coming back in the morning. "I can cook for you and the others," she said. "Smokey can help you."

"I know you can," Reese said, "but the major don't want you cookin' for nobody but him." He shook his head patiently and she nodded her understanding. She remained at the door to watch him climb on his horse and ride off behind the barn, toward the south range, before returning to her preparation of supper. *Reese is a good man*, she thought. *He doesn't belong here*.

Reese nudged his horse up to a fast walk when he passed behind the barn and struck out on a trail to the south range. He immediately reined the horse back when he spotted something moving in the distance, then pulled to a stop while he squinted in an effort to identify what appeared to be a couple of riders. After a few moments, he was able to see it was a rider leading another horse. *Juan?* he thought. *Maybe Seth?* He pulled his horse into a stand of young oaks beside the barn and waited to see who it was. The rider was following the trail from town and he appeared to be carrying something on the back of the horse he was leading. A little closer and Reese recognized the flea-bitten gray Deacon Pratt rode. In the next instant, it struck him. The rider was Cullen McCabe and the load on the back of the gray horse was the body of Deacon Pratt!

Unaware that he had been spotted approaching the ranch headquarters, Cullen watched the house and the barn for any chance of a reception. His rifle was cocked and ready for instant use. He was counting heavily on the notion that the few men Dixon had left would be taking care of the cattle. It was getting close to suppertime, so he was also counting on the probability that the men would be occupied with that. At any rate, he was prepared to react quickly in the event Nathan Dixon fired at first sight of him. He did not discount the fact that his visit to the Double-D was not the wisest thing to do at this point. But he found himself weary of the whole assault on the town of Bonnie Creek and the insane determination of Dixon to continue it, no matter the cost. This latest act of the major's, sending for a gunfighter to eliminate him, was enough to exhaust his patience with the conscienceless maniac. He was beginning to wonder if he was going to have to shoot Dixon to end Bonnie Creek's problems with him. With that solution as a possibility, Cullen felt it his duty to try to negotiate a lasting peace between the major and the town first, so he was determined to try to talk to the man.

Seeing no sign of anyone around or near the barn or corral, Cullen rode up to the front porch of the house and dropped the gray's reins on the ground. He was about to call out to Dixon, when the door opened and the major stepped out, a revolver in his hand. When he saw his hired killer draped across the gray's saddle, the fire of frustration burning in his veins threatened to cause them to explode. His first thought was to kill this demon who had destroyed his empire. But with Cullen's rifle aimed at him, he hesitated to raise his pistol and fire. "You've got your nerve," he roared defiantly, "riding up here on my property. I could have you shot."

"You make the first motion to raise that pistol and I'll cut you down," Cullen warned him. "I brought your hired gun back home 'cause I'm sure you wanna give him a proper burial."

"I don't know who that man is," Dixon claimed. "He's not one of my men." Somewhat assured now that if McCabe had come to kill him, he would already be dead, Dixon demanded, "Get off my property!"

"You're finished, Dixon," Cullen calmly informed him. "You ain't got enough men left to run the cattle you've got. The best thing you can do is make your peace with the people of Bonnie Creek and run this ranch like everybody else along the river. You'll still have the biggest range of all the ranches in this valley, and you can use the town's supplies and services. Whaddaya say, Dixon, you about ready to call off this stupid war and declare a truce? There's room for both you and the town. Take my advice and make peace with the town before it's too late."

"Who the hell do you think you are?" Dixon roared in answer, still unable to accept defeat. "Riding in here on my land, telling me what I can or can't do," he railed. He could feel his hand tightening on the grip of his revolver, wanting desperately to raise it and shoot, but knowing he couldn't get the shot off before McCabe pulled the trigger. "Damn you," he swore. "Get off my land."

"All right," Cullen said. "I'm goin', but you think it over, and if you're ready to live in peace like everybody else in this valley, it ain't too late. I'll set up a meetin' tomorrow with the mayor and the town council—say ten o'clock in the hotel dinin' room—and we'll put an end to this war between you folks." Dixon did not speak but continued to glare at the man he had come to hate like no other in his life. "No harm will come to you, if you're ready to talk like civilized people," Cullen promised. "But I warn you, send another hired gun after me and I won't stop with killin' him. I'll come after you. Best you make your peace with the town people. Bring your men with you if you want." His appeal finished, he backed his horse slowly away from the porch, his rifle still aimed at Dixon, lest he decide to take that shot he so desired to take.

From the grove of oaks beside the barn, Reese Cochran steadied his rifle against the trunk of the tree he had been hiding behind. He had heard only part of the talk between his boss and McCabe, most of that being Dixon's words because they were fairly shouted in anger. He heard enough from the major's responses to get the gist of the confrontation. He carefully set the front sight of the Henry on the broad back of the man the major had tried so hard to have killed. He thought about the satisfaction he could give the major with one squeeze of the trigger. The act of killing McCabe would also increase his value in Dixon's eyes, a quality that had fallen severely in the last few days.

Still backing away, not taking any chances on Dixon's insanity, McCabe turned his back slightly more, giving Reese an even bigger target, one he could not miss. He pulled the hammer back and slowly squeezed the trigger. He recoiled, startled, when the hammer clicked dully on an empty chamber. He had forgotten to crank a cartridge into the chamber. Confused, he quickly levered a round into the chamber, and with the hammer automatically cocked, ready to fire, he returned the front sight to the back of the unsuspecting victim. He still had time to take out the man standing in the way of the major's grand plan. He hesitated, not certain, then he lowered the rifle as McCabe wheeled his horse and loped off up the trail to the front gate. Still confused and not certain why he had not fired, he eased the hammer back down and walked back to his horse. Somewhere deep in his conscious mind, that metallic click of the hammer falling on an empty chamber must have been a signal that he was about to kill the wrong man. From the few words he had been able to hear, it sounded as if McCabe had offered a truce. Whether the major was able to consider a truce was still a question and not likely to happen.

Reese's mind had been troubling him for some time over the right and wrong of working for the major. He thought of young Jeff Hammond. Just as Jeff made the decision to shoot Ike Roper, Reese had decided it was wrong to shoot McCabe. Like Jeff, maybe he was finally reaching the point where he had had enough of the major's employ and it was time to make an attempt to live out the rest of his years as an honest man. "I just don't know," he muttered under his breath, so he climbed up into the saddle and rode out the back of the grove.

After a ride of two miles, he reached the creek and the camp where Smokey had parked his chuckwagon. Seth and Juan were sitting by the fire and eating supper. "You fixin' to eat?" Smokey called out to Reese when he rode up, and after an affirmative nod, dished up a plate of beans and bacon for him.

Reese stepped down and helped himself to a cup of coffee, took the plate from Smokey, and sat down with Seth and Juan. "You'll be goin' back in the mornin'," he said to Smokey. "We'll all be workin' out of the bunkhouse, so you'll be cookin' back there again."

"Damn, Reese," Seth complained at once. "We sure need Smokey to help me and Juan. Why the hell can't Consuelo cook for the four of us?"

"She told me she could do that," Reese replied, "but the major won't let her. She just does the cookin' for the big house." When Seth grunted and started to complain again, Reese said, "Besides, you and Juan are lucky. I'm gonna be helpin' you." His attempt to lighten the moment fell flat and his next statement caused them to forget that issue for a moment. "The major had a visitor right after I left." He told them then about the visit by Cullen McCabe and the delivery of Deacon Pratt's body. "He left that bastard's body layin' across the saddle of that gray he rode, left it in the front yard."

"I swear," Smokey exclaimed. "Did he come after you and the major?"

"I didn't have nothin' to do with it," Reese answered. "I had done left to come back here, but I stopped in that bunch of oaks by the barn and watched what happened." They were eager to hear what had taken place between the major and McCabe, so Reese painted the picture for them. When he finished, they all had questions.

"I can't believe the major didn't take a shot at him soon as he showed up," Seth remarked. "Too bad you didn't take a shot at him. It woulda been worth two hundred dollars for you."

"I thought about it," Reese said, "but I never got a clear shot." He didn't confess to having had second thoughts about killing McCabe.

"I swear," Smokey drawled, "I can't figure that feller out. He didn't hesitate to shoot Tom Yates or any of the other boys, but he didn't shoot the major? He's a hired killer, ain't no doubt about that, but you think he was talkin' about a truce?"

"That's what I think," Reese said. "And he was settin' on his horse right in front of the major, with his rifle on him the whole time. He coulda killed him anytime he took a notion to."

"Damn," Seth swore. "I bet the major wasn't too tickled about that." He raked the last of the beans off his plate and washed them down with a gulp of coffee, obviously in deep thought. "Wouldn't it be somethin' if the major quit thinkin' about runnin' everybody out of this valley and we could do some honest-to-God cattle ranchin'?" All three of the others immediately stared at him as if he had spoken blasphemy. "Don't go lookin' at me like that," he responded. "You know damn well you've all thought it sometime or other."

"Mighta thought it," Smokey said, "but I had better sense than to say it out loud." He looked at Reese, expecting some reaction from him.

"Every man's got a right to think what he wants," Reese said. "We all hired on, knowin' what kinda work we were hired for. We've all rode on the wrong side of the law."

Juan Hernandez, silent to that point as he listened to the discussion, was especially uncomfortable with thoughts that had recently troubled him. He had served the major longer than any of the Double-D crew, having acted as Dixon's valet when he was in the army. Was the major's increased disregard for human life and wanton elimination of anyone standing in his way actually a sign of an ailing brain? If the major was actually losing his sense of right and wrong, how long would it be before he would lose everything he had built up since leaving the army? What would become of Consuelo and her son? Juan was not sure what he should do. He had taken orders from the major for too long and his sense of loyalty weighed heavy on his mind. His thoughts were interrupted when Reese gave the order to go back to work. "We'll work 'em a little farther up the creek in the mornin'. That'll keep 'em in a little closer to headquarters and we won't have to worry about 'em strayin' off our range. I've gotta go back to the house tonight to see what the major wants to do." He hadn't mentioned that McCabe had invited Dixon to come into town in the morning to talk peace, and he was anxious to see if the major would consider doing that. It would be one hell of a surrender for the old man, and Reese found it near impossible to believe that could happen.

When Reese returned to headquarters, he was surprised to find Dixon in the barn. "Where the hell is Juan?" the major demanded when Reese rode in to unsaddle his horse. When Reese reminded him that Juan was helping Seth and Smokey with the cattle, Dixon responded with, "I pay Juan to take care of this house and barn. I don't pay him to work cattle, I have other men to do that."

"Yes, sir," Reese said. "I'll tell him you need him here." He hesitated to remind his boss that he had only three other men to work the cattle, including himself. He could see the major seemed to be out of touch with what was going on. He was trying to decide whether or not to ask him if he was planning on going into town in the morning to talk with the town council, when Mateo came out of the barn.

Relieved to see Reese, the boy said, "I took care of the gray horse, but I don't bury the man's body yet." He looked at Dixon nervously as he spoke. "The major say to dig a hole back of the barn."

"That's right," the major barked. "Bury him where I can't see him. I can't abide a man who can't do his job. Damned if I'll pay him for it."

Reese and Mateo exchanged glances, both thinking the old man was definitely out of his mind. "I don't reckon you're thinkin' about ridin' into town in the mornin' to talk to those folks," Reese said, hoping to bring Dixon back to reality.

"What would I want to do that for?" Dixon asked. "I

have no business with any of those people in that town. They're squatting on my range and I intend to get rid of them like the lice they are."

Reese knew then that the major was out of his mind. He hadn't even asked how Reese knew about the proposed meeting. The question to think about now was, what to do about it? "Yes, sir, I'll help Mateo dig a hole for Deacon Pratt, and we'll make sure all the other chores are took care of, too."

"Right," Dixon replied. "Carry on." He did an about-face and headed back toward the house, leaving Reese to think about some serious decisions to be made.

"You think maybe the major acting funny?" Mateo asked as they watched Dixon march back to the house. "He's been talking crazy things ever since that man brought the body back."

"I don't know, Mateo," Reese answered. "He might be a little off his rocker. Maybe he'll be right again in the mornin'. It might just be a temporary thing. I guess we'll see."

"I worry for my mother," Mateo said. "I think maybe he hurt her if she make a mistake."

"I wouldn't think he'd do anything to hurt your mama. It's just all this killin' that's got him actin' a little loco, and that feller McCabe has got into his head. Maybe he'll come out of it. But right now, let's grab a couple of shovels and dig a hole for that big-time gunslinger." In spite of what he had just told the boy, Reese was not at all convinced that Dixon's insanity was a temporary thing. It might be time to step up and take the responsibility for his own future. He had obviously made a mistake when he put his fate in Dixon's hands.

CHAPTER 17

Mayor Mitchell and the two men who made up the town council, Marvin Winter and Malcolm Howard, were more than a little skeptical when Cullen informed them of the meeting he had proposed to Nathan Dixon. "Talk about a leopard changing his spots," Howard had responded. "There's no way in hell that ol' busybody is gonna come in here to talk about peace." His response was seconded with grunts of agreement from both Mitchell and Winter.

"You may be right," Cullen readily agreed, "but I thought it wouldn't hurt to let him think about it. He's taken a helluva beatin' in this war with you folks. Right now, he's down to four men. He might be ready to call it quits if you folks let him know you're willin' to start over with him."

"I don't know, McCabe," Percy Mitchell said. "He might come in here with the idea of shooting us all down. Even if he said he wanted peace, I'm not sure I'd want to trust his word." They were still puzzled by the fact that Cullen had decided to take Deacon Pratt's body back to the Double-D and make such arrangements for a meeting. This without telling anyone that he was going to do it. The question that had lately been forgotten, but now surfaced again among the town council, was what motive could McCabe have for acting in the town's interest? They had talked anew about the reason a drifter, who was just passing through town, could possibly have for his actions. He had no apparent business he was thinking of starting up here. He had no interest in taking the job as sheriff, although that was an occupation he showed the most potential for. His most unnerving characteristic was a seemingly constant seriousness without ever relaxing his guard.

"Well," Malcolm Howard summed up, "we're here this mornin', just like you asked. Just to take some precautions, we've asked the sheriff and his deputy to come to the meetin', too. I don't think Dixon will show up, after you chased him outta town the last time he was here. Daisy agreed to make us a big pot of coffee, so the meeting won't be a total loss. We might as well drink it up for her and then we can all get back to our businesses."

"It's about time we had a council meeting, anyway," the mayor said, "just to see where we stand, now that we've got the cattle out of our backyard."

"What about that nephew of yours, the doctor?" Howard asked. "Is he still thinkin' about startin' up a practice here? We could sure as hell use a doctor. I ain't sayin' nothin' against you, Norman, since you do the best you can. But you're a helluva long way from bein' a doctor."

"I ain't never claimed to be a doctor," Freeman immediately responded. "You folks are the ones who keep comin' to me with your cuts and bruises. It'll suit me just fine if we get a bona fide doctor to settle here."

With that discussion under way, Cullen walked over to one of the smaller tables and sat down next to the postmaster. Daisy, carrying a coffeepot and a cup for him, came over to the table. She had no real business at the meeting but contributed her services simply because of her incurable need to know everything. Since it was an official town meeting, she even relaxed her standing order about no weapons in her dining room but permitted only the sheriff and his deputy—as well as Cullen—to wear their sidearms. "You didn't really think that ol' coot was gonna come ridin' into town this mornin', did you?" she asked Cullen while she poured his coffee.

Without changing his somber expression, he answered her question truthfully. "No, but I thought it was worth a shot."

"If you'd asked me, I'da told you it wasn't," she said, smiling smugly.

"I didn't," he responded, and she playfully stuck her tongue out at him. Set to reply again, she was interrupted by an exclamation over by the window.

"Well, I'll be . . ." Jeff Hammond started. He quickly moved to the door from his position by the front window. His remark caused all heads to turn toward the door. "I wonder what in the world . . ." he started again.

"What is it?" Percy Mitchell asked.

"It's Reese Cochran and Smokey Jones, and they're headin' this way," Jeff answered.

"Damned if they are." Marvin Winter snorted in disbelief, got up, and walked to the door to see for himself. "Damned if they ain't," he announced after a few seconds.

"Just them?" Percy asked. "The major isn't with them?" When Shep, moving up beside Jeff, confirmed that it was just the two ranch hands, Percy said, "They couldn't be coming to meet with us. They might be coming to eat."

"It's too late for breakfast and too early for dinner,"

Daisy said, her head in the window now. "They oughta know that."

Curious as well, Cullen patiently waited to see if the two Double-D hands were actually coming to meet with the town council. Just in case, however, he got up from his chair and walked to the back door, thinking it wouldn't hurt to check it. He had realized after the fact that it might not have been wise to set the town's leading citizens up together in one room. From recent history with Nathan Dixon, he couldn't discount the possibility that Dixon's other two men—or Dixon, himself—might come through the back door, blazing away. With a thought toward caution, he turned the knob and eased the door open. There was no one in the hallway. Just to be sure, however, he walked to the end of the hall to be certain no one was coming into the hotel lobby. Finding no one there but John Taylor at the desk, Cullen nodded in response to Taylor's curious expression and quickly returned to the dining room. Once inside again, he locked the door behind him and stood waiting while Marvin Winter and the others stepped back away from the front door.

A few seconds later, Reese and Smokey appeared on the front step and peered through the glass before cautiously opening the door to step inside. Like two animals approaching a baited windfall, they stood looking around the room at the people gathered there, their gaze stopping to focus on Cullen. Reese nodded to him as if to acknowledge him as the critical danger in the room. Cullen returned the nod. Only then did Reese turn to address the three men seated at the head of the long table. Cullen imagined it must appear to the two much as a courtroom might. "We come to talk," Reese said.

"We were hoping Nathan Dixon was coming to talk," Percy said. "Did he send you to talk for him?"

"No, sir," Reese answered respectfully. "Me and Smokey came on our own. The major don't know we came." His statement caused a wave of puzzled glances and a few grunts in response.

"Well, what good is that?" Malcolm Howard was the first to ask. "Dixon's the man givin' the orders. He's still goin' on with his plan of killin' the whole town, then."

"We came in to let you folks know we ain't at war with you no more," Reese said. "The major ain't got but two more hands besides me and Smokey and we came in to tell you where the four of us stand." He glanced at Smokey for support, not quite sure how to explain himself.

"What we want you to know," Smokey said, stepping in, "is there ain't no more gunslingers left at the Double-D, and the four of us still tryin' to take care of the ranch ain't interested in the fightin' and killin' that's been goin' on. We druther work on buildin' up the ranch and be on friendly terms with the town, too. I reckon the reason me and Reese came in this mornin' was to ask you for help on that."

"If Dixon is ready for peace, why didn't he come in, himself?" Percy asked.

"Well, sir." Reese hesitated. "That's kind of a problem. The major ain't as ready for peace as we are." Percy threw up his hands in frustration in response to Reese's statement.

Marvin exclaimed, "It doesn't do a bit of good for you two to come telling us this. The Double-D is Dixon's claim. He's the boss and there ain't much anybody can do till he decides he's had enough. All we've been doin' the whole time is defending ourselves from the Double-D's attacks."

"There's another problem," Smokey said. "You see, the major's not exactly in his right mind lately. He's been actin' funnier and funnier ever since you folks hired McCabe, there." He nodded toward Cullen, standing near the door. "It got to him so bad till he sent word to Waco and hired him a gunfighter of his own. And when your gunfighter killed Deacon Pratt, the major went plum loco."

Poss Rooks, silent for longer than he could ordinarily stand, piped up then. "Hell, we thought he was loco from the start. You mean he's worse than he was?"

Before either of them could answer Poss, Percy interrupted. "I think it's important for you to know that we didn't hire Cullen McCabe. He's his own man and chose to help because it's the right thing to do, just like Jeff over there." He nodded in the deputy's direction. Both Reese and Smokey appeared to be surprised by that. They had been convinced that Cullen was a hired gun. "If he's a hired gun," Percy went on, "he's not here in that capacity."

"If you say so," Reese declared, "but he sure looks like one. The four of us that's left could build that ranch up to be a fine-workin' spread, if the major spent his money on breed cattle and a few more hardworkin' men. It'd be good for the town, too, if you folks could get some of the Double-D's business. It'd be a sight easier for us, instead of drivin' a couple of wagons eighty miles to pick up supplies at San Angela, over by Fort Concho."

The two men seemed to be sincere, but as far as anyone in the room could see, they were facing a problem with no solution. "Let me say right off that we'd be happy to work with you men, but I don't know what we could do to help as long as Dixon feels the way he does," Percy said. "Give us a few minutes to butt our heads together on this to see if we can do anything. Daisy, get 'em a cup of coffee while they're waiting. Might as well be sociable. We're all trying to do the right thing here." Reese's comment about buying supplies was enough to cause Percy to want to try to find a solution.

While the three-man city council huddled together to discuss the problem presented to them, Daisy got two more cups from the side table and filled them for Reese and Smokey. Unable to resist, Reese took his and walked over to talk to Cullen. "I just took my arm out of the sling yesterday, but I'm still carryin' some lead in my shoulder that belongs to you."

"You're welcome to keep it," Cullen said, his face as expressionless as usual. "It you're lookin' for an apology, I'd like to remind you that you were fixin' to shoot me through that window."

"I reckon I was," Reese admitted, "but I thought you was about to shoot my boss down in the doorway."

"I'm sorry now that I didn't," Cullen said. "It woulda solved the problem you've come here with this mornin'."

"Might have, at that," Reese replied. "No hard feelin's?"

"No hard feelin's," Cullen answered. "Just don't try it again."

"Seein' as how we're all friendly-like this mornin'," Smokey spoke up, "what's your real name?" He was convinced that Cullen was a hired gun and he was willing to bet that he was probably famous by his real name.

"Cullen McCabe," he said. "Is your real name Smokey?"

"No, it's Clarence," Smokey replied before he thought.

"Clarence?" Reese blurted. "Your name is Clarence?"

"What's wrong with that?" Smokey immediately shot back indignantly. "I got a sister back in Missouri named Clarise. My mama named us both after her daddy. His name was Clarence. The only problem was when Grandpa came to live with us, he didn't have no teeth and sometimes when he called us, we didn't know whether he was callin' for me or my sister." He chuckled in appreciation of his story, looking up at Cullen, but stopped when he saw no change in the somber man's expression, other than a look of puzzlement. "I swear, you're a lot bigger than I thought you was now that I stand up next to you," he declared, his humor seeming out of place at this meeting.

Long with a habit of ignoring much of Smokey's ramblings, Reese was focusing his thoughts on the man Cullen McCabe, as well. Finally, he asked, "You thinkin' about plantin' your roots here in Bonnie Creek?" He was still curious to know why Cullen decided to involve himself in Bonnie Creek's problems unless there was something in it for him.

"Nope," Cullen replied. "I don't plan to plant my roots anywhere. I woulda already been gone if your boss hadn't sent Deacon Pratt to kill me."

His answer did nothing to satisfy Reese's curiosity, and it was obvious that Cullen wasn't going to share any plans he might have. There was no time for further questions because the council came out of their huddle at that moment. "Like wc said before," Percy Mitchell began, "there isn't much we can do to help you. The only way there's gonna be any peace between Bonnie Creek and the Double-D is for Nathan Dixon to give up on the idea of closing up the town. We appreciate you two coming in to try to work something out between us, and we'll give you all the support we can—and you'll certainly be welcome in town. But at the same time, we have to be on our guard in case Dixon hires more gunmen to cause us trouble."

Reese was disappointed, but hardly surprised. He and Smokey had not held out much hope for any miracles but thought it important to let the town people know that they, personally, had no plans to continue the war. "And that goes for Seth Wiley and Juan Hernandez," Reese reminded Mitchell. "Well," he sighed, "I reckon me and Smokey best get back to the ranch before the major knows where we are. Thank you for meetin' with us, and thank you, ma'am, for the coffee." They walked out the door, thinking they had accomplished very little except possibly not getting shot if they showed up in town again.

Jeff Hammond walked outside with them. "I reckon everybody back at the Double-D must think I'm a low-down dog for what I did," he said.

"Nobody but the major," Reese replied. "It ain't much different than me and Smokey ridin' into town to talk peace, is it? Tell you the truth, you just weren't cut out to be an outlaw, anyway." He smiled and added, "And now, look at you, wearin' a deputy's badge." He climbed up into the saddle. "Be seein' you," he said as he wheeled the horse away from the rail and loped off to catch up with Smokey, who was already at the end of the street.

Malcolm Howard walked over to talk to Cullen, who was standing at the window, watching the two men ride away. "Well, you had your meetin' but it doesn't look like it accomplished much, does it? Now we know we're not just dealin' with a greedy man, we're dealin' with a greedy lunatic."

"It does look that way," Cullen replied. "But it helps to know there's four men who ain't gonna fight anymore." He was possibly more frustrated than the people of Bonnie Creek, because it was his job to solve the town's problem. Part of his job had been finished—there were no more roughshod outlaws terrorizing the town on a regular basis. It was tempting to call the job done, but what would keep Dixon from starting over and hiring another gang of outlaws? Now, after hearing how strange Dixon had begun to behave, Cullen thought the major might actually be insane. How could he deal with that? Then, again, had Dixon really gone loco? *Maybe Reese just thinks he has. Maybe I'd best find out for myself.*

The sun began to filter through a cover of patchwork clouds, making it seem warmer than it really was by the time Smokey and Reese had ridden the four and a half miles back to the front gate of the Double-D. They hadn't talked much about their meeting with the people in Bonnie Creek while they rode, but there was very little else on the mind of each man. Reese, especially, was not sure they had accomplished anything. He decided he would talk it over with Seth and Juan to see if either of them had anything to suggest. Juan had been a faithful servant to the major since his military days. Maybe he had seen Dixon stray off the trail mentally before and might reasonably give them hope that he would find his way back to normalcy. It was plain to Reese that in order for the Double-D to recover, the major's best hope was to make peace with his neighbors, both in town and with the small ranchers. The major was a proud man, and Reese was not sure he could accept the total defeat of his ambitious plans.

Seth walked out of the barn to meet the two riders when they rode in. "There ain't much to tell you," Smokey volunteered upon stepping down. "How are things goin' here?" He thought it kind of odd when Seth didn't respond right away, and he was about to comment as much, but paused abruptly when the major walked out of the barn. He knew at once that Dixon was on the warpath again, if only by the way he was dressed—cavalry pants and boots, his hand-decorated deerskin shirt, and his Boss of the Plains Stetson. To add to his military attire, he was wearing his officer's sword, as well. If there was any doubt as to the major's state of mind, it was immediately confirmed when he spoke.

"Where the hell have you two been?" Dixon demanded. Before either answered, he continued, addressing Smokey. "The men have to be fed, but you're not in the cookhouse preparing their food!" Back to Reese then, he asked, "Is this the way you run my regiment? Why isn't the cook preparing the food for my men?"

Both men were speechless for a moment, not certain how to answer and afraid to offer any excuse. It was apparent that the major was still traveling mentally between his ranch and his regiment in the army. Reese was the first to attempt to reason with him. "I was just checkin' on the herd," he lied. "I thought it'd be all right if Smokey rode along with me, seein' as how he already fed the men breakfast this mornin'. You remember, there ain't but four of us to feed now, don'tcha?"

"Damn you!" Dixon roared. "I want all my men fed!"

"Yes, sir!" Smokey replied, aware that the major was really talking crazy. "I've got beans soakin' for dinner already. I'm gonna take care of the men, all of 'em."

"See that you do," Dixon said. "I'll return to my quarters. Where is Hernandez?"

"I'm right here, Major," Juan answered, and stepped forward from his position beside the barn door.

"Good. Hernandez, I'm going to need my sidearm

cleaned and I'm finding a bit of rust on my saber. I want all to be in tip-top shape for the battle ahead of us."

"Yes, sir," Juan said. "I'll follow you to the house, and I'll take care of your weapons." He looked over to meet Reese's gaze, both men aware that Dixon's mind had snapped, mentally leaving him with his feet in two different worlds at the same time. Reese nodded to Juan to let him know that he understood.

Dixon spun on his heel and started toward the house with Juan following close behind him. Then Dixon paused long enough to order Reese to report to him at his headquarters, which Reese took to mean in his study. "Yes, sir," Reese replied, "just as soon as I take care of the horses."

"Loco," Seth Wiley said when the major had marched out of earshot. "Crazy as a damn June bug." He looked at Reese and Smokey, who were both still amazed by the major's antics. "He's been like that all mornin'," Seth went on. "Marchin' around the barn and the bunkhouse, lookin' for you, Reese, most of the time—talkin' about a campaign against the enemy at Bonnie Creek. Me and Juan had to tell him you and Smokey were gone to make sure everything was ready for the attack." He shook his head, resolved. "Only I ain't fixin' to go on no attack against Bonnie Creek to get my ass shot off for him and his imaginary army. I'm gonna pack up my little bag of possibles and ride out of here before he gets us all killed."

"Well, don't go ridin' off right away," Reese urged. "You're right, he's gone plum loco, but he might come back to his senses just as quick as he lost 'em. Then he won't have no choice except to try to take care of the cattle and get along with everybody in the valley. This ain't a good time to ride the grub line, anyway, so you'd as likely as not wind up robbin' some poor soul just to keep from starvin'.

I ain't got no intention of ridin' against Bonnie Creek, either, neither has Smokey, so let's see what happens. The major's got Juan and Consuelo to settle him down off his warhorse. He might be back to normal by suppertime, and we need you to help with the cattle." Seth hesitated, not convinced the major would ever accept defeat of his plans to build his cattle empire, so Reese tried to appeal to his prospects for a path out of a life of rustling and killing. "If the major comes around to facin' the way things are, he ain't got much choice, he'll have to run an honest outfit, and we'll be workin' a top-producin' cattle business. That's worth a day or two, to see what happens, ain't it?"

"I reckon," Seth reluctantly agreed. "What the hell?" It was a relief for Smokey as well. Like Reese, he was feeling too old to strike out looking for work. If it was in the spring or summer, it might have been different, but winter was a hard time to go looking.

"Wait till Juan comes back from the house," Smokey said. "Then maybe we'll know a little more about how things are goin'." They remained there, staring at the front door of the house long moments after Dixon and Juan went inside, unaware of the rider on the bay horse coming up behind them. It was Smokey who first discovered their unexpected visitor. Turning to go to the bunkhouse, he suddenly yelped, "Jumpin' Jehoshaphat!" for the second time that week to find himself facing the formidable mystery man no more than fifteen yards away.

Seth reacted immediately, reaching for his .44, only to be stopped by Reese before he drew it. "Hold on, Seth!" Reese ordered, afraid Seth might get himself shot. He noticed the rifle resting across McCabe's thighs right away, ready for instant use if necessary. "McCabe," he asked then, "what are you doin' here?" He quickly looked around him as if afraid someone might see them talking.

"After our meetin' this mornin', I figured I'd like to see if Dixon is as crazy as you said he was. I'm thinkin' he might be ready to talk this problem over now that he's had a little time to think about it. I figured it wouldn't hurt to ride out here, so he could hear it from somebody from Bonnie Creek. You know, maybe settle our differences." He actually had no such hopes, but he thought it the right thing to do just in case Dixon had reformed. He made the trip out to Dixon's headquarters with the firm notion he was dealing with a mad dog. And he expected he might have to end this problem with the Double-D in the same way he would end a problem with a mad dog. And that was to shoot it. Unless he was wrong and Dixon had decided to call off the war, he feared that was the only solution.

"Damn, McCabe." Reese hesitated. "I ain't sure that's a good idea right at this particular time." He looked at Smokey and saw him shake his head in agreement with him. "The major's already been actin' like he's a little bit tetched."

"That's right, McCabe," Smokey said, stepping in to help Reese. "Right now, the major ain't sure if he's still in the army or tryin' to raise cattle. It wouldn't do no good for you to show up on his doorstep till he knows for sure where he stands."

"If you're worryin' about us lettin' the major lead us on another raid on the town," Reese said, "that ain't gonna happen. We've all agreed we ain't gonna fight you no more. This war's over, and as soon as the major's had time to get it settled in his mind, he's gonna see there ain't no sense in fightin' a whole damn town. I understand you're tryin' to make peace between the major and Bonnie Creek.

Why, I'll be damned if I know the reason, but you're the last man he wants to see right now, and I can understand why." Reese was too far into speaking his peace by now, so he decided to say everything on his mind. "The major was like a king over this valley until you showed up, and I reckon he's still tryin' to figure out why you did. The folks in Bonnie Creek say they don't know what your stake in this fight is. They say they didn't send for you, don't even know where you came from." He threw his hands in the air in frustration. "Who the hell are you, anyway, and what are you after?"

When Reese paused, unable to say more, Cullen looked at Seth and Smokey in turn. They wore the same faces of frustration that Reese wore. Cullen realized at once that his theory to approach the "mad dog" was probably not the right thing to do and may have been inspired by a simple wish to have his job finished. He was at once aware of Reese's frustration and thought that he deserved an answer. "I'll be honest with you, Cochran, the only thing I'm after is to ride away from Bonnie Creek, knowin' those folks don't have to worry about gettin' wiped out by outlaws ridin' the Double-D brand."

The three Double-D hands stood staring at him in disbelief. "You ain't takin' no money from that town to do their killin'?" Reese spoke first.

"Nope, no money," Cullen answered.

"What are you, some kinda preacher or somethin'?" Seth reacted.

"Reckon not," Cullen replied, "but I might as well talk to Dixon. He's gonna have to come face-to-face with somebody from Bonnie Creek before this trouble is finished. What I need to know is whether or not he's in his right mind. If he ain't, then it'll most likely be up to you three and Juan to keep this ranch from goin' down."

"I've thought about that," Reese confessed.

"Every day you wait, is one more day of losin' cattle and strained relations with the people in town," Cullen tried to reason. "Let's get the cards on the table and see what we've got to deal with." He paused to let Reese think about it, then urged, "Let's go up to the house and call him out now."

"You're crazy, man," Seth charged. "You're as crazy as he is!"

"Maybe he is and maybe he ain't," Reese spoke up, "but I think he may be right. We're just foolin' ourselves thinkin' the major's suddenly gonna get over bein' loco." He turned to face Cullen. "If you're sure that's what you want, I'll go up to the house and see if I can get the major to come out to talk."

CHAPTER 18

Nathan Dixon stood warming his backside before the fireplace, a glass of his favorite brandy in his hand. After a few minutes, he stepped over to look at a passage he had read in his Bible about Joshua and the conquest of Canaan before returning to warm his behind again. He could identify with Joshua, for he was a mighty leader of men. Tomorrow, he would set his regiment on the march for the final conquest of the tiny village that dared to stand in the way of his destiny. "Hernandez!" he summoned loudly. In a few seconds, Juan hurried into the den from the kitchen, where he had been huddled with Consuelo and her son, listening to the major's constant raving in his den.

"Yes, sir," Juan reported, making a point to stand at attention, knowing that the major was mentally in the army at this time.

"Did you clean my weapons as I ordered?"

"Yes, sir, I cleaned and oiled them."

"My sword, too?" Dixon demanded. When Juan replied that he had removed the spot of rust from the sword as well, Dixon ordered, "Bring my weapons in here. I need to see them around me." Juan did an about-face at once and started for the door. "And send that whelp of a boy in here with some more wood," Dixon yelled.

When Juan passed through the kitchen on his way to fetch the major's weapons, he paused before a worried Consuelo and her son. "What does he want his weapons for?" Consuelo asked anxiously. She could see no good purpose for them when the major had been raving like a maniac all morning.

"He says he wants to have them close to him," Juan replied. He turned to Mateo. "He said for you to bring more wood."

"I heard him from here," Mateo said. "I brought wood already, enough to last a week for that fireplace."

"I know, but bring some more in," Juan insisted. "We have to humor him when he is having one of these fits."

"Where will I put it? The box is full, and I have already stacked some in front of it. The man is crazy."

"Hush, don't let him hear you," Consuelo whispered. "Go get the wood."

Both the man and the boy hurried to their tasks then and when they were finished, they went back to the kitchen to huddle once again to await any further orders from the major. With Juan and Mateo seated at the kitchen table, Consuelo continued her preparations for the noon meal. She was rolling out her biscuits when they heard a knock on the back door. She opened it to find Reese standing on the top step. Behind him, Seth and Smokey stood with a man she had never seen before. She felt a little skip in her heartbeat, for somehow, she knew the man was Cullen McCabe, even though she had not seen him when he brought the major's hired gun's body back from Bonnie Creek.

Juan Hernandez got up from the table and went at once

to the door when he saw Reese through the screen. "What is it, Reese?" he started but stopped when he saw McCabe standing with Seth and Smokey. His next reaction was to look behind him to make sure the major wasn't in the kitchen. "You go crazy? You don't say you gonna bring that man here!"

"I know, I know." Reese hurried to calm him down. "I didn't know he was gonna show up here, but he did, and he's come to make an honest effort to make peace. And me and Smokey and Seth think it's worth a try. It's the only way we're all gonna make it on this ranch."

Listening in, as she always did, Consuelo spoke up. "He is right, Juan. The major's war was not the right thing to do. Now is a chance to live on here for all of us."

"You have heard him in there talking to people you cannot see," Juan insisted. "He cannot listen to reason now—maybe when he is well again." Having been a faithful servant for too long, Juan was fearful that McCabe had come for no purpose other than to kill Dixon. He had agreed with the other three men that there should be no more war with Bonnie Creek, but he was still protective when it came to his master's safety.

Reese understood the Mexican's problem, and in a way, he admired him for his loyalty, but it was past time to stop the major's insane determination to rule the valley. "Nobody wants to do the major any harm," he patiently explained. "All we're wantin' to do is to hear what McCabe has to say about livin' beside each other without goin' to war. I'll go in and tell him McCabe has come to make peace and ask him to listen to what he has to say." Juan hesitated, thinking it over, but assumed a protective stance in the kitchen door, so Reese made a suggestion. "How 'bout you goin' in and tell the major what McCabe's here for? You can tell him we'll all be right there to make sure everything's all right."

Still not sure, but from the urgent faces of Consuelo and Mateo, Juan decided it was the best thing for everybody, especially if the major agreed to a truce. "All right," he said. "I will go tell the major. It would be best for me to tell him. He trusts me."

"Good," Reese said. "We'll go around to the front door and wait on the porch where he can see us. Tell him he ain't got nothin' to worry about, there's three of us to keep an eye on McCabe." He glanced at Cullen, but Cullen showed no reaction to his remark.

Juan turned at once to go to the den. Consuelo closed the kitchen door and Cullen and three nervous Double-D hands walked around to the front of the house. Without the customary feeling of comfort he usually enjoyed with his rifle in hand, Cullen casually nudged his .44 a couple of times to make sure it was riding loose in the holster. He wasn't sure what to expect when Dixon came out that door, but he was going to be prepared to take him out, if he came out shooting. From what Reese and Smokey had told him, he figured he was dealing with a crazy man, so he positioned himself beside a window. This was in case Dixon chose not to come out and tried to shoot through the window.

Inside the house, Juan stood before the door to the den, hesitating before knocking. He could hear Dixon talking, as if someone else was in the room. He took a deep breath and told himself that if things didn't go well, he must be ready to defend the major. He tapped lightly on the door and the talking stopped. After a moment, Dixon called out, "Who's there?"

"It's Hernandez, Major."

"Oh . . . well, come on in, Juan," Dixon said. When Juan entered the room, he found the major seated in his favorite chair, his rifle on the table next to his Bible, his army revolver in his lap. Before Juan could speak, Dixon remarked, "You did a first-rate job as usual on cleaning my weapons, especially my saber." He nodded toward the sword, now in its usual place above the mantel. Juan was immediately aware of a calmness about his master. Of significant importance was the fact that the sword was back over the fireplace, when only that morning the major had been ready to strap it on. Maybe, he hoped, the major was no longer thinking he was in the military and preparing to go into battle. "What is it, Juan?" Dixon asked. "Is dinner ready?"

"Uh, no, sir," Juan replied. "Not quite yet. Consuelo's fixing it. It won't be long." He was at once hopeful. The major appeared to be recovered from his mental lapse. Reese may be right, it might be the right time to talk peace, so Juan began, "I came to tell you that Reese is out on the front porch with someone from the town. They have come to talk about making peace between the Double-D and the town."

Juan's words ignited an explosion in the brain of Nathan Dixon. He sprang immediately to his feet and turned to face the startled Mexican. "You brought that enemy assassin to my door?" Dixon roared. "You, of all people! I trusted you to be loyal!" Without further warning, he bellowed, "Judas," raised the revolver he still held in his hand, and fired one shot that struck Juan Hernandez in the middle of his forehead.

Out on the front porch, it was as if the explosion had happened there. All four men reacted as if under attack. Of the four, all but Cullen stood motionless, undecided what to do. He didn't hesitate. He ran at once to the door, colliding with the heavy oak door when he discovered it locked, which probably saved his life, because the door was immediately struck with four more shots from inside. Convinced that he couldn't break in the heavy door, he ran back to the window and peeked inside in time to see Dixon run out a door in the back of the room. "He ran outta the room!" Cullen exclaimed. Then shifting to get a better angle to see into the room, he spotted the body on the floor. "Damn," he exhaled, causing Reese to squeeze in beside him at the window.

"He shot Juan!" Reese blurted. He joined in with Cullen then and the two of them kicked at the window until they broke out the lower sash. Cullen, his six-gun in hand, was the first one through the window, but Reese was right behind him. Cullen turned and told Smokey and Seth to run around to the back door in case Dixon tried to escape that way. He saw the dazed expressions of confusion on both faces and hoped they would act to stop Dixon if he came out the kitchen door. He was afraid they would not be able to turn on their boss after obeying his every command for so long. But there was nothing he could do about that at the moment, he was too busy trying to stop Dixon before he killed anyone else.

"Where does that go?" Cullen demanded, pointing to the door he had seen Dixon vanish through.

Reese, standing stunned, unable to stop staring at the hole in Juan's forehead, shook his mind free long enough to answer, "To the hallway! He mighta gone to the kitchen!" He finally realized just how insane Dixon had become.

Cullen's main concern was the danger of running into an ambush, especially since Dixon knew the house and he didn't. It was not enough to slow him down, however, for he was too far past the point where he wanted the Bonnie Creek situation settled for good. So with one mighty thrust with his foot, he kicked the door open, with his .44 ready to shoot whatever he found on the other side. It was an empty hallway, just as Reese had said. Moments later, he heard a woman cry out beyond a second door down the hall. He guessed it to be the kitchen. Another moment found Reese behind him. "Consuelo," Reese exclaimed. "She and her son were in the kitchen. He must be in there with 'em."

Inside the kitchen, a dazed and desperate man held Consuelo and her son at gunpoint. The wild look in his eyes caused the tiny Mexican woman to cry out in terror when he had charged into the room with his revolver in his hand. "Throw the bolt on that back door," Dixon ordered Mateo.

"Please don't hurt my mother," Mateo begged as he ran to obey his order.

"You just do as you're told," Dixon snapped, "or I'll shoot the both of you." Back to Consuelo then, he asked, "How long have you been plotting behind my back with your fellow conspirators?"

"I don't plot with nobody," she pleaded. "I know nothing about conspirators. I cook, I clean the house. I take care of you. That's all I do, and Mateo does the chores for you. We don't plot with nobody. We work for you, long time."

"Yeah?" Dixon replied. "Juan worked for me a long time, too, but he made a mistake when he sold out to the enemy. Maybe I'll give you the same as Juan got."

"Please, sir," Consuelo begged, "let Mateo go. He is just a boy. He has done you no harm."

"Shut up!" Dixon barked when he heard noises outside the kitchen door. Moments later, he heard McCabe when he called out.

"Dixon, don't make this any worse than it already is. Come on out of there and I give you my word, I won't shoot."

"Hah!" Dixon yelled back. "What good is the word of a hired gun? I'll give you my word, the word of an officer and a gentleman. If you don't ride out of here, and off my land, right now, I will send my regiment to destroy everyone in that irritating little town on my range."

"I can't do that," Cullen returned. "Not till you let those people go." There was no question now that the major was completely delusional.

"If you don't, I swear I'll kill them both, right here in this kitchen."

"You do that, and I'll kill you," Cullen threatened, "and that's a promise."

"You think I'm afraid of death?" Dixon called out. "I'll die before I surrender my flag to the likes of you, and I'll take the woman and her son with me. You'll have to burn this house down around me, and you'll be burning the woman and boy with me."

"Whaddaya gonna do?" Reese whispered to Cullen. "I think he's crazy enough to do it."

"I ain't sure," Cullen answered truthfully. They were at a standoff for sure. He was worried about the two hostages, certain that Dixon wouldn't hesitate to kill them. Suddenly, they heard a low grunt of pain from the other side of the door, like that from someone receiving a hard blow. Certain that Dixon had begun to make good on his threat to kill the hostages, Cullen could wait no longer. He rammed his shoulder against the door hard enough to cause it to slam against the wall. Inside, he came face-to-face with Dixon, his eyes staring sightlessly at him before he suddenly sagged and collapsed to the floor, an eight-inch butcher knife buried almost to the hilt in his side. Looking at once for the woman, he saw Consuelo crying as she held her young son tightly to her bosom. He understood immediately—the tiny woman was not strong enough to drive the knife blade that deeply into Dixon's side. As a precaution, he walked over and kicked the revolver Dixon had dropped well away from the body of the dying man. "Keep your eye on him," Cullen said to Reese. "He ain't dead yet." Then he walked over and placed a reassuring hand on the boy's shoulder. "You did what you had to do."

Mateo looked up into the face of the powerful man towering over him. "He was going to kill my mother," he said tearfully, still shaking as a result of the action he had been forced to take.

"I know, son, you saved your mother's life. You had no choice and you rid the world of an evil man." If he hadn't, Cullen figured he and possibly Reese, too, would have charged right into a blazing .44 pistol. Thanks to something he hadn't counted on, however, that didn't happen. He walked over to see how badly Dixon was wounded while Reese went to let Smokey and Seth in. Soon, they were all gathered around the wounded man, the man who had ruled their lives.

Gazing down at the pool of blood forming under Dixon, Smokey was inspired to say, "And this ain't really no valley, anyway."

* * *

The death of Nathan Dixon left an unsettled atmosphere on the Double-D ranch. There had been nothing they could do to ease the major's passing, short of putting a bullet in his brain to end his suffering, which none of the surviving crew wanted to do. Mateo's knife thrust had evidently pierced a lung, and although Smokey tried, he could not stop the bleeding. So Reese and Seth carried him to his bedroom to let him pass on out of this world on his bed. Never comfortable with the major out of sight, Smokey continued to check on him until he finally took his final breath. Juan Hernandez's body was removed from the den floor and carried to the spare bedroom, where it lay wrapped in a blanket, ready for burial. There were graves to be dug, but Reese decided it best to wait until morning. In the meantime, the kitchen floor had to be cleaned of blood, so Seth volunteered to do that unpleasant chore to save Consuelo from having to do it. The tiny woman was shaken to the bone by the horrible incident, having to be consoled by her son, whom she held close to her side. Juan had been like a cousin to her and an uncle to her son. His senseless killing was almost more than she could understand.

After the bodies were removed from sight, Seth cleaned the floor as best he could, even though he ended up spreading a quilt over the stains he was unable to mop up in order to hide them. With that task finished, it wasn't long before Consuelo regained the strength she was normally noted for and announced that, in spite of the terrible thing that had just happened, they still needed food. She set in again to finish the dinner she had started before her whole world exploded, peeling more potatoes and rolling out more biscuits to feed the extra mouths. Cullen suspected the woman was wise enough to know that the killing of

Nathan Dixon would result in a better situation for the Double-D.

When a quiet meal was finished, everyone remained at the table to decide what to do now. In spite of everything that had happened, there was still a mystery surrounding the quiet stranger, Cullen McCabe. Reese could not help but wonder if the real reason McCabe involved himself so thoroughly in the destruction of the Double-D gang was in order to eliminate the major and move in to take control, himself. Reese was not alone in his thinking. Smokey held the same suspicions and thought back on the day McCabe startled him in the camp by the river. He reasoned that he wasn't killed because McCabe had a use for him after he took over the ranch. Consequently, they were all surprised when it was Cullen who proposed a course of action they could consider. He first asked a question. "Does Dixon have any family that might possibly have any claims for this ranch or the land?" Reese told him that there was none. "In that case," Cullen continued, "I think those of you left here have a good opportunity to rebuild this ranch and run it the way it shoulda been run all along. Whatever you decide to work out, maybe you might form a partnership where the five of you are the owners, and you can start lookin' for honest, hardworkin' cowhands. And I expect there are quite a few ridin' the grub line this time of year. Whaddaya think?"

"I think that's a helluva idea," Reese replied at once. There was a chorus of agreement around the table and after it died down, Reese asked, "How 'bout you, McCabe? You interested in goin' into the cattle business?" Seth and Smokey both looked up in interest to hear his answer.

"No, reckon not," Cullen answered, "but I 'preciate the

notion. I expect I've stayed over in Bonnie Creek long enough. It's time to move on."

"If you don't mind me askin'," Seth spoke up, "where are you headin'?"

"Oh, nowhere in particular," Cullen replied. "It's just time to move on. I expect I'll head back to Bonnie Creek and tell the folks there that there's new owners at the Double-D, and they're lookin' forward to doin' business with the town."

"I swear, I like the sound of that," Smokey commented. There were even a few soft chuckles in response, even though there was still an eerie cloud of uncertainty hovering over the former employees of Nathan Dixon. Cullen could see that it would be some time yet before the spirit of the would-be king of the Texas cattle business would finally fade away.

Cullen wished them all the best of luck and took his leave. Reese, Smokey, and Seth walked out with him and wished him luck as well, while he stepped up into the saddle, then turned the bay gelding back toward the river. "Damned if that ain't a big turnaround, ain't it?" Seth asked. When Smokey asked what he meant, Seth said, "Couple of days ago, we was shootin' at each other, and now we're downright neighborly."

"It's a damn shame, though," Reese speculated. "There's somethin' chasin' that man that makes him keep on the run."

It was late by the time Cullen returned to Bonnie Creek and just about everything was closed up for the day, with the exception of the Rose. Still content after the late dinner at the Double-D, he felt no need to visit the dining room at the hotel. He thought about stopping in to have a drink to celebrate the completion of the job he had been sent there to do. After a moment's thought, however, he decided he didn't really want a drink, so he rode on down to the stable. Ross was not there, evidently having gone to supper, but the barn was open, so Cullen unsaddled Jake and put him in a stall. Before leaving, he scooped out a portion of grain for the bay and his sorrel packhorse. Then with his saddlebags over one shoulder and his rifle in his hand, he walked back to the hotel. As he walked, he took a good look at each door he passed, each one familiar to him now, as well as the folks who worked there. Only a handful of days, but it seemed much longer. There were some good people there, and maybe they would make it, he thought. At least he hoped so.

When he arrived at the hotel, there was no one at the desk, so he climbed the stairs and went to his room. After dumping his saddlebags and weapons, he removed his hat, shirt, and boots, picked up his towel, and went down the back stairs, where he found the night clerk cleaning up the washroom. "Evenin', Mr. McCabe," the clerk greeted him. "If you're lookin' for a bath, you got here just in time. I was just checkin' the stove to make sure the fire had gone out. It has, but there's a tub of water that's still fairly hot."

"Glad to hear it," Cullen replied, "'cause I feel like I need a bath tonight. If the water had already gotten cold, I mighta even took a cold bath." He didn't express it, but he felt like he needed to wash all the business with Nathan Dixon off him. As he filled the tub with the hot water, he thought about the news that he carried back from the Double-D. It was important news that the people of Bonnie Creek had long hoped for and should be a cause for celebration. But he didn't feel like trying to get the word out that night. *It'll keep till morning*, he decided. *I need some sleep*.

After a good night's sleep, he woke up early the next morning. Once he was dressed and ready for the day, he decided the first person he would contact should be the sheriff, even though he had a stronger hankering to visit the dining room. It was early, anyway, and his appearance at the door wouldn't surprise Daisy Lynch, but he passed up the dining room and walked down to the sheriff's office. Sheriff Shep Blackwell was just getting up from his cot in the corner behind his desk when Cullen walked up to find the door locked. Shep came at once when he saw him through the window. "Good mornin', McCabe, I was just fixin' to put some coffee on the stove. I'll add a little more water and some more grounds."

"'Preciate it," Cullen said. "I could use a cup." He glanced at the cot against the wall. "I figured you'd be settin' up house in here."

"Yeah, but it's just till I can get me a permanent place again," Shep said. "I tried sleepin' in the cell room when there weren't nobody in there, but the bunks are so hard I decided to set up this cot." He shrugged indifferently. "What brings you around so early?"

"Figured there were some developments goin' on at the Double-D last night that you needed to know about." He immediately had Shep's attention. "There's been a change in management out there and I think you oughta know that the new managers plan to be on peaceful terms with all the merchants in Bonnie Creek."

"Is that a fact?" Shep replied, not certain he wasn't being japed. "What happened? Did ol' Nathan Dixon suddenly pass away?"

"As a matter of fact," Cullen answered.

Shep started to smile but paused when the look on Cullen's face remained solemn. "You ain't foolin', are you? Is that where you were last night? I was thinkin' I didn't see you around town. I figured it was only a matter of time," he said, coming to the wrong conclusion.

"I didn't kill Nathan Dixon, if that's what you're thinkin', but it's a fact, he is dead." He went on to tell Shep what had happened at the ranch and how young Mateo Sanchez had to kill a crazed Dixon to protect his mother. "That's what happened," he said when he had finished. "Dixon went loco, shot Juan Hernandez in the head, and threatened to kill the woman. Reese Cochran, Smokey Jones, and Seth Wiley were all trying to stop Dixon, and now that he's stopped, they will be running the Double-D and tryin' to make an honest living at it."

"Well, I'll be damned," Shep uttered, and sank down in his chair, scarcely able to believe what he had just been told. Cullen pulled the coffeepot over to the edge of the stove when it threatened to boil over. Then after it settled down a little, he poured Shep a cup and another one for himself. "You need to tell Percy and the rest of 'em about this," Shep said. "They ain't gonna believe it."

"I thought maybe you oughta tell 'em," Cullen said. "Make it an official announcement from the sheriff's office. I'm gonna go to breakfast, soon as I finish this cup of coffee."

"I expect they'll wanna hear what happened from you,"

Shep replied. Just as he had, he felt sure they would want to hear every detail.

"If they do, I'll be in the hotel dinin' room," Cullen said. His intention was to play down his part in the whole operation that finally brought down the Double-D. In line with that, he thought it a good idea to have the sheriff inform the town council. His thinking was that it would be good for both the council and the sheriff if he appeared to have been a part of the newly declared truce. Cullen finished his coffee and left the sheriff to handle the situation.

"Well, good mornin'," Daisy greeted him cheerfully when he walked into the dining room. "You even waited till the dinin' room was open. What's the matter, you off your feed this mornin'?"

"Good mornin'," Cullen answered simply.

By now accustomed to his lack of conversation, she continued, "Didn't see you all day yesterday after breakfast. I thought maybe you'd decided to leave us."

"Thought about it," Cullen replied, "but I decided I'd try one more of Bertha's breakfasts."

"I'll get you some coffee," Daisy said, but turned around, almost bumping into Fanny, who was already bringing a cup for him. "Was that quick enough?" Daisy joked.

"Reckon so," he replied, then said, "Good mornin', Fanny." She responded with a cheerful smile, no longer shy in his presence.

He enjoyed a hearty breakfast, and as he ate, it seemed to him there was a more peaceful and pleasant atmosphere in the room this morning. He knew it was just his imagination, but it was almost like the few diners in there were already aware of an end to threats from the Double-D. It gave him a feeling of satisfaction and he recalled Michael O'Brien's words when he offered him the job—"*do something positive with your life, something that might help the people of Texas.*" It almost made him smile. He paid for his breakfast and went out the back door that led to the hotel.

Approximately forty-five minutes after Cullen had left the dining room, Percy Mitchell and Malcolm Howard came in, accompanied by Shep Blackwell. "Has McCabe been in this morning?" Percy asked Daisy. She informed him that Cullen had come and gone. Back to his room, she presumed, since he left through the inside door to the hotel. They promptly went out the same door. At the front desk, they were told by John Taylor that McCabe had paid his bill and checked out. Out in the street again, the three men hurried past Mitchell General Merchandise, where two horses were tied at the rail, but the men thought nothing of that fact. When they got to the stable, Ross Horner told them that McCabe had settled his bill and had taken both of his horses. Realizing then that there had been two horses at the hitching rail, they hustled back to Mitchell's store, relieved to find the two horses still there.

Inside, they found Jane Mitchell and her son, Chip, gathering the supplies that Cullen called off to them. "McCabe," Percy said, "are you fixing to leave us?" When Cullen said that he was, Percy asked, "Without even telling us what went on out at the Double-D?"

"I figured Shep would tell you what happened out at the ranch," Cullen replied, then turned back to Jane. "And a sack of that ground-up coffee, and that oughta do it."

"He did," Marvin said, "but we'd like to hear all the details."

"Shep knows everything that's important, mainly that Dixon has been goin' crazy for quite a while, and he finally went plum loco and started killin' his own people. The woman's boy killed him when he went after his mother. The people left out there took over the ranch and intend to run it honestly. End of story." He paid Mrs. Mitchell for his supplies, picked up the sacks, and headed for the door. They followed him out and watched him while he tied his supplies on his packhorse.

"Now that everything's lookin' peaceful, ain't you gonna stay around awhile?" Marvin asked. "You've done a helluva lot for this town. I think it's way past time when somebody should have told you so. If you hadn't happened to hit town when you did, we'd probably still be getting regular destructive visits from Dixon's men."

"Oh, I don't know," Cullen pondered. "Things just happen the way they happen. I think it's about time I moved on. I've already stayed longer'n I planned to. I wish you folks the best of luck, though. Maybe I'll get back this way sometime." He shook hands with each one of them, then stepped up into the saddle. "I think Reese Cochran's got his mind on the right track. You might find you can work with him." With that, he wheeled Jake around and rode out the south end of town at a fast walk.

"Good luck to you, too," Percy called after him. They stood watching him until he disappeared around a bend in the road. "And I hope whoever's chasing you never catches up with you," Percy said. He looked at Shep and Malcolm and they both nodded in agreement. "I know I'm going to write the governor another letter and tell him we don't need his damn help. We took care of our problem ourselves."

"Amen," Malcolm responded.

He took two and a half days to make the one-hundred-mile trip back to Austin. All the way, he reflected on the time he had spent in Bonnie Creek, the killing he had done, and the changes he had caused. He had to admit that the town and the small farmers and ranchers around it were better off now, but he knew it was time to decide if he was ready to take on another such assignment for the governor. He mulled the question over and over, and by the time he arrived in Austin at the end of the day, he had made his decision. In a way, it was a sorrowful choice but one that he could not deny he was well qualified to make. His life ended with the deaths of his wife and children, leaving him with no fear or dread for his own death. If he could be of service to the state of Texas until his appointment with the Grim Reaper, then so be it.

He found himself a place to make camp for the night outside of town, having no desire to return to the rooming house where he had been eaten by bugs before. He went into town the next morning and ate breakfast at a small restaurant close to the capitol, taking his time, since he knew O'Brien wouldn't be in his office until eight o'clock.

"McCabe!" Michael O'Brien exclaimed when he looked up to see the formidable agent led in the door of his office by his secretary, Ben Thacker. "The governor and I were talking about you just yesterday. We were wondering when we might hear from you." He paused, waiting for Cullen to respond. "Well, tell me about it. What have you got to report? Governor Hubbard and I were hoping this was a good idea. Please tell me it was a success."

Cullen shrugged. "Well, I'm satisfied I did what I could," he said. "The town ain't got any trouble with the Double-D ranch anymore, so I reckon you got what you wanted."

"That sounds good," O'Brien said, "but the governor's going to need more details than that. Let's go in and talk to him now."

There followed a nearly two-hour session with Governor Hubbard, during which he canceled two scheduled meetings in order to complete the interrogation to his satisfaction. He questioned Cullen extensively until he had a picture of the entire operation from the first day Cullen set foot in Bonnie Creek. Finally satisfied that Cullen was truthful in his responses, the governor said, "It sounds to me like we have an efficient program working here. I think you need to take a little time off now and we'll think about whether or not to go forward with another assignment." He didn't say so, but Cullen assumed he would wait until he could check his story for accuracy before contacting him again. "You're still on the payroll," Hubbard went on, "and I'll wire you at that same telegraph office in Two Forks. Will that be satisfactory?" Cullen nodded, they shook hands, and Cullen started home to his unfinished cabin near Two Forks, hoping no one had found it and moved in while he was away.

Wearing a confident smile now, O'Brien walked him out to the hallway. "We'll be in touch," he said, and extended his hand.

* * *

"I called you all to this little meeting tonight," Percy Mitchell said, "because I thought you might be interested in some mail I got today. You know I wrote to the governor and told him we got tired of waiting for help from the state of Texas, so we took care of the problem ourselves."

"We never needed the damn Rangers in Bonnie Creek in the first place," Poss Rooks commented. Several of the other men grunted in support.

"Well," Percy continued, "Buford brought me a letter from the governor today, answering my letter. He goes on about how glad he is to hear we were able to work out our problems, and I wanna quote you this last sentence. *'I'm happy to hear that Bonnie Creek has eliminated the problems previously caused by members of the Double-D ranch. I hope that you were aided in your endeavors by Special Agent Cullen McCabe.'*"

There was a full moment of profound silence following the statement, broken only when Poss Rooks spoke out. "I knew that feller was a lawman from the first time he set foot in Bonnie Creek." His claim was met with a full chorus of groans.

CHAPTER 1

Making a journey he had made many times before, Will Tanner guided the buckskin gelding through a gap in a long line of hills that led into the San Bois Mountains. The gap was actually one end of a narrow passage that led through the hills and ended at a grassy clearing at the foot of a mountain. On the other side of the meadow, built against the base of the mountain, stood the log cabin of a man named Merle Teague. A little, gray-bearded man, Merle had become a friend of Will's, just as the original owner of the cabin had. It was built by a quaint elflike man named Perley Gates, who had also become a friend of Will's. But one day, Perley abandoned his cabin and left for parts unknown. Will had gotten into the habit of stopping to camp there whenever he was traveling into certain parts of the Nations. It was on the way and a convenient distance from Fort Smith. And he was always welcome because he usually brought coffee and tobacco. More times than not, he was able to enjoy a supper of fresh venison. So, one of the first things he looked toward was the large oak next to the porch where Perley, and now Merle, hung their fresh-killed venison to skin and butcher. He smiled to himself when he saw the carcass hanging from that tree on this occasion.

Merle spotted him as soon as he left the cover of the trees at the end of the passage. He dropped his skinning knife, picked up his rifle, and brought it to his shoulder before he realized who it was. "Will Tanner!" he exclaimed, delighted. "You musta smelled some of that fresh meat on the fire over yonder." He nodded toward the firepit at the opposite corner of the porch.

"Howdy, Merle," Will said. "That's something new. That firepit wasn't here the last time I came by. You're makin' a regular palace outta this place." He was glad to see the little old man was getting by. He pulled the buckskin and his sorrel packhorse to a stop in front of the cabin. "That's a dandy firepit you built there, with that low wall of rocks around it. You can sit right there on the rocks while you tend your cookin', can't you?"

"You sure you wasn't here since I built it?" Merle asked. "Has it been that long since you was here?"

"Six or eight months, I expect," Will answered. "Anybody up in that cave?"

Merle knew Will was referring to a cave up on one of the mountains that was a popular hideout for fugitives on the run. It had earned the name of Robbers Cave. "I ain't been up that way in a week or so. But if there is somebody holed up there, they ain't stumbled on me yet. And they usually do, so I reckon ain't nobody up there right now."

"Well, the least I can do is help you get rid of some of that deer meat," Will said. "I'll take care of my horses first." He pulled his saddle off Buster and the packsaddle off the sorrel, then turned them loose to go to the stream that cut through the meadow. He put his saddle and the packs up on the porch, then he commented, "I like a good cup of coffee with my venison, and I don't see your coffee-pot settin' out anywhere."

"I'm sorry about that," Merle said. "I've been outta coffee beans for three months."

"Did you throw your coffeepot away?"

Merle grinned sheepishly. "No, I didn't throw it away. I knew you'd show up here again, so I kept it ready to go."

"Well, get it out and put some water in it," Will said, chuckling. "Here's a twenty-pound sack of coffee, ground, it ain't beans. That oughta last you a little while." Merle could not speak, for grinning so wide. "I brought you a sack of sugar, too. What about smokin' tobacco? Did you give that up, too?"

"About two days after I gave up coffee," Merle managed, still beaming like a kid at Christmas.

"Well, I reckon you can start again," Will teased. "You didn't throw your pipe in the fire, did you?"

"I swear, Will, if I had the money, I'd be happy to pay you double for this stuff."

"Hell, it's a fair trade for some fresh deer meat," Will replied. "I don't get to go deer huntin' like I used to. I brought you some flour. I bet you're outta that, too."

Merle just shook his head as if he couldn't believe his good fortune. Without further delay, he ran into the cabin, came back with his coffeepot, and went straight to the spring to fill it. "I knew this was gonna be a good day when I woke up this mornin'." They enjoyed a big supper of venison and fresh coffee and a long visit while Merle finished butchering his deer and prepared a good portion of the meat to be smoked on a rack that Perley Gates had made for that purpose. It was later than either man's usual bedtime when they finally turned in, Merle in the cabin, and Will in his bedroll on the porch.

"I swear," Lester Camp whispered to his partner, "I didn't think they was ever gonna go to sleep, but I reckon it was worth the wait."

"I'll say it was," Carl Babcock replied. They had trailed the old man after he had killed a deer they had been following for more than a mile. Lester had wanted to shoot the old man and take the deer right then and there, but Carl talked him out of it. He persuaded him to wait and follow the old man to see if he had anything else they could use. He figured the deer was theirs for the taking, even if he didn't have much else they could use. "I don't know if we woulda ever found this place, if he hadn't led us here. Then this other feller comes along, ridin' a dang good-lookin' buckskin horse and leadin' a packhorse loaded with supplies. It can't get much better'n this." He grinned wide with pleasure over the happenstance, knowing it was just plain luck.

"Ain't no trouble takin' care of the feller on the porch," Lester figured. "That old man might be a chore to get outta that cabin. Might have to burn him out."

"I hope not. We could use that cabin," Carl reminded him. "We mighta made a mistake waitin' for dark to take care of that old man."

"I thought it was you that wanted to wait and let him skin that deer and butcher it for us," Lester declared. "Besides, you saw how quick he had that rifle up when the other feller showed up. I don't care how old he is, it don't take much strength to pull the trigger on that Henry rifle he was holdin'."

"I say we oughta wait a little bit longer to make sure they go to sleep," Carl suggested. "And while we do, I'm gonna slip up to that little corral they put the horses in and lead that buckskin over closer to our horses back there. I mean to have that horse, so if anything goes wrong, and we have to run, I'm takin' that horse with me."

"Hell, ain't nothin' gonna go wrong," Lester insisted while he watched Carl sneak back to the horses they had tied on the other side of the meadow to get a rope. He almost chuckled as he watched Carl going to the trouble of sneaking up to the corral, where he removed the two rails that served as a gate. The horses started walking out of the corral, so Carl waited and stopped the buckskin. He quickly fashioned an Indian bridle with his rope, then led Buster halfway across the meadow before tying him to a small bush. Then he returned to take his place beside Lester.

"You ready?" Lester asked, and Carl said that he was. Lester drew his long skinning knife from his belt and tested the edge of the blade with his thumb. "When I cut this jasper's throat, if he don't make enough noise, I will. And when that old coot comes running out to see what's wrong, we'll give him a belly full of lead. All right?"

"Why don't you just shoot him?" Carl asked.

"If I shoot him, that old coot inside will grab his gun and bolt the door, and we'll have to shoot up a lot of cartridges tryin' to get him outta there," Lester explained. "Might have to set fire to the cabin to get him outta there before it's over. But if I cut the other feller's throat, I'll holler like hell, and the feller inside will come a-runnin' to see what happened. He might have his gun with him, but he'll be out of the cabin. And that's when you'll cut him down."

"All right," Carl answered. "You be careful."

"Always am," Lester replied. "Don't worry, I'll leave him with a great big smile, right under his chin." He got to his feet again and, hunkered over in a crouch, he approached the sleeping figure on the porch. Carl aimed his pistol at the cabin door and waited.

Lester paused at the edge of the porch to listen for sounds from the sleeping man. There were none, thanks to a contented belly, Lester figured. *Good*, he thought, *best way to die, with your belly full of deer meat*. He climbed onto the tiny porch and crawled over to his victim, whose back was turned to him. Even though he was on his side, his victim was turned more toward his stomach, so Lester didn't have a clear view of his throat. He laid a hand gently on his shoulder and slowly rolled his body toward him. The sleeping man offered no resistance, but as the body turned, the barrel of a Colt .44 six-gun came into view, and it was aimed straight at his face. "Was there something you wanted?" Will asked, his voice soft and calm. Lester Camp made the last and worst mistake in a long line of mistakes in his life. His reaction was to try to stab Will. With no time to think, Will pulled the trigger at the same time he tried to block the hand holding the knife. The result was a .44 slug sent into the forehead of Lester and a cut on Will's left arm.

Shocked almost to a state of paralysis, Carl nevertheless managed to fire a couple of rounds at the porch, but Will held Lester's body in front of him to catch both bullets. He returned fire then when he saw the spot the shots came from and rolled off the porch to take cover behind Merle's firepit. In a panic then, Carl didn't like the position he now found himself in, so he decided to run when he realized that Will didn't know exactly where he was in the darkness.

It was so dark in the narrow valley between the mountains that Will didn't know Carl was running until he caught an image of a dark figure moving across the meadow. He had no way of knowing how many attackers were there before, but now he felt sure there had been only two. So he scrambled out from behind the low rock wall of the firepit and gave chase, ignoring the fact that he was without his boots.

Running as fast as he could manage, Carl was already out of breath when he came to the buckskin he had left tied to a bush. He untied the horse and jumped on his back. When he kicked the buckskin with his heels, Buster kicked his rear legs straight up in the air, with only his front feet on the ground, causing Carl to go flying over his head to land hard on his backside. Stunned for a few moments, he looked back to see the dark form of Will Tanner running toward him, and behind him, Merle Teague jumped off the porch to give chase as well. Again in a panic, Carl reached for his six-gun, only to find it missing from his holster, having lost it when Buster bucked him off. Almost crazy with fear now, Carl looked all around him for his missing handgun, crawling one way, then another until finally he found it. With Will almost upon him, he frantically fired one round and missed before he was struck in the chest by a round from Will's .44. He went down at once and never moved again. Hearing Merle puffing behind him as he ran to catch up, Will said, "He's done for. It's over." He then knelt beside the body and took the pistol out of Carl's hand, then slowly released the hammer. He realized then, that had the man been able to pull the trigger again, he probably would not have missed, for he was so close by that time.

"What in tarnation?" That was all Merle could think to say at the moment. "Was there any more of 'em?"

"Don't think so," Will replied.

"Are you all right?"

"Yeah, I'm all right. That one back there at the porch managed to give me a little cut on my arm, but that ain't my worst problem. I ain't got my boots on and I feel some sore spots on the bottom of my feet from runnin' after this jasper."

"That horse of yours is kinda particular about who rides him, ain't he?" Merle asked.

"Not so much," Will answered. "He'll let pretty much anybody ride him as long as it's me." That prompted him to remember. "The direction he was runnin' in was that way." He pointed to some trees on the other side of the meadow. "So I reckon we'll find their horses over that way somewhere. I'll go see if I can find 'em."

"While you're doin' that, I'll go back to the cabin and get a lantern, so we can take a look at these two buzzards," Merle said.

"That's a good idea," Will japed. "They mighta been some of your relatives come to visit you."

"If they are, we treated 'em the right way," Merle replied, then turned to go back to the cabin to fetch the lantern. Will walked toward the edge of the clearing until his eye caught the movement of forms big enough to be horses in the darkness of the trees. At that point, he drew his weapon again, confident that he wouldn't need it, but cautious enough to make sure he didn't blunder into a third person left to hold the horses. There turned out to be just the two horses, as he expected, so he untied their reins from the tree branches and led them back toward Merle's corral. He put all the horses in the corral and pulled the saddles off the two would-be assassins' horses. Then he went over and joined Merle, who was taking a close look at Lester on the porch. He picked up his boots, but decided against putting them on, since he had already torn the bottom of his socks and caked them with dirt.

"I brought their saddlebags over," Will said. "Thought I'd throw 'em on the porch, so you can look in 'em to see if there's anything worth something in 'em. I'll bring the saddles up, too, and you can see if you can trade them for something, but I wouldn't get my hopes up on 'em. You recognize him?"

"Never seen him before," Merle said. "He's just another one of those drifters who robbed somebody, or killed somebody, and came up to the mountains to hide. Don't know him, and I don't know his partner, but they were sure fixin' to settle your grits, weren't they?"

"Yep. Neither one of 'em gave me any choice. I had to shoot both of 'em."

"I sure thank the Lord you came along. This was my lucky day when you showed up."

"Well, I'm glad I happened to be in a position to help," Will responded. "Those two weren't plannin' to leave anybody in this cabin alive."

"Oh hell," Merle snorted. "I weren't talkin' about them two tryin' to kill me. They'da played hell tryin' to smoke me outta this cabin. I was talkin' about the coffee and the tobacco you brung me."

"Right," Will replied. "What was I thinkin'? Bring your lantern and let me take a look at the other fellow." They walked back out in the meadow to Carl's body and Will took a quick look. "I don't know him, either," he told Merle. "Did he have anything on him?"

"A Colt .45 Army revolver and a knife, eighty-five cents

in his pocket, and that's all," Merle answered. "Oh, and a pocket comb. You want it? You've got hair."

"I don't want it," Will told him. "You feel like diggin' a hole tonight to put these two jokers in, or you wanna wait till mornin'?" Merle chose morning, saying he'd rather go back to bed now. That suited Will fine, so he dragged Lester's body off the porch to lie in the yard till morning. He moved his bedroll away from the puddle of blood Lester had left on the porch and retired to try to make up for some of the sleep the visit had cost him.

They were up early the next morning, in spite of the little interruption in their sleep the night before, and enjoyed another meal of fresh-killed venison for breakfast. They gave their two guests a rather undignified burial on the backside of the mountain before Will set out again on the trail to Atoka. "How long you figure you'll be down that way?" Merle asked. He was wondering if Will might stop by on his way back to Fort Smith.

"I don't know for sure," Will told him. "After I see Jim Little Eagle in Atoka, I'm gonna ride on over to the other side of Tishomingo. Tom Spotted Horse wired Fort Smith about some cattle rustlin' goin' on over near the Red River. So I don't know how long I'll be gone."

"What about all this stuff we ended up with after we stuck these two fellers in the ground?" Merle asked, already pretty sure what Will's answer would be.

"I figured it might be a little more trouble for you, but the next time you ride over to McAlester for supplies you'll have a lot more to trade for 'em. And you won't have to wait for me to show up to have coffee."

"I 'preciate it, Will. That's mighty generous of ya. I might keep one of them horses, that roan. He looks in pretty good shape and that sorrel I've been usin' for a packhorse is gettin' so dang old he ain't gonna be good for much of anythin' pretty soon."

"Yeah, that roan looks like he's got a lot left in him, and you oughta get something for the bay, too," Will allowed. "Well, I'd best get in the saddle. I've got a good day and a half's ride to get to Atoka. Maybe by the time I get there, Jim will have taken care of the problem, himself."

CHAPTER 2

Will and Buster put in a long day after leaving Merle that morning. He wanted to arrive in Atoka around noon the following day because he planned to eat dinner at Lottie Mabry's dining room, which she had recently started calling Lottie's Kitchen. It was next door to a rooming house owned by her husband, Doug, and started out as the dining room for her husband's boarders. In short time, the quality of Lottie's cooking became quite well known, and consequently, the favorite place to eat in the little town. As much as he had enjoyed the fresh venison, he was hankering more toward a good homestyle dinner with some biscuits or corn bread and butter. So after a day's ride that he figured to be close to forty-five miles, he rode into Atoka a little after noon. He decided to eat first, then ride out to Jim Little Eagle's cabin on Muddy Boggy Creek. He knew Jim's wife, Mary Light Walker, would insist on fixing him something to eat, if he had not already eaten. The food would be good but not what he was hankering for on this day.

He pulled Buster up before the hitching rail in front of Lottie's and dismounted, wrapped the reins of both horses around the rail, and paused only a moment to admire the

new sign that proclaimed the dining room to be LOTTIE'S
KITCHEN. "Will Tanner!" Louise Bellone called out when
she saw him come in the door. "I thought you musta died."

"Howdy, Lou-Bell," he greeted her by the name she was
called by all her friends. "I couldn't die till I had one more
dinner at Lottie's."

"So you're sayin' one more dinner here will kill you?"
Lou-Bell replied. "I don't know if you oughta tell Lottie
that or not."

"You know what I meant," he said. Knowing she was
japing him, he gave up immediately. He knew better than
to get into a battle of wits with Lou-Bell. "What's for
dinner today?"

"Lottie made meat loaf," Lou-Bell said, not willing to
give up that easily, "and it's pretty deadly. But if you wanna
be sure, we can fix you up with something that's guaran-
teed to do the job."

"Just bring me the meat loaf and whatever else goes
with it and maybe that'll do the job," he said. She shrugged
and headed for the kitchen to fill a plate for him, passing
Lottie on her way out of the kitchen with the coffeepot.
He went into the back part of the room and sat down at
one of the small tables, instead of taking a seat at the long
table in the center.

"Howdy, Will," Lottie greeted him. "Is Lou-Bell giving
you a hard time?" She turned the coffee cup right side up
on his saucer and filled it with hot coffee.

"She always does," Will admitted. "I think she knows
she's got a sharper wit than I have, and I know when I'm
overmatched."

Lottie chuckled and said, "Sometimes I think I oughta

put a gag in her mouth, but I'm sure half my customers come in here just to swap lies with Lou-Bell."

"Well, I'm in the other half," Will said. "I come in here because the food is the best in this part of the country."

"Why, thank you, sir," she responded, "I certainly appreciate that." She stepped to the side then to give Lou-Bell room to place his dinner on the table.

"Here you go, Deputy Tanner," Lou-Bell announced as she set his plate down. "Hope it does the job," she japed, and gave him a wink. She turned to Lottie then and said very softly, "Look who's coming in the door. I kinda hoped they wouldn't be back today."

Forgetting Will for the moment, Lottie said, "Well, let's not sit them at the big table today. Go tell Fred to clear the dishes off that table over there by the window. I'll seat them there." Lou-Bell went at once to the kitchen and Lottie turned toward Will again. "I'll check with you in a little bit." She started to leave, pausing only a few seconds when Will asked a question.

"Who's Fred?" During the many times he had eaten there, he had never seen anyone named Fred.

Lottie quickly explained, "You probably remember Lila, the elderly lady who used to work here as our dishwasher. She came down with arthritis so bad she couldn't work anymore. We couldn't find anybody to take her place, so her husband came in to do her job till we found someone else, and he's still here." She hurried away then to intercept the two men coming in the door.

"Good afternoon, gentlemen," Lottie greeted them. "You've come back to see us again."

"You said that like you're surprised," Clyde Vickery

responded. He turned to look at his partner. "Didn't she, Sonny?"

"Maybe she's sayin' we ain't welcome," Sonny Doyle answered.

"We try to welcome everyone here," Lottie said. "We hope that everyone who eats with us is considerate of everyone else who's eating here. I'll call your attention to the table we've provided in the corner for firearms and ask if you'll be considerate of the other customers in the room and leave your weapons on the table until you're ready to leave. Yesterday, you refused. I'm hoping that today you'll leave them on the table. How 'bout it, you wanna make the rest of my customers feel more at ease?" Her earnest request failed to wipe the smirks off either face.

"How 'bout it, Sonny? You wanna make her customers feel more at ease?"

"I don't give a fat rat's ass whether her customers feel at ease or not," Sonny answered him. "I just care about how I feel, and I feel uncomfortable when I'm settin' in the back of the room full of sodbusters and my .44 is layin' on a table up front."

"Well, there you go, sugarplum," Clyde told her. "I reckon you've got your answer. Now the smartest thing for you to do is to bring us plenty of food and don't let none of them other customers bother us, and everythin' will be just fine."

Lottie hesitated. She glanced over at the opposite back corner at Will, already eating, apparently paying no attention to the two men she was talking with. She couldn't decide whether to ask him to order the troublesome two out of the building, or not. Maybe these men had no intention of causing anyone any trouble and just wanted to eat and get on their way. Finally, she made a decision. "All right, gentlemen, I'm gonna seat you right over here at a table by the window, best table in the room. It'll be cleaned off and set up with clean knives and forks." She led them over to the table. "Have a seat and I'll go to the kitchen and get your dinner ready."

Clyde and Sonny looked at each other with surprised grins on their faces. "Now, that's more like it," Clyde declared.

Watching from the kitchen door, Lou-Bell grabbed Lottie's arm when she walked into the kitchen. "What did you tell them?"

"I decided the best way to handle them is to treat 'em like a couple of kings, feed 'em good and fast, and get 'em out of here as quick as we can. Don't give 'em anything to complain about."

Surprised by her plan of action, Lou-Bell was quick to remind her, "We've got a genuine U.S. Deputy Marshal settin' right across the room from them. Why don't we just tell Will to order them out of here?"

"That was my first thought, too," Lottie answered while she set two plates next to the stove and put two healthy slices of meat loaf on each one. "But those two refuse to take their guns off, and if we get Will to throw them out of here, I'm afraid there might be a gunfight. Then we would be endangering the lives of all our good customers in here. I'd rather try this approach first and save Will for the last resort."

Lou-Bell thought about it for a moment, then shrugged. "I don't know. Maybe you're right. It wouldn't be too good if it turned into a gunfight in here. But I ain't sure your idea will work on those two ignorant saddle tramps. I don't think they're housebroke."

"I'll wait on 'em if you don't wanna," Lottie suggested, even though she was of the opinion that Lou-Bell was far more bulletproof to insults and crass remarks than she was.

"Oh hell, no," Lou-Bell came back at once. "I'll serve 'em with a sweet smile, no matter how bad they misbehave." Fred came from the back sink with an empty dishpan and walked around them on his way to clear off the table by the window. "Clear off those dirty dishes, Fred, and we'll set those gents up with enough food to keep their mouths shut."

Out in the dining room, Will cleaned the last little bit of grease from his plate, using a piece of biscuit for a mop. Contrary to what Lottie and Lou-Bell thought, he was very much aware of the guns still riding in the holsters of the two rather raunchy-looking men seated at the table by the window. He knew that Lottie had a policy of no firearms in the dining room, unless you were a lawman. He was curious as to why Lottie was making an exception for them. So he decided to have another cup of coffee and stick around for a while. He made an attempt not to be obvious about his interest in the two drifters. They hadn't broken any laws that he was aware of, just refused to remove their weapons in the dining room. That was Lottie's law, but not one a deputy marshal was called upon to enforce. *Hopefully, they'll just eat and be on their way,* he thought. It didn't take long for him to find out.

"Let me clean up this table a little bit for you fellows," Fred Polk said, and started picking up the cups and dishes left on the table.

"Who the hell are you?" Clyde demanded, thinking the

old man had been sent to wait on them since they wouldn't surrender their guns. "Where's that sassy gal that waited on us yesterday?"

"Lou-Bell," Fred replied. "I reckon she'll be servin' you. I'm just cleanin' up the table for her."

"He's just the dishwasher and the cleanin' woman, Clyde," Sonny remarked. "Ain't that right, old man?"

"I reckon you could say that," Fred answered. "I'm just tryin' to help Lottie out a little bit till she finds another dishwasher."

"We wouldn't want him handlin' our food, anyway," Sonny continued taunting the old man. "If somebody drops a dish on the floor, he has to clean it up. Ain't that right, old man?"

"I reckon I'd most likely be the one to clean it up," Fred allowed.

"Oops." Sonny grinned and slid a coffee cup to the edge of the table to let it drop off and smash into pieces. He and Clyde both chuckled as Fred tried to clear the rest of the table before any more dishes fell. "You better check this table," Sonny continued. "I don't believe it's level."

"I didn't know you was a carpenter, Sonny," Clyde blurted gleefully. "Maybe you oughta take a look at this table to see if you can see what's wrong with it." He took hold of the edge of the table and came up with it till all the remaining dishes slid off on the floor. "Sorry about that, old man. Looks like you've got a bigger mess to clean up. Come on, Sonny, we're gonna have to move to another table."

"You're gonna be movin' farther than that."

So absorbed in their harassment of an old man, neither Clyde nor Sonny was aware of the man who got up from the table in the opposite corner until they heard him speak behind them. Both turned to discover the dead-serious eyes of Will Tanner. Sonny was the first to challenge the stranger. "Mister, you'd best turn your behind around while you still can and mind your own business."

"This is my business," Will replied. "Now, you and your partner have shown everybody that you're not fit to eat with civilized folks. So both of you start walking toward that door."

Amazed, the two drifters exchanged puzzled glances before Clyde sneered, "And what if we don't? You gonna throw us out?"

"I'm gonna give you the chance to walk out of here peacefully," Will answered him, and pulled his vest aside to show his badge.

"A lawman!" Clyde exclaimed, then broke out with a grin. "This is Injun Territory. You ain't got no jurisdiction in Injun Territory. So you can just go to hell."

"I'm gonna explain this to you just one time," Will said. "This badge says I'm a U.S. Deputy Marshal. I *am* the law in Indian Territory for every white lawbreaker like you two sorry scabs who think you can do anything you want in the Nations. That ends all the discussion we're gonna have on that subject, so start walking toward that door. You better hope you've got enough money to pay for all those dishes you broke. You're lucky that table ain't broken." He glanced at Lottie, who was standing frozen like everyone else in the dining room now. "How much are those dishes worth, Lottie?"

Still too flustered to think straight, Lottie could only stammer for a few seconds before she blurted out, "It's not that much. Just take them out of here. They don't have to pay for them."

Seeing she was too upset to think, Will asked, "Would a dollar cover it?" She said yes immediately, so Will looked back at Clyde and said, "Put a dollar on the floor beside those dishes." He could almost see the thoughts racing through the crude man's head as he snarled and raised a hand that hesitated over his holstered pistol. "Don't even think about it," Will warned, and drew his .44 to enforce the warning. He had hoped to avoid the appearance of a gun in the dining room, but Clyde had hesitated long enough to warrant his concern. "A dollar," Will reminded him.

His eyes blazing with anger, Clyde reluctantly reached in his shirt pocket and pulled out a small roll of bills. He peeled a dollar off the roll and dropped it to fall in the middle of the broken dishes, then looked defiantly at Will. "I wonder how tough you'd be if we took it outside and you faced me with that pistol back in your holster."

"That would make me as stupid as you," Will answered. "Now, I'm tired of messin' with you two, so walk right on out that door." With little choice, since his gun was already out and aimed at their backs, they did as he ordered. Once outside, he said, "I'm arrestin' you for disturbin' the peace and destruction of private property. That's three days in jail."

"Three days in jail?" Clyde exploded. "Hell, man, I paid for those broke dishes!"

"That's right," Will replied. "The jail time is just for disturbin' the peace. It woulda been five days for both counts." He let them stew over that for a few seconds, then continued. "I'll tell you what, I'm in a pretty good mood today, so I might cut you fellows a little slack. We ain't got no real jail here in Atoka, so I use the Choctaw jail, which ain't nothin' but an old smokehouse they turned into a jail. It's gonna be a little cramped up for ya, dependin' on how many drunken bucks the Choctaw policeman has in there right now. So, I'm gonna give you a choice—the Choctaw jail, or get on your horses and ride outta town right now. What's it gonna be?"

"I reckon we'll ride," Clyde said, and untied his horse's reins and backed it away from the rail. Sonny, the silent witness to the confrontation between Clyde and the deputy marshal, was astonished by his partner's apparent surrender, especially when they had the deputy outnumbered two to one. And when Clyde's horse backed away from the rail and blocked Will's vision of him for a couple of seconds, Sonny didn't hesitate. He reached for his six-gun and raised it halfway before Will put a round into his right shoulder, causing him to drop his weapon and stagger backward several steps.

"You ain't had time to grow any common sense, have you?" Will asked. "I oughta put a round in your head, so you'd have something inside that empty space." Stunned for a few moments, Sonny clutched his wounded shoulder with his left hand. When he thought to pick up his six-gun and made a motion to do so, Will said, "Leave it right where it is. Can you ride?" Sonny didn't answer, so Will looked at Clyde and said, "Get him outta here, before I decide to throw him in that smokehouse jail and throw the damn key away." Clyde immediately went to help Sonny, and Will watched while he got the wounded man in the saddle. While Clyde was busy with that chore, Will picked up Sonny's .44 and emptied the cylinder and checked to be sure there was not one in the chamber. Then he dropped the gun into Sonny's saddlebag. "You gonna be able to take care of that wound?" Will asked.

"Nope, but I know somebody who can," Clyde answered. "Maybe we'll see you again sometime."

"Is that a threat?" Will asked, his six-gun still in his hand.

"No, it ain't no threat. I was just sayin', that's all," Clyde quickly replied.

"Get on your way, then," Will said, and stepped back out of the way. He stood there to watch them ride out of town. Near the end of the street, they passed a rider coming into town, who gave them a concentrated looking-over. Will smiled when he recognized the rider as Jim Little Eagle.

"Will Tanner," Jim called out as he pulled up next to him and slid off his horse. "One fellow back there look like he been shot. Was that you?"

"Yeah, that was me. Couple of drifters makin' trouble in Lottie's. It got outta hand, so I had to ask 'em to leave."

"You not put 'em in jailhouse?" Jim wondered.

"I'll be honest with you, Jim, I didn't wanna burden you with 'em, and I sure as hell didn't wanna take 'em with me. I didn't bring a jail wagon with me, and I've got to go on out to the Chickasaw Nation after I leave here. That's why I decided to run 'em outta town and hope they don't come back for a while."

"Better you shoot 'em. Then they don't come back," Jim said. "I hear one shot just before I get to town."

"I put a bullet in one of 'em's shoulder. He tried to go for his gun when I'm standin' there with mine in my hand. His partner said they didn't have to see the doctor, said he knew somebody who could take care of it. I don't know where he was talkin' about."

"I know where they go," Jim declared. "That's the reason I send wire to Marshal Stone and ask him to send somebody for little problem we got." Will knew Jim always asked Stone to send him, and it was usually for the sale of whiskey to the Indians.

"Has to do with those two fellows?" Will asked.

"Them and others just like them," Jim said, nodding slowly to emphasize the gravity of the problem.

"Don't tell me those women we left to operate Mama's Kitchen down the road have started sellin' whiskey, after all their promisin' to run a law-abidin' eatin' place," Will remarked. It had not been that long ago that he and Jim Little Eagle had worked together to close down an illegal saloon and whorehouse no more than three miles from Atoka. Run by a crude man named Tiny McGee, in partnership with a Texas cattle rustler named Ward Hawkins, Tiny was selling whiskey in Indian Territory to white man and Indian alike.

"No," Jim quickly assured him. "Those women do like they promise, sell food and rent rooms." He nodded toward the door of Lottie's Kitchen. "They give them some competition. What I wire Marshal Stone about is new place. Man named Reese Trainer build cabin on Clear Boggy Creek, twelve miles east of Atoka. I think he build big house, must have big family, but he not build house. He build saloon, sell whiskey. I tell him no sell whiskey in Choctaw Nation. He tell me mind my own business. I tell him deputy marshal come to see him. He tell me mind my own business."

"I'll take a ride out that way after my horses are rested

up. You ready to go with me?" Will asked. Jim said that he was and suggested that Will could leave his packhorse at his cabin, assuming that Will would camp at his place on Muddy Boggy Creek, as he often did. Will was agreeable with that, so he went back inside the dining room to pay Lottie for his dinner. She and Lou-Bell both thanked him for getting rid of their troublesome customers even though there was no guarantee they would never come back.